DAY
OF THE
DEAD

Also by the author:

Reaching Out to Moscow:
From Confrontation to Cooperation

With Pamela Sanders
ICELAND, Isle of Light

Translator and Editor:

Three Modern Icelandic Poets
Steinn Steinarr, Jón úr Vör, and Matthías Johannessen

The Naked Machine
Matthías Johannessen

DAY
OF THE
DEAD

a Novel

Marshall Brement

MOYER BELL
KINGSTON, RHODE ISLAND AND LANCASTER, ENGLAND

Published by Moyer Bell

First Printing

**LIBRARY OF CONGRESS
CATALOGING IN PUBLICATION DATA**

Marshall Brement, 1932-
Day of the dead / Marshall Brement.
448 p.   21.6 cm.
1. Vietnam–History–1945-1975–Fiction.
2. Americans–Vietnam–Fiction. 3. Young men–Fiction.
4. Consuls–Fiction. I. Title.
PS3602.R448D39   2005
813'.6–dc22   2005019491
ISBN 1-55921-387-6   CIP

Printed in the United States of America
Distributed in North America by Acorn Alliance,
549 Old North Road, Kingston, Rhode Island 02881,
401-783-5480, www.moyerbellbooks.com and
in the United Kingdom, Eire, and Europe by
Gazelle Book Services Ltd.,
White Cross Mills, High Town,
Lancaster LA1 1RN England,
1-44-1524-68765, www.gazellebooks.co.uk

For Pamela

compañera de mi vida

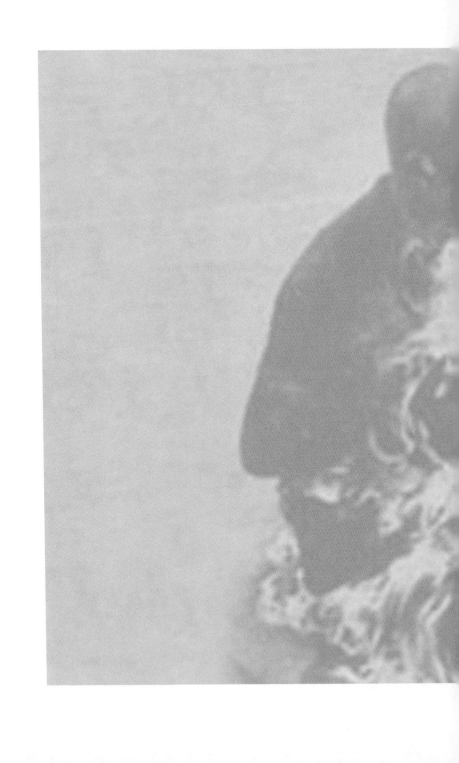

DAY
OF THE
DEAD

Chapter 1

MASTERING THE BASICS

Nobody assigned to Saigon in mid-1962 did not at odd moments feel at least a twinge of fear at the prospect, although the enemy, tough and ruthless as he was, had not yet started targeting Americans. Most of the killings—shootings, knifings, eviscerations—were directed at GVN officials in the boondocks, not the capital. But on the long flight out, thumbing through a briefcase of unclassified reports and "sitreps" on a security situation that was continually worsening, over and over his mind returned to it—not that he was actually afraid, but rather that he was interested in whether he would react to physical fear with a toughness he hoped he possessed. He was soon to find out.

David Marnin left Washington on Thursday at noon and, flying straight through with good connecting flights in San Francisco and Tokyo, arrived in Saigon on Saturday morning. In those halcyon days all Foreign Service Officers on "Permanent Change of Station" (PCS) travel, even the lowliest, went first class. This was at no real cost to the taxpayer, since the government on national security grounds made up the deficits the American airlines regularly ran on their Pacific routes. Nevertheless, it was a regulation that the Kennedy Administration, for form's sake, rescinded the following year, exiling our diplomats to steerage class, from whence they have yet to emerge.

Marnin was one of the last of the lucky ones. The DC-8's were just being introduced by Northwest Orient Airlines, who were in head-to-head competition with Pan American and its 707's for the trans-Pacific route, and those in first class got berths to sleep in. So he was in good shape when he arrived—ready and eager for the fourteen hour workdays and hopefully for long evenings of play to round them off. His boss, Ambassador Augustus Corning III, gave him two days to get acclimatized and all his administrative processing done before putting him to work.

He was met at Tan Son Nhut airport by Phillip Combs, a lanky, bespectacled junior officer in the consular section. Combs had finished his tour and would be leaving Viet Nam for a Washington assignment in the Economic Bureau of the State Department. Marnin had been slotted by the Admin section to take over Combs's flat, a small, one bedroom unit—furnished entirely in dark rattan—in a three story apartment house just off Nguyen Hue Street, very convenient to the Embassy. Combs had written, nicely offering a bed until his departure and Marnin had gratefully accepted—and ended up taking over not only Combs's flat, but his ancient Citroen and his servant Ba Lop, a cheerful and efficient old soul.

Saigon, with its broad boulevards, its great leafy blossoming trees, its charming restaurants, and its lovely graceful girls in their flowing *ao dais*, was with considerable justification still considered in the Service to be one of the jewels of the orient. Not only were wonderful houses and superb servants plentiful, but the cost of living was inconsequential, and the style of life more gracious and agreeable than at any other post in Asia.

It was true that the war was heating up—1,118 assassinations in 1962 alone. But Americans in Saigon, on the "front lines," lived undeniably well. Their life style was considerably enhanced by the twenty-five per cent "hardship allowance" on top of their normal salaries that was given to them for service in a dangerous country.

And they not only lived well, but at the same time felt themselves to be at the cutting edge of the "Free World," serving in the most significant American mission anywhere. Write an important cable in Saigon and it would end up on the desk of the President of the United States. There were few other posts, not even places like Moscow or Tokyo, where this was true. That led to an intensity of concentration on the job at hand and a solidarity on the part of the official American community that was exceptional.

Marnin's principal task in Corning's office was to organize the ambassadorial reading. Every morning at six, after writing down the events of the previous day in the journal it became his custom to keep throughout his diplomatic career, he culled a selection of cables from the hundreds the embassy had received overnight and the dozens sent out over the Ambassador's signature the previous evening. (All embassy cables went out signed "Corning," but the Ambassador, like most of his brethren at big posts, only had time to look at ten per cent of them before they were sent to Washington.)

At seven, he took those cables to Corning at the Residence, along with The Saigon Post and the summary of Asian news in the American press, prepared daily by the Office of Public Affairs of the State Department's Bureau of Far Eastern Affairs. He also brought the daily yellow-papered Clandestine Summary from the local CAS (i.e., CIA) station as well as the "intercepts" from and to foreign embassies and other sensitive cable traffic caught up in the net and decoded by the National Security Agency—the latter two each in one manila envelope inside another—sealed with tape and stamped "TOP SECRET UMBRA."

On top of the morning folder, to be wrestled with before breakfast in order to avoid tea and fruit stains, were those half dozen outgoing cables that required Corning's scrawled personal initials in the lower right hand corner of the first page and on the last page as well, under his name. Outgoing cables were typed in at least septuplicate, with enough red-papered carbon copies to reach all the relevant recipients in Saigon's large official American community. The top form was green and headed "Department of State"—another casualty of the computer age. In those days, after a draft was approved, a secretary would be told to "put it on green."

Corning, a handsome Virginia gentleman, would go through his morning labor invariably dressed in black swimming trunks and a white monogrammed terrycloth bathrobe, making changes in violet ink, using a Waterman fountain pen purchased in 1925 when he was a young man on the Riviera. He worked in the cool of the morning near a wonderfully fragrant frangipani tree on a white wrought iron glass-topped table on the veranda overlooking the pool, after he had breast-stroked his ten laps, and while he breakfasted on toast, mango from his own tree, papaya, and chrysanthemum tea.

While he dressed Marnin took the worked-over cables back to his office, and made sure the necessary changes were made accurately and the cables dispatched. Washington was exactly twelve hours behind Saigon. This meant that an "Immediate" telegram—and all cables that the Ambassador personally approved were by his dictum slugged "Immediate"—that left Saigon before nine in the morning was read in the White House, at CIA Headquarters, and at the State and Defense Departments at opening of business the same day. But if a cable were significant enough, it could reach Washington the previous evening, before the President and the Secretary went to sleep, and before they read the next day's editions of the *New York Times* and the *Washington Post*. So it was important for Marnin to ensure that cables aimed for the highest policymakers were sent out by the code room by eight at the latest.

Marnin then went back to the Residence to make the five minute drive to the Embassy with the Ambassador in his Checker limousine, where they could go over the daily schedule together. David entered the car first and sat to the Ambassador's left, so that Corning could be last in and first out. The Checker was a prototype—the first armored car commissioned by the Department for ambassadorial use. It weighed five tons and got four miles to the gallon, but the interior was roomy, with lots of leg and head space. Unfortunately, its air conditioning system, also a custom designed prototype, like the elevators in the embassy, only worked one day in three, and because it was a fully armored car the windows did not open. This meant that even at nine on a tropical Saigon morning the inside of the vehicle was unbearably hot. To combat this, Mr. Bac, the chief local employee in the Admin section, had rigged up two small, revolving electric fans at either side of the back seat, next to the reading lights. The heat bothered Marnin, not yet acclimatized to the ever-present humidity of Southeast Asia, much more than it did the Ambassador, who hardly perspired, even on the tennis court.

Climate notwithstanding, David enjoyed these double morning drives from the Residence to the Embassy and then back again through the city, through broad boulevards lined with eucalyptus, poinciana, and jacaranda shade trees, going by pastel colored French villas with bougainvillea and yellow allamanda tumbling over garden walls. Near the Rue Catinat there were ochre yellow office buildings with dark green louvered shutters. Shops were often just opening, with their owners pulling back the iron grates with which they locked up at night. Some swept and sloshed down the sidewalks, others were buying noodle soup or congee for their breakfast. On apartment balconies above the shops, aerial gardens throve and people were doing their morning tai chi amidst potted palms and hanging orchids.

They would arrive precisely at nine o'clock at the front door of the embassy. This regularity of movement was frowned on because of the terrorist danger. Assassination of Vietnamese was a daily occurrence in Saigon and embassy personnel were all urged to vary their habits and specifically their routes to the office. Knowing where the ambassadorial limousine would be at any given time of day obviously made an assassin's problems that much simpler. The embassy Security Officer, in fact, had had the temerity to send a memo urging the Ambassador for his own protection to adhere to established embassy security procedures, on which Corning had scrawled, "I am not about to change my habits for the VC or anybody else."

The embassy itself was a converted six story apartment house adapted in a slapdash manner to the sudden increase in demands that the new security situation had thrust upon it. Nothing about it was suitable for an embassy chancery, but Corning had been told that until funds were found he and his staff would have to do the best they could in what was admittedly a very bad working environment. Corning's office on the fifth floor, although suitably large and ambassadorial, had the singular disadvantage of being separated by only a ten foot alleyway from the building next door, and had an excellent view of the kitchens of the two adjacent apartments—thereby forcing the Ambassador to keep his windows closed and his shades down. Nevertheless, the easygoing Corning, an avuncular, pipe-smoking professional diplomat, put up with the shabbiness of his surroundings with seeming good humor.

The calls Marnin made on the various senior officers who com-

posed the Mission Council were amiable and inconsequential, except
for his first dealing with Carl Bilder, the short, pinch-faced Deputy
Chief of Mission (DCM), Corning's Number Two. When Marnin
entered his office on his second day in Saigon, Bilder was seated at his
desk working on a cable which, judging from the scowl on his face,
seemingly displeased him. After a minute or two he scrawled
"REWRITE" across the top and threw it in his out-box. Only then
did he look up, giving Marnin a non-committal once over.

"So you're Marnin," he said.

"Yes, sir."

"You'll like it here—provided you and I are reading off the same
sheet of paper."

"I don't quite understand."

"You'll soon learn that the Ambassador deals largely with policy
and that I control the paper flow around here. If there's anything
going on I have to know about it right away. Keeping me fully
informed is one of the most important aspects of your job—in fact,
the most important as far as I am concerned. Keep in mind that
Efficiency Reports are what get you ahead in the service and that I'll
be writing yours."

Marnin gazed at him, hoping that his real feelings were not reflected on his face.

"I'll do my best," he finally said.

"Good. I'm sure you will. And now if you'll excuse me, I'm crash-
ing on a cable that has to be out of here in the next half hour."

He clicked on his intercom. "Effie," he said, "get me Curly Bird on
the phone right away."

The interview was over. As he left Bilder's office Marnin heaved a
huge sigh. "What a prick," he thought to himself.

The two people who were most useful in breaking him in to his
new job were Chick Rizzo, a young USIA officer temporarily seconded to the Political Section, and Miss Ky, the Vietnamese Protocol
Assistant and social secretary. She ensured that matters went smoothly at the cocktail receptions and dinner parties that the Cornings gave
once or twice a week. She was a beautiful woman, above average
Vietnamese height, invariably looking lovely dressed in a pastel *ao dai*.

Marnin took her to be about his own age—twenty-eight. He was later amazed to discover that she was married to an ARVN Colonel and had a seventeen year old daughter.

Miss Ky kept a book in which everyone who had ever visited the Embassy Residence was characterized, defined, and then listed in protocol order. This was invaluable in seating guests at a formal dinner, where the placement of high ranking military officers and diplomats was always screened with a professional eye by those in attendance to ensure that their seating was commensurate with their rank. It was especially useful to have when there had to be a last minute rearrangement of a formal table because of the non-appearance of one of the guests, a constant occurrence in a wartime environment. In such a situation ensuring that no protocol gaffes took place was no simple matter. In fact, it was nerve-wracking, principally because it necessitated dealing with the fumbling and muttering of Corning's high strung wife, Patty Lou. Miss Ky's handling of such situations was nothing short of masterful.

Next to most names in her protocol book were comments in pencil by Miss Ky about the preferences and sometimes the character of Residence guests—"drinks scotch," "always arrives late," "not to be seated next to a young woman." In going over that book with her name by name in order to learn the cast of characters at the top of the Saigon social world, Marnin soon discovered that the demure, self-effacing, attractive Miss Ky was as cool and as tough as a person can be. Further experience soon taught him that while Vietnamese men talked tough, Vietnamese women *were* tough.

In the front office itself he was shown the ropes by Chick Rizzo, who helped out when things got too hectic in the Ambassadorial Suite. Rizzo, who had been through a year's Vietnamese language training at the Foreign Service Institute (FSI) in Arlington Towers across the Potomac from the State Department, taught him the meaning of the various acronyms in cables and reports, whom to watch out for when screening reports for the Ambassador, what the various components of the Mission were responsible for, and how these various components were expected to interact with the Ambassador. Rizzo could be counted on to absorb all the gossip making the rounds of the

American community. More important, as far as Marnin was concerned, after work Rizzo taught him the rules of the game in the night clubs of Saigon, where he went every night "to practice his Vietnamese," Rizzo said with a wink.

It took several weeks for Marnin, who was given what had been literally an old broom closet for an office on the fifth floor twenty feet away from the Ambassador, with the help of Rizzo and Miss Ky, to get used to his new surroundings, to distinguish between the various Government of Viet Nam (GVN) players and to master the special vocabulary and the bureaucratic alphabet soup of the Department, the Embassy, and the various American and Vietnamese governmental agencies, and how they related to each other.

"Why are some cables signed and others unsigned?" he asked Rizzo at one point.

"Anything in State channels are signed by the highest ranking officer at post in the Department or at an embassy or a consulate. In CIA and Defense channels cables are unsigned," Rizzo replied.

Once Marnin got the hang of this, the job boiled down to making sure that established procedures functioned efficiently, and, except for the long hours, was not overly taxing. In any case, the one thing he and his newly-commissioned colleagues had imbibed from course chairman Handelman and the A-100 course at the Foreign Service Institute—mandatory for all entrants to the Foreign Service—was La Rochefoucauld's maxim: *Surtout, pas trop de zèle!* (Above all, not too much zeal!) Do what you have to, was Handelman's message, but do it with as much languid grace as possible.

Although Marnin had taken that message to heart and done his best to temper any signs of visible enthusiasm, the truth was that he was thrilled to be where he was and to be doing what he was doing. His instincts told him that there could hardly be a better post than Saigon, a better role model for a beginning Foreign Service Officer than Gus Corning, or a better job than to be his aide.

Chapter 2

OPENING NIGHT

It was October 7, 1962, and Marnin's first performance assisting the Ambassador and his wife at the residence. The occasion was a formal reception for the Commander in Chief of the Pacific (CINC-PAC), Admiral Bill McGrath, who was on one of his periodic visits from his headquarters in Honolulu.

Marnin arrived twenty minutes before the guests, the requisite arrival time for embassy staffers, wearing a light blue striped Haspel tropical suit that, along with half a dozen members of his entering class, he had gone to Baltimore to purchase at diplomatic discount at Swartz's. In the foyer he was greeted by Miss Ky, dressed in a demure blue *ao dai*.

"Good evening, Mr. Marnin," she said with old fashioned formality. "I hope you are completely recovered by now from your long journey?"

"Yes, thank you, Miss Ky, I'm very well, just—" David hesitated. "Well, to tell you the truth," he grinned ruefully, "I'm just a bit ...warm."

"Oh, no need to be nervous," she said solemnly. "I shall introduce each guest to you. Would you care for something to drink?"

She led him to a long table covered with a white cloth and he ordered a Seven-Up from the barman. They stood chatting in a stilted fashion, strategically positioned near the top of the stairs lest a guest jump the gun and arrive prematurely. The foyer where they stood was a large, high-ceilinged hall typical of Indochina at the time, with tiled floors and tall windows with their louvered shutters thrown open, and sparingly furnished with a few pieces of wicker, potted palms and hanging ferns that swayed lightly in the breeze of the overhead fans. The drawing room beyond was much the same, except that its hardwood floors were partly covered with oriental carpets and somewhat more ornate furniture.

Over Miss Ky's shoulder, Marnin could see a half-dozen servants in white tunics and black trousers gliding back and forth carrying trays of glasses and hors d'oeuvres which they were setting up on tables. Some members of the embassy "family" drifted about, making desultory conversation in subdued voices. Presently, Ambassador and Mrs. Corning entered the drawing room from a side door, greeted the other staffers and their wives, and then approached Marnin and Miss Ky.

The Ambassador, with his pepper-and-salt hair, erect carriage, and well tailored white linen suit, looked the very model of a diplomat. Patti Lou Corning was another story. Marnin had not yet met her, but had heard her characterized by Phil Combs as an "aging Georgia peach." So he was not unprepared when he saw her plump figure cinched into a ruffled pink cocktail dress and her blonde curls sprayed into a too-youthful bouffant flip.

"Patti Lou," said the Ambassador in his courtly manner, "this is David Marnin, my new aide, just arrived from the States."

She appraised him approvingly, and said in a broad, down-home accent, "You will have to meet mah Amanda when she comes out for her summah vacation."

With the swiftness of a shrike, she reached out and snagged a martini from the tray carried by a passing houseboy.

"I'd be delighted," David replied.

She could spot his anxiety.

"This your first post?"

"Yes it is, Mrs. Corning."

"Well, don't you worry 'bout a thing. Rose here knows everyone."

"Patti Lou," said Corning, taking his wife firmly by the arm, "I believe the Admiral is arriving."

"Fall in, young man," said Patti Lou. She winked broadly and handed him her empty martini glass. "To the barricades!"

Nonplussed, Marnin stood looking at the glass in his hand as the Cornings moved toward the front door. Glancing around, he stowed it in a potted palm and then joined Miss Ky at the top of the veranda stairs. It was from this vantage point that he watched the ascent of the military brass and their respective retinues. First the Americans: the guest of honor, Admiral McGrath, his Executive Assistant and his aide, all in full dress whites, followed by Generals Donnelly and Parker, their assistants and aides, all in dress blues. Then the Vietnamese: triple-starred and triple named, beribboned and bemedalled, the five white-clad Generals—Tran Van Don, Tran Tra Bich, Tran Van Minh, Duong Van Minh, Le Van Kim—descended from a flotilla of black Mercedes sedans and ascended the steps in a flying wedge to run the gauntlet of the receiving line. As guests were passed along, from Miss Ky to Marnin to Mrs. Corning and on up the line to the Ambassador and Admiral, David noted that a conspiratorial "of course" seemed to be in order.

"Mrs. Corning, you of course know General Tran Van Don . . ." his voice ending on a hopeful note.

"Of course I do, you silly boy." Patti Lou by that time clutched another stemmed martini glass in her left hand and swiveled toward the General, extending her right. "Dear General Don, how lovely it is to see you on this wonderful Saigon evening. You are doing such great work, not only for your own people, but for the whole Free World. My husband has talked so much about you."

And since Augustus Corning was more than an Ambassador—he was America's proconsul, the one man everyone in the country, of whatever political stripe, felt was empowered to decide the ultimate fate of Viet Nam—General Tran Van Don seemed to eat up her southern locutions and cornbread mannerisms, as did the other Vietnamese, at least as long as she was sober enough to stand upright.

"Mrs. Corning, you of course know General Duong Van Minh . . ."

"I should say I do!" exclaimed Patti Lou, as though she were greeting Robert E. Lee.

Ursine and taciturn, "Big Minh," as he was called, to distinguish him from "Little Minh" (General Tran Van Minh), was clearly a man's man, someone not at ease in a social situation. Thus David was surprised to hear Patti Lou say, "Dear General Minh. . . I so hope that one of these days soon you will spare me just the teensiest bit of time to show me your orchid collection—I understand you grow the finest cymbidiums in the whole country."

Big Minh rose to the occasion. Taking Patti Lou's hand and looking shy and pleased, he said, "I shall be honored, Madame."

At that point Marnin was distracted by the arrival of an exquisite young Vietnamese woman in a white silk ao dai poised on the top step framed by the palms. As she approached, he observed that her hair was drawn severely back into a smooth chignon and that she wore no jewellery.

"Madame Do Ba Xang," said Miss Ky, introducing them.

She unsmilingly extended her hand and he saw that he was wrong about the jewelry, for on the fourth finger of the right hand she wore a gold wedding band.

"*Enchanté*," she said. Their eyes locked briefly. Then he released her hand and passed her on to Mrs. Corning, who seemed to know her well and to be very solicitous about her.

"Who is she?" he asked Miss Ky.

"The widow of the famous General Do Ba Xang, who was killed in the war last year."

He turned away to look at her again before she disappeared into the crowd. Then he felt a sudden clap on the shoulder and heard Miss Ky saying, "Mr. Willis Mandelbrot of the *New York Times*."

Marnin turned and found himself face to face with an old friend— a tall, rangy man his own age, dressed in a rumpled linen jacket, chino trousers, blue button-down shirt, madras tie and wearing horn-rimmed glasses that he had a habit of punching back onto the bridge of his nose.

"David, you old sonofabitch!" he grinned, giving Marnin a hearty handshake. "I heard you were coming."

"How are you, Billy?"

"You know each other!" Miss Ky exclaimed.

"Billy and I were classmates at Princeton," David explained.

"Class of 'Fifty-seven—a vintage year!" Billy said to Miss Ky. "I used to trounce him regularly on the tennis court." Then he laughed. "Nah, just kidding. Dave was captain of the tennis team. . . used to give me lessons." He turned back to Marnin, cuffing him lightly on the arm. "So what the hell's a straight arrow like you doing in a wonderfully wicked city like this?"

"Playing tennis, man."

"Hey, great! We'll get some doubles going. You know I'm working here for the *Times*.

"So I gather. I hear you've pissed off everyone in Foggy Bottom."

"Oh yeah? You heard that?" Mandelbrot looked pleased.

Marnin felt a piercing hiss in his left ear. With a jump he turned to find Patti Lou's face an inch from his own.

"Move that line, young man," she commanded, sounding like a Parris Island drill instructor. "Keep that line moving!"

Over Mandelbrot's shoulder, Marnin saw a line of guests stalled on the stairs and backed up down to the driveway.

"Yes ma'am!"

Mandelbrot grinned.

"Everybody makes his living in his own way," he said. "See you later, kiddo. I'll give you a call."

Extending his hand to the Ambassadress, he laid on a down-home accent of his own, saying, "Hello there, Mrs. Corning, sure is nice to see you again."

Patti Lou smiled graciously like the old pro that she was and said, "I surely do wish I could say the same, Mr. Mandelbrot."

After what seemed to Marnin like three hours but was actually forty-five minutes, the receiving line broke up and he spent the rest of the evening treading water in the wake of his Ambassador as Corning and the Admiral trolled along in tandem from one shoal of guests to the next, exchanging pleasantries.

Ambassador Casimir Berman, the Polish member of the three-nation (Poland, Canada, India) International Control Commission, had just returned from one of his frequent trips to North Viet Nam. Corning respected Berman and found him a useful source of information. He introduced McGrath and greeted him affably.

"How were things in Hanoi, Casimir? Did you learn anything?"

Berman, a dark heavy-set man with an equally weighty demeanor, replied in a thick Polish accent, "I learned that it is time to bring peace to this unhappy region."

"Nobody wants peace more than we do," Corning said amiably.

"So you say. But I can tell you that the other side is ready to talk."

"Of course they're ready to talk," Corning said, "they're losing the war."

Berman bristled.

"Just a year ago," he growled, "you told me the insurgency was making alarming strides and that you could not negotiate from a position of weakness. Now I'm told you can't talk because your faithful Southern allies would not understand it if you engaged Hanoi in conversation at a time when you're supposedly winning the war."

"We are winning, Casimir. Two things happened this year—we introduced helicopters to give the ARVN more mobility and the GVN implemented the Strategic Hamlet program. We're cutting the insurgents off at the knees. Isn't that right, Admiral?"

"That's absolutely right," said McGrath.

"You'll have to aim higher than the knees in order to stop them."

"But we are stopping them, Casimir," Corning argued. "We've turned a corner—we're winning this war!"

"What you Americans don't understand is that time is on their side, not yours."

"Make no mistake—you can tell your friends in Moscow that our commitment here is total. Too much depends on this place, including the situation in Germany and in Eastern Europe. That's why we'll be here for as long as it takes. Tell that to your friends in Hanoi as well."

Berman pointed his finger at Corning and said emotionally, "It's you who are making the mistake, Gus—a very tragic mistake. Listen, I'm a Pole, a communist Pole. I know these people in Hanoi. They are not to be trifled with. Make a deal with them while you still can. And I tell you this is a war that can't—believe me—cannot be won."

Marnin watched with interest the manner in which his boss at this point smoothly decelerated the conversation without yielding to his adversary, and then disengaged, having decided that it had escalated too far in this social setting,

"I suppose that was just the usual Commie bullshit," McGrath said to Corning. "Or do you think Ho is really ready to talk?"

"The question is," said Corning, "are Diem and Nhu ready to talk? That's what really worries me."

Chapter 3

THE CERCLE SPORTIF

On his first full Saturday in Saigon, Marnin had appeared at seven in the morning on the composition court in back of the Ambassador's residence in his whites and with his three tightly strung Dunlop Maxplys to serve as partner in Corning's weekly doubles game with the MAAG chief, General Harold "Blix" Donnelly, and his aide, Captain Tom Aylward. As far as Corning was concerned, this was institutional combat—the Embassy vs. MACV, the civilians against the military, the equivalent of the Detroit Lions against the Chicago Bears. Unfortunately, the Lions had not been holding up their institutional end. Since Aylward had been singles champion of the Seventh Army in Germany and Donnelly was a steady player and good at the net, the two military officers had previously had no trouble wiping out Corning— who had good strokes and had played as a student for the University of Virginia—and Sam Sabo, the Political Counselor, who had been the Ambassador's regular partner, but was clearly the weakest of the foursome.

The Ambassador was the courtliest of Virginia gentlemen. His son Harry (Augustus Harrison Corning IV) was the seventh generation of Cornings to attend the university in Charlottesville. But there was nothing about being a Virginia gentleman that implied a willingness to be beaten regularly on the athletic field. He was, in fact, despite an avuncular nature, intensely competitive and was convinced (as was Marnin, once he was in a better position to judge Aylward's non-tennis talents) that the main reason for Aylward's assignment to Donnelly's staff was his backhand.

Having been newly offered an aide of his own, thanks to the enormous growth of the official community that in 1962 had turned Saigon from a Class Three to a Class One embassy (only Ambassadors at Class One posts get aides), Corning had decided that two could play at that game and had written a fateful letter to Handelman asking him to find an aide for him from the newly entering A-100 class who was a crack tennis player. Donnelly had trumped, but Corning had overtrumped.

Marnin subsequently often suspected that the "outstanding" Efficiency Reports Corning gave him (an FSO was rated from one to six, with six as "outstanding", a relatively rare rating), had more to do with their subsequent victories on the court than with the eighty-hour weeks he put in at the embassy. That first Saturday, however, had been a disaster. The court was slow, David's reflexes were not yet in tune, and he kept overhitting the ball. The scores—6-1, 6-2, 7-5—were dolefully recorded without comment in his journal.

Corning took this disappointment with a characteristic mixture of outward equanimity and inner determination to correct the situation at once. When the victors had departed, he invited Marnin to join him in a *citron pressé* beside the pool.

"I'm awfully sorry to let you down," David stammered. "I surely didn't cut the mustard this morning."

"Well," said Corning graciously, "it takes awhile to adjust to the heat. And you're obviously a bit rusty—had other things to do, I don't doubt. But you've got great form. It's just a matter of time," he added encouragingly.

"Thank you, sir," David mumbled.

Corning thought for a moment.

"There's a chap here, a Central American diplomat who plays a hell of a game of tennis. Name's Claudio Pepe. He's the Guatemalan Consul General. I've played doubles with him at the Cercle Sportif and he's the best in town. He can get you up to speed. I'll give him a call today. I'm sure you'll want to get on it right away. My hope is that next Saturday we'll have a different story."

"Yes, sir," David agreed.

The Ambassador was as good as his word and on the following afternoon Marnin and Pepe met at the Cercle Sportif where they played four sets of singles. With his hooded eyes framed in dark half circles, his sallow complexion, his powerful chunky body, and a constant cigarette dangling from the corner of his mouth, occasionally even on the tennis court, Pepe was not the person a Hollywood casting director would have chosen to impersonate an athlete. Unorthodox and deceptive, he never struck a ball hard or flat. Every groundstroke was hit with a slice that made the ball skid a foot off the ground instead of bouncing up and into his opponent or with a topspin that could kick over an opponent's head if the ball were allowed to take a full bounce. He was also surprisingly quick, retrieved everything, and rarely made an unforced error, drunk or sober. And the harder Marnin hit the ball, the tougher were Pepe's returns. So while the Ivy Leaguer had the form, the Guatemalan won every set. (Marnin's coach at Princeton had always told him that the guys with great form were all on the third team.)

The Cercle Sportif, like most other colonial institutions in the Far East, had been established exclusively for foreigners, in this case the French. Since the war, however, its membership included upper class Vietnamese, as well as the usual assortment of diplomats, foreign businessmen, and those of the French community who had stayed on. The layout was typically colonial: a large two-story clubhouse with veranda set back from the street in verdant gardens with tennis courts, swimming pool and, this being French, a court for boules.

Weekends, of course, were busiest: guests came and went; children trotted up the path to the pool, followed by anxious amahs and suntanned mothers. Pot-bellied old men in white pants and sun hats played boules. Waiters hovered, carrying drinks from inside the clubhouse to people on the veranda. Weekdays were given over to women and children except at noon, when the men arrived, and again in the evening in that happy interlude between office and home.

Despite the heat and the overhead sun, which made it difficult to serve, David and Claudio began meeting at the club every day at twelve. Twice during that first week they were joined for a game of doubles by Billy Mandelbrot and Dennis Chang, a local Chinese businessman who was sometimes called "the mayor of Cholon," although he held no municipal office. Chang was a strong, steady player, while Mandelbrot was enthusiastic but wildly erratic. Tall, powerful and ungainly, he dearly loved to serve an ace, but had trouble controlling his service. At one point when this happened he erupted in a noisy but short-lived series of oaths.

David, who was usually Mandelbrot's partner, dryly admonished him, "Keep your eye on the ball, Billy—"

"Oh really?" Mandelbrot replied. "Say, I never thought of that."

"—instead of on the ladies watching us."

A foursome that included Mrs. Sabo and Mme. Do Ba Xang, had played tennis at eleven o'clock and then lingered afterwards on the veranda overlooking the courts, sipping their drinks and watching the men play, occasionally applauding and exclaiming over good shots. Mme. Do Ba Xang, who was small-boned but quite tall and long-legged for a Vietnamese, looked exciting in her white tennis outfit. Mandelbrot, no less observant than Marnin, took in the young widow's charms. Giving her another once-over on his way to the locker room, he said to Claudio, "I'd sure like a piece of that action."

Claudio shrugged.

"Forget it. Next to her the Virgin Mary is a hot tamale."

In the locker room, as they drank their *citron pressés*, Marnin said to Pepe, "Do Ba Xang must have been quite a man."

"The Lion of I Corps they called him," said Claudio. "He was a great friend of mine. A hell of a guy—the toughest general in the army, a real killer."

"How did he die?"

"His helicopter was shot down by the VC somewhere near Hue."

"That's for publication," Mandelbrot said. "But as I get it the chopper was sabotaged by the *cailles*."

"The *cailles*?"

"Chinese tongs," Mandelbrot said. "They control the under-world—gambling, protection rackets, prostitution. They're into everything. Rumor has it Xang reneged on a deal, so they killed him."

"You journalists lead a rich fantasy life," Claudio said. "Come on; let's go to the Continental for a drink."

"Not me," said Chang. "Got to meet with my *caille*."
They all laughed.

Like the Cercle Sportif, The Hotel Continental Palace was a venerable colonial institution. Located in the heart of the city, the hotel veranda, known to Americans as "the Continental Shelf," was a prime place for *al fresco* drinking and people-watching. Around seven o'clock on any given evening, one could find an assortment of journalists, diplomats, military officers and visitors chewing over the day's events and gazing out at the various forms of traffic and trafficking taking place on the busy street just one level below them.

"Best place in the city for bird-watching," Mandelbrot observed enthusiastically.

As the shops and offices closed, a parade of pretty girls passed by on their way home, walking, bicycling, or perched demurely on the backs of motor scooters, their long hair flying out from under conical straw hats tied beneath their chins with colored ribbons and their pastel silk ao dais floating behind them in the dusk like banners in the breeze.

"Enchanting, aren't they?" Claudio said, looking with an amused smile at Marnin, who was watching with obvious interest.

"Like. . .butterflies," David said with a kind of wonder.

Claudio gave a short laugh.

"Iron butterflies."

"No man—lollipops!" Mandelbrot corrected them. "Delectable, delicious little lollipops! All colors, all flavors—mm-mm!"

"The women of this country," Claudio said reflectively, "have a wonderful tactile quality—a unique feel to the skin, a special scent. There's something in the air of Saigon—"

"It's the smell of noodles, man!" said Mandelbrot, jumping up. "I'm famished! Let's go eat!"

They headed for a restaurant called The Diamond in Claudio's chauferred Mercedes. It was located in Cholon, the Chinese sector of the city. They made their way slowly along the congested streets teeming with sidewalk shops and stalls that stayed open as long as there were customers. In the glare of naked light bulbs people were swilling soup, having haircuts, unrolling bolts of fabric, and pawing through every sort of merchandise from buttons to bicycle tires. Cyclo drivers weaved through the dense mass, repeatedly ringing their bells to attract potential customers, and coolies hauled their loads of heavy goods in carts; radios blared and Chinese opera screeched over loud-speakers.

The three men emerged from the car and pushed their way through the shouting, shoving crowd and into the Diamond, where the din was nearly as deafening. The restaurant was blazing with lights and pulsing with activity—it was *re nau*, as the Chinese would say. Diners shrieked at each other in Cantonese or Hakka, suggesting to the foreigner that they were having furious arguments, but then they would burst into raucous laughter; waiters scurried about yelling orders and imprecations and slinging clattering plates.

Claudio, a steady customer, was greeted like royalty by the manager, who led them to a table. "Please see that this is chilled, Mr. Lee," Claudio said, handing him two bottles of white wine.

"Christ, Claudio, you're too much!" Mandelbrot exclaimed. "Beer's the drink to have with crab."

"My dear Billy," Claudio replied, "Don't feel compelled to drink any of this sublime Montrachet. Mr. Lee, be good enough to bring Mr. Mandelbrot a warm Budweiser."

The waiters set huge platters of hot spicy crab on the table with chili pepper sauce and bowls of fried Singapore noodles. A third waiter poured the wine and a fourth brought large bottles of Ba Mi Ba beer, mineral water, Orange Fanta and a box of miniscule paper napkins. Mandelbrot and Pepe wrapped the napkins around their fingers before picking up the hot crab pieces, then cracked the shells with their teeth and sucked out the pungent meat.

Marnin watched how it was done, then followed suit. The string bean chili pepper sauce was so spicy it burned a couple of small cuts he had on his finger. Sweat soon poured from the foreheads of all three men.

"Hey," Marnin gasped, "this is fantastic!"

He had played seven sets of doubles that day—four at the Cercle Sportif and, this being Saturday again, three with the Ambassador early that morning (in which the embassy finally defeated the MAAG two sets to one.) He was ravenously hungry and thought nothing in his life had ever tasted as good as that crab washed down by Montrachet.

Halfway through the meal they were joined by Klaus Buechner, a German photographer who worked for the Associated Press. Buechner, who shared a villa with Mandelbrot, had just returned from a combat mission. One of the unique benefits of covering the war in Viet Nam was that one could leave Tan Son Nhut with the choppers at five in the morning, spend the day tramping around the Delta, and be back in Saigon at five in the afternoon in time for a bath and a good dinner.

The four men plunged into the food and ate in silence, sucking out the crabmeat and tossing the empty shells onto a platter that was periodically whisked away by aged gentlemen in white jackets and black trousers. Most of the Chinese and Vietnamese customers simply threw the shells on the floor, to be swept away by busboys who looked about ten years old.

Finally, his appetite slaked, Mandelbrot turned to Buechner. "How'd it go?"

"Samo samo." Buechner, who had a reputation for courage in the field, grunted with disgust. "Another long, hot walk through the Plain of Reeds. The ARVN managed to make plenty of noise, so of course we didn't find the enemy. But I found the exact location of every leech in the district—mostly on my body. I pulled fifty-four beauties off me when we reached dry ground. I gave them a feast—at least a pint of good red Bavarian blood. In the four months I've been here I've been on maybe fifty combat missions and the results have been the same on every one—zilch. I'm beginning to wonder whether Victor Charlie really exists, or whether he's just a ploy by Diem to extract more aid money from all you generous Americans."

"You know why that is, don't you?" Mandelbrot demanded rhetorically. "Because the aim of the ARVN is to avoid Victor Charlie, not to fight him. And why is that? Simple—Diem doesn't want to take casualties. So the aggressive generals get shit jobs, while the toadies kiss his ass and get promoted. Donnelly knows this, Corning does too. But when you ask them about it, what do they say? They quote Kipling. You can't hustle the East, they say. And you know what I say to that?" He pounded the table. "I say bullshit!"

There was a pause while he glared around him pugnaciously. Marnin looked uneasily at the neighboring tables, but nobody seemed to be paying Mandelbrot any notice.

"It's hard to get Billy to express an opinion," Claudio said and laughed.

"I can understand Donnelly," Mandelbrot continued. "He's a military man and he's trained to accomplish a mission. So if you're given mission impossible, the trick is to keep ten thousand balls in the air in order to obfuscate what's really going on. It's only a two-year tour and hopefully you'll be living on General's Row at Fort Myer by the time the shit hits the fan. But Corning's something else. Diem trusts him. An Ambassador pays a price to achieve that kind of trust. But once he has it, he ought to use it. What's the point of having that trust if you're not willing to tell Diem the truth? If this government is what Corning says it is in his cables—"

"You read our cables?" David broke in.

"A few. But our guys in New York get them all! There's White House leakage you wouldn't believe. And don't think I'm bitter just because the President of the United States tried to fire me. . ."

"Come off it, man!" David exclaimed.

"Scoff if you like. But it's no secret in New York that JFK himself called in Cy Sulzberger last month for a chat in the Oval Office to suggest that our man in Saigon be replaced by someone more. . . mature."

"Not a bad idea, actually," said Claudio.

"Cy told Kennedy, politely of course, to shove it. And what was I accused of? Reporting with too much zeal. I was overzealous! I'd said we were in big trouble—that Diem sits in his palace isolated from his people, that Nhu brags that he controls everything Diem hears and sees." Mandelbrot shook his head. "Those guys are in the bunker. We're seeing the last days of Hitler all over again."

There was a loud snort from Buechner. Mandelbrot rushed on.

"If you ask me—"

"Somehow I think we're going to hear this even if we don't," David interjected.

"—We should take this whole fucking rotten government and dump it in the Saigon River. Corning says sure there are problems, but there's no one who can run this country better than Diem and Nhu. But I think there's no one who can run it worse. Any coolie rickshaw driver would be better. The fact is we need new leadership on the Vietnamese side and on the American side as well. You can tell Corning I said so. He feels free to advise Kennedy to get me fired. Well, I feel free to advise Kennedy to fire him."

"Whatever happened to journalistic objectivity?" David inquired.

Mandelbrot ignored the question. Suddenly pounding the table, he rose and furiously declaimed, "One thing's for sure—if we stick with Corning and Diem, then it's all going down the tubes. We're going to lose this war. Did you hear me? We're going to lose!"

There was a long pause. Marnin looked at the surrounding tables once more, but none of the other diners were paying the slightest attention to Mandelbrot's antics. Pepe and Buechner looked at each other, and then back at Mandelbrot, who remained standing, his finger raised prophetically.

"Kennedy's right," said Claudio. "You do have too much zeal."

Mandelbrot grinned a bit sheepishly.

"Let's go to La Cigalle," he said. "I'll buy."

"Who can resist an offer like that?" Claudio rejoined.

La Cigalle was an upscale nightclub on the Rue Catinat. As they entered, a Vietnamese vocalist in a red mini that barely reached her thighs was gyrating onstage and, backed up by a Filipino orchestra, was belting out "Let's Twist Again Like We Did Last Summer." Customers were tapping their feet and bouncing in their chairs in time to the music, but the dance floor was empty. In the dim light the party of foreigners threaded its way to a table at the front of the room. There they joined three more journalists: Miranda Pickerel, a knockout blonde stringer for Time-Life, Larry Burrows, a famous Life photographer, and a Vietnamese cameraman named Ha Thuc Can.

Claudio, who sat down next to Miranda, observed that Madame

Nhu, who had recently infuriated everyone by introducing a ban on dancing, was destroying the economy. "This place used to be so crowded you couldn't get in. Now look at it," he said, "it's nearly empty."

"Better watch it," Mandelbrot warned, "the Dragon Lady's lackeys are listening." The nightclub was said to be patronized by spies and agents provocateurs of all sorts, including Nhu's security police. "She doesn't take kindly to criticism, especially from foreigners."

"Well, I don't take kindly to her edict," said Claudio. "Dancing was the only way I could get close to Miranda. Now—what hope do I have?"

"None," said Miranda. "As a matter of fact, I just interviewed her on this very subject. And she said—and I quote—(here she lapsed into an exaggerated French-Vietnamese accent)—"Dahn-ceeng? Why ees everyone so ahn-gry about thees bahn on dahn-ceeng? Eef they 'ave so much enairgy they should go out and fight! Do you theenk they are dahn-ceeng the Pee-pair-meent Tweest een Hanoi?" Miranda paused for the ensuing laughter and turned to Claudio. "Madame Nhu also said people should practice more sexual abstinence. She had you in mind, Claudio."

"Me? But I am like a priest."

A curvaceous Vietnamese in a tight yellow ao dai handed some sheet music to the bandleader, then swung into an energetic rendition of "It's My Party and I'll Cry if I Want To," lifting her arms and vigorously gesticulating.

Buechner groaned.

"Oh my God! Help me, I'm falling! Get me an ambulance!"

"What is it, man?" Mandelbrot asked in mock alarm.

"See that little triangle of flesh at the waist when she lifts her arms? It drives me mad! *Complètement fou!*"

A pretty Vietnamese with long straight hair down to her waist and wearing a traditional *ao dai* entered and walked to the bandstand. She, too, carried a portfolio of sheet music under her arm, which she handed to the bandleader. Then she began to sing a Vietnamese ballad in a high plangent voice. When she had finished, Mandelbrot went over and talked to her.

Marnin, who was sitting on the other side of Miranda, said to her,

"Who are these girls?"

"They're minstrels," she replied. "They make the rounds every night, going from one club to the next, carrying their sheet music with them."

"That's a lovely girl," David said to Mandelbrot when he came back to the table.

"Yeah," he agreed. "It's hard to believe she's actually a Viet Cong Colonel."

Nights like this were heady stuff to a careful young man like Marnin just embarked on a diplomatic career. While he loved his new ambiance, he was disturbed at Mandelbrot's personal attacks on Corning. The following morning he felt it necessary to give his Ambassador a brief *précis* of the *Times* correspondent's remarks. In response, Corning looked at his aide bemusedly, but refrained from any comment. Two days later, however, he handed Marnin a neatly typed version of Mandelbrot's monologue, turned out by the ubiquitous South Vietnamese secret police, who had obviously tape recorded it.

"Watch what you say around this town," the Ambassador said laconically.

Three weeks to the day after his arrival in Saigon Marnin had been awakened at two by Cal Mehlert, the embassy duty officer. A "Flash" cable was in announcing that the President had reserved the networks to make a speech "of the highest national urgency" at seven P.M. Washington time. All ambassadors were directed to bring the contents of the speech to the attention of local chiefs of government and heads of state immediately. Specific instructions were to follow.

Marnin decided to call the DCM, Carl Bilder, before rousing the Ambassador, who had problems getting to sleep. The two of them agreed, the Department's instructions to the contrary, that there was no point in waking Corning in the middle of the night.

"It's a Flash cable to all posts worldwide," Bilder said. "So this can't be a Viet Nam focus. If it were, we'd know about it. It has to be something else."

He instructed Marnin to get in touch with the secretariat at the Palace and make an appointment for the Ambassador to see Diem at eight o'clock on a matter of the highest urgency. He said he would wake Corning at five-thirty himself.

Marnin hung up and then called the Palace on a line that was supposed to be manned twenty-four hours a day. He gave it twenty-five double rings on that French telephone system that was like playing roulette—there was a one in thirty-seven chance of hitting your number—but nobody answered. He tried the Palace five times in all. Then he called Mehlert to get the duty numbers for the Foreign Ministry and the Prime Minister's office, but had no luck at either place.

Marnin finally telephoned MACV and asked to speak to Tom Aylward, who was on within thirty seconds and said they would use the General's radio net to get through to ARVN channels, which could be trusted to be in touch with Diem. He promised to call if they could not make contact or if Diem were not available. Marnin gratefully went back to sleep.

It was Tuesday, October 23, 1962, seven A.M. and they were in the Ambassador's fifth floor office. Bilder was pacing back and forth across the width of the room. Marnin was in his usual seat facing the Ambassador's desk. Corning was perched on the table next to the window. At Pattie Lou's urging, he had taken to using an amber "medicated" cigarette holder with removable hairy plastic filters, changed with each new pack, thereby eliminating fifty per cent of the nicotine and eighty per cent of the "tars and resins." Putting the device to the ultimate test, he was smoking one after another, lighting a new one from the burning end of its predecessor, as he hunched over a Zenith Transoceanic short wave radio listening to the president's speech on Voice of America through heavy static.

Kennedy was laying out the problem in a measured, deadly serious tone, in that unforgettable New England twang:

". . .This urgent transformation of Cuba into an important strategic base, by the presence of these large, long-range and clearly offensive weapons of sudden mass destruction, constitutes an explicit threat to the peace and security of all the Americas. . . . This secret, swift and extraordinary build-up of Communist missiles in an area well known to have a special and historical relationship to the United States and the nations of the Western Hemisphere. . .this sudden, clandestine decision to station strategic weapons for the first time outside of Soviet soil, is a deliberately provocative and unjustified change in the status quo which cannot be accepted by this country, if our courage and our commitments are ever to be trusted again by either friend or foe. . . .

"Our unswerving objective, therefore, must be to prevent the use of these missiles against this or any other country, and to secure their withdrawal or elimination from the Western Hemisphere. . . . The path we have chosen for the present is full of hazards, as all paths are, but it is the one most consistent with our character and courage as a nation and our commitments around the world. The cost of freedom is always high, but Americans have always paid it. And one path we shall never choose, and that is the path of surrender or submission. . . ."

There was a long pause after Kennedy concluded. Bilder broke the silence.

"That's something," he said. "That is really something."

"It means war," Corning said. "If Russian ships are stopped on the high seas, Khrushchev will counter in Berlin."

Bilder glanced at his watch.

"I think I better look to the running of this embassy. Not too many people are going to feel like working this morning."

"The operational order of the day is business as usual," Corning said. "I want everyone to carry on. We're to be steady at the helm."

"We have a war to win right here," Bilder chimed in.

"That's right. And in terms of U.S. policy in this country, so long as we keep our nerve and don't panic and go to all out war this could even turn out to be fortuitous. For the Vietnamese, the big question mark has been will we stay the course. Now they'll see that when we make commitments we mean to keep them."

A grandfather clock was striking eight as Corning and Marnin were ushered into Diem's huge corner office on the second floor of Gia Long Palace by Ambassador Luyen, the Chief of Protocol. Marnin was there as note taker, as was Dinh Trieu Da, Diem's aide and second cousin. Luyen stopped at the threshold and left the four of them alone.

Diem's pudgy, agreeable face was well known to all readers of the Western press, but it was the first time Marnin had seen him up close. The President was wearing the familiar white sharkskin suit, white shirt, and a navy blue ecclesiastical club tie. Every inch of Diem's carved mahogany antique desk was piled two feet high with neatly stacked folders—hundreds of them. On the right hand side of the desk the folders were tied up with red ribbon; on the left hand with blue ribbon. Other than the desk, the room was furnished almost entirely in black and red; black lacquer tables, cabinets, and empty bookcases, and deeply upholstered red armchairs. Modern prints of old Chinese paintings, not very skillfully reproduced, hung on the walls. It felt less like an office than a hotel lobby.

Diem greeted Corning warmly. There was clearly a close rapport between them. The Americans had finally sent him an Ambassador he could trust. Corning and his aide were ushered into armchairs facing the President and his assistant across a low black lacquer table. On it was an oxblood red vase containing a stalk of four large white orchids. Palace servants dressed entirely in white entered with trays of local mineral water, Budweiser beer, Coca Cola, Fanta orange soda, Whitman Sampler chocolates, bitter tea, a thermos of coffee, and even a bottle of Remy Martin VSOP Cognac which tempted nobody at eight in the morning.

Both Diem and Corning were constant coffee drinkers and chain smokers. The President admired the Ambassador's new cigarette holder, asked to look at it, pulled out the filter and examined it, put the filter back and then inserted his own Gauloise and tried a few puffs and laughed happily.

"The wonders of modern science," he said.

"Mister President," Corning began his presentation, "I've asked to see you under instructions from my government and thank you for being good enough to receive me at this early hour."

"It is not early for me, Excellency. I take mass every morning of my life at six," Diem said in that peculiar, piping tenor voice.

"I was ordered by Washington to ask for an urgent appointment with you, Mr. President, to bring to your personal attention the extraordinary speech that your good friend, President Kennedy, just made within the hour."

"I have read it. Your USIS has delivered me a copy."

"It is in my view a speech for a lifetime. It reminds me of one of Churchill's perorations calling on the English to resist Hitler."

"It is very significant, very powerful," Diem agreed. "And it has great importance for this country, for the struggle we are undertaking against the communists. It also reminded me of Churchill. Your Vice-President Johnson, after visiting us last year, was good enough to call me the Winston Churchill of Asia. That moved me deeply. But making stirring speeches like Churchill's is not the Asian way. We try to stick to facts and figures, to talk to our people as a father does to his children. Whenever I go off to the countryside and talk with the peasants about their problems, your USIS chief Mr. Mecklin wants to make a newsreel about it. But that is not the Asian way either. The Asian way is simplicity and strength, to show by doing, to be modest, not to claim what you are not. Speaking frankly, Your Excellency, after the fiasco of the Bay of Pigs when you mounted an attack against Cuba and then changed your minds right in the middle of the operation, many of your friends began to worry about you. Without you we are lost. Every Vietnamese knows this, whether he is a democrat like me or a neutralist in Paris or even a communist in Hanoi."

"Exactly the conclusion I came away with, Mr. President. Our willingness to face up to the Soviets in Cuba should be an extremely encouraging development for you and your countrymen. There are five points I am instructed to emphasize."

It was Marnin's first effort as a note taker—that quintessential diplomatic skill—and he was beginning at the Chief of State level and was nervous. The armchair was so deep and plush he had difficulty taking notes on the yellow legal pad brought along for that purpose. As the conversation progressed, he noticed with mounting uneasiness that his counterpart Da never put pen to paper.

"First of all," Corning said, "this action by the Kremlin was done entirely clandestinely. At the time it was happening the Soviet government flatly was denying that anything untoward was taking place, even in the face of unimpeachable photographic evidence. . . ."

"These Communists cannot be trusted, Excellency," Diem interjected. "Lying, cheating, killing is all right for them if it serves their purpose. After the war they seized Khoi, my oldest brother, and threw him in a cell with fifty other prisoners, a cell built by the French for two people. You can imagine the conditions. Then they asked for his family to send warm clothes. It was winter and there was no heat in the jail. My brother, he suffered from consumption. My sister-in-law, she was sick in bed and decided to send her oldest son, who had been hiding in the house of one of our servants. But when the boy came with his father's clothes they arrested him too. They dug a big pit and threw them both in, the boy and his father, and buried them alive. Alive, Excellency!

"Later Ho Chi Minh, he sends me a message. It was all a big mistake by local cadres. We should forget about it and work together for the good of the country. As if these communists care about our country. These people are lackeys. They are bootlickers. They are servants of the Kremlin. And these people are animals. Just yesterday in Tay Ninh province they went into a village and got hold of this farmer with two hectares of land—two hectares!—and said he is a landlord, an exploiter of others. This is a poor man with one water buffalo, five pigs and some chickens and ducks."

Diem said something to Da in Vietnamese, directing him to go over to the desk and bring him one of the hundreds of folders. Da fished in the pile and came up with one. Diem gestured impatiently. It was the wrong folder. He gave Da further directions and the correct folder was retrieved. There were about a hundred sheets of paper in it. Diem put on his black, horn-rimmed reading glasses and pulled out a report. He translated from it, reading slowly and with emotion.

". . .They declared him a landlord and held a trial and convicted him. They cut him in fifty places and hung him upside down and let him bleed to death slowly, like a chicken, and made his wife watch, and his seven children watch. They are animals."

Diem paused for effect. After a surreptitious look at his watch, Corning seized his opportunity.

"The second point I would like to underline, Mr. President, is that there was no cause whatsoever for this Kremlin move. Mr. Khrushchev represents it as legitimate defense of an ally in peril. He says that his action was undertaken as legitimate self-defense, in line with article fifty-one of the United Nations Charter. . . ."

"This is typical, Excellency, typical, of the way the communists operate," Diem asserted. "They are the same in Russia, in China, and here. These people who lie and steal and cheat every day in every action they do, in every word they utter, have no shame about using the democratic legal guarantees of the civilized nations for their own purposes."

He snapped an order to Da, who went to the desk and fetched

another folder, the twelfth down in the pile.

"In Binh Dinh province just last week a VC squad entered a village after dark and seized the village chief. Then they called out all the villagers and made them take part in a trial that lasted six hours. They said the chief was an exploiter, that he robbed the people. They of course found him guilty of all charges. They took off all his clothes and made him roll around in a pig pen till he was all covered with mud and pig dirt. Then they laid him out on the ground as though he was being crucified, with three men holding him down, one on each arm and one holding his legs. And a fourth man took a large pungee stick, thick as a javelin, dipped it into human excrement and plunged it into his heart."

Taking advantage of Diem's brief pause for effect, Corning leapt in to make his next point.

"I am also under instructions to stress, Mr. President, that this move by the men in the Kremlin is unprecedented. Never before have nuclear-tipped ballistic missiles been stationed outside the territory of the Soviet Union itself."

"Cuba is only the first place, Mr. Ambassador," Diem interjected. "Let them have their missiles in Cuba and soon, you'll see, there will be missiles in Egypt and Indonesia and in Hanoi too. The communists, they cut you up and eat you piece by piece, like thin slices of salami. They come into a village and say to the village chief we have to hide in the jungle. All we want you to do is look the other way. We don't ask you to do anything for us. We don't harm you and your people. You don't harm us. Just mind your own business. Two more months go by and they say some of their people have been killed and they need three recruits from the village. After that the village is hooked. Just let them inside the door and soon they are sleeping in your bed. And that's just what Khrushchev will do. He will say that he's only putting those missiles in Cuba as a defense, as though anyone practices aggression against them. Fifty years ago they did not exist. Now the Communists have two billion people under tight control—half the world. And they have the nerve to say they are worried about the rest of us attacking them and that there's no reason for us to worry about them attacking us."

Corning had several meetings scheduled for the late morning, including an eleven o'clock briefing of a visiting Congressional delegation (CODEL Murphy) headed by Congressman Thomas Murphy of Massachusetts, Chairman of the House Armed Services Committee. He glanced at his watch once more, then resolutely resumed.

"The fourth point I'm under instruction to underline, Mr. President," he said, "is the moderate and prudent nature of the American response. Nobody wants war, least of all my country. Despite the grave nature of the threat, we are meeting it cautiously, with a real determination not to be provocative."

"This shows the real cleverness," Diem interjected again. "No, no, no, not cleverness, I should say brilliance of my friend John Kennedy. It was he, you know, who found me in Ossining and who was my champion—he and Cardinal Spellman. He was a brilliant young man. And so handsome, a young prince. Yes, it is clever in the extreme to give the other side a chance to think matters over before they do something rash."

This reminded Diem of the dilemma faced by Trieu Da after he conquered Au Lac and set up the first Government of Viet Nam in 208 B.C.—how to preserve his gains without unnecessarily upsetting the Han Dynasty in China. Trieu Da, at each milestone along the road, faced problems similar to those encountered by Diem's good friend President Kennedy in his efforts to lead the Free World against the depredations of the Communists. The travails of Trieu Da, in turn, reminded him of the wisdom of Emperor Dinh Bo Linh, who managed to maintain the independence of Viet Nam at the height of the Sung Dynasty, when his army was incomparably weaker than that of China. Diem then chronicled various high points of Vietnamese history, stretching from 208 B.C. to 1772 A.D. and the start of the Tayson rebellion, when the Nguyen clan was unseated from power. At that point, Corning, having drunk six demitasse cups of coffee and filled two ashtrays to overflowing, stood up, looked at his watch for the fifteenth time, and announced, "I'm terribly sorry to leave, Mr. President, but Congressman Murphy and a delegation of seven other

Congressmen, whom you're scheduled to see tomorrow afternoon, are due in my office in fifteen minutes."

Diem rose as well, seemingly reluctantly.

"Of course, Excellency, of course. I can finish my little history lecture some other time. And you've heard it all before, haven't you?" He laughed gaily in that special, high-pitched way he had as they all walked toward the door. Suddenly, he stopped.

"But Excellency, what was the fifth point?"

"The fifth point?"

"The fifth point you wanted to stress."

"Oh, yes, the fifth point." For a second Corning could not remember. "Of course, the fifth point. I'm glad you reminded me, Mr. President. The fifth point was to ask for your support in explaining the American quarantine of Cuba to your people as well as to your counterparts in neighboring countries who might be more persuaded by a fellow Asian than by us."

"I will issue a statement later this afternoon. I'll write it right now, as soon as you leave. But as for my neighbors, I am afraid they pay little attention to what I think."

The Ambassador and the President both laughed.

"What did you think of Diem?" Corning asked on their way back to the embassy in the Checker.

"He certainly is a talker," Marnin said.

"It can be a lot worse than this. This was only three hours. Sometimes I want to see him about four or five subjects and I can only get through the top one on the list. Once he starts talking, there's no known way to get him to stop."

"But I liked him," Marnin said. "There's something about him that's very likable."

"He has lots of charm. It's a little known fact."

Back in his office, after the briefing of CODEL Murphy in the Embassy conference room on the sixth floor, Marnin asked Corning how he wanted him to handle the twenty-seven yellow pages of notes he had taken of the conversation that morning. Corning was feeling expansive. One way of cutting back on cigarettes was to use a pipe. He had a dozen in the table behind his desk on which the Zenith Transoceanic was set. He selected a Sherlock Holmes curved meerschaum and filled it with a special aromatic mixture, smelling strongly of cloves, blended for him by P. Coomaraswamy, his tobacconist in Hong Kong.

"Try your hand at a memcon. I'll dictate a brief cable to Helen when I get back from lunch that will cover the salient points."

"I felt a little foolish," Marnin said, "sitting there and scribbling away while the President's aide did not take a single note."

"Don't be fooled by that," Corning replied. "Da, who by the way is Diem's cousin, has something close to a photographic memory. I've seen him in negotiations refer to conversations that took place a year previously that I've then checked against our own memcons and found them to be near verbatim recollections of exactly what was said. He has a doctorate in particle physics from Cal Tech—studied with Murray Gell-Mann."

"Do you think Diem was really as encouraged as he sounded?" Marnin asked. "Not too many Americans around here are very optimistic right now."

"It's not surprising they feel that way. I have a lot of experience with the Russians and I don't think there's a chance of Khrushchev backing down in Cuba without doing something about it elsewhere, with Berlin being the odds-on favorite. Monkey around with Berlin in the current mood and it could mean war."

"But do you think this can really make a difference here? We're an awfully long way from Moscow, or Havana for that matter."

"That's dead wrong," Corning replied. "That's what Mandelbrot thinks, what all the young reporters think. Youth has its virtues. But patience is not one of them. It's natural for the young to simplify, to think that what's important is moving ahead quickly to win the war. The fact is, every bit of statistical evidence we have proves it, we are winning the war. But it can't be done overnight. There's not going to be any armistice agreement like we have at Panmunjom in Korea. There won't be any surrender on the deck of the Missouri. This is a war that's just going to fade away. We're going to win it gradually, place by place, hamlet by hamlet. The indicators of victory are going to be statistical. Once we get below a certain point, the insurgency will degenerate into isolated banditry.

"But every time a Delta farmer brings his crop to market it's a victory for the GVN. Every time a new school or factory is opened, this country strengthens. We'll have almost 300,000 tons of rice for export this year. The number of students in primary and middle schools has doubled over the past five years. Manufacturing has gone up by over seventeen per cent. Diem is a Confucian. People don't understand what that means. They try to measure success by popularity, as though this were Waukeegan or Oshkosh. What counts is whether a functioning state is becoming more entrenched with each passing day. Of course Diem has defects. But so did the Kang Hsi emperor and he was probably the most successful single ruler in Asian history."

"But perceptions are important," Marnin rejoined. "And there seems to be a widespread perception here, not just from Mandelbrot but from the Vietnamese themselves, that Diem's government and his dictatorial style are not what this country needs."

"Of course there is. Everybody who ever went to a *lycée* in this place thinks he's more qualified to run this country than Diem. And they don't mind telling you about it either. You can't sit down at a sidewalk cafe without someone coming over to explain to you why this government is doomed to walk the plank. That's why I have to laugh when they call South Viet Nam a dictatorship. Worse than Hanoi, they say. I'd like to see any North Vietnamese talk that way to a foreigner about Ho Chi Minh or any Russian talk that way about Khrushchev. Twenty years in a labor camp if they're lucky, that's what they'd get for talking that way. But you're right. Perceptions determine willpower and I'm convinced that if we have the will, the United States can't lose.

"The only question is how much time it will take to win. Diem is right. The one thing that all Vietnamese—Communist, neutralist, or nationalist—agree on is that the Viet Nam war won't be decided in Moscow or Peiping, or even, for that matter, in Hanoi or Saigon. It will be decided in Washington. Once Americans agree that there are certain rock bottom interests we're willing to put our lives on the line to defend, then we'll never have to go to war to defend them. It's only when the other side senses confusion that it will dare to provoke us. That's why our willingness to stand up to Mister Khrushchev is going to mean so much in Viet Nam. Everybody knows we're winning the peace. This means that we'll win the war as well. We've reached a turning point. We're going to win."

Three days later, on October 26, Corning and Marnin took their seats at the National Day celebrations in the section of honor reserved for the diplomatic corps, having arrived at the prescribed time—seven in the morning. What would normally have been a three minute drive from the Residence had taken twenty minutes. The streets along the Saigon River had been closed off and, despite the early hour, traffic jams blocked the center of the city.

Bowing to Diem's preference, the Ambassador was in a white suit, a white shirt, and an All Souls tie. Marnin was sitting next to him, substituting for Pattie Lou, who had given up attending Vietnamese ceremonial occasions, which combined stultifying heat and impenetrable boredom as speech after speech droned on in Vietnamese, interspersed with marching songs played by the enthusiastic but not very adept Vietnamese Air Force band.

They spoke in whispers, although it was not really necessary to do so. Like the rest of the corps, they paid little attention to the ceremony as it proceeded. Sitting next to them was the British Ambassador, Sir Neville Boggs, who had recently given up smoking and now knitted whenever he felt the nicotine urge. That morning he finished almost a quarter of an alpine sweater, with Lady Boggs holding the carmine yarn in her lap.

Diem arrived at seven-thirty, after everyone was seated. Nobody was permitted to enter the ceremonial enclosure once he made his entrance. The band played "Diem Thong Tong," the song that had become the Vietnamese equivalent of "Hail to the Chief." Following the Minister of the Interior, the Archbishop of Saigon, and the provincial Governor, the President was the fourth of six speakers on the program and the briefest of them all. In a high-pitched monotone he read from a text over a pair of half spectacles, hardly looking up and with almost no expression, as though this were a painful duty that had to be fulfilled. A translation had already been furnished to the embassy. The Missile Crisis is a great boon to our country, he said. The Soviets will back down in Cuba. The Communists are on the run everywhere. The masses are starving in China. North Viet Nam is in terrible shape economically. The Vietnamese people know this. They have seen the steadfastness of their American allies. As a result, the Viet Cong will lose faith in Communism, an alien ideology, and in Communist victory, a forlorn hope, and will stop fighting. Equitable reconciliation between the North and the South can then, and only then, take place.

Knowing that Marnin's Memorandum of Conversation with Diem was the first written effort of a nascent diplomatic career, Corning had been kind enough to make a special effort to show that he was pleased with it. He had it with him in a manila envelope and handed it to Marnin and patted him on the right shoulder. The younger diplomat thumbed through the manuscript. The Ambassador had made numerous corrections. But on the top right hand corner of the first page he had written, in the violet ink he used to differentiate himself from others in the Embassy, "Excellent. Good Work!" Marnin felt a tingle of pride suffuse his body.

"Your reconstruction of what Diem said is really most interesting, David," the Ambassador said in a low voice, paying no attention to what was going on around him. "Particularly the parts that draw on Vietnamese history to make a point. In the two years I've been here I don't know of anyone who's bothered to get down the totality of one of Diem's monologues before. The old hands are so anxious for him to get done so that we can get a word in edgewise on the Strategic Hamlet Program or the CIP or whatever, that we no longer listen to what he's saying. But there's more coherence, and even wisdom, in those excursions into Vietnamese history than we give him credit for."

"I wasn't really sure whether I was spinning my wheels or not, whether trying to get down everything he said was worth the effort."

"It is. And you should keep doing it. Get in the habit of putting your impressions on paper while you're looking at things with fresh eyes. My advice is always make a written record of what's happening to you. Otherwise, you'll forget. We all forget. Youth has a touching faith in the constancy of its memory. But its faith is misplaced. If we win here, our efforts will become part of a fading tapestry that nobody will care about, but that you'll want to keep very straight in your own mind. And if we lose. . . ."

He turned away at this point, finishing the thought without looking at Marnin, as though he were embarrassed even to raise it.

"If we lose, then each event will simmer in the mind and be recooked by what happens next. The separate ingredients will fuse and the flavors will gradually fade until it all becomes a large, undigested stew."

Chapter 5

THE GUATEMALAN SOLUTION

The following evening, after three sets of singles under the lights, Marnin and Pepe, towels slung around their necks, sat on the verandah of the Cercle Sportif, savoring their gin and tonics. Filled with newly imbibed wisdom about Viet Nam, David tried out his theories on the older diplomat.

"The missile crisis," he said, "is going to make a big difference here."

"I shouldn't think so," said Claudio, reaching for the peanuts. "Nobody's paying any attention to it."

"You're wrong. Hanoi is, and Saigon too. Because Kennedy has now definitively demonstrated that the U.S. will defend its interests."

Claudio grunted noncommittally.

"The one thing all Vietnamese agree about," David continued, parroting Corning, "is that the counter-insurgency effort and the eventual outcome of the war depend on a lasting U.S. commitment. The missile crisis proves to both the North and the South that we won't fold if and when the war heats up here. Kennedy has shown we won't be pushed around."

"You're getting confused. What Kennedy has shown is that he wants to get reelected in sixty-four."

"Come off it!"

"I'm a Guatemalan and I see things a little differently from you Yankees. You talk a lot about counter-insurgency, but you don't have a clue how to deal with one—even though you've already won one.

That's what you ought to be studying—instead of the works of Chairman Mao; you ought to be figuring out how you won against the Indians."

"You mean we should slaughter most of the Vietnamese and put the rest on reservations?"

"Isn't that the basic idea behind the Strategic Hamlet program? You stick the good guys inside and those who remain outside—you kill them."

"That's ridiculous," David said heatedly.

"But that's what you should be doing." Claudio smiled. "Now, in my country, we just happen to know a great deal about insurgencies. We've had at least one and maybe three of the largest insurgencies of the twentieth century, not to mention the seventeenth, eighteenth and nineteenth. You want to know how to deal with an insurgency? Simple, compadre—you kill all the insurgents. That takes care of it for one generation. Then when they come back, you kill them again. You grind them into powder—as often as it takes."

"Guatemala is hardly Viet Nam."

Claudio shrugged.

"Basically, the problem here is the same one the conquistadores faced in Latin America, and the same one you faced in North America: how do you keep a bunch of dumb indios in line? And the solution is the same—those with the guns you kill. The rest you make so fucking afraid they wouldn't pick up a gun if you handed it to them."

"That's simplistic. You're totally disregarding ideology, geography, politics, economics. . ."

"These have nothing to do with it, my friend. The real problem is boredom. Life in the boondocks is very uninteresting. A sixteen-year-old boy squatting fourteen hours a day planting rice—this is no fun at all. Now give this boy an automatic rifle, send him off to the jungle and train him to be a soldier—this is fun. He has excitement, adventure, compadres. Then when some foreigners or stooges of those foreigners tell him he should lay down his rifle and go back to squatting on his haunches fourteen hours a day in the boiling sun for the sake of "democracy," do you think he is going to do this? No. Once he has a rifle in his hands, you have to kill him. That is the Guatemalan Solution."

Claudio called for the bill and when it came he signed the chit. As they walked out to their cars, Claudio companionably put his hand on David's shoulder. "*Basta* with this stinking war," he said. "What do you say we head down to the Texas Rose and gather some rosebuds while we may?"

"Can't do it, sorry. Got an early staff meeting tomorrow."

"Are you saving yourself for your wife?"

"No," David smiled.

"This is not a good idea." Claudio's expression was grave. "Nothing is worse in the tropics than celibacy. It's bad for your health. It's bad for your tennis. Look what's happened to Diem."

"What?"

"He's gone crazy."

Marnin laughed. "From celibacy?"

"Definitely," Claudio said. "This is no joke."

Driving home, Marnin thought about Claudio Pepe. Viet Nam, he had begun to suspect, brought out the worst in everyone.

At six o'clock one morning in early November, as Marnin was leaving for the Embassy, he opened his front door and to his surprise found himself face to face with a fat Chinese woman of about sixty dressed in the black trousers and high-necked white jacket that cooks and amahs generally wore. Bubbling over with good humor, she introduced herself as Madame Chung.

"Mistah Claudio, he send me," she announced, and proceeded to make clear that her trade was the purveying of young girls, all of them, according to her, sweet, virginal and slavishly obedient.

"Money-back guarantee," she chirped, "if you no satisfied."

Marnin's mind went back to the conversation two weeks earlier after the tennis match. Was the appearance of this unlikely genie meant to be a test of some kind? Or was it merely a joke? Claudio was notorious in Saigon for his practical jokes. He had once slipped an exploding cigar into the Papal Nuncio's cigar box, with dire results at Monsignor's dinner party for the Archbishop of Hue, who happened to be the President's older brother, Ngo Dinh Thuc.

Or could this be a provocation? Preposterous as that seemed, there surfaced in his mind the memory of a three-hour security lecture given in the A-100 course, during which a sharply dressed agent with slicked-back sandy hair from SY named Cassidy, bolstering his case with anecdote after anecdote of code clerks and diplomats gone astray and photographed ass up through keyholes, stressed that sexual entrapment was the principal means the KGB used to enmesh Foreign Service Officers in its web of espionage. Although the thought of Claudio as a KGB agent was bizarre, Burgess and McLain had fooled their American colleagues in Washington and London for years. If the British diplomatic service could be penetrated, why not the Guatemalan?

David, nevertheless, could not resist asking the cost of her services.

"For you," she grinned, "first time no charge. Mistah Claudio, he say charge to his account."

"I could never accept that," David said firmly.

That was a mistake, because to Mme. Chung it implied that he was willing to agree to other arrangements.

"I'm really not interested at all," he added hastily, trying to rectify his error.

"Monsieur David," she said earnestly, "I give you best price in town. You go see. You compare, do bargain shopping. You no get bettah price nowhere. And these no bar girl shit. These good girl from good family. Go to school. Become doctor, judge—you see."

"How much?" he asked again.

Like many negotiators, she remained elusive, pushing her product, but refusing to name her price. "These Numbah One girl, they like daughter to me. You be nice. No hitting, no slap around, no belt, no hairbrush, no nothing like that. Kissing all right though," she laughed.

"How much, Mme. Chung?" David insisted.

"How much?" she repeated, as if this were a new concept. "Price for you. . .very special price is—"

She paused.

"—twelve hundred piastre. You take two girls each week, get one girl free. Three girls week, twenty-four hundred P. Numbah One girl—clean, young, pretty, tight pussy. What you say?"

David laughed.

"You're a hell of a saleswoman, Mme Chung. But I think I'm going to pass on this opportunity."

An expression of suspicion replaced her grin; she looked him up and down, her left eyebrow cocked.

"You pansy boy?" she asked.

"No. No. I like girls. But I. . .well, I like to find them myself," he concluded lamely.

"I find you bettah girl than you find yourself," she countered angrily, her professional pride piqued. "Younger, prettier, do anything you want, anything you even think you want. You be satisfy. Best pussy in town. Best pussy in whole world. Viet Nam girl sweet like mango. You be one big happy man."

At this point he realized what he should have known at the start—she would never get off his doorstep as long as he said no.

"I'll think about it."

Her grin returned, lighting up her fat face. She dug into the pocket of her jacket and withdrew a stiff, gold calling card at the top of which was a crossed-out printed telephone number and another one above it scrawled in pencil. In the center of the card there appeared, in embossed French lettering:

Mme. Chung
Objets d'art
Bought and Sold

Chapter 6

LOOKING FOR SOMEONE

More than once Marnin took Mme. Chung's card from amidst the cuff links, collar stays and loose change in the top drawer of his dresser, looked at it, and put it back. Nowhere in the world were there more attractive, available women than in Saigon. Yet in two months he had not had a date, let alone slept with anyone. So women were on his mind. But he did not want a bar fly, who would be little better than a prostitute, nor a pubescent alleged virgin. He wanted someone in between, but told himself that he was too busy to go out hunting, or perhaps too lazy. Girls had never been a problem and he knew someone would come along.

"Someone", as he defined her, was a woman who was smart, funny and beautiful—in that order. To date, only Miranda Pickerel filled that bill. The problem with Miranda was that her lifestyle precluded attachments and, while he was not interested in anything permanent, he did not want to follow in Mandelbrot's wake and be just the latest on her Leporello list of casual conquests. Thanksgiving (turkey and trimmings at the Cornings) came and went. The cool season (a relative term) arrived and the weather became relatively drier. Some of the trees, to David's surprise, actually dropped their leaves. Within a week, after the shortest winter on God's earth, they began to grow again. The war continued to be quiet, but as the number of battlefield incidents fell off, the number of visiting congressional delegations (CODELS) picked up, as though there were some sort of inverse correlation between the two.

In mid-December "CODEL BOWMAN" arrived for a three-day swing; the congressmen and their staffers choppered to the four Corps headquarters while their wives remained in Saigon Christmas shopping. (Starting the following year, when things heated up, congressional wives rarely came to Viet Nam, and did their shopping in Bangkok or Hong Kong.)

On their last night in Saigon, Carl Bilder and his wife Ursula gave a dinner for the Bowman party at their villa on a quiet side street not far from the embassy. At first the guests stood outside on the patio beneath a string of Christmas tree lights—the women in long bare dresses, the men sweating in coats and ties—drinking gin-tonics while "Frosty the Snowman" and other seasonal tunes emanated from the outdoor speakers.

Bilder had rounded up the usual hangers-on for this affair—the Minister of Finance, a couple of high-ranking Foreign Ministry types, a two-star ARVN General, the Thai Ambassador, the director of USOM, a senior CIA agent, all with their wives, and, to fill in the blanks, Marnin and Mme. Do Ba Xang. Once again, she was dressed in a white silk *ao dai* without ornament but for a small sprig of jasmine tucked into the chignon at the nape of her neck. Once again, she greeted him without the trace of a smile.

As they sat down to dinner at a long table set for twenty-two, Marnin happily found that the widow was seated to his right. To begin the festivities Ursula Bilder, a bossy schoolmarmish woman with a graying bun—who was actually the principal of the local American elementary school—tapped the side of her water glass with a knife, thereby asking for silence.

"Now gentlemen," she said with officious merriment, "everyone turn to the lady on your right so we don't have any wallflowers. And remember, this is the holiday season, so no shop talk!"

Marnin, happily following orders, turned to Mme. Do Ba Xang.

"I'm David Marnin, we met at—"

"I remember you, Mr. Marnin," she said without expression. Her English was overlaid with a thick French accent. "Also, I have seen you play at the Cercle Sportif. You have a beautiful game."

"Thank you," said David, tongue-tied with pleasure. "I uh. . . well,

I've been playing a long time."

"Really?" She studied his face impassively. "Then you must have started when you were very young."

"Not that young," David replied.

"So difficult," she said coolly, "to tell the ages of you Westerners."

A servant cleared away her soup bowl and placed a ramekin of Coquilles St. Jacques before her, leaving Marnin with the conviction that they had not gotten off to a happy start.

When the servant had withdrawn, she said to him, "Now if you'll forgive me, I must speak to the gentleman on my right before I am reprimanded by my hostess."

The man on her right was Frank (formerly Francois) Gascon, the chief liaison between the CIA and the ARVN senior officers, and a pal of Mandelbrot's. He was a large, bullet-headed man with an enormous protruding stomach who was always chewing on a dead cigar.

Gascon had been raised in Marseilles, having arrived in the United States at the age of sixteen after his mother married an American seaman. When the war started he had gone to London to enlist in De Gaulle's forces and had served for fourteen years in the French military. At the end of the French Indochina war, while still serving in Hanoi as a Lieutenant Colonel in the Foreign Legion, he had joined the CIA.

"He's thick as thieves with the ARVN brass," Mandelbrot had said to Marnin. "Don't forget, when he was in Hanoi every one of these generals was a non-com or junior officer in the French Army."

From screening intelligence reports for the Ambassador, Marnin knew that Gascon's access to the higher levels of the ARVN was total and unparalleled. He was regarded by the Vietnamese as a colorful, sympathetic and macho senior officer, an impression that was helped along by his native French overlaid with a Marseilles accent, his tough guy veneer and his good natured self-absorption. He was no shrinking violet. Among the many stories about Gascon were persistent tales of his exploits in the jungles of Viet Nam in the early fifties and the numerous exotic alliances he had contracted—including "marriages" with daughters of montagnard tribal chieftains and Laotian princesses—though the present wife, a morose metisse named Suzy, seemed unremarkable enough.

Like dancers in a quadrille, the dinner guests punctiliously changed partners with each course—Ursula Bilder was one of those hostesses who did things by the numbers—so that Marnin spoke to Mme. Do Ba Xang with the soup, roast duck and camembert, and to Mme Huang Thuc Nhai, the wife of the head of the America section in the Foreign Ministry, during the scallops, salad and apple tart. (After dinner the ladies withdrew upstairs and he had cognac and coffee with the men.)

At one point, during the salad, as he was asking Mme. Nhai the ages of her children, he heard Gascon, loud and well lubricated by then, attempting to regale the widow with his amorous adventures.

"After Dien Bien Phu," said Gascon in his guttural Marseilles French, "I walked into the jungle with nothing but a toothbrush and came out five years later with three wives, six gold bars. . .and the same damn toothbrush. Those gold bars were heavy, let me tell you."

A servant brought the cheese tray to Mme. Xang; she turned to her left and, meeting Marnin's eyes, sighed expressively. He leaned toward her.

"What do you suppose," he said under his breath, "happened to those other wives?"

Her lips curled faintly. "*Tiens*! I suppose he bored them to death."

David laughed.

"At least it must have been a mercifully quick demise."

"Sh! Mme. Bilder is observing us—if she thinks we're enjoying ourselves she'll be very cross." She helped herself to some camembert from the tray. "I heard you speaking French just now to Mme. Nhai. You're very fluent."

"I lived for a year with an uncle in Montreal."

"But you don't have that disgusting French-Canadian accent."

"I was at a *lycée*," he said, not much liking her superior tone, "not a logging camp."

"Yes, of course." She looked at him. "So, Monsieur—"

"David."

She nodded slightly.

"So. . .David. . .I perceive you are a man of many talents. . ."

Now she was teasing him, and he did not much like that either.

"I'm also a good driver. Could I give you a lift home after dinner?"

"You're very kind," she paused, "but I came with your director of USOM, Dr. Bird."

Marnin glanced up the table at "Curly" Bird, bald and good-natured, conversing stolidly with the Finance Minister, then back at the widow.

"Perhaps another time," she said.

She turned back to Gascon and he to Mme. Nhai, and they spoke no more until the party broke up.

In the foyer she turned to him and wordlessly extended her small hand. He took it and said, "*Au revoir*, Madame."

She made a little *moue* of impatience. "Oh please—you needn't be so formal. My name is Lily."

Chapter 7

THE STREET OF FLOWERS

The holidays arrived and so did Amanda Corning—blond, sweet, pretty and seductive, a genuine southern belle, back from her freshman year at Sweetbriar. David took her to dinner at the Diamond, for local color, to Attarbea, the best of Saigon's excellent French restaurants, and escorted her to various embassy parties. In the darkened Residence living room afterward he went as far as one could and have her still remain a virgin, which had its frustrations, but was nevertheless a great relief to him.

He was sure he could have bedded her too. He considered it. Where and when was the problem. Taking her to his place was risky in the highly charged atmosphere of Saigon, where secret police agents were known to be tracking the movements of embassy officers. Perhaps more to the point, he had heard somewhere that you could look at a girl's mother and see what the girl would be like. Testing this out in Attarbea one evening after two martinis and a bottle of medoc, as he gazed at the lissome Amanda through the candle flame and squinted slightly, he saw in the blurred image leathery old Patti Lou. That settled it.

On December 21st, the Cornings gave a Christmas dinner dance in Amanda's honor, with the music supplied by the six man Filipino orchestra that played regularly at the Officers Club at Tan Son Nhut. That afternoon, Mrs. Corning, finding she needed extra flowers for centerpieces for the eight round tables of ten guests each, dispatched Marnin to Nguyen Hue to buy more roses.

While normally this would have been an annoyance, nothing was happening at the embassy and Marnin was glad of the opportunity to get out of the office on an unusually pleasant day, the temperature barely above eighty. He walked along the broad boulevard known as "the street of flowers," enjoying the afternoon sunshine and the sights—stalls filled with fruits and sweets, vendors selling red paper lanterns in the shapes of stars and animals, and flower carts overflowing with narcissus and giant poinsettias and roses from Dalat. He bought four dozen scarlet roses and was threading his way past the stalls to his car when he literally bumped into Mme. Do Ba Xang, cradling two pots of jasmine and in the process of picking up a third.

"Oh, Monsieur Marnin," she said.

Before he had time to respond, the third pot of jasmine, with which she was struggling, started to slip from her grasp and Marnin, encumbered as he was, just managed to grab it.

"Here," he said, "let me help you. Where are you going?"

"Home. But my chauffeur has gone to pick up something for me. I was going to take a cyclo."

"May I offer you a ride—once again?"

She hesitated.

"Yes, why not? That's very kind. Here," she said, handing him the pots, "you take these, I'll take the roses."

As they walked in the direction of the car, David, speaking French, said, "What a beautiful street this is!"

"Yes, it's especially pretty at Christmas and Easter."

"It never occurred to me that Christian holidays would be so celebrated here."

"Many of us are Catholics, after all. As you know, the President spent years in monasteries all over the world, including New Jersey."

As they reached the car, Marnin opened the door and put the pots of jasmine and the flowers in the back seat.

"It's too bad Diem didn't become a priest like his brother," she continued. "He would have made a better priest than a president and his brother would be a better president than a bishop."

"Why do you think that?"

"Because Diem likes to give sermons, is ill at ease with people, and doesn't like women."

She laughed gaily at her own observation, which was a standard bon mot in Saigon. Marnin thought he had never seen anyone so ravishingly lovely.

"Well, I do," he said.

Taken aback by the candor of his gaze, Lily lowered her eyes. "So I see," she murmured. Then she looked up. "And are all these roses for a friend?"

"Yes," he laughed, "for my friend, Mrs. Corning."

The Deux Chevaux was old and run down and Marnin had had continual trouble with the transmission. He hunched over the wheel, trying to get the car in gear.

"This damn thing," he muttered, "it's not a car, it's an egg beater. Why are you laughing at me?"

"You're too big for this car—you look like Gulliver in Lilliput. You should be driving an American Chrysler like Curly's."

"I inherited this—" he said, finally jamming the car into gear and bucking out into the street "—from my predecessor. Where to?"

"Phan Dinh Phung."

They were silent a few moments. Then David asked, "Is Dr. Bird a good friend?"

"Yes, he has been very kind to us since my husband's death."

"Us?"

"My two daughters and me. You must meet them some time. Turn right here. . ."

They pulled up before the iron gate of a villa in the First Quartier. A Kha guard with a carbine peered in at them and Mme. Xang impatiently motioned him to open the gate. The house was not a traditional French colonial villa, but a large modern stucco building. Marnin carried the pots of jasmine to the front door, which was opened by a servant.

"I'm going to have some tea," Lily said. "Will you join me?"

He accepted and they walked through the entry hall into the drawing room, where she excused herself. The large room in which he stood was filled with heavy, ornate Chinese arm chairs, ottomans, end tables, consoles, chests, settees and coffee tables, all illuminated with standing floor lamps—like the display room of an overstocked furniture store. In one corner of the living room was a new Frigidaire, a symbol of wealth and status in many Vietnamese households, but surprising in the home of one so sophisticated. He was inspecting a garish painting on velvet of a tropical sunset when she returned.

"Hideous, isn't it?"

Turning guiltily, he stammered, "Well. . .I. . .no. . ."

"Oh come, come, Monsieur Marnin—"

"David," he reminded her.

"—No need to dissemble. It's an atrocity, like all these other furnishings." She turned on one of the lamps. "Please sit down." She gestured toward a settee and sat in an adjacent chair.

"I don't understand. Aren't you. . .isn't this your house?"

"Let's just say. . .it's in my name. But I didn't buy it."

"But who then. . .does it belong to your family?" She looked at him silently and he added, "Sorry. . .I didn't mean to pry."

She shrugged. "Not at all. It belonged to my late husband's friends. A group of Vietnamese. . ." she paused, "patriots. They're really Chinese. After his death they gave it to me—the destitute widow of *un grand chevalier*. They wanted to put a plaque beside the door, but I wouldn't let them. Was that very selfish of me?"

He did not know how to answer her.

"I don't know," he said thoughtfully. "I can see how they'd want to honor him. . .the General was a great hero."

She smiled. "Haven't you heard, Monsieur Marnin—?"

"David."

"David. . .the old saying that no man is a hero to his wife?" She gave a brief, self-deprecating laugh and, looking down, said in a low, quavering voice, "Of course Xang was a hero. . .a very great hero." She looked up, her eyes shining like onyx in the lamplight, moist with tears. Marnin felt his own eyes tear.

A pretty, young servant girl entered with a tea tray. Setting it down before her mistress, she picked up the teapot to pour, but was curtly dismissed. The girl nodded sullenly and left. Lily served him jasmine tea and a kind of almond cake.

"Your parents," David inquired, "are they—"

"They live in Paris," she said.

She drank some tea and then went on rapidly. "My people came from Hanoi. When the French left in 1954, so did they—those who could. What's left of our family is in Paris. My father was an official of the court and then a diplomat. I grew up in France. I doubt I'd ever have come back here, but I met my husband in Paris while he was taking a course at the École Militaire. *et voilà!* We married and came to Viet Nam."

"And then?"

"Well," she sighed, "it's an old and not so very interesting story. While my husband was alive, we lived well. Of course, there is always an element of anxiety when one marries a soldier, but we had a good life. When he commanded I Corps in the north we lived in Hue, a very beautiful city. We raised our daughters. . ." She hesitated, continuing more slowly. "And then he was killed. . ." She broke off, then seemed to change tack and brought her story to an abrupt end. "And I moved to Saigon with my girls and accepted this. . .gift. *Mon Dieu!*" she said, looking rather annoyed, "I don't usually talk so much. I don't usually have anyone to talk with."

"But you must have many friends here."

"Not many. I was abroad for so long. Anyway, I'm really very busy. You may not believe me, but I have no time for such—"

"Time! Oh my God!" Marnin leapt to his feet, nearly knocking over the tea tray. "I'm so sorry. . .I completely forgot Mrs. Corning."

"That is not a good idea," she smiled.

"I'll say! You have no idea. May I see you again?" he asked as she walked him to the door.

"Yes."

"Really?" he said, startled at her easy acquiescence. "When?"

"Tonight."

"But tonight—"

"Tonight you shall see me at the Cornings."

"That's not what I meant."

"I know, but you shall see me there anyway. . .and then   " She opened the door.

"And then?"

"And then we shall see."

Chapter 8

THE WARRIOR

It was December 30, 1962. Christmas (another turkey at the Cornings) had come and gone, and so as of that morning had the nubile Amanda, whose healthy sexual appetites, as her vacation had come to a close, had the previous evening in the darkness of the Residence sun parlor, nearly undone his good intentions.

Having accompanied the Ambassador on a courtesy call on the Prime Minister, he had arrived late at Claudio's dinner party to find that the other guests were having drinks on the terrace. Glancing at the seating chart, he noted the usual sprinkling of journalists—Miranda Pickerel, Klaus Buechner, Mandelbrot; Embassy types—Frank Gascon and his wife, the Public Affairs Officer John Mecklin, and Helen Eng, the Ambassador's secretary; and some Vietnamese—Dinh Trieu Da, the President's aide; a girlfriend of Mandelbrot's named Hung who owned a dress boutique; and, to his delight, Lily Do Ba Xang, with whom he had danced several times at the dinner for Amanda given by the Cornings. But they were at different tables and their contact—other than the sedate dancing—had been minimal.

Collecting a whiskey from the houseboy, Marnin walked out onto the terrace to find the assembled guests in the evident thrall of a scrawny American recognizable by his haircut and demeanor as a military man. Short, about five feet seven, and dressed in khaki slacks, GI shoes, and a lavender Hawaiian sport shirt worn outside his pants, he was totally undistinguished. Only his pale blue eyes—washed-out yet strangely intense, as though back lighted—were remarkable, the eyes of a fanatic.

He turned out to be the fabled John Henry Mudd, who had made an unannounced trip up from the Delta for some holiday "Rest & Recreation." In his particular case, this meant arranging through Claudio, with whom he was staying, for six of Mme. Chung's star "pupils" and fucking them in relays, two at a time, for the next forty-eight hours, after which he intended to chopper back to My Tho, ready for what the New Year would bring.

Few men become legends to their friends, associates, and contemporaries: still fewer among those mired in the middle of the chain of command of a military bureaucracy, where intolerance and jealousy are endemic for those cut from a different mold. Yet if asked to name such a legendary figure, the one man who would immediately occur to those who were actors in the Viet Nam drama—whether American or Vietnamese, journalist or soldier—was Lieutenant Colonel John Henry Mudd.

Nobody had put the newly-arrived Hueys and the M-113s to better use than Mudd. His seventh division had been ready to go, ready to use them to their full effect as soon as they appeared on the scene. This made Mudd something of a local celebrity, the darling of MACV's Public Information Officers. He was one of three advisers out of the hundreds in Viet Nam who were allowed to extend their tours for a second year because of their exceptional effectiveness. As a result, when Willis Mandelbrot wrote an article for the Sunday Times Magazine on "The American Adviser," it amounted to a paean of praise for John Henry Mudd. But Mandelbrot's hero-worshipping article raised hackles in American military circles in Saigon, particularly because it more than implied that if only the other Americans in Viet Nam could soldier as well as Mudd, the war would have been over a long time ago.

At the moment, the Colonel was in the process of entertaining the company with an account of the Battle of the Bassac River, in which, the previous July, the crack VC 514th had come within an ace of being wiped out—the greatest victory of his Seventh Division. The guests were seated in a semi-circle on white wrought iron chairs and he was standing behind a matching center-pedestal table before them, pacing back and forth as he talked. They were obviously riveted by Mudd, a man who knew better than most how to hold an audience.

"This is a night operation," Mudd was saying. "That's the key to it. We have good intelligence that he's out there, know where he is, and even know the name of the unit, the 514th. But that don't mean much. The same thing has happened ten times in the last twenty days. So we didn't get excited about it. Because then we went out into the field and discovered that Charlie just isn't anywhere to be found. The truth is our boys are pretty goddamn careless in the way they communicate with each other, so that the other side half the time knows we're coming. But this time it's a little bit different because they don't expect us to go after them in the dark.

"Tiger Cao, our division commander, is itching to get those guys. He owes them a licking. But his staff is urging him to hold off. I tell him that we've got the choppers, but that if we wait till morning they can be taken away from us for a higher priority mission. One of the goddamn things about this war is that the helicopters are under a separate command and are only released by MACV on a case by case basis. The ARVN doesn't have its own dedicated air assets. So you can plan, but then you find you can't carry out those plans because there's no way to transport the troops into action.

"Well, I'm at division headquarters with the Tiger, on the radio to Major Jock Waggoner, a first-rate airborne officer who's with the troops in the lead chopper. They're coming in for a landing at the coordinates we had fixed and all of a sudden Waggoner says, 'holy shit,'—excuse me ladies—'holy shit, we're right on top of them.' Then he goes off the air. I can feel that something big is happening. I grab a radio and some flares and call for my spotter plane. In fifteen minutes we're over the battlefield. We drop a flare. It's all there beneath us, clear as day. . ."

At this point, Mudd did an extraordinary thing. From a standing position he jumped to the center of the pedestal table in front of him, making a squat landing. Without breaking stride, he continued the story looking down at Claudio's guests, as though he were in the air looking down at the battlefield. It was an exceptional athletic feat, particularly in ordinary street shoes. Had he not landed exactly in the center of the precariously balanced table it would almost certainly have tipped over and made him look a fool. But he had the balancing skills of the trained gymnast. From his new elevated vantage point he surveyed the terrain.

"The village is here. . .the tree line is here. . .the Bassac River is here. And Charlie's main force is camped right here. And yes sir, we've caught them bareass with their pants down, excuse me ladies. Total surprise. Our guys are as shocked as the VC, but they're good little troopers and give a good account of themselves in the right situation. And here it was dog eat dog, kill or be killed. They're right on top of them, in the middle of their camp.

"Our guys let loose with everything they've got. Charlie is creamed, totally disorganized, in full retreat. It's a rout. But what's left of him is getting away. I throw down another flare. They're all heading for the Bassac River. Cross the river and they're in Cambodia. They're looking for safe haven. That's another crazy thing about this war—safe haven! They're running as fast as their legs can carry them and they're about three kliks from Cambodia and I'm on top of them radioing for M-113s to cut them off and for our Hueys to come in and strafe them, finish the goddamn job. Sorry, they tell me from Saigon, no Hueys available. They're all earmarked for a big operation tomorrow. Sorry, they say in Can Tho, our M-113s can't come to the party. So there I am, watching two hundred of the enemy in full retreat, running as fast as they can, right on top of them, and there isn't a goddamn thing I can do about it, except shoot a few of them with my M-16."

Mudd paused.

"Yeah. We had a victory, all right. But we could have wiped out the entire 514th. As it is, they've now regrouped and are giving us a lot of heartburn."

His yarn ended, Mudd jumped backward off the table, landing exactly where he had been when, at Mandelbrot's request, he had begun his story. The company applauded, whether for acrobatic skill or in admiration of this warrior, nobody was sure.

As they sat down to dinner, Claudio announced that they were allowed to talk about sex, religion, anything they wanted, but not about war or politics. Everyone laughed and nodded approvingly, then immediately fell to arguing about war and politics.

The war was everyone's meat and drink; they could never get enough of it. In fact, it was Lily Do Ba Xang who first violated her host's interdiction by asking Mudd, who was scheduled to leave Viet Nam in a month, to sum up his opinion of the ARVN—did they have what it took to win? To Marnin's surprise, the Colonel turned out to be quite the diplomat. Whether this was out of respect for the lady's late husband, or out of consideration for Dinh Trieu Da, one of Diem's closest aides, was not clear. The ARVN, he said, had advanced considerably during his two years in Viet Nam. There was room for improvement, of course, but no reason to think that such improvement could not be made.

This was a red flag for Mandelbrot, who then tried to goad Mudd into repeating one of his myriad stories of Vietnamese ineptitude. But Mudd refused to take the bait. Noting his own previous service with the French Army, Frank Gascon observed that Vietnamese made very good soldiers, particularly on their own territory. He added that one of these days the ARVN was going to be a top rated fighting force.

Gascon, feeling upstaged by Mudd, had been uncharacteristically quiet up to that point, but he now launched into an account of his adventures with the Montagnards in the early fifties, monopolizing the conversation for the better part of the dinner. By the time he had finished with his jungle exploits, they were on to dessert. Gascon had been part of the American clandestine mission headed by General Ed Lansdale, who had played Svengali to both Magsaysay in the Philippines and to Diem. Pushing his plate away and lighting a cigar, Gascon proceeded to describe the problems Lansdale faced in setting up the Ngo Dinh Diem government in Saigon in 1954.

"If you think the situation is risky now," he said, stabbing the air with his cigar, while Helen Eng on his right shied back in evident alarm, "you should have seen it in those days. People forget we're a thousand per cent better off today in this country than we were seven years ago."

"Frank, you're full of shit," Mandelbrot interjected. "In 1955, there was some hope. Now this place is finished. It's going down the tubes."

"If it does," Gascon rejoined, "it'll be because people of your ilk sent it down."

"Just what the hell does that mean?" Mandelbrot demanded, leaning forward aggressively. "My ilk? What ilk are you talking about?"

"If you don't know," answered Gascon, equally truculent, "then it's no wonder you write the crap you do."

"If you want to see what my ilk is really like, why don't we step outside and I'll show you."

Mandelbrot scraped back his chair and got to his feet. Gascon rose heavily and the two men faced off, the aging jungle fighter planting himself in a crouch like an old bulldog, his bullet head and grizzled chin thrust up pugnaciously at the journalist who loomed over him. Mudd, the bantam rooster, and David right behind him, jumped between them.

"You guys have been drinking too much of the hard stuff," Mudd rasped. "It's time to cool it. Let me remind you there are ladies here."

"All right, all right," Mandelbrot said, but could not resist adding prophetically, "but mark my words, things are going to get a lot worse this year!"

The party began to break up and Mandelbrot, who cooled down as quickly as he fired up, made peace with Gascon, an important professional source of his, and on the way out apologized to Claudio as well.

"Great party," he said. "Sorry I lost my temper."

Claudio shrugged it off.

"You ought to watch your mouth, *coño.*"

Mandelbrot grinned. "My mother's been telling me that for twenty-eight years."

When Mandelbrot and Gascon had gone, Miranda said, "Well, another elegant Saigon dinner party."

Claudio rolled his eyes. "*Caramba!*" he said, putting his arm around her. "You hot-blooded Yanquis are too much for me."

None of this was preoccupying Marnin. His goal since first glancing at the seating chart had been to drive Lily home, and in this he succeeded.

Chapter 9

THERE ARE NO ACCIDENTS

She left him, as she had before, in the large, cluttered sitting room. Two overhead bulbs, covered with pink paper shades, cast a pall of dim light across the dark furniture and faded silk upholstery, reminding him of cheap hotel rooms. Restless, he walked over to the fridge and opened the door; the light went on and it hummed. Inside were three bottles of Coca-Cola.

David heard a slight sound and turned to see her enter, carrying a tray of Remy Martin cognac and two snifters. He walked over and sat down on the settee.

"So chic to have a fridge in the drawing room, isn't it?"

"Why don't you get rid of it? Why don't you change what you don't like?"

She handed him a glass and sat at the other end of the settee, angling her body gracefully toward him.

"Because," she said slowly, "if I move even a single piece of furniture, I shall perceive it as a sign of permanence. As long as I leave it exactly as it was when I received it I can convince myself that this is only temporary, a situation that will end."

"But why don't you—?"

"Why don't you stop asking me so many questions beginning with 'why'?" she said irritably. "No! No, you are not going to do this to me again."

"Do what?"

"Get me to talk my foolish head off. Tonight," she said, and her voice grew lighter, more bantering, "you are going to talk. And I am going to be the merciless interrogator. First, where did you grow up?"

"In New York. I lived there with my. . .with my father."

He took a long sip of cognac.

"Did you have brothers or sisters?"

"An only child."

"So lonely. . ." She paused. "And your mother?"

"My parents were divorced."

"Divorced! This could never happen here. Divorce is not allowed."

"It didn't happen much either where I grew up. Hardly at all. I didn't have a single friend with divorced parents. I was horribly embarrassed by it, never even admitted it to anyone—not to my closest friends."

"How sad for you."

David felt uncomfortable talking about his childhood. He wanted to turn the conversation around, steer it back to her.

"Were you educated in Hanoi or in Paris? he asked.

"I studied at the Dong Khan Girls' School in Hue, as did Mme. Nhu, our so-called first lady. It was a Catholic school, very strict. There is also a seminary for boys, but there is no contact between the two. President Diem studied there." She laughed. "So he and I have something in common."

"What did your family do in Hanoi?"

" They were merchants. . .very successful, with close ties to France. But my father had no interest in business—my mother had the business head," she said, laughing. "My father was a younger son, so the family was able to spare him. And he became an official and then a diplomat. And your father—what did he do?"

For a moment, David made no reply. He recalled Kipling stating that the first proof a man gives of his interest in a woman is to talk to her about his own sweet self; if she listens without yawning, he begins to like her. He took another swallow of brandy. Then he did what he had never done before: speak honestly to another human being about his childhood.

"My father," he said, beginning slowly, "was an immigrant. My mother, too, emigrated from Russia. When they arrived in America they spoke no English. The only job my father could get was as an 'operator' in the garment district in New York. He ran a sewing machine in a dress factory. The cutters cut the dresses on a pattern and the operators sewed them together. It was a job he hated. He did it for forty-seven years."

"And your mother?"

"My mother." He thought for a moment, and then said abruptly, "I didn't see her much. She had mental problems. My father had custody of me."

They were silent while she refilled his glass.

"And Montreal? You told me you—"

"Yes, my father's sister and her husband lived there. They had a small patisserie. I spent a year with them while my parents were getting divorced."

"How old were you?"

"Thirteen. Then I went back to my father. We shared a rented room in a house in Flatbush—" He could scarcely believe he was telling her all this.

"I would meet him after work. We used to eat dinner at the Automat—"

"The what?"

"That's a kind of self-service restaurant. Horn & Hadart was the name of the company that owned them. There were different kinds of food inside in little glass boxes —"

"Ah, like Japanese displays."

"No, this is real food. You select what you want and put your coins in the slot, and then you open the door and take out your food."

"It sounds quite clever."

"It was awful, but fun for a kid. They're all gone now. But at the time I thought they were terrific. You could get a piece of pineapple pie and a glass of milk for a dime."

"Not a very good diet."

"I ate a lot else besides. At thirteen, I was already over six feet and still growing. So I consumed plenty. But I couldn't stand eating with my father. We used to sit there and he was always pointing out some other kid eating with an adult and he'd say, 'Look at that young man

there. Look how respectful he is, how nicely he talks to his father.'
And I'd say, 'How in hell do you know what he's saying to his father?
Or even if it is his father?' I never was very nice to him, I'm sorry to
say."

"It's a difficult age. My own daughter, as sweet as she is, is not
always so nice to me either."

David was astonished. A teenage daughter? She read his expression
and said quickly, "I was married when I was just seventeen and had a
baby within ten months."

That made her thirty-one or thirty-two at least. But so what?

"I'm curious about one thing," she said. "Didn't you tell me you
went to Princeton University?" He nodded and she said, "But this is a
very expensive school, is it not? How could your father afford to send
you there?"

"He couldn't. My father never made more than four thousand dollars a year in his life. He never owned a car, never even owned a wash-
ing machine. We had no telephone. He couldn't afford to send me to
any university. I went on a scholarship. Not that I was such a good
scholar. I was always skipping school, so my grades weren't all that
great. And I didn't straighten out till the end of my junior year in high
school—too late to turn my average around. But the Navy runs an
Officer's Training program. They gave you a long multiple choice test
and if you scored well they sent you to college on full tuition, after
which you had to serve five years in the navy. That was the catch—
five years. But my only other option was either City College or a bas-
ketball scholarship to a third rate school in West Virginia. So I went
for it."

She was quiet. They both sipped their drinks. Then she said, "I'm
interested in what you say because I'm thinking of my girls. I want
them to be educated. Not like me. It's time to start planning for their
future. My oldest daughter is a very good student. Soon she will graduate from the *lycée* and I must try to get her into a good university,
maybe in France or the United States. It's not easy for a widow. . .with-
out resources. . ." Her voice trailed off.

"But Lily," said David, "One thing I don't understand. Your position, the way you live. . . surely you must have resources—"

"That's what I thought. But in fact, I don't."

"But your husband was well connected—"

"Yes, he was that. Vietnamese marriage is a strange thing. The wife is expected to raise the children and run the household. She's supposed to manage all the family finances—but without ever knowing how much money there is. My husband never confided in me about his business affairs. We lived so well. . . . I never worried. It wasn't until he was killed that I found out we hadn't a sou; that we owned nothing and owed everyone; that everything I thought was ours belonged to someone else—to the men who owned this house."

"Who are they?"

"Ask your good friend Claudio if you want to know who these people are."

"Claudio?"

She became agitated, her hands fluttering at her throat and nervously fingering the silk fastenings at her neck.

"Yes, he is an. . .associate of theirs."

He placed his hand over hers. Looking silently at her small white palm, he gently drew her right hand to his lips and kissed it.

A grandfather clock somewhere on the second floor chimed twice. She withdrew her hand from his and rose.

"I'm sorry," she said stiffly, "It's so late. I must say goodnight. I'm leaving tomorrow, quite early."

"Leaving?" His heart fell. "Where?"

"My girls and I are going for a few days to Hong Kong."

She moved toward the front door and he followed her.

"When will you be back?" he asked.

"On the sixth of January."

"Can I see you then?"

"On the sixth?"

"Yes, why not?"

"I'm afraid it's not possible."

"The seventh?"

She shook her head. "Why don't you call me," she said.

"No," he said. "Let's make a date right now. How about the eighth? I'll just keep going, Lily, till you say yes."

"The eighth. . .that's a Sunday." She thought for a moment. "All right. I'll meet you after mass."

"Great, I'll pick you up here."

"No, no," she said quickly, "not here. The Continental, in front. At noon."

She opened the door. He put his hands on her waist and bent to kiss her. His fingers touched the small triangles of bare skin above her silk trousers where the *ao dai* parted and he felt her body tremble. She averted her face. His lips brushed the top of her head and he smelled the scent of jasmine in her hair.

"You must go," she said nervously.

"I'll do what you want now," he said. "But I make no promises for the future." He started out the door, then turned to look at her again. "What a stroke of fate. . .to meet you." He shook his head. "What a glorious accident!"

"There are no accidents," she said solemnly.

Chapter 10

THE BLACK CAT

The Black Cat, one of the new sleazy bars on Catinat, like its siblings, was dark and noisy. It had a small (empty) dance floor and a large horseshoe bar. On the wall behind the bar was a mirror, over which was draped a paper banner scrawled with the message, "HAPPY NEW YEARS G.I." Above the mirror was a green and red neon sign alternately flashing "Cold Beer—Hot Women." At the back of the room, next to the toilet, was a door on which hung another scrawled sign reading "Tonsil Parlor," which led to a cubicle where the ladies who worked the bar could take American soldiers in need of a quick oral fix. Next to that was a plastic Christmas tree strung with blinking lights and topped with a gold tinfoil angel.

Late in the afternoon on New Year's Day, Marnin sat drinking with Claudio and two of the regulars—Claudio's favorite, a girl with wavy hair and frosted coral lips, whom he had christened "Hedy Lamarr" because of her tangential resemblance (except for a gold eye tooth) to the actress, and Ruby Ky, who had a pretty face and a mopey expression. The two men were drinking cognac, the women weak tea disguised as whiskey. "White Christmas" was blaring, courtesy of Armed Forces Radio, and Hedy Lamarr crooned along lustily with Bing Crosby, her gold tooth catching the light and twinkling in the murky darkness. Every few minutes she absentmindedly gave Claudio's crotch a friendly feel.

Ruby Ky, morosely pushing back the cuticles on her fingernails, did not sing. Marnin, no less melancholy than Ruby, and hung over as well from too much champagne at a New Year's Eve party at the British Embassy, stared gloomily into his glass and thought of Lily.

"I don't like to complain, *coño*," said Claudio, "but it's New Year's Day, a time for joy and revelry."

"The holiday season gets me down," David replied. "We make too much over Christmas."

He sighed and took a swallow of cognac.

"Well—it's not every day you have a virgin birth."

"Or even a virgin."

"Ah-hah!" said Claudio with interest. "You want virgins? I can get you virgins."

"Not so fast," David laughed. "I never said that."

Claudio shrugged.

"They're a taste I never acquired myself. I prefer at least a modicum of experience. But *chacun a son goût*, eh? The Chinese—they're loco for virgins. The younger the better. Some of my business partners can't get a hard-on with anyone over twelve."

"Business partners?"

"War has always been good business. Why not be a good business-man?"

"But what business?"

"Any business. Thanks to your splendid country, it makes no difference."

David frowned.

"I don't get it."

"Look," Claudio explained patiently, "the government of Vietnam desperately needs investment, but thanks to the Viet Cong, no foreigner in his right mind will invest a centavo here. So the only hope is the local business community—i.e. the Chinese, with whom I am happily in a most lucrative partnership."

Suddenly, Ruby Ky began to weep loudly, the tears streaming down her cheeks.

"Ruby," David said with concern, "why are you crying?"

"I so sad," Ruby wailed.

Claudio shook his head in mild exasperation.

"She's hopeless, this girl. She cries all the time."

"Ruby, she care 'bout everything," Hedy Lamarr volunteered cheerfully. "She cry a lot."

"This song," Ruby sobbed, "it make me so sad."

"This song?" David raised his head to listen. Tony Bennet at that point was singing "I Left My Heart in San Francisco."

"But Ruby," he said with surprise, "have you ever been to San Francisco?"

"No," Ruby wept, "I nevah been."

Hedy Lamarr got up to pacify Ruby.

"I nevah cry," she said in passing. "I don't give one shit."

David watched the two women for a moment, put it down as another of the unfathomable mysteries of the East, and turned back to Claudio.

"But what's the United States got to do with this?" He asked. "What are you talking about?"

"I am talking about becoming a fucking Commodity Import Program millionaire. Give me two more years here with the CIP in effect and I'll be set up for life, my five sisters will be set up for life, not to mention my old mother, and even you, my friend, will be set up for life if you allow yourself to partake of my fabled generosity."

"I still don't know what you're talking about."

"I am talking, my young friend, about the CIP, instituted in its wisdom by your splendid government. The CIP—conceived, implemented, administered by your own embassy—not only ensures that the GVN will prevail over the commies, but that I will grow old in dignity and respect."

"What in hell do you mean?"

"Thanks to the CIP, I make six dollars for every dollar I invest. If I can do that every month I end up making seventy-two dollars a year for each dollar, a return of 7,200 per cent. Not too bad! The only trick is knowing how to turn the money over, to keep it moving and not let it stop moving."

He ordered one more round.

"If nature were left to take its course, shortages of consumer goods would generate an inflation that would drive the economy into the ground. The GVN therefore desperately needs, and your government desperately wants, foreign investment in this country, or at least some stanching of the flight of capital that leaves here every week for points north and west. As your compatriots learned in post-war Europe, and what the Marshall Plan was all about, was that enough goods must be made available to sop up consumer demand and hold down inflation. But the more troubling the insurgency, the greater the difficulty the GVN will have attracting capital from abroad. The only real hope for investment is the local business community—and that means my friends the Chinese, who are right now still very pissed off at this government, especially after Diem's crackdown on them last year. Why should they help him out when he pissed all over them? All these guys can invest their money in Hong Kong and get a guaranteed twenty-five per cent return. They can invest it in Bangkok and get eighty per cent, but that's far riskier. But the risk is nothing compared with investing it in Viet Nam. On the other hand, they're making money hand over fist here. So they have lots of piasters burning holes in their pockets. But it is just so much red paper. What they need are dollars—green paper. That's where I come in. I've got diplomatic immunity. I can carry anything I want into or out of this country. The last thing this government wants is an incident with a friendly nation. The official exchange rate is 35 to 1. The going rate is 70 to 1. The black market rate is 110 to 1. And I get 150 to 1, and can use it to generate wonderful convertible dollars, thanks to the CIP."

"How do you get to use the CIP? I don't understand."

"The CIP has worked beautifully. Show me a country at war with a smoother functioning economy than this one. And all because some genius in Washington has figured out that if you supply South Viet Nam with the consumer goods it needs, the economy will take care of itself. The free market wins again! And if you can get local capitalists to keep their investments channeled into this country you're obviously far better off than having all that money escape to Hong Kong, Bangkok, Singapore or Switzerland.

"As a practical result, this means that on Monday morning when they deal at the Finance Ministry in import licenses, if I turn over to my good friend Mr. Hung, who is in charge of these transactions, 150 piasters that cost me one dollar, he very nicely gives me a license to import, at the official rate of thirty-five to one, four dollars worth of foreign commodities to be sold on the local market. And if these commodities are then dumped into the Saigon River it wouldn't bother me too much. The big thing is getting the licenses, which can be bought and sold for profit like any other business product. But if this license is turned into badly needed consumer staples and then sold on the local market, it brings me back on top of the four dollars I have already made still another two, a total of six dollars back, which is a pretty good return on a dollar invested. And if I can do this, let's say, once a month, my return is seventy-two dollars for one, 7,200 fucking per cent. A man can get rich that way."

"But why doesn't everyone do this?"

"Mr. Hung and the other Vietnamese economic mafia, all of whom seem to have been trained at the University of California, understand that there has to be an obvious limit to this process. They control it by issuing just enough import licenses for consumer goods to sop up demand and keep things in balance. So scotch and condensed milk only get you so far and no further. But if you're actually investing in this country and you need to import material to enhance that investment, for a factory or what have you, then there are no limits. You can get whatever you want. And since I'm the only Cantonese and Hakka speaking Guatemalan in the history of the world, and since the local Hakka community is anxious to turn its piasters into Hong Kong gold, I'm now the owner, or at least the front man and partner, of three rice mills, two textile factories, a cinnamon processing plant, a pig farm, a dairy, a chicken factory where we produce those damned birds like pencils, a slaughterhouse, a sausage plant, and a sugar refinery. And all of them in this overheated economy are making money. Not only that, but we spread the money around and help the local economy further. Everybody gets paid off—Mr. Hung at the Ministry, the Minister himself, the chief of customs, the Saigon police chief, the province chiefs where our factories are located, the mayors of the towns, the division commanders charged with protecting those areas—even my Foreign Minister in Guatemala, who gets his monthly cut, but doesn't seem to think it's enough and keeps threatening to have me transferred to some less lucrative post like Oslo. So everyone gets his piece of the CIP pie, everyone except the American advisers, all of them honest as the day is long. David, my boy, you work for a great country!"

Armed Forces Radio began playing a bouncy number called "You Talk Too Much," then a top-ten hit in Saigon.

"That you," Hedy Lamarr said sulkily to Claudio, "you talk too much. Last night, you Numbah One. Today you Numbah Ten." Getting worked up, she escalated her figures. "Numbah ten hundred. Numbah ten thou!"

At that point a Special Forces Sergeant, walking by on his way to the john, waved a casual greeting.

"Hey babe," he said affably, "how 'bout a tonsil massage for the New Year with ol' Big Red?"

Hedy Lamarr looked at him churlishly.

"How 'bout you fuck off, fuckface?"

The soldier advanced a step and struck a menacing stance, but then thought better of it.

"*Madre mia!*" exclaimed Claudio. "Let's get out of here." He handed a wad of piastres to Minh, the one-eyed owner of the bar, and took each girl firmly by the elbow.

"Which one you want?" he asked David as they reached the sidewalk outside.

"Can't do it. Got to stop at the office and check the cable traffic."

"Well," Claudio said, a girl on each arm, "I guess I'll just go home myself and have a Saigon sandwich. *Hasta luego, chico.*"

Hanky-panky of the magnitude described by Claudio required further guidance. So the following morning, Marnin went to see "Curly" Bird, chief of AID and administrator of the CIP, and handed the bald, avuncular official, who was smoking a pipe, a memo reporting the gist of what Claudio had said. Bird at first—when told Marnin wanted to see him—had thought this was something from the Ambassador that required expeditious handling and practically snatched the memo from the aide. But after he ascertained that the Ambassador had nothing to do with the matter, he took a deep pull of aromatic tobacco and a smile gradually spread across his face. Finally, he laid the memo on his desk and shook his head.

"There's no substance here. Just a lot of mouthing off in a bar. I know these Latinos. I've spent a dozen years in South America. And in any case, even if all this loose talk while under the influence in a disreputable joint has some kernel of truth to it, then so what? It isn't our business. As long as we're generating capital investment in the Vietnamese economy that would otherwise have fled to safe havens abroad, the CIP program is doing what it was designed to do. All local business practices have aspects that are not meant to see the light and that we wouldn't countenance in the United States. Everyone here is a little bit crooked. That's just the oriental way."

Marnin stared at Bird, hardly believing he had heard him correctly. Then he rose and took his memo off the AID chief's desk, folded it in three and stuck it in the breast pocket of his jacket.

"In that case," he said, "you won't need this."

Bird pulled at his pipe and nodded assent.

Marnin pursued the subject no further. Bird's meaning was clear: Welcome to Asia, sonny boy!

Chapter 11

"WE ARE ALL NHU'S PUPPETS"

Marnin drove directly to the Embassy, intent on catching up on the Ambassador's traffic that he had missed over the holiday. He picked up his cable folder, which was kept in the code room on the fourth floor and from there walked up the flight of steps to his cubbyhole.

Chick Rizzo was duty officer that day. He was sitting at Helen Eng's desk just outside the Ambassador's office reading a Modern Library edition of *The Red Badge of Courage*. Rizzo was the gungest of the gung ho officers in the embassy. He had already volunteered to do a two year tour with the Special Forces as a Vietnamese-speaking political advisor, but had been turned down by MACV because Donnelly thought him a shade too unorthodox.

"I finally met your hero," David said to him.

"You mean Mudd?"

He nodded. "He's in Saigon for a little rest and recreation. He's quite a guy."

"That he is," Rizzo grinned, grasping David's meaning. "Anyway, the job he's done in the Delta has been simply phenomenal. He's taken the worst division in the ARVN and transformed it into the best, and all in the course of less than a year.

"As I said, he's quite a guy," David repeated.

"The boss is in there," Rizzo said, gesturing toward the Ambassador's office.

Corning was slumped over his desk, writing in violet ink on a yellow legal pad, twisting his body to the right, as left-handed people do. He usually dictated all his cables to Helen Eng, but had decided to give her the day off. He was deep in thought, working on a year-end wrap up, trying to put 1962 in Viet Nam in some sort of overall perspective. Many ambassadors made it a practice to do these year-end summaries, although it was not a State Department requirement. But Corning's "think piece," entitled "Victory in Sight—the Year That Was in Viet Nam," was one of the few New Year cables from any embassy in the world that first day of 1963 that had been specially slugged "FOR THE PRESIDENT."

He continued writing as Marnin entered and only looked up when he had finished the paragraph. Marnin waited quietly.

"Happy New Year," Corning said. He gestured at the yellow pad. This is my year ender. I should be finished in an hour or so. I'd appreciate your getting it typed up by the duty secretary once I'm done with it. It should go out first thing tomorrow morning. I'll want to look at it again as soon as I get to the embassy."

An hour later, Corning's draft cable in hand, Marnin attempted to carry out his instructions. Angela Cartini, the duty secretary, was supposed to be on call, but Rizzo could not reach her. They found out the next morning that she had had a date with one of the MAAG Colonels and had arranged for Mary Rhodes, the secretary in the economic section, to replace her for the evening. Thinking Mary would do it, she had neglected to inform Rizzo.

Marnin did not want to spoil Helen Eng's first evening of the New Year by calling her in—she worked an average of thirty hours a week overtime as it was. So he decided it would be all right to leave the typing for the first thing the following morning. That was a mistake. The cable was fourteen pages long. It was after nine by the time Helen had finished typing and proofreading it. Corning did not hide his annoyance that the cable had not been typed up the previous evening. He was fuming. And he was not much interested in miscommunications between duty secretaries and duty officers or in Marnin's reluctance to summon Helen Eng to fill the gap.

"Damn it, David," Corning said, "I wanted that message on the President's desk by this afternoon. I still have to make a few more points and I won't have time to do it till we get back to the embassy. Now it will skip a whole day and get to Washington along with a bunch of other year-enders from ambassadors all over the world. There's no point in sending a fourteen page cable that some GS-9 summarizes in two lines."

But there was nothing to be done. Corning and Stu Markoff, the Station Chief, had to leave immediately for an appointment with Diem to talk about problems that had arisen in the Strategic Hamlet program. (The Americans were being blamed in the Vietnamese press, controlled by Ngo Dinh Nhu, for failures to supply the hamlets with lumber and barbed wire, whereas existing shortages were actually caused by crooked contractors and local officials who, instead of turning these American goods over free as they were supposed to, were charging the peasants full market price for them.)

The demarche had only been scheduled to last an hour but, as was often the case with Diem, it took almost four, and Corning had to go straight on to a luncheon with Sir Neville Boggs and the Foreign Minister at the British Embassy. From there he proceeded to a ceremony at MACV where six of the American advisors, including Mudd, were to receive medals for heroism under fire. Mudd, who was to get a Distinguished Flying Cross for exceptional bravery during the Battle of the Bassac River, was the only honoree not present for the occasion.

One of the big gripes of Americans in the field had been that although they were daily risking their lives there was no official recognition of this fact. The fiction had to be maintained that they were non-combatants. This meant no medals, not even the Purple Heart when they were wounded. Medals being the meat and drink of the soldier, the morale problem had been considered serious enough for Donnelly to send a message urging that the policy be changed. Over the objection of the State Department, which thought it important to maintain the distinction between combatants and non-combatants, the President decided in the General's favor.

This was, therefore, the first awards ceremony of its kind and required an Ambassadorial presence. The Vietnamese government was represented by the burly General Duong Van Minh, "Big Minh," military adviser to the President, and by the extraordinarily handsome

General Tran Tra Bich, who was as French as a Vietnamese can be. Partly because of their long service in the French Army and their remaining links to France (including French citizenship), partly because of the surveillance reports from Nhu's agents which documented the way they talked to others about him, Diem distrusted both these generals and, despite their impressive titles, carefully saw to it that they had no authority to deploy or command fighting units. Since the coup attempt of the paratroopers in 1960, and especially after the aerial attack in February on Independence Palace by a disgruntled South Vietnamese Air Force First Lieutenant he was taking no chances.

The Ambassador was given the seat of honor in the reviewing stand on the parade ground under a red, white, and blue canopy. Marnin was to his left and General Bich to his right. Next to Bich was Big Minh and to Minh's right was General Donnelly. General "Ace" Parker, Donnelly's Deputy and the head of the Military Assistance Advisory Group (MAAG) and therefore the chief of all the advisors in Viet Nam, was in charge of pinning the medals on and making the speech that would end the ceremony. Halfway through it, Tom Aylward came up to Donnelly and whispered in his ear. Donnelly made his apologies to Minh and left. He did not return.

Corning and Bich spoke in French, a language nobody seated in the vicinity, other than Minh and Marnin, could understand.

"Well, my dear General, I'm delighted to see you here on this great occasion. In my view, diplomatic rationales always should play second fiddle to human feelings. It is time that our heroic advisors received the recognition they deserve."

"I completely agree, Excellency. Your advisors, they are so to speak *la crème de la crème*, the very best people of your entire army. I am constantly inspecting our fighting units and I can assure you that, thanks to the efforts of your countrymen, our troops are constantly improving, learning new skills, getting better weapons and better equipment. At last we have what it takes to give a good account of ourselves. This is, mind you, at the lower levels."

"And at the higher levels?" asked Corning, taking his cue.

"That is a different matter. I probably should not be saying this to you, Excellency. But I am a simple soldier and must speak frankly. From private up to field grade officers the ARVN is getting better all the time. However, the improvement is technical, not operational. We now know how to do things, as you say, 'by the numbers.' The problem lies from Major through flag officer rank. There things have become much, much worse. At that level people are trying to look good without doing any fighting. They mount large operations and aim them where the enemy is not, rather than where he is. An army runs on its fighting esprit. Take away that esprit, and it becomes a big lump of mud. That is what is happening to us."

"Why is that?"

"Because to have esprit in an army the brave have to be honored, as we are honoring your brave men today. The foe we are facing is experienced. He is cunning. He is smart. The only way to counter him is to reward the brave and punish the cowards—that is the way you build an army! But we are doing just the opposite. We punish the brave and promote the cowardly. There is only one criterion for promotion in Viet Nam today. And that is loyalty to the Ngo Dinhs. Every military advancement, every deployment of a military unit, is controlled by the Palace. The President personally approves every promotion of every officer in this country, even from Lieutenant to Captain. Promotion lists stay on his desk for months. It is impossible to run an army under such conditions. I am packing up and going back to Paris."

"That would be a tragedy for this country, my dear General," Corning said. "But have you discussed this matter with the President?"

"I have tried. But it is impossible to get him to listen. He is more interested in his own safety and the safety of his family than in the struggle against Communism."

At this point, Minh, who had been listening to Bich and nodding, grunted his full agreement.

"I think you are surely being too harsh on him."

"I am not being harsh enough. The President, I know, has some sterling attributes and some very great accomplishments. He rallied the country against the Communists and absorbed a million of our anti-Communist countrymen from the North. With the help of my friend General Minh over here, he defeated the Cao Dai and the Hoa Hao sects and convinced us this could become a viable country. But all this was years ago. In those days he would go out on his own and see the country for himself. He was a popular leader. But now he is almost entirely controlled by his brother. We are all Nhu's puppets. When Nhu gets suspicious of you, he calls you in and gives you a so-called promotion. ("Grunt," went Big Minh.) Then he takes away your responsibilities and only sends you to ceremonies to represent their family. ("Grunt, grunt.") Worst of all is that woman, Madame Nhu. She says whatever she pleases, usually the first thing that jumps into her head. She insults high ranking officers. She openly threatens us. ("Grunt.") I tell you, Excellency, it is intolerable."

Large beads of sweat dotted Bich's forehead.

"The main thing," Corning said, "is the war effort. President Kennedy is for anything that helps the war effort and against everything that hurts it."

"I quite agree," Bich retorted hotly. "But that's just what's suffering—the war effort. My friend Blix is doing a colossal job. But you are being fooled by the victories the APCs and the choppers are bringing us. This is a matter of tactics. Over the long run, the VC will adjust their tactics and figure out what to do. You don't win wars through gimmickry. And I can assure you, Excellency, that the leadership of the ARVN is much worse today than it was even a year ago and that nothing will reverse this trend until the Nhus stop accusing the General Staff of treachery and let us get on with winning this war."

Big Minh, who sat silent throughout the entire ceremony, a gloomy scowl creasing his ursine face, gave one great, final grunt. He nodded at Bich and with the forefinger of his right hand tapped his right temple three times. This gave the Ambassador to understand that, in his view, Bich was a deep thinker.

"Thank you for your frankness, General," Corning said. "I'm glad you've chosen to confide in me. I appreciate such frankness. We are friends and allies, fighting together for the same vital cause. We have our disputes and disagreements. But the main thing is that we're confident, and President Kennedy is personally confident, that we're going to win this thing."

"Of course we are," Bich quickly agreed. "Nobody can defeat the United States of America."

PART TWO

THE TURNING POINT

Chapter 12

AP BAC

Two messages marked "URGENT" were on Marnin's desk when he returned to the office. The first was from John Mecklin, the Public Affairs Officer, the second from Mandelbrot.

"There's a big battle going on in the Delta," Mecklin said. "According to the press, it's the biggest battle of the war. And it seems to be going badly. . .very badly. AFP reports twelve of our choppers shot down. . ."

"Twelve?"

"Wait a minute. They've issued a correction. They now say eight."

"And where's this happening?"

"It's a place called Ap Bac, about fifteen miles northwest of My Tho. The press are all screaming for transportation to the Delta."

Marnin then called Mandelbrot, hoping to get more information.

"Hello, Billy," he said. "What's on your mind?"

"What's on my mind? We're in the process of suffering the worst defeat since Pearl Harbor and you ask me what's on my mind. Listen, I've got to file in four hours and the readers of the *New York Times* want to know what's happening out there. And when I ask for a simple thing like transport to the battlefield or at least to My Tho all I get is a runaround. Fill out some forms. Put it through channels. BULL-SHIT! What I want is assistance from the embassy in getting my ass over there. But before that I want a fucking statement from the Embassy on just what the hell is happening."

"Calm down, Billy. Talk to John Mecklin. The Ambassador's been away all day and only got back to his desk three minutes ago."

"That's fucking typical. The biggest story of the year and the American Embassy hasn't heard about it."

"All I know is there are press reports of some of our helicopters shot down near a Vietnamese hamlet called Bac. . . ."

"It's Ap Bac, not Bac."

"Ap means 'hamlet' in Vietnamese."

"Thanks! That's the first bit of information I've gotten out of your embassy all day."

And he hung up. Marnin burst into Corning's office.

"Goddamit," the Ambassador said, "I'm trying to finish this damned cable. I told you I didn't want to be interrupted!"

"Sorry, sir, but there's a big battle going on in the Delta. The press is claiming that eight of our choppers are down. Mandelbrot is calling it the greatest single American defeat since Pearl Harbor."

"What?"

"They're screaming for the embassy to make a statement."

There were three telephones on Corning's desk. He reached for the green one, which connected him on a secure line to Donnelly's office and to the world-wide military communications network.

"This is Ambassador Corning," he said. "I want to speak to General Donnelly. . .Hello. . .Blix? Yes, it's a bad connection. You sound like you're at the bottom of a well. What the hell is happening? They're saying eight of our choppers are down. . .No. . .You're sure?. . . Is it still going on? Look, I'll need an update. Are you coming to the Residence tonight? Good, it'll show people nobody around here is pushing the panic button. . .OK, swing by the embassy first and we'll have a chat in the tank. I want to know what to say to people. . . I agree. . .This thing has definitely got to be kept in perspective. I'll see you soon."

"He says it's only five," Corning said abstractedly to Marnin.

"Five choppers are more than we've lost to enemy action in the whole war up till now."

"Donnelly says Colonel Mudd's watching the whole thing from a spotter plane. In fact, it looks as though the whole thing is Mudd's fault."

He paused.

"It's a good thing you didn't get that cable typed up earlier after all," he said. "It might not have gone over too well with the President if it had arrived just before these news stories. I'm going to have to make a few little adjustments before I send it out." Lighting a cigarette, he said, "Did I ever tell you about the dispatch from Taipei that arrived via the pouch in the Department in 1957 a week after a Chinese mob burned down our embassy? It had been written by Paul Meyers, the Political Counselor, five days before the mob attacked and only reached people's desks in Washington two weeks after he wrote it. That dispatch had a wonderful sentence in it saying, 'In my twenty-three years of dealing with the Chinese, I have never known US-Chinese relations to be in a better state.' There's a lesson in that, David. Get your thoughts in to the Department pronto so there'll be enough time for people to forget about them if things go the other way."

The tank was a tiny room off the Ambassador's office that was as impenetrable to bugging as the technology of the day could make it. It was furnished with a wooden table and six secretarial chairs. Heavy red drapes were hung along the plastic walls. The room had three switches—for the lights, for the air-conditioning, and for the taped sounds of a cocktail party that were intended to foil a potential eavesdropper by acoustically drowning out the talk going on inside it. Since it was poorly air-conditioned and had no windows, since nobody was too concerned about KGB infiltration of the embassy in those days, and especially since the cocktail party clamor drove people crazy, it was seldom employed except by the local CIA station.

Donnelly, who was as nervous as a cat, kept jumping up, but was restrained from much lateral movement by the size of the room and the fact that the Ambassador, disturbed by the taped cocktail chatter, could only hear clearly when the General yelled in his ear. Donnelly was suffering from some sort of tropical eczema and both his arms from the wrist to the elbow were painted in gentian violet. He talked and scratched, talked and scratched.

"This damn thing has got to be put into the proper perspective," Donnelly said, shaking his head. "I've told those monkeys in the press that I'm goddamned if I'm going to comment on a battle that's in the process of being fought. Right now we've got the VC pinned down. There's going to be an airborne drop any minute that should cut off their line of retreat. There's about three hundred out there caught in a noose. If we can tighten the noose and kill them or, better yet, capture them alive, this won't be the biggest defeat of the war. It'll be the biggest victory! What happened quite simply is that we had good intelligence that a sizeable force of Viet Cong, the 514th Regional Battalion, was camped in a village northwest of My Tho, named. . ." He paused.

"Bac," David said.

"Yeah. Ap Bac. That's it. That's the hamlet—belongs to the village of Tan Phu. Our plan was to attack them from three sides and leave an open rice field as their escape route when they withdrew. It would have been a perfect killing zone for our choppers. We would have chewed them to shreds. The only trouble was that the bastards didn't withdraw. For the first time since I've been in this country they stood their ground. Now this is just what we've been waiting for. All along we've been saying if only the raggedy ass little bastards would just stand up and fight we'd wax their clocks. And that's just what should have happened today and may happen yet. The plan was perfect. But the execution stank. And it looks right now as though it was the fault of that goddam Mudd—the hero of Viet Nam the press calls him. You know what the chopper pilots call him? They call him MMQ, the Monday morning quarterback. He's got a lot to answer for."

"What did he do?"

"He was up there in a spotter plane watching the whole thing unfold—in fact, using the damn plane as a decoy to draw enemy fire so he could figure out where they were. Oh, he's brave enough, no question about that. Well, the best regiment of the 7th Division was coming in to the west and he guided them down just a hundred yards from the tree line where the enemy was dug in. It was far too close. It was goddam foolhardy. Mudd couldn't see the VC because they were smart enough not to fire at his plane from those entrenched positions. So we were right on top of them and instead of us bushwhacking them, they ambushed us. We came in on ten H-21s guarded by five Hueys. And they didn't start firing till three had already landed. It was an ambush. They were waiting for us. One of the choppers couldn't make it off the ground. His rotary shaft had been hit by a stray bullet, just one single lucky shot.

"Well, it's S.O.P. that we don't leave a helicopter crew on the ground under enemy fire without trying to rescue them. So two of the others went back to get their buddies. This was against the advice of Mudd, who's got to take the original blame for sending them in there in the first place. But he was overruled by the pilots on the spot. And instead of landing far enough away from the VC field of fire and letting the crews walk or be carried to them, they chose to go right back to the goddam heart of the battlefield. Very macho, but very stupid. Mind you, we had two men badly wounded at that point and speed of rescue was important. And you don't want to let paddy water seep into a wound. That water is filthy. It would mean a sure infection. But by this time the enemy had the range and their machine gunners chewed up those two choppers so badly that they couldn't get off the ground either. Now we had three down and the commander of our chopper battalion was going crazy. Suddenly his unit had four men wounded, two of them badly, two men killed, the remnants of three chopper crews hunkered down in the paddies under withering enemy crossfire, and absolutely no goddam way to get them out of there until the APCs reach the scene.

"We were confident that these M-113s would eventually do the trick. Based on past experience, we figured that when the APCs showed up, the VC would see their position was hopeless and withdraw. But the goddam APCs were three hours from the scene and the wounded were losing blood. And then that gung ho chopper commander really did a dumb thing. He sent in four more choppers to rescue the ones that were down and lost two more of them. What a fiasco! I've been telling these guys ever since I got here never to underestimate the other fellow. We've been operating in an environment where whenever the VC saw a chopper or an APC they would do one of two things—they would run or they would hide. Well, whoever was commanding the other side today did neither. He came ready to fight. And he gave a damn good account of himself.

"But all of us were still confident that when the squad of thirteen

M-113s got there the VC would do what we expected him to—retreat through the killing zone. But he didn't oblige us. The ARVN captain in charge of the unit, instead of massing his firepower and attacking with all his APC's at once, sent them in one at a time. And Goddamit, they picked off the machine gunners on the first four 113s. The machine gunners are the top non-coms in those units. They're the most experienced men, have seen the most action, are the ones to rally the others to get on with the fighting. When you lose four of them like that, you've crippled your unit.

"There was still hope, though. The fifth 113 was mounted with a flamethrower instead of a machine gun. The VC was dug in beautifully. We had to push them out of their positions. VNAF fighter-bombers were called in to napalm their positions, but the pilots missed the target and hosed down the village instead of the Western tree line. And our guys were now so close to the tree line that the ARVN regimental commander was afraid to call for more napalm, afraid they'd miss the target and fry his own men instead of the enemy. But the flamethrower on that 113 could still have done the trick for us. It's got a range of fifty meters and should have been able to roust out the VC. It looked like a sure thing. The APC lumbered into position thirty meters from the tree line. Mudd was on the radio, broadcasting the whole thing like a sports announcer. And you know what? The goddam Vietnamese crew had mixed the gel wrong and instead of firing fifty meters it fired forty. That was as far as the flame went—ten meters short of the Viet Cong lines. It had all the force of a zippo lighter.

"It was the last straw. By that time morale was shot. The best officers and non-coms had been killed and that unit was afraid to close with the VC. They turned around and withdrew. They withdrew! We threw the best we had at them, first the choppers and then the APC's. And instead of running, as we expected, they looked us in the teeth and said come on, give us all you've got. It was a gutsy show. You've got to give them that. But don't you worry. If they get the idea that they can slug it out toe to toe, that's just fine with me. It will be a lot shorter war. What wins wars is firepower. And that's what we've got and they don't. And even if they get away from us this time, we'll make the necessary adjustments.

"That's what war is—making adjustments. They make some progress. And we bring in Hueys and M-113s and shove that progress down their throats. Now they're adjusting. They were lucky today. Next time they won't be so lucky. And we still have a good chance of breaking their backs this afternoon. So let's not panic. Let's try and keep this whole thing in perspective. This is not the Battle of the Bulge. It's a goddamn skirmish."

Chapter 13

A MISERABLE
DAMN PERFORMANCE

Normally Marnin would have gone back with the Ambassador to the Residence. Instead, Corning, who had a dinner at the Papal Nuncio's, asked him to stick around the Embassy, pick up all the information he could, and then meet him at the Residence on his return from dinner. Tom Aylward, who also ordinarily would have been accompanying Donnelly on his social rounds, was tracking the military situation at MACV and served as Marnin's main source of information. John Mecklin, following what was being reported in the press and on the networks, was also useful, as was Colonel McCloud, the advisor to General Dinh, the commander of IV Corps in Can Tho. Chick Rizzo had good sources all over the country, both American and Vietnamese, and knew the geography of IV Corps. Marnin needed lots of help in order to paint a coherent picture of what was happening. He had no idea of the terrain bordering the Plain of Reeds.

The parachute drop that the ARVN promised for four o'clock did not materialize until six, shortly before dark. The plan was nevertheless to try and cut off the 514th, to illuminate its escape route with flares and then to pound it all night long. Nobody was giving up hope yet.

Marnin called Dinh Trieu Da at the Palace. Da was very excited, said that it was a terrible thing, but that it wasn't the fault of the ARVN. There was an American Colonel flying over the battlefield repeatedly trying to countermand the orders of the division commander and creating great confusion. The press had got hold of the story and was exaggerating it entirely out of proportion. President Diem and General Donnelly were both in full agreement. This was a minor event—a minor event—in the course of a long war.

Marnin called Mudd three times. But a black staff sergeant answered each time and said, in a bemused tone, that Mudd was out on the battlefield.

"When there's fighting going on, that's where the Colonel's gonna be," he said.

Marnin wrote his update on the situation and had Rizzo check it out sentence by sentence. Then he drove to the Residence and waited outside until the Cornings returned shortly before eleven. When the Ambassador had read Marnin's report, he said, "Not a very pretty situation."

"No, sir."

"Pity the press has got hold of it. In any case, thank you, David. Let me know if anything further develops. Right now I'm going to fix up my year-ender. You'll have it first thing tomorrow morning."

It was eleven-thirty when David, exhausted after a very long day, pulled into his own driveway. He was walking toward the door when, to his astonishment, he saw a young girl sitting on the front step. Fifteen at most, her pretty face was freshly scrubbed and she was dressed in the uniform of the Saigon *lycée*. As he approached, the girl stood up and curtsied.

"*Qui. . .qui êtes vous? Qu'est-ce que vous voulez?*" David stammered.

She replied in Vietnamese. David could not make out what she was saying. He tried again, but she did not understand him. Despite her uniform, she clearly had never been a student of the *lycée*, where all courses were conducted in French. Digging into the pocket of her pinafore, the girl fished up a card which she handed to Marnin. He opened it and, in the dim light, read:

> Attached please find one certified virgin. Purity guaranteed. Use as desired. Warranty good until 7 A.M.
>
> Feliz año nuevo!

"Oh for Christ sake!" Marnin crumpled the card. He grabbed the girl by the arm. "*Où est votre. . .*"

The girl let out a shriek. "No hurt me!" she cried.

Marnin dropped her arm. "Oh my God!" he exclaimed, realizing how this would play to the neighbors or to any passing police. "Don't be frightened," he said, switching to English, in what he hoped was a soothing manner. "Listen, I'll take you home. You just tell me—" He heard the telephone ringing in the house. "Shit!"

He pulled the girl inside and grabbed the phone.

"Marnin here."

It was Rizzo.

"David, did I wake you?" Without pausing for a reply, he said, "Listen, we have an IMMEDIATE just in. Washington's gotten the press play on the Ap Bac battle and they want to know what's going on."

Rizzo paused to consider.

"Shall I call the Ambassador?"

"No!" David answered decisively. "Let him sleep."

"Okay, I'll call Bilder."

The girl, still standing in the middle of the room, began to cry.

"Oh Christ," David said in distress, "Don't do that!"

"Why not, man?" said Rizzo. "He already eats ten rolls of Tums a day—let him have a few more. I'll keep you posted."

"Great," David muttered. "Do that."

He rang off and stood for a moment looking at the girl and wondering what to do. Goddam Claudio, he would kill him for this. He went to the girl and led her to the sofa.

"Please don't cry," he said. "If you tell me where you live I'll take you home."

"I no go home," she said flatly. "I stay here. If I go way, Madame Chung, she kill me."

"Madame Chung brought you here?"

"Yes, she bring me. She tell me I do everything what you say." The girl giggled.

"Fine," he said brusquely. "Go away!"

"I no go away!" she wailed, her voice ascending to a high pitched howl. "She kill me!"

"Stop that!" David shouted. "Right now!"

To his relief, she stopped. He cast about for a solution. "Listen," he said, "would you like a Coke?"

She nodded, sniffing. He went out to the kitchen and when he came back he found her sitting on the sofa, drying her tears. He set down the Coke and a bowl of potato chips. The telephone rang again.

"It's John Mecklin, David. Sorry to bother you. I wake you?"

"No, it's okay, Mr. Mecklin."

"The wire service stories on Ap Bac are coming in on the ticker," Mecklin said, sounding unusually ruffled. "The shit's really hitting the fan. I know you'll be taking the news updates to the Ambassador in the morning, so I thought I'd stop in on my way home and drop them off."

"Oh Christ no," David blurted. "I mean. . . it's really nice of you, Mr. Mecklin, but it's not necessary."

"Oh, no problem," Mecklin assured him. "I go right by your house. I'll be there in five minutes, if not less."

David slammed down the phone.

"Look, you go in there," he said to the girl, pointing at his bedroom door. "Shut the door and go to bed. Okay?"

She looked at him uncomprehendingly. He grabbed her by the arm and pulled her toward the bedroom, whereupon she began to cry again.

"Madame Chung say I no make you happy she kill me."

"Listen, if you don't get into that bedroom, *I'll* kill you." Marnin pushed her into the room, then, seeing her distress, addressed her more gently. "You sleep, okay?" he said, pantomiming sleep. "*Dormez-vous.*"

Hearing a knocking, Marnin slammed the bedroom door shut and hurried to the front door. Mecklin was outside, holding a huge wad of teletype paper. Marnin wrenched the paper from Mecklin's hand.

"Thanks a lot, Mr. Mecklin. Don't want to keep you. Goodnight, sir."

He had a last photographic image of Mecklin's open mouth as he shut the door.

At three o'clock that morning, as Marnin lay asleep on the sofa, the telephone rang.

"You awake?" said Mandelbrot.

"I am now. What do you want, Billy?"

"Dave, I want a statement from Corning."

"No sweat, he's right here. I'm sure he'll be glad to give you one."

"Listen, smart ass, are you aware that Mudd is in deep *kimchee*?" Mandelbrot demanded angrily. "Both the ARVN and the Palace are saying this whole debacle is his fault. He should know this, but I can't reach him. Can you help out?"

"By doing what?"

"You can reach him on the Embassy or the military line. All you have to do is give him a heads-up."

"As a matter of fact, I tried to reach him earlier and failed," David said. "But I'll try again. Why not?"

He hung up and then called My Tho on the embassy line. Mudd picked up on the fourth ring.

"What's on your mind, my boy?"

"I called earlier, but you weren't there. I needed your input to update the Ambassador on the battle. You also ought to know that I just got off the phone with Mandelbrot, who says the ARVN and the Palace and MACV, they're all blaming you for this Ap Bac disaster."

"Well, they fucking well won't get away with it."

"I've also got all the wire service play here. They quote an American adviser as saying the ARVN didn't cut the mustard. . .that it was a quote miserable damn performance unquote."

"It was that. Who could deny it? Listen, Dave, hold onto those wire service stories, will you? I want to read them before I get flayed by the General. And, hey, thanks a lot."

At 6.30 Marnin lay dozing on the sofa when he was roused by a sharp rapping on the front door. It was Mudd, freshly shaved and smelling of cologne, in a spit and polish uniform, looking entirely rested and very sharp. This was striking. Marnin had, after all, been on the phone with him not three hours before, after a day that he had spent entirely in battle. With him was a black Air Force Staff Sergeant. Marnin invited them into the living room and offered to brew a pot of coffee.

"I don't have much time. We have to be at a briefing at MACV by seven-fifteen. This is Sergeant Washington. He works in the advisor's office in My Tho. Tell him what you do, Sergeant."

"I'm a radio operator."

"And what were you doing yesterday morning at ten-thirty?"

"I was monitoring the battle between the Seventh and Victor Charlie's 514th Regional Battalion."

"And what was happening at ten-thirty?"

"The ground fog had cleared and ten Flying Bananas were ferrying in the first reserve company from the airstrip. You were in your L-19 guiding them to a landing place."

"And what was I saying to them?"

"You was saying that they were coming in too close to the Western tree line, that there was a whole bunch of VC in there and that they should bring in the troops no closer than three hundred meters or all hell was gonna break loose."

"Who was I talking to?"

"Major Markham in the lead chopper."

"And what were my exact words?"

"You said, 'you fucking asshole, you gonna get your ass shot off.'"

"And what did he say?"

"He said it was his goddamn decision as to where those troops were gonna land and that he knew a good landing place when he saw one."

"And you recorded all this? You've got this all on tape?"

"Yes, sir. That's S.O.P. We use those tapes when we do our after action reports."

"Thank you, Sergeant," he said. He turned to Marnin with a pleased smile on his face.

"What happened to Markham?" Marnin asked.

"He's dead. Shot through the head. That asshole."

David took a deep breath. Then he said, "You ought to make sure you get your own version of what happened on the record. You owe it to yourself."

"Let me tell you something. This battle is going to become famous. I'm going to write up every detail and my report will be stud-

ied in staff colleges centuries from now. The only thing that might
stop this from happening is that MACV will classify it TOP SECRET.
Because what it will show to anyone who has eyes to read is that the
ARVN didn't cut the mustard today and isn't likely to in the future,
that this was a miserable damn performance, A FUCKING MISER-
ABLE DAMNED PERFORMANCE. . . ."

The front door opened. It was Mme. Chung.

"*Bonjour, bonjour*," she said, and then marched resolutely through
the living room into the bedroom. In a few moments she emerged
with her charge in tow, still dressed in the uniform of the Saigon lycée,
her hair uncombed, her eyes puffy, and looking very sleepy and
grumpy and much the worse for wear. Mme. Chung bade them a fond
farewell with a happy wave and marched out. The girl did not say a
word and did not even glance at Marnin. Colonel Mudd and Sergeant
Washington looked at each other. Mudd cleared his throat showily
and then asked Washington to wait for him in the jeep.

"Son," he said to Marnin when they were alone, "you be careful
with that Vietnamese poontang. Your base is Saigon. The one thing
the Vietnamese don't like worse than anything is having foreigners
messing with their women. We've got a job to do in this country. And
that comes first before anything. If you really feel that you just got to
have a taste of that sweet Vietnamese pussy, you come down to My
Tho and I'll fix you up. But in the meantime remember that no dog
shits in his own back yard."

Marnin was speechless.

A week later, on January 10th, he received by military courier a
small package from My Tho. It was from Mudd and it seemed to contain personal papers, perhaps a manuscript. In a covering note Mudd
asked Marnin to hold onto it for a little while and only to open it if
something should happen to him. Marnin put it in his desk drawer
and forgot about it.

It took four days for the Paris-based *Herald Tribune* to reach Saigon and the *New York Times* took a week. The first American newspaper the Embassy saw was *Stars and Stripes*, Pacific edition, printed in Okinawa, which arrived the day after it was published, and was of no interest to anyone looking for a serious account of world events. The Embassy, of course, did not lack for news. The USIA Wireless File described the public position of the United States on the whole range of foreign policy issues and the Voice of America, largely at Embassy Saigon's behest, had stepped up its signal to Southeast Asia.

The embassy ended up regretting this as VOA news broadcasts critical of the South Vietnamese became a running sore in its relations with the Government of Viet Nam. There was no way to contend to the GVN, to Diem or Nhu personally, or to any other Vietnamese for that matter, that VOA was meant to be a medium for broadcasting the news "objectively." They laughed in Corning's face when he tried to make such an argument. This put Corning, who sent cable after cable complaining about distortions in VOA broadcasts, in a head to head conflict with Ed Murrow, the influential director of USIA, whose aim was to give VOA a BBC-like panache of "total objectivity," and who insisted, therefore, that the bad news from Viet Nam picked up by the *New York Times* be rebroadcast to Southeast Asia.

The Embassy also had access to numerous press summaries. The one prepared by the Department's Far East Bureau was the most thorough. And USIS Saigon subscribed to the *Associated Press Ticker*. Further, despite the terrible trans-Pacific connections in those pre-satellite days, Bilder was on the phone every evening with Paul Kattenberg of the Viet Nam Working Group in the Department, catching him at the beginning of his working day and getting a sense from him of what Washington was focusing on that morning. The Ambassador therefore well knew what was being reported about the "catastrophic Battle of Ap Bac," as the wire services termed it. In fact, he and Diem had traded observations on it two days before when he dropped by the Palace for a congratulatory drink to celebrate the President's sixty-first birthday.

They found that this was one subject about which they could pretty well agree. The title Corning gave to one of three cables he sent to the Department on January third, based on that birthday conversation with the GVN leader, was "Battle of Ap Bac, a Tempest in a Teapot Says President Diem." Nevertheless, despite all the preparatory warning, the January 4 edition of *Stars and Stripes* turned out to be a shock. It was received in the ten-thirty mail run on the fifth of January. Marnin brought the newspaper to the Ambassador as soon as he saw the front page. Corning was in his office with Bilder going over the schedule for the return visit of Commander-in-Chief for the Pacific (CINCPAC), Admiral Bill McGrath, due to arrive that afternoon.

"I thought you'd want to see this right away," Marnin said.

Normally the Ambassador did not even look at *Stars and Stripes,* a tabloid aimed at the average nineteen year old army corporal. This time he took it and stared at the front page. The eighteen point headlines screamed, "VIET CONG DEFEATS ARVN IN BIG BATTLE." In smaller type were two subsidiary stories, "THREE AMERICANS KILLED, FIVE CHOPPERS DESTROYED," and "WHITE HOUSE CONCERNED, PRESIDENT DEMANDS SPECIAL INVESTIGATION." The bottom half of the front page showed an H-21, a "Flying Banana," tipped over on its side. The caption of the photo read, "American helicopter, one of five destroyed by Viet Cong. Three Americans reported dead."

Corning handed the newspaper on to Bilder, who began flipping through it. "I don't have to read this," Corning said. "I know what it says. I've had twelve personal calls from the States in the past two days. None of them official, mind you. All of them from friends. And every one of them starts out by asking, 'what the hell is going on out there, Gus? I thought we were winning that thing. What in the world is happening?' And I tell every one of them that they had it right. We are winning. But I can sense that there's a good deal of skepticism on the other end. They're not hearing what I'm saying. A whole bunch of Americans are going to bed tonight thinking that we're in desperate straits out here."

"This is the story," Bilder said. "This is the one Kattenberg was telling me about, the story you ought to read."

He folded the paper back to page five and showed it to the Ambassador. "A MISERABLE DAMN PERFORMANCE," the headline shrieked. And then, in smaller type, "U.S. ADVISORS BLAME ARVN COUNTERPARTS FOR GIVING AWAY THE STORE." There was a photo of an American Captain on a stretcher being carried by two Vietnamese. He was waving to the camera. The caption underneath read, "Wounded U.S. Advisor Evacuated from the Battlefield after Major ARVN Defeat." The story had originated on the *New York Times* wire and carried a Willis Mandelbrot byline. Bilder read the first two paragraphs out loud.

"American advisors in the Delta, South Viet Nam's fertile rice bowl, were stunned at the crushing defeat inflicted on the Seventh Division January 2 by the 514th Field Battalion of the Viet Cong. Words like "cowardice," "fecklessness," and "incompetence" were used to describe the efforts of our Vietnamese allies. One senior American, summing up a day of frustration and bitterness at the loss of close comrades in arms, expressed the view of all his colleagues when he said, 'it was a miserable damn performance, just like it always is.'

"Too emotionally upset to engage in the usual cover-up that the Americans adopt when talking about the ARVN, this U.S. military man said, "those three Americans didn't die from gunshot wounds. They bled to death. They died because they didn't get the attention they should have from ARVN commanders who weren't on the scene supervising their forces as they should have been. The failure to act was then compounded by the failure to react. The real pity was that the enemy was pinned down and cut off. All we had to do was block his retreat. We could have annihilated the whole 514th—the best unit they have. The airborne could have closed a trap in the afternoon and vindicated the ARVN after its god-awful show in the morning. But when they finally made the parachute drop, its aim was not to engage the enemy. Its aim was to avoid the enemy. It was a miserable damn performance, just a miserable damn performance. . . ."

"That's enough," Corning said. "I get the drift."

"It's just what I told you. It's practically treason," Bilder said. "They ought to find the son of a bitch that said that and fry his gonads. We spend hundreds of millions of dollars training these people, molding them into a first rate fighting army, and then some dumb hothead who can't see the forest for the trees comes along and shoots off his mouth and does more to ruin what we've been doing than the whole Viet Cong main force. They should find that guy and make an example of him."

"It shouldn't be too difficult to figure out who Mandelbrot's source was," Corning said. "It was obviously that fellow Mudd, the subject of the story that Mandelbrot wrote in the *Times Magazine*. He's got a mouth to match his ego. He's the adviser to the Seventh Division. He was following the action from beginning to end. He's the one the Palace thinks is entirely to blame for the whole fiasco. He's obviously reacting to those accusations. What other so-called senior military man would have been quoted as saying a thing like that? But that's assuming somebody actually said that. I wouldn't put it past Mandelbrot to concoct it out of whole cloth."

"I doubt that he made it up," Marnin said.

Corning tilted back in his chair and looked up at him.

"You know Mudd. Don't you think that he was the source of that article?"

Marnin shifted uneasily.

"I don't know. I've only talked with him once or twice. He seems very committed to the war effort. I'm. . .not sure he'd make rash statements like that. By all reports he's a pretty cool customer. I talked with him the morning after Ap Bac. He was all spit and polish and very composed—amazingly so after a battle like that."

Marnin was sweating—embarrassed to be telling a lie to his boss, whom he venerated. He knew very well that Mudd had been the source of the story. He was therefore greatly relieved when Helen Eng announced on the intercom that the Agency chiefs were gathered for the regular twice weekly Country Team meeting.

The principals were sitting around a long brown polished table in the conference room. Besides the Ambassador and DCM, this included MACV (General Donnelly), the MAAG (General Parker), USOM (Dr. Warren "Curly" Bird), the CIA station (Stu Markoff), USIS (John Mecklin), the Embassy Political Counselor (Sam Sabo), the Economic Counselor (Bob Jaspers), the Consul General (Lou Holbein) and assorted Embassy hangers on. Various ancillary figures, including Marnin, were seated in chairs along the walls behind them. When Corning entered they all rose, only seating themselves again after the Ambassador did. He took his usual place at the head of the table. General Donnelly sat to his right and Bilder to his left. Before Donnelly's promotion it had been the other way around. When MACV came into being it gave Donnelly not only a fourth star, but also a separate organization that transcended Viet Nam by including Thailand. This allowed him the right to communicate with Washington independently, without ambassadorial clearance. And anyone with bureaucratic experience understands that unfettered communication is the first requisite of true power.

Back channel messages from Donnelly to Maxwell Taylor, the Chairman of the Joint Chiefs of Staff, or to McNamara, the Secretary of Defense, therefore became entirely his own prerogative. This meant that although in some senses Donnelly still worked for the Ambassador, in other senses he did not. It therefore behooved Corning to treat him as something of an equal while at the same time maintaining his own supreme status.

With many, if not most, high ranking officers, who are picked to rise in their profession not only for their dedication and their military skills but also for their aggressiveness, this could have been a big problem. But not with Donnelly, the quintessential military diplomat, unusually sensitive to cultural factors that could be the breaking point in accomplishing his mission. In moments of frustration, when they were alone together, or sometimes when they were relaxing with a *cit-ron pressé* after a tennis match, Donnelly might complain to Corning that building the ARVN into a fighting force was like teaching a bunch of corporals how to fight the battle of Stalingrad. But this kind of comment never escaped his lips when talking to a subordinate on his staff. On the wall of his office was the anonymous motto, "Nobody fights well until he thinks he can lick the other guy." .

"Unless someone has something urgent they wish to raise during this meeting," Corning said, "I intend to devote it entirely to a briefing by General Donnelly on the Battle of Ap Bac. I can tell you that the President and the Secretary are deeply disturbed by the fuss that's been generated about an incident which has been mindlessly blown up out of all proportions. On that score I would urge every one of you to read three documents that try to give it some balance. The first is General Donnelly's cable, drafted by General Parker, that went out yesterday and was entitled 'AP Coverage of the Battle of Ap Bac—the 95 Inaccuracies.' The second cable, which also went out yesterday, was drafted by Chick Rizzo and Sam Sabo and was entitled, "Tepid Vietnamese Reaction to the Battle of Ap Bac." It pretty well summarizes the lack of response in this country to that engagement. The third cable that you should all read is my own account of the conversation that I had with President Diem on the subject the day before yesterday. With that I want to turn over the floor now to General Donnelly. Blix, it's all yours."

Donnelly rose and gestured for Aylward to come forward and set up the portable screen and the viewgraph machine at the foot of the long table. Bilder and Sabo exchanged amused glances. The military never conveyed information without resorting to audio-visual techniques which would have been the worst kind of bad form in the State Department, where the slide projector was regarded as a crutch for simpletons. Donnelly reached into his shirt pocket and pulled out a collapsible metal pointer and extended it.

"This briefing is classified Top Secret. First slide, please," he said to Aylward.

The viewgraph flashed on the screen.

"The Viet Cong have the initiative and most of the control in the jungle foothills of the High Plateau north of Saigon all the way down to the Gulf of Siam, excluding the big city area of Saigon—Cholon. . . .South Viet Nam should be handled as a combat area of the cold war, an area requiring emergency treatment."   —General Ed Lansdale

"That," said Donnelly, "was written in 1960—just two years ago—in a Top Secret report from General Lansdale to the President. It was Lansdale's first trip back to this country since 1956. For those of you who don't know it, Lansdale was instrumental in helping President Diem in 1955 and 1956 survive the threat from the sects, the Cao Dai and the Hoa Hao, and from the Binh Xuyen, the gangster force that controlled Saigon. Lansdale left Viet Nam on the upswing. He was shocked at what he found when he came back.

"Eighteen months ago this country was in the process of going down the tubes. The ARVN as an instrument of war was entirely useless. This is the big forgotten fact about Viet Nam. The goddam press is screaming about the screw-up at Ap Bac. Hell, if those puppies who are writing these stories had been old enough to fight in Korea, not to mention World War II, they would have seen screw-ups that made Ap Bac look like a masterpiece of military planning. Before you start screaming about the ARVN you ought to take a good long look at what happened to the U.S. Eighth Army after the Battle of the Chosen Reservoir.

"More to the point look at the ARVN itself. What happened at Tan Phu and Ap Bac, and this is beyond disputing, is that a force of two thousand ARVN attacked a Viet Cong unit in the morning and that this force was supplemented by a thousand airborne troops that attacked in the afternoon. Sure there were screw-ups. But the point is that eighteen months ago the ARVN was physically incapable of mounting an offensive action involving even five hundred troops, not to mention three thousand. It didn't have the leadership. It didn't have the doctrine. It didn't have the logistics. It didn't have the mobility.

Eighteen months ago we had three to four engagements a month worse than Ap Bac. But nobody knew about it. Nobody was paying any attention. And nobody remembers it. Why not? Because our advisors come here and serve eleven months and get the hell out. And that's even truer for the reporters. And who are those reporters? They are children."

He snapped his finger and Aylward came up and handed him a series of index cards. As he read from the cards, photos and names of each of the reporters were flashed on the screen.

"UPI. Twenty-six years old. First experience overseas. Never covered a war before. Been here eight months. Previous academic study of Southeast Asia or experience outside the United States: none.

"AP. Twenty-nine years old, and a goddam Australian at that. Experience and academic qualifications—absolutely none! These guys think their job is to throw rocks.

"*New York Times*. The worst of the lot, twenty-eight years old. Formerly something called an investigative reporter. Covered the civil rights movement in Alabama. Tells my guys right up front that he personally intends to get rid of the president of this country. I'm old fashioned. I always thought a reporter was supposed to be objective. In this case, there's lots of doubt as to who he wants to win this war—us or the commies.

"The most charitable way to look at it is that they've none of them ever seen a war before. They think they're at the movies and watching John Wayne. On the silver screen nobody gets hurt. Or if they do it's all very pretty. But here, when they see a few dead bodies with their guts spewed out who don't smell so good in the tropical sun, it's a tremendous shock. So I'm not saying that any of these guys are out and out subversives. They may mean well. And they may just be misplaced idealists. But I'm also not saying that they're not subversives. As far as I'm concerned, the jury is still out on that particular question. Next slide please."

The second viewgraph showed three blue and red maps of South Viet Nam, the first marked July 1961, the second July 1962, and the third January 1963. Red indicated areas of Viet Cong control; blue, areas controlled by the government.

"This shows what's happening in this country. Eighteen months ago—right here—the Viet Cong controlled 39.4 per cent of the land and the government 60.6. Now here you see the situation six months ago—VC 19.4, government 80.6. And here's how it looks today—VC 8.5, government 91.5. Next slide, please."

The third viewgraph consisted of the same three maps, but expressed in terms of population, rather than area.

"We give the Communists credit for control of a lot of empty territory," Donnelly went on. "The GVN, on the other hand, governs every population center in this country. So when you look at those three maps again, you find that eighteen months ago the VC held sway over 13.7 per cent of the South Vietnamese people. Six months ago it was 8.3 per cent, and today only 3.9 per cent. Next slide.

```
VIET CONG KIA
July 1, 1962–December 31, 1962......................13,321
VIET CONG-ARVN KILL RATIO...................2.3: 1
```

"Now this viewgraph tells us pretty much why the dramatic improvement in government control took place in this country, why we've gone from a government on the ropes to one ready to deliver a knockout punch in the short space of a year and a half. The reason is that we're eliminating the best people the Viet Cong have. It takes at least a year to train and equip a combat soldier. And we're killing Viet Cong faster than they can recruit them. Those are front line soldiers, men who carry weapons. Next slide, please."

```
ARVN (AND OTHER GVN SECURITY) FORCES...432,157
MAINLINE VIET CONG....................................21,135
OTHER VC FORCES.........................................74,359
TOTAL.............................................................95,494
GVN: VC RATIO................................................9:2
```

"Now I'm not happy with a 9:2 ratio. We can't win this war until that ratio becomes 8:1 or better. But there's no denying that any engagement in which we take as many casualties as the enemy has got to be considered to the advantage of the side that has a 9:2 force ratio in its favor. I don't want to take fifty thousand ARVN casualties. But if I could do that and inflict fifty thousand dead on the enemy while I was doing it, I'd be a pretty happy man. If I could do that in the next six months, then I'd have my 8:1 ratio and the war would in effect be over. Well, let me tell you. I intend to do just exactly that. The ARVN is going to win this war, and win it within a year. I'll tell you how we're going to do that. But first I want to talk about the so-called Battle of Ap Bac that I call the Battle of the *New York Times*. Next slide, please.

```
THE BATTLE OF AP BAC
ARVN KILLED......................................................61
US KILLED.............................................................3
VC KILLED............................................................94
US HELICOPTERS (OUT OF COMMISSION)..............1
ARVN APC DESTROYED.........................................0
```

"Now I want everybody to absorb those figures. When we're talking about the so-called Battle of Ap Bac, we're not talking about Gettysburg, or the Wilderness, or Chateau Thierry, or the Ardennes, or Iwo Jima, or Tarawa, or the Chosen Reservoir. We're talking about a skirmish in which exactly three Americans got killed. That's three more Americans than we wanted to see get killed, but it's not exactly a turning point in this war."

"You say there was only one chopper knocked out," Sam Sabo interjected. "I thought there were five."

"There were five disabled on the morning of January second. Four of them have been repaired and are now flying. They're in the air. One is still in the shop. But it should be ready to go by the beginning of next week. Do you have anything to add Ace?"

"No, sir!" replied Ace Parker, an Air Force general who looked as though he had just fallen off a radish truck, but who was nobody's fool. "Our boys were a little courageously over-opportunistic at Ap Bac. People should remember that Victor Charlie hasn't been fighting this way ever before and he may not do so again. We may just be dealing with one particularly gutsy local commander. There's no question that our boys weren't ready. Well, we're going to be ready the next time."

"And that's another thing," Donnelly added. "We've been wanting those raggedy ass little bastards to stand up and fight with us for a long time. So far they've been smart enough not to do so. But if they want to slug it out, nothing could make me happier. They're going to lose anyway. But in head to head combat they're going to lose a lot quicker. Next slide, please."

```
                    HEADWAY REPORT
   KILL RATIO ...............................................71%
   OPERATIONS LAUNCHED................137%
   SORTIES FLOWN................................243%
   BOMB TONNAGE...................................368%
   INCREMENT TO ARVN.........................38%
```

"Now these are all figures taken from my year end 'Headway Report.' For those of you who don't know it, the Headway Report is a weekly document that we compile for CINCPAC in which we lay out in an absolutely objective manner exactly what has taken place during the past week. These percentage figures all represent increases in the July to December framework over what they were from January to July. Militarily speaking, what this shows loud and clear is that the ARVN is getting bigger, smarter, better, and above all it's getting more aggressive. These same cowardly generals who, according to the *New York Times*, are afraid to engage the enemy, have initiated 137 per cent more operations and are now killing 71 per cent more of the enemy than the enemy is inflicting on their forces. Next slide, please."

```
   HOW WE WIN THE WAR
     THE THREE M'S
   MEN——MONEY——MATERIEL
```

"Why am I so sure we're going to win? Why won't fifty battles like Ap Bac make me change my mind, even if the *New York Times* version of the battle were the true one, which it isn't? Because military history teaches us that the side with the men, the side with the money, and above all the side with the materiel is the side that's going to win in war. It's all there in Clausewitz. No amount of operational art is going to make up for deficiencies in men, money, and materiel. That's what Ulysees Grant taught Jefferson Davis and Robert E. Lee.

"The Wehrmacht were man for man and division for division by far the most effective fighting forces in the Second World War. But ultimately it didn't do Hitler any good. Because no matter how good your troops and how good your generals, if you don't have the money, and you don't have the men, and you don't have the materiel, then you can't win. Victor Charlie's days are numbered. We've expanded the ARVN by 30,000 men—two new infantry divisions that are going to be the best they have. The same kind of thing is happening in the Civil Guard and the Local Forces, which will be tripled by the middle of next year. We've upped our military and economic aid from $215 million to $337 million over the past year. All this is having its effect. It's giving these guys the one thing they've always lacked—confidence. Ap Bac is not going to undermine that confidence. Next slide, please."

```
OPERATION EXPLOSION
PHASE ONE............................................PLANNING
PHASE TWO...................................PREPARATION
PHASE THREE...................................EXECUTION
PHASE FOUR...........................FOLLOW UP AND
                                        CONSOLIDATION
```

"This is Top Secret and I don't want it to go outside this room. But this group should understand that what we're doing here has been worked out with the Ambassador and with President Diem in a clearly thought through plan. It's been okayed by the Chiefs and by Secretary McNamara and signed off by the President. It's an articulated four phase plan to win this war and get the United States out of this country with dignity and honor. This plan is not just ready to roll. No sir, it has been rolling. It started in May of last year and we're seven months into it. The first two phases, Planning and Preparation have already been completed. And now we're starting on Phase three—execution.

"Each phase is worked out in the finest honed detail. To get from phase two to phase three, for example, we had to meet forty-two statistical indicators that had been set up six months ago when we conceived this plan. We were not prepared to go from phase two to phase three until we met at least thirty-eight out of those forty-two indicators. But we met them all. And we're going to meet our phase three indicators as well. We're going to mount a nationwide offensive that will continue until the Viet Cong as an organized force will be ground down to powder.

"I expect this to be done by next January, a year from now, or at the very latest by June of 1964. Once we begin Phase Four, the problem will be to mop up the guerilla remnants and restore the authority of the government in every village, in every hamlet, in this country. The GVN will be able to do that by itself because by that time the ARVN will rule supreme. There'll be no way for Victor Charlie to stand up to it. The Free World is going to win this war. The tide is going to stop right here."

When Donnelly was finished there was a long pause as he walked back to his seat at the head of the table. Then Sam Sabo stood up and started to applaud. At the end of his third clap Gus Corning also stood and joined Sabo. And then all the others joined in—a standing ovation to a briefing in an embassy conference room. Marnin was never to see anything like it anywhere else in his whole career. This group of embassy leaders felt beleaguered. For them the lines were clearly drawn—US Embassy Saigon versus the *New York Times*.

Marnin too joined the applause and was as carried away as anyone by the controlled fervor of General Donnelly. And perhaps he applauded with even more ardor than any of the others, for at that point he was still deeply puzzled and ashamed of his action an hour before. Without thinking, operating on instinct, he had taken sides. And it had been the wrong side. Donnelly once more had convinced him of that.

Chapter 15

ON THE TEAM

There was only one sour note to the January 5 visit of Admiral Bill McGrath, Commander in Chief in the Pacific—his "exit" press conference at Tan Son Nhut, just before his departure. All the Saigon based press were there, as were forty or fifty other newsmen who had descended on Saigon in the wake of the Battle of Ap Bac—the most press attention to any event in Viet Nam over the previous several years. The press had been scrambling for days for a story and was frustrated that the Embassy, ARVN, and MACV insisted officially that there was no story. In the *Times* Mandelbrot had speculated that the purpose of CINCPAC's visit had been to investigate the Ap Bac fiasco. The fact of the matter, as Marnin could attest, was that McGrath's visit had been laid on long before any of the correspondents in Viet Nam could have told Ap Bac from Sarasota.

The resident press in Saigon were all young men. Their editors at home, while not wanting to undercut them, were nevertheless not anxious to pick a fight with the United States government. Before that press conference normal decorum between newspapermen and high officials had been observed. When reporters questioned Corning or Donnelly about something, "Mister Ambassador," "General," or at least "sir" were the usual forms of address. But after the McGrath visit that stopped happening. The press and the Embassy openly went to war.

The press conference took place in the VIP area at Tan Son Nhut airport. The air-conditioning was not working and sixty people were jammed into a space that was inadequate for half that number. To add to the level of irritation, because of security procedures at the airport that went into effect with the New Year the press was asked to be there at nine for a conference that was not scheduled to begin until ten.

McGrath and Donnelly had no idea that they would be facing a crowd of hot, angry, impatient, and hostile newsmen. The MACV Public Information Officer, Lieutenant Colonel Hodgkins, opened the meeting. He discovered the microphone was not working.

"Sorry about that, gentlemen. We'll have to ask the Admiral to speak up. Now this is all going to be on deep background."

This announcement was greeted with hisses, whistles, and boos.

"What the hell's going on?" someone asked. "Nobody said anything about deep background."

"That was agreed on," Hodgkins said. "It was announced yesterday at our five o'clock briefing."

"Who the hell goes to that? We've got to write a story, man. Deep background won't work. How about if we source it to a high administration official or to a key military commander?"

Hodgkins left the podium to confer with McGrath and Donnelly, who were standing uncomfortably by the entrance, along with Ace Parker, wondering if they had been sandbagged. Marnin was there next to them.

"Maybe we should call the whole thing off," Parker said tentatively.

"We can't do that," McGrath said. "The whole purpose was to mollify these guys. Hell, let's make it on the record. I've got no problems with that. Do you Blix?"

"We've got nothing to hide," said Donnelly.

Hodgkins walked back to the podium.

"This press conference will be on the record. Admiral McGrath has agreed to that."

There was a smattering of applause from the press.

"Lawdy, lawdy, thank you massa," Mandelbrot, sitting in the first row, said loudly. "Ise gwine be evah so grateful."

Everybody laughed, including McGrath and Donnelly, but there were glints of steel in those four-star eyes. John Mecklin, a former

Time correspondent, was standing next to Marnin.

"This is going to be a disaster," he said.

"You all know who Admiral McGrath is," Hodgkins said, "so I won't bother with the normal introduction. He's in charge of our fighting forces in the Pacific and is one of the most senior military men now on active duty. Admiral McGrath."

"Thank you, Lou. It's a pleasure for me to be here. This is my eighth trip to Viet Nam since I took over as CINCPAC. So it's not exactly terra incognita for me. I've had a very good visit—good talks with President Diem, with Ambassador Corning and the Country Team, and with MACV and my old friend Blix Donnelly, who's doing a great job here. The progress since my last visit has been tangible, more than I realized, more than you can get from a bunch of reports and briefings. You have to look at things on the ground in order really to understand what's happening. I did that. And I'm very pleased at what I saw. In fact, I'll be in Washington next week and will be reporting on all this progress to the President when I see him next Thursday. Are there any questions?"

Twenty hands shot up. But Mandelbrot stood up—all six feet three of him—and raised both hands over his head. McGrath, who had taken an instant dislike to him, for a minute contemplated freezing him out, but then thought better of it.

"New York Times. I have several questions," Mandelbrot said. "Let me start with three related ones. You say you were impressed with all the progress that's been made here since your last visit, which I believe was five months ago. Then how do you fit the disaster at Ap Bac in that framework? Secondly, did you have a chance during your visit to talk with the American advisors who were working with the Seventh Division and with the airborne forces during the battle? If so, what did they say about it? If not, why not? Thirdly, you made only one trip outside Saigon during your visit—to Can Tho. But the Seventh Division, the force that actually fought at Ap Bac, is stationed in My Tho, only an hour's drive or a ten minute chopper ride from Saigon. Why didn't you go to My Tho?"

"I'll answer your questions in reverse order, if I may," McGrath said. "In terms of my schedule and where I went, I was more or less in the hands of General Donnelly. So I think I'll ask him to comment."

Donnelly moved to the podium, looking very unhappy.

"I'm not sure I understand the import of the last question," he said. "As you know, Admiral McGrath is on a very tight schedule. He goes from here to Singapore, Honolulu, and then Washington. So we couldn't stretch his schedule. And it was most important that he spend as much time as possible conferring at the national level with our GVN allies. It was essential that he see the President, the Foreign Minister, the Minister of Defense, the heads of the ARVN, the State Secretary, and so forth. There was time for one trip outside the capital. And in view of all the fuss that you gentlemen have made about events in Tan Phu and Ap Bac earlier this week, it seemed a good idea for the Admiral to have a full briefing on the subject. The best place for such a briefing is at corps headquarters, which happens to be in Can Tho, not in My Tho. . ."

"Isn't it really," Mandelbrot interrupted, "because you knew that things could be covered up in Can Tho, but not in My Tho. . ."

"Now just one cotton-picking minute," Donnelly shot back hotly, "I'm not going to stand here and have my integrity impugned by you or anyone else. Nobody was thinking of a cover-up. Nothing happened at Ap Bac that we need to cover up. But if something ever does go wrong out here, and in war screwups are absolutely inevitable—I've fought in three wars and I know—if something goes wrong this headquarters will never, I repeat never, be guilty of trying to hide anything from our duly constituted superiors in the chain of command."

"Are you saying," said Wilbur Durfee of NBC, who had come down from Hong Kong to cover the story, "that if you had to do it all over again, you would advise the ARVN to operate in the same way that they did in Ap Bac January 2?"

"Nothing is ever perfect in war. Nothing works out exactly as you planned. The reason for that is there's an enemy out there trying to frustrate your plans. Now moving two thousand men into battle and supplying those men with the necessary requisites to fight successfully may seem a simple thing to those of you who have never had to do it. But let me assure you that it isn't easy, that the ARVN did it relatively well January 2, and that it wouldn't have been able to carry out an operation of this kind a year ago. So I saw good things and bad things at Ap Bac. We and the ARVN leadership are going to make those good things better and we're going to correct those bad things and make sure they don't happen again."

"Can you tell us what those bad things were?" Durfee asked.

"You guys have me here all the time," Donnelly countered. "I'm going to turn this thing back over to Admiral McGrath."

By this time there was a tangible air of tension in the room.

"Admiral, could you answer my questions," Mandelbrot said. "You've now had a chance to talk them over with your advisors. I want to know your view of Ap Bac. I want to know what they've been telling you about it. I want to know whether you think that the worst defeat that we've suffered in this war is really a sign of progress. Are we marching through the looking glass? Is this a real war or Alice in Wonderland?"

"It sounds to me," McGrath said, "as though you've already made up your mind and that there's nothing that I or General Donnelly or anyone else could say to you to make you change it. OK, that's all right with me. You're an American and you're free to think whatever you want to. But let me tell you that military affairs are a science as well as an art. And when you want to know something about a science you go to a scientist, you go to an expert. And General Blix Donnelly is an expert. And when a soldier with his background, and his training, and his expertise tells me something about a battle I give him a lot more credibility than I would to a bunch of amateurs or even to a bunch of junior officers, no matter how well meaning and patriotic those amateurs and junior officers may be. Now everything I've heard about the Battle of Ap Bac leads in one direction. War is basically about seizing and holding and controlling territory. And that's what happened at Ap Bac. The enemy took some positions and tried to hold them. So we mounted an operation and dislodged them. They had their objective, we had ours. They failed to achieve their objective and we achieved ours. It's as simple as that."

McGrath was growing hoarse from trying to shout over the constant buzz of the reporters talking to each other. The acoustics were bad and the din made it difficult to hear anyone past the first row, where Mandelbrot held court. He leaped into the breach.

"Then would it be fair, Admiral, to quote you as saying that the Battle of Ap Bac was an ARVN victory?"

"Yes. They gained their objective. Why not? Sure it was a victory. Wouldn't you say so, Blix?"

"Victory is maybe a little strong. But they certainly gained their objective. The Viet Cong was dislodged. If you define victory as the achievement of one's objective, then it clearly was just that—a victory."

This was a little too much for Anthony Durch of the London Times, also down from Hong Kong.

"Do you realize," he asked, "that the people in this room have been reporting for the past five days that a colossal defeat for ARVN and American forces has taken place in the northern Delta, that a mainline Viet Cong unit for the first time not only stood and fought—but stood, fought, and prevailed? Now do you really expect us, based on a simplistic definition which as far as I can see has not much relevance in this kind of war, to change our tune, to leave this room and cable our editors that we're awfully sorry, but we had it all wrong? The Battle of Ap Bac was not a defeat after all. Please hold the presses. It was a VICTORY!"

The entire room burst into applause.

The press conference lasted fifteen minutes more and went from bad to worse. At the end of it the wits in the press corps were having a field day and the group was actually laughing at McGrath and Donnelly, a sensation that few people can bear with equanimity and those with four stars on their shoulders less than almost anyone else. There was no way to redeem the situation. Getting the high sign from McGrath, Hodgkins went up to the podium and declared the press conference over.

Mandelbrot, like the true picador he was, raced after McGrath, who was getting a bitter post mortem assessment of what had occurred from John Mecklin. Mecklin, for politeness sake, introduced Mandelbrot to McGrath.

"I've heard a lot about you, Mandelbrot," the Admiral said. "What's eating you, man? Why don't you get on the team?"

For once in his life, Willis Mandelbrot was speechless.

He and Marnin were parked next to each other in the VIP lot. He was with Buechner and they were going back to their respective offices to file stories and photos. Marnin would have liked to avoid him, but there was no comfortable way to do so.

"I'd like to congratulate you," Mandelbrot said, "for being a cog in the wheel of the great machine that just turned a stunning defeat into a crushing victory."

"Very funny."

"Did you hear what he said?"

"I heard."

"The Japs are holding on to Iwo Jima. You attack them. Now you're holding on to Iwo Jima. That's a victory. The VC is holding on to Ap Bac. You attack them. Now you've got Ap Bac. That's also a victory. Could you believe your ears? Could you believe your fucking ears?"

"Get on the team, man," Buechner said. "Get on the team."

The phrase "get on the team" became a byword among the Saigon press, guaranteed to evoke gusts of unrestrained glee. After McGrath's admonition to Mandelbrot made the rounds, whenever anyone in the press corps gave vent to skepticism or criticism of official Vietnamese or American efforts, one of the others would pipe up, "Get on the team, man. Why don't you get on the team?"

Chapter 16

THE COUNSELORS

The rest of the company had been gathered on the Sabo veranda for twenty minutes when the *Conseiller du Président*, his only official title, came up the driveway in a large black Cadillac limousine. The Sabos' houseboy opened the door of the limo and Ngo Dinh Nhu emerged wearing a navy blue bush jacket over matching trousers. The other men were in dark tropical suits, the ladies in long dresses. The Sabos had not let on who the guest of honor was going to be. This was at the request of the Palace, for security reasons. Capturing the second man in the country for a dinner party was a real social coup in Saigon.

But not everyone was impressed by this feat. As Nhu emerged from the limo, Lady Boggs turned in surprise to Stu Markoff, standing next to her, and said in her clarion tones, "Ah, there's Counselor Nhu. Horrid fellow!"

Sabo walked down the steps to greet the Counselor.

"Welcome my dear friend," he said in French. With Nhu's arrival, despite his excellent English, all those who could switched to French.

"*C'est un grand plaisir*," said Nhu, with the sardonic grin that almost never left his face all evening.

Grace Sabo greeted him as he was climbing the steps.

"And Madame Nhu?" she asked tentatively.

"She has decided not to come," he said, still smiling.

No apologies, not even lame ones. Grace Sabo was quite tall, at least five feet nine. She towered over Nhu. There were occasions when she had difficulty in forgetting that she was a Guggenheim.

"She's not coming?"

"No."

"This is a small sit-down dinner," Grace said coldly. "There were going to be fourteen of us. Now there will be thirteen, an unfortunate number. You'll excuse me. I will have to rearrange the table."

She turned on her heels and went inside and did not emerge until it was time to summon the guests for dinner. Nhu took not the slightest notice. He coolly asked Sabo for a *pastis* over ice and nursed it as he made the rounds of the veranda shaking hands and greeting the other guests.

In addition to Lady Boggs, the company consisted of the CIA Station Chief Stu Markoff, who at that point was working with Nhu organizing what was ultimately to turn into the Phoenix Program, and his wife; Warren "Curly" Bird, the USOM director, a widower who regularly consulted with Nhu about material support for the Strategic Hamlet program that also belonged to Nhu; Ton That Tuyen, the senior civil servant in the South Vietnamese government and his wife; Nguyen Hung Binh, the head of Nhu's internal intelligence unit and his wife; and Madame Enonu, the wife of the Turkish Ambassador, who was on consultation in Ankara.

Rather than going around the veranda greeting each guest in turn depending on where they were standing, Nhu chose to greet the company in the order of their protocol rank, beginning with the Vietnamese—first Tuyen, then Binh. He thereupon shook hands in similar fashion with the others—first Lady Boggs, then Bird, then Markoff, then Marnin. Other than Lady Boggs, he never acknowledged anybody's wife. It was outrageous.

Just before he reached Marnin for his introduction he put down his *pastis* and asked Sabo, who as the host was following in his wake, for a vodka on the rocks. He said he preferred Polish vodka. Wyborowa was his brand. Sabo confessed that there was only Smirnoff available. In that case it would have to do.

"So," Nhu said coldly. "you're Marnin. I wasn't told you were coming. You must have been a last minute invitation. We know a lot about you, Marnin. A lot. There is an old saying that you know a man by the company he keeps."

Marnin was unable to say a word. That the second man in the country—some would say the most powerful—even knew who he was, much less was keeping track of him, was astounding. Nhu then walked over to Tuyen and began talking with him in Vietnamese. At that point Grace Sabo emerged to summon the company to dinner.

As guest of honor Nhu should have been put to the right of the hostess. But Grace had rearranged the table to seat thirteen instead of fourteen and had put Nhu on Sam's right instead. If Nhu noticed that anything was amiss, he gave no indication of it. Marnin was seated in the middle of the table below the salt, with Adele Markoff to his right and Madame Tuyen to his left.

Nhu looked nothing like his brother. Diem was pudgy and pleasant with a happy, mobile face. There was something sacerdotal about him—he could be easily pictured as the jolly abbot of a large monastery. Nhu, on the other hand, was an exceptionally handsome man with high cheekbones, flashing eyes, and a head that seemed slightly too large for his body. The word everyone used to describe him was "leonine" and there was indeed something of the caged lion about his demeanor. He gave the impression of someone forced by circumstance into playing a role he neither liked nor admired.

The first course was a fricassee of five wild mushrooms from the Dalat highlands served in a white wine, cream and ginger sauce and accompanied by a 1959 Puligny Montrachet. Nhu waved the wine away and asked for more vodka.

"I suppose you are wondering where my wife is," he said to Sabo. "The truth is she has been deeply offended by you Americans, by the way you are treating the skirmish near the Plain of Reeds last week. At this point she does not want to pretend that everything is all right between us, when all the publicity surrounding the battle makes it clear that you see us as inferior beings, lesser than yourselves."

"But surely Madame Nhu doesn't see all Americans as alike," Sabo protested. "It's no secret that we in the Embassy are at odds with our own press for the way they've been reporting that battle."

"That's just the point. What is it that the Embassy and the press are disagreeing about? Is it the strategic location of the battle? Hardly that. One could look far and wide in this country and not find a more insignificant place. Then was it the carnage? No, it was not that. Sixty killed on our side. We say ninety on theirs, but maybe it was less, maybe it was forty. Anyway, let us say a hundred-fifty Vietnamese. Good men, every one of them. Good men on both sides. Now in the last six months we've killed 14,000 VC. And they've killed, one way or another, counting assassinations and irregular actions maybe 6,000 of our people—20,000 Vietnamese overall. That averages out to 3,500 a month, not very much by world war standards, but quite a lot by ours. But where were the news stories when those people were killed? Why the sensation in the world press now? Because three *Americans* were killed. Because five *American* helicopters were shot down."

He was interrupted by the arrival of the second course, a classic turtle soup, in which floated tiny, one inch dumplings filled with goose liver. The wine was a 1949 Chateau Margaux. Nhu again waved it away and asked for vodka.

With the changing of the course, Adele Markoff turned left. She began to regale Marnin with servant stories she had obviously dined out on for many years. She told of a newly hired maid in Djakarta who had mistakenly served aluminum foil wrapped rectal suppositories to her startled guests instead of similarly wrapped after-dinner mints.

"And the one thing one doesn't require in Southeast Asia is a cure for constipation. . ."

Marnin laughed and did his best to listen politely to her chatter, while at the same time trying not to miss anything that passed between the two Counselors.

"I am not anti-American, not at all," Nhu was saying. "That is a canard repeated constantly by members of the local press corps and is about as accurate as all the other things they write. I am not anti-American. I am anti-stupid. I get along well with you not because you're not an American, my dear Sam. . ."

"But I am an American," said Sabo, "more of an American than most people who were born in the United States. That's what distinguishes ours from every other society on earth. Not only was I immediately accepted as an American, but I'm even allowed to represent my country abroad."

"That may be," Nhu said. "But what makes me angry, and what has confused some people into thinking I'm anti-American, is that your countrymen seem to feel that just because they're Americans they have the right to give me advice about my country, about which by the way they don't know next to nothing—they know absolutely nothing."

"Yet we've done great business this past year. We've made progress. We've turned the corner."

"That is true, my dear Sam. And I'm not talking about you. You at least have the good sense to refrain from telling me what to do in my own country, about which you also know zero. No. Not zero. The square root of minus one—an imaginary number."

"But you're exaggerating, my dear Counselor."

"Not in the least. I spent six years studying in France. I organized and led demonstrations there to support the Popular Front of Leon Blum, which was anti-colonialist. I demonstrated as a Vietnamese, not as a Frenchman. Yet I would not have the gall—and plenty of people call me arrogant—to tell a Frenchman what to do about the politics of France."

"No Frenchman would listen to a foreigner's advice on politics," said Curly Bird, who had previously had two postings in Paris.

"But why not?" replied Nhu. "After all, I am a graduate of one of the *grandes écoles*. I finished at the top of my class ahead of all the real Frenchmen. I have slept with French girls. Half the dreams I dream are in French. And as intelligent and well informed as I am, I would not in my wildest imagination advise De Gaulle on what to do about the *pieds noirs*. Now, does this work the other way? I ask you that. Give me a fair answer."

"The advice I have to offer," responded Sabo, "has to do with my own country, not with yours."

"No, no, no. I'm not talking about you, my dear Sam. If I were I wouldn't be here tonight. I'd be at home with my wife. I have not so much time that I can afford to waste it with fools. You at least, like Leon Blum, are Jewish and intelligent. I'm talking about the others. I'm talking about people who haven't the foggiest idea of what has happened in this country over the past two centuries, who don't understand that Tonkin is different from Cochin China, who have no grasp of how we educate our children, of how and why we hate the Chinese and have taken away their economic power in this country, of the anti-colonialist feeling that dominates the thinking of all Vietnamese—North and South—of the determination we all share that no outsider, no Caucasian, no Chinese, and certainly no Russian is going to replace the French in telling us what to do. I'm talking about people like that telling the President, telling me, why it's essential to introduce American political practices in order to influence something called 'the grass roots.' And these same 'regular guys' shake their heads in bewilderment when I tell them that they don't know their chins from their assholes and then call me, *ME*, arrogant."

Nhu, who had been constantly sipping vodka all evening and paying no attention to the magnificent meal being put in front of him, was becoming noticeably drunk, slurring his words, having difficulty in focusing his eyes. Grace Sabo, obviously fed up, stood abruptly and announced that coffee would be served on the veranda. The guests rose, the women to go upstairs, the men to the veranda.

When they got outside Tuyen spoke to Nhu in Vietnamese, clearly urging him to go home. Nhu instead seated himself in a deep wicker armchair, signifying that he would leave when he was good and ready. The houseboy brought out cognac and liqueurs and coffee in demitasse cups. Nhu took a large snifter of Courvoisier.

"The reason nobody understands what is going on in this country," Nhu continued, addressing the gathering at large, "is that the whole world confuses left and right. They think our brothers in Hanoi are progressive and left and that we are reactionary and right—exactly the opposite from reality. Ever since the days of Phan Boi Chau and Prince Cuong De the Vietnamese have been struggling against colonial rule. Ho Chi Minh, insofar as he's been effective, has used this for his own purposes. But the fact is that Ho is just as bad as any of the running dogs of the French; only he's a running dog of the Russians and the Chinese. Whenever they snap their fingers he gets up on his hind legs and begs for a cookie. We're supposed to be a reactionary regime. But how many people are aware that we take our ideology from the left? How many Americans have heard of Emmanuel Mounier? You there, Marnin, did they teach you about Mounier in college?"

"No, sir," David replied.

"They will," Nhu said. "A hundred years from now nobody will ever have heard of Sartre, but everyone will know of Mounier, who combined Christianity and existentialism into our philosophy of personalism."

"But a great deal in this country doesn't seem consonant with the teachings of Mounier," Sabo said.

"Sam, you are the only American in the world who's ever heard of Mounier. It's of course true that you cannot run a country according to the doctrines of Mounier. But you cannot run a country according to the doctrines of Jesus of Nazareth either. You know what he did to the money lenders. Imagine what he would do to your Wall Street. No. We listen to Mounier. But politics is an art. It has to be adapted to the times the artist lives in and the medium in which he works. Your countrymen seem to have the absurd idea that your political system with its political parties that have no separate identity, your Republicrats and Demicans, can be transplanted across oceans. There are no potential Republicans and Democrats in Viet Nam, just a lot of people who will tell you that this country needs democracy because they think that you'll give them good American dollars to hear it."

"Nobody is seriously suggesting that you duplicate the American system here," Curly Bird said.

"But that is exactly what they tell us. How do you have the nerve to send to me, who has studied in one of the *grandes écoles* of France, people who have never read the writings of James Madison to talk about the establishment of political parties in this country? Political parties make no sense in a Confucian society. That's why there is no democracy in China, Taiwan, Singapore, or in both Viet Nams and why I've organized the Can Lao the way I have and why the Republican Youth contains more than one million members. These are not political parties. They are millions of Vietnamese patriots joined together with a single aim—the independence and glory of their fatherland. Give me ten years, even five, and we'll have in this country millions of people committed to our cause who know what will happen to them if the other side takes over. Once more than half of the adult males are with us, we'll be invulnerable. But. . ."

And here he paused and looked at each of the Americans, fixing his eyes on them one by one, and grinning his sardonic grin.

"But you don't plan to give us five years, do you? So when we get advice to put aside our ways and adopt yours we have to conclude that the people who are giving that advice are fools. The fact is that we give our people as much freedom as we are able to—more than any other country in the world in our position. Compare the situation of the opposition in this country to the opposition in Hanoi."

"Just a minute," Markoff said. "There is no opposition in Hanoi."

"Exactly! The opposition here can say pretty much everything it wants. We don't send them off to be reeducated in camps in the jungle. Look around you. Not just Hanoi. Look at Rangoon. Look at Djakarta. There is no war in those countries. Does the opposition in any of those places have more freedom than they do in Saigon?"

He finished with a flourish, his right hand above his head, waving in a circular motion, a fixed grin on his face, his words slurred but fluent, delivered rapidly and forcefully. He tried to rise, but fell back into his seat. Sabo rushed over and helped him up. He escorted him down the stairs and into the black limousine, holding on to his left elbow. Before Nhu got in the car he placed his palms on each side of Sabo's jaw and kissed him on both cheeks, French style.

"Goodbye, my friend, my smart redheaded Jew," he said. "I hope we'll both still be here to celebrate the New Year a year from now."

On Sunday the eighth of January, Marnin arrived at the Hotel Continental at ten minutes to twelve for his engagement with Lily Do Ba Xang. He had with him a copy of Purcell's *The Chinese of Southeast Asia* and he took a table on the veranda, ordered a beer, and prepared to wait for her.

He opened the book and tried to read but, unable to concentrate, found himself looking at his watch every two minutes. At twelve-fifteen she had not appeared and his anxiety increased. By twenty-five after, he was convinced she would not come. She had forgotten or, worse yet, decided to pass. But at twelve-thirty she appeared, breathless and apologetic. Someone had unexpectedly showed up at her house and she had been unable to get away.

"I'm so sorry to keep you waiting," she said.

"I'd wait all day for you," David said truthfully. "Would you like something to drink, or some lunch?"

"I thought we'd go for a drive. I'll show you the countryside and we can have some lunch out there, if you'd like."

"Wonderful."

They drove north in his Deux Chevaux and were soon out of town, traveling along the Saigon River on Route One toward Bien Hoa. As it was Sunday, the traffic was relatively light, mostly bicycles and pedicabs.

Lily was dressed, for the first time, in Western style—beige slacks and a cream silk blouse. Her hair, as usual, was combed straight back and tied in a bun and she had on small pearl earrings. Her lipstick was pale pink, much lighter than the scarlet shade she wore at night. As they drove, she spoke about her childhood and her family, about the love/hate relationship they had sustained with the French ever since her great great grandfather had managed a string of highly profitable tea and rubber godowns on the Red River outside Haiphong for French merchants in the 1880's.

Just before Bien Hoa she told him to turn off onto a side road that paralleled the river.

"I just can't get over how beautiful this country is," David said.

Lily waved her hand toward the groves of trees that they were passing.

"These are the old rubber plantations that used to belong to the French. The VC chased them out in 1960."

"Who owns them now?"

She shrugged.

"Government by day, VC by night. This is no-man's land."

Marnin was a regular reader of the "Incident Report," a secret publication put out daily by the GVN security services which chronicled each Viet Cong outrage, many of which occurred along secondary roads. He looked up the long empty track ahead and began to grow wary. At last they turned left through a gate overgrown with trumpet vines. On the arch above it a legend in wrought iron script read:

Paix — Tranquilité — Fraternité

"What's the significance of the motto?" David asked.

"Just the conceit of some French manager who lived here, I suppose, ruling over hundreds of workers. Maybe he thought it would pacify the peasants. If so, he was wrong."

They drove on over a dry and dusty potholed road.

"How much further is it?" he asked.

"Oh, not too far. Are you worried about the car?"

"I'm worried about the fact that we haven't seen another car since we left Route One."

"No one will bother us," Lily said reassuringly. "Everyone's been paid off."

At that moment, a man in a camouflage uniform suddenly

emerged, standing in the middle of the road and waving a submachine gun. Marnin screeched to a halt. The man, a hill tribesman, peered into the car and, seeing Lily, grinned, snapped a salute and waved them on.

"Who was that?"

"One of Xang's montagnard bodyguards. Now they work for me."

They drove in past another, smaller gate through a fence topped with barbed wire and pulled up before a modest house. In the background were five concrete outbuildings and, beyond those, more rubber trees. Lily turned to him with a happy smile.

"This is my farm," she said with pride.

"What kind of farm?"

"Pigs and chickens. This farm is the only thing I really own." She caught herself. "Correction—the Michelin Tire Company actually owns it, the land anyway, but they've gone—got tired of paying protection money—and I don't think they'll be back for a while."

They got out of the car and Lily stretched her arms out wide like a little girl and inhaled deeply, as if she were breathing crisp, alpine ozone, instead of Southeast Asian air thick with dust and humidity.

"But how did you happen to get this place?" David asked.

"When Michelin left, my husband acquired it. . . . I really don't know how. When he died his. . .'friends' could have taken it over, like they did all the rest of our property. But they didn't want it. They thought it was worthless—too far from Saigon, too many VC. From here to the river is all VC. But I love it. I spend every minute I can here, even though everyone thinks I'm crazy."

"Me too."

"But I told you—the VC are paid off. Anyway, I treat my workers well. They're loyal—and fierce. They would kill anyone who hurt me. The VC know that. Come," she said, "let's go into the house."

Over the front door, the year "1928" had been painted in purple letters above the lintel.

"Whose house was this?"

"Maybe the foreman. The manager's house is up the road. It's much too big." She looked down at his feet. "First I need to find some boots for you."

The house was rustic and small, with exposed beams and white-washed walls. Old mezzotints of Paris were the only decoration. In a few minutes she was back, wearing a straw peasant's hat and a pair of Wellingtons, and carrying another pair of boots.

"These are the biggest we have," she said. She set them down next to his feet, then, looking from one to the other, burst out laughing. "*Mon Dieu! Ça ne marche pas. Pas du tout.*" She stopped to think, frowning. "But you have to see the farm. What can we do?"

"Here's a simple solution," David said, and removed his loafers and socks. "I've had dirty feet before."

As they walked around, she explained to him how the farm was operated. "It's a simple but effective system," she said. "We feed the hogs and chickens on the agricultural surplus that we get from your AID mission. And when they're fat and healthy from all your vitamins and hormones we supply the VNAF base at Bien Hoa with pork and eggs. It's turned out to be a great deal more profitable than any of us ever imagined. I'm getting twice the price I was originally counting on from the Americans and almost as much from the Vietnamese government. Your Mister Bird has been an angel to us. And your General Donnelly has also been very helpful. Oddly enough, one chance in a thousand, he met my husband in London during the war. Donnelly was working for General Patton and my husband was on De Gaulle's staff."

"How many people do you have working for you here?"

"About fifty, if you include the wives and families who feed the hogs and chickens and collect the eggs. They are tribesmen we got to know when we were stationed in Kontum—very loyal. And very tough—not to be trifled with. So I don't worry about the Viet Cong. Anyway, I think the VC respected my husband. He may have fought the Communists, but he also fought the French. Like Diem, he was a true Vietnamese nationalist."

She led him on a brisk tour of the five outbuildings, all of them built of concrete, obviously during the past year, each with a red tile roof, unpainted on the outside but freshly whitewashed within. The closest one was the henhouse. The door to it was only five feet high.

"Watch your head," she said.

He ducked down. Inside, the ceiling was barely a few inches above him. The cages were stacked in rows of four, one on top of the other. The hens were red and white—Rhode Island reds. On each cage was a piece of slate, with colored chalk marks on them—red, yellow, white, blue, green, orange, and purple.

"What does the colored chalk mean?" Marnin asked.

"That's my own system," she said proudly. "Each piece of colored chalk represents the day of the week. When these Montagnard women take an egg from a cage, they mark it with the colored chalk of that particular day. This way we know what every hen is doing."

"What happens to a hen that doesn't produce enough eggs?"

"Three chalk marks missing and they go right in the pot. We all eat chicken salad. I tell each of those hens that there's a war on and they have to produce. No place for VC hens around here."

The back room contained neatly stacked rows of crates for the eggs and fifty pound bags of chickenfeed marked "made in USA," and sparkling new incubators for the chicks. The room smelled strongly of disinfectant, like a hospital ward. Everything was stainless steel and brand new. Lily was clearly pleased at the profuse compliments Marnin, who had never before visited a farm, heaped on her.

The piggery consisted of three large buildings and barnyards with food troughs on one side and water troughs on the other. Seventy or eighty sows were nursing ten to fifteen piglets each. Inside, where the feed was mixed, the machinery—supplied by Curly Bird's aid mission—was all spanking new.

"Curly was very helpful," she repeated. "He was the only one who really encouraged me.

As David questioned Lily about how the farm was run, where the pigs were purchased, what they were fed, when they were weaned, how they were fattened up, who were their ultimate purchasers and what price they were sold for, it became clear that she had every detail at her fingertips. When they had finished the tour it was after two, the hottest part of the day. He was sweating and his feet were filthy. She sat him down on the front steps and told him not to move.

She returned with a bucket of hot water, a bucket of cold water, some large yellow towels draped around her neck, and a bar of brown laundry soap under her right arm. Ignoring Marnin's protestations, she got down on her knees on the step in front of him and rolled up his pants legs to just under the knees. She then seized his muddy left foot and plunged it into the bucket of hot water.

"Ouch!" He yelled out.

"What a foot!" she said, ignoring his cry of pain. "It's almost too big to fit in the bucket."

She smartly slapped the bottom of the foot four times. Then she made a lather by rubbing laundry soap briskly along the instep and washed from the big toe to just under the knee. Afterward, the foot was immersed again in the hot water, soaked in the cold water, and then dried with the rough yellow towels. When finished with his left foot, she held it in both her hands, like a carpenter surveying the results of his labor. With a solemn face she explored the bottom of his foot with the tips of her fingers, only breaking into laughter when he did. Then the whole process was repeated with the right foot, including the tickling, until he begged her to stop. She bent over him and mopped his brow with a fresh hot towel, her body brushing up against him.

The dining room table had been set with grey ceramic hand painted plates and bowls—birds and fish done in a "quickbrush" style, ceramic spoons also hand painted, and ivory chopsticks with blue and green dragons carved on them. They ate Pho, a delicious beef noodle broth, an asparagus omelet, and salad, and drank Algerian red wine. Over lunch they talked of the political situation. Would Diem survive? Would South Viet Nam survive?

"I can't imagine that it won't," Marnin said. "Washington can't afford to let South Viet Nam fall. There were terrific political repercussions in the United States over the loss of China. Viet Nam is long and narrow and faces the sea, which the United States Navy will always control. If the U.S. wants to, it can hold Viet Nam indefinitely. Sending our own armed forces into the country would be a tough decision for an American President, but letting it go down the drain would be much tougher. There's no way we wouldn't prevail."

"What if the Chinese or the Russians came in on the other side?"

Marnin considered himself an expert on the USSR, and especially on the Soviet Navy. He had been trained in Russian by the Navy for fifteen months at Anacostia and spoke the language well. Altogether he had spent five years as a Naval Intelligence officer, two of them on a carrier and three years seconded to CIA to work on Soviet affairs and to follow the ins and outs of Moscow's burgeoning maritime buildup.

"There's no chance of that happening. Our fear of Chinese expansion is what motivates us here, but the Chinese are undergoing a general collapse of the 'Great Leap Forward.' People are starving there. As for the Soviets, Khrushchev's not about to play games in Southeast Asia, especially after the missile crisis. He'd never support an attack by Hanoi on Saigon."

"But would Hanoi listen? Doesn't the quarrel between the Chinese and Russians give Ho Chi Minh the ability to maneuver between them?"

"Ho can't do anything without the Soviets and the Chinese. He manufactures no weapons of his own. He has no oil. The Soviets call the tune on this. They have the resources."

"This isn't a matter of political theory for me," Lily said. "It's a very practical question. If I want to invest more in this place, all I have to do is chop down a few rubber trees and there will be plenty of new land that I can use as I see fit. I'm thinking of starting a dairy and maybe raising cattle as well. Within the next year or two I should be inheriting a bit of money from my father. He's in Paris and quite sick. The best place to invest that money, the best return I can get, is right here. But I don't want to do that if the country is going down the drain."

"Kennedy would feel compelled to put our forces into Viet Nam to prevent it from falling to the communists. And the same would be true of Rockefeller, Sedgewick, Goldwater, or any other Republican I can think of. If you have doubts, read the Kennedy inaugural speech."

"So the Americans know what they're doing? It doesn't always seem that way to us."

"We still have to convince your government to make the ARVN more aggressive. Then we can get rid of this insurgency and win the war."

"You Americans think that if you throw enough of your money

and of our troops at the VC, you'll end up winning. You forget that this war is not against the Viet Cong. It's against Hanoi. And Ho cannot be beaten militarily unless you're willing to march north. And you're not. Diem understands this. But you don't."

"Our advisors say Diem restrains the ARVN from becoming a first rate fighting force. They say he's too afraid of casualties."

"Diem sees himself in a struggle with Ho for the soul of all his people, not just those in South Viet Nam. His real security problem is to insure that the North Vietnamese Army doesn't invade his half of Viet Nam. But this is going to take decades. So it therefore makes no sense, from Diem's point of view, to throw away the lives of the bravest of his soldiers to achieve meaningless local military victories."

"Does he expect Washington to support him for decades?"

"Diem hopes that won't be necessary. He knows, in any event, that there's never been a case in the two thousand years of Vietnamese history when a Cochin Chinese army defeated a Tonkinese one. The Cochinois are farmers, the Tonkinese soldiers. Any fight between them is a mismatch. Diem's army is run by Cochinois mercenaries— every one of them in the pocket of a Chinese businessman. If it took on the NVA, it would be a fight between disciplined professional soldiers and hired guns more devoted to their mistresses and swimming pools and Mercedes than to their country."

"General Donnelly says the South Vietnamese soldier can be every bit as good as the North Vietnamese. So does Colonel Gascon."

"Blix is a nice man. Gascon is a fool. Both of them know less about this country than you do."

"I don't know anything. I admit it."

"That's why you know more than they do. They think they know everything and they understand nothing. To them all Vietnamese are alike. But believe me there are big differences. In the Delta the earth is rich, the population lazy and happy. Eat a mango today, throw the pit in your back yard, and tomorrow a mango tree will be growing. In the North the living is hard. The people are tough, obstinate, wily. Over the centuries they defeated first the Chinese, and now lately the French. The Cochinois defeated nobody. Never. Look at the top ranks of the ARVN. They all joined up to help the French fight their own people. These were Corporals and Sergeants in the French Army. While they were on the Paris payroll as enlisted men, Ngo Dinh Diem was being offered by the French one job after another—a Ministry here, a Prime Ministry there—but he refused them all because these governments he was being asked to join were controlled from Paris."

"If the ARVN can't do it, then maybe U.S. forces will be needed. There are plenty of Americans here who think this is inevitable."

"Diem's nightmare is to become a creature manipulated by Washington. As far as he's concerned, American combat troops should only be used to inhibit the North from attacking the South. The contest with Ho Chi Minh is to prove which of the Viet Nams—North or South—is truly independent. Ho says that the Americans have replaced the French. Diem says the Russians have replaced the French."

Marnin was hungry and finished the last of the salad. Lily rang a little bell shaped like an elephant and Ding Ding, the young Kha maid, brought in cheese, water crackers, and two glasses of Port. Marnin looked up at the girl and smiled at her.

When she left the room, Lily asked, "Do you like that girl? Do you find her attractive?"

"Why do you ask me that?"

"I was just wondering if she appeals to you."

"She's much too young."

"For what?"

"For me."

"Vietnamese men find girls that age the most sexy. If my husband were still here, I wouldn't allow Ding Ding to serve us. He'd be after her like a fox after a rabbit."

"I guess I prefer women to rabbits. . .older women."

"Really? My husband liked them young. He was incorrigible. It was the thrill of the chase, the vanquished prey."

"A true warrior. How long were you married?"

"Many years. We were betrothed when I was fifteen and married a year later. He was twenty-eight years older. *Mon Dieu!* What a chatterbox I've become! It's late. And one must have a nap before driving back."

"A nap?" he asked hopefully.

"Yes, it's the custom here in the country—just a half hour. Come."
She led him out of the dining room into a hallway and then pushed
open the door of a bedroom.

"Here's your room. I think you'll find everything you need. There's
a shower next door if you want to wash off the dust of the farm. You
can inaugurate the new hot water heater. I'll call you when it's time to
leave."

Marnin changed into an ill-fitting red terrycloth bathrobe and got
into bed. He thought about bathing, but could already hear the
sound of the shower. Then it stopped. A door opened and light foot-
steps receded down the hall and into a nearby room. He could hear
a muffled voice. He rose and walked barefoot into the hallway. The
door of the bedroom facing opposite was slightly ajar. He could see
the foot of the bed. She was lying there under mosquito netting. He
tapped lightly.

"Yes? What is it?" she asked.

David tentatively pushed open the door.

"Sorry. . .I didn't mean to alarm you."

He could see Lily only as a hazy form beneath the mosquito net.
She raised herself up on one elbow and spoke sharply.

"What do you want?"

David stood awkwardly in the doorway.

"I couldn't sleep. I was on my way out to the car to get a book.
Then I heard a voice. I thought you were awake."

"That was Antoine."

"Antoine?"

"My boyfriend."

David did not know what to say and held his tongue. Laughing,
Lily pushed aside the mosquito net and pointed. In a corner of the
room on a perch was a large gray parrot regarding Marnin with a
beady eye. David smiled, but at that point was more interested in Lily,
naked under a thin white sheet that she clasped tightly under her
arms. She had let down her hair and it fell loose and tousled over her
shoulders. Transfixed, he remained motionless, staring at her.

Seeing his expression she said, "No, David. . .it would be a mistake."

He moved to the bed and took Lily in his arms.

"No. . .no, you mustn't! Please! This cannot be!"

Lily clutched the sheet to her body while David kissed first her neck and then her shoulders.

"I wanted a friend," she said. "This is wrong. Don't you see. . . ? You can force me. . .but it's wrong. . ."

David paid no attention to her words; kissed her, first lightly, then passionately. At first she resisted, her body stiff.

At that point Antoine interjected, "*Ma foi! C'est très interessant.*"

Lily laughed and fell back against the pillow.

"The door," she said, "shut the door."

"*Je t'adore,*" squawked Antoine. "*Je t'adore. . .*"

"You're not still angry with me?"

She smiled.

"Perhaps just a little," she said. They had been talking for hours.

The only man Lily had ever slept with before was the General. She had been married for seventeen years to a husband twenty-eight years her senior, a husband who could only be physically aroused by the unusual and bizarre and who, despite the lack of sexual interest in his wife, was known to her as a chaser after every girl he could get his hands on.

"For him," she said, "it was not the sensuality, but the conquest. He had to keep conquering his own wife. And in order to do that, he insisted on things that were revolting to me."

"What did he want?"

"Many things. I can't tell you. It's too disgusting. And once I got used to something or agreed to anything with any kind of willingness, it lost all interest for him. Then he had to push on to the more forbidden, the wilder, and the more sinful."

Her love life, she said, became and remained stormy, perverse, and intermittent at best. In the year before he was killed they had only made love half a dozen times. The General did not care. He had women all over the place, including a mistress in Danang whom he kept in a big house near China Beach.

"Where is she now?"

"She's still in Danang and runs a French restaurant there on Rue

Pasteur. She claims her two sons were the General's. But it's a lie."

"Why not divorce?"

"Out of the question."

Her family were strict Catholics. Her father would not tolerate divorce, she said. The youngest of five children, he had been almost fifty when she was born. He remained a remote and patriarchal figure, more like a grandfather to her all her life. And while Viet Nam was not India, the prospects for a good second marriage for a widow with two children, even one as beautiful as she, as soon as it became generally understood that she had lost all her money, were dim, and her uncompromisingly withering view of the conduct of Vietnamese men and her fearless way of expressing herself made them even dimmer.

As a young woman in her teens she took readily to the arts of love—including the arcane variations that her husband was teaching her. But as she came to realize that her husband was an incorrigible womanizer, trying out on her the various tricks he was picking up from other women, the sexual act had filled her with such loathing that she had determined to give it up altogether once she was rid of him. Married when barely sixteen, she became a mother before her seventeenth birthday and a mother the second time before her eighteenth.

"But this is all about me. Why is it always I who do all the talking? What about you? Who introduced you to the art of love?"

"It was my cousin Myra. I had moved to Montreal to stay with my uncle and aunt when my parents were getting divorced. I was thirteen and she was fifteen. She seduced me just as I was reaching puberty. Her parents spent all their time in their store. She had no brothers or sisters. We were left alone to take care of ourselves. And we did. We made love sometimes four or five times a day, talking all the time. That's really how I learned French so quickly and so well. After a year of this paradise we were, to make a long story short, caught in the act and I was shipped back to New York in disgrace."

He looked over at her and she was sleeping. They rested, dozed off, and then awakened and made love again. Afterward they lay in bed under the mosquito netting, she in his arms, and talked first about the history of some of his other love affairs and then about her other problems—the practical difficulties she had faced since the death of her husband; the problems of nurturing her daughters since the loss of their beloved father.

The sun had set long before. It was pitch dark in the room, not a glimmer of light anywhere. "You've made me very happy," he whispered.

"And you me, more than you know."

They slept, but Marnin thought it could only have been for a minute. Gently, he nudged her awake.

"Shouldn't we be getting back?" he asked.

"Aren't you hungry, *petit frère?*"

"Famished.

She slipped on her clothes and went in back to awaken the servants, from whom there were no secrets and for whom there were no normal working hours. Then she led him to the shower, which she made hotter than he would have preferred, and washed every part of him.

It was well past midnight when they entered the dining room, where Ding Ding was waiting for them with a sleepy smile on her face. They wolfed down their late supper greedily—cold chicken and potato salad—and finished the rest of the Algerian red. The wispy and knowing look on Ding Ding's face did not please Lily at all. The girl, Marnin knew, was in for a severe dressing down at the first opportunity. After dinner Lily took him by the hand and led him back to the mosquito netting. But she sensed his hesitation.

"It's probably not a good idea to drive around here after dark. Can you stay the night?" she asked.

"I shouldn't, but I can be convinced," he said.

Donnelly's red and blue maps that Marnin had just seen in two separate briefings flickered across his brain. On those maps that whole area was red.

A trace of light could be seen beyond the shutters. Dawn was just breaking. It was very still. Lily was awake, David sleeping. Slowly the cicadas began to sing and the frogs to croak. In the servants' quarters a radio was switched on and a female voice began singing "Chieu

Mieu Binh Xei." David turned over on his back.

"Are you awake?" She asked.

He reached for her and she nestled in the crook of his arm, her head on his shoulder.

"Good morning," he said.

"Good morning to you."

For a moment they were silent.

"What's this song about?" he asked. "It's beautiful."

"A soldier. He longs to be with his lover, but the war keeps them apart. It's called "A Rainy Night on the Frontier." For awhile it was banned because Madame Nhu, who was at school with me, said it was sentimental and subversive. It sapped our fighting spirit."

David turned to her and took her in his arms and kissed her.

"I can't tell you how happy you've made me," he said again.

"And you me," she repeated. "More than you can know."

She pushed the hair back from his eyes.

"I've never known a young man before. When I was born, my father was fifty. When I was married, my husband was forty-four. I had no brothers. There were only girls at the *lycée* in Hue. I never had a male friend. Will you be my friend?"

"Yes, we'll be friends. . .always."

They kissed and began to make love again.

"*Ma foi! C'est très interessant!*" said Antoine.

The thought of her was constantly with him. It eclipsed all else. Those thirteen-hour workdays that he had previously found so stimulating now seemed merely to be keeping him from the side—and the back, front, bottom and top—of his secret love. Even his tennis went into a tailspin. The Corning-Marnin string of victories came to an end. They lost to Donnelly and Aylward three Saturdays running, which mightily displeased Corning. In fact, David sensed a certain cooling toward him from the front office—both from the thin-lipped DCM who had always been less than encouraging and, worse yet, from the Ambassador, who noted his slackening of attention to his work.

An aide's function is to preside with meticulous care over routine, often uninteresting, and sometimes even boring matters. Lack of concentration and attention to detail can be fatal. Marnin felt that he could be riding for a fall. But he was so besotted with Lily that he ignored the portents.

No one but her household servants knew of their liaison. Had it been up to him, he would have shouted it from the roof of the Continental. But Lily was doggedly insistent on this point and David, who saw from her deep concern that this was a matter that brooked no discussion, never betrayed her trust.

They were together on Tuesday and Thursday nights and for as much of the weekend as he could spare from the office and she from her daughters, whom he had yet to meet. On the afternoons prior to their assignations he telephoned her at exactly four o'clock on a private line that only she answered. If something prevented him from calling at four o'clock, he rang her back only on the quarter hour—precisely at quarter past, or quarter to, any of the succeeding hours. She did not answer the phone otherwise.

The ritual of their rendezvous was unvarying. After work, at around seven-thirty, he went home from the embassy, bathed and changed into a sport shirt, walked to Tu Do Street, hailed one of the little Renault putt-putt taxis and took it to a block away from her villa. He got out on the southeast corner of the street, made sure he was not followed, and walked to the house. The Kha guard at the gate waved him through, gesturing with the M-1 in his right hand. Entering through a side door left open for him, he went up a back staircase that led directly to her bedroom.

There he might find her waiting for him, reclining on a wicker chaise longue in a revealing, pale pink lace peignoir or—and this was the one variable in the routine—the room might be empty, in which case he would help himself to a drink from a butler's table bearing a silver ice bucket and assorted bottles and glasses.

The airy, high-ceilinged room, unlike the downstairs living and drawing rooms, had been decorated to her taste. Like Lily herself, it was feminine and seductive, an eclectic combination of Vietnamese and French decor, the air infused with her scent of jasmine. A bottle of Veuve Cliquot lay cooling in a silver ice bucket. Waiting, he removed his shoes, closed his eyes and, beneath the swish of the ceiling fan, could feel himself succumbing to her enveloping presence. He had not long to wait before she entered, attired on these occasions in a less revealing but still suggestive silk kimono sashed at the waist, and carrying a tray of spring rolls and cold shrimp, a plate of lemon-grass chicken, and a bowl of fruit.

Along one side of the room, beneath a Chinese brush painting of birds and almond blossoms was an antique carved opium bed covered in pale green silk. Here they ate, sitting cross-legged before small lacquer tray tables and propped up against a bank of cushions.

When they had finished, she placed the dishes on a sideboard. With a smile she drew him to his feet and, between kisses, undressed him slowly, letting her gown slide from her shoulders and slip to the floor. Then Lily extinguished the light and in the darkness taught David one more of the General's clever tricks.

The Battle of Ap Bac refused to die. Mandelbrot and his colleagues in the press kept thinking of new angles that kept it in front of their readers. When, during the third week of January, Mandelbrot decided to go to Bangkok for his first vacation since arriving in Vietnam, the Mission Council breathed a collective sigh of relief. The "Ap Bac flap," as they referred to it, seemed to be finally winding down to the insignificance they thought it deserved.

But fate decreed otherwise. One of the American advisors wounded during the battle, a handsome black Captain named Corky Thomas, contracted a tropical infection in the military hospital in Thailand and suddenly, unexpectedly, died of sepsis. Thomas had won a bronze medal for the javelin throw in the 1956 Olympics and, as a giant of a man and as a famous track and field coach to the Vietnamese in his off hours, was almost as well known in the Delta as John Henry Mudd. As luck would have it, since Thomas was something of a celebrity as well as a friend of his, Mandelbrot was notified of the advisor's death by his office. He went to the Captain's house on a condolence call and there obtained from the dead man's widow, who had been living in Thailand, the diary Thomas had been keeping during his tour in the Delta.

Captain Thomas's diary was permeated with disgust and loathing at the behavior of many of his charges in the ARVN. Skillfully edited by Mandelbrot, excerpts from the diary were featured for a week in the *Times*. They ran the gamut of crimes big and small, ranging from chickens stolen from unwary Vietnamese farmers to young girls raped and old peasants murdered. The diary contained graphic examples of members of the ARVN committing each of the seven deadly sins, most especially sloth. To all these derelictions Thomas felt obliged, because of the nature of his mission and the strictures of the MAAG, to pretend that he just didn't see. This burned in his conscience. The decency of the man and his moral dilemma were painful. Nothing could have conveyed more vividly the problems the American advisors faced in trying to mold credible military forces from the recalcitrant, feckless, and occasionally cowardly clay of the ARVN.

Nothing could have irritated the Government of Viet Nam more, or created a bigger stir than the Thomas diary. It confirmed the gravest doubts of Diem and Nhu about the wisdom of the American advisory effort in their country. The *Times* of Viet Nam and the rest of the Vietnamese press ran excerpts designed to show, ironically enough, that Thomas was a racist who was hopelessly prejudiced against the Asian people. If anything, this feature story by Mandelbrot nettled Corning and Donnelly even more than his tendentious posturing about the battle of Ap Bac itself. The idea that he would go off to Bangkok on vacation and manage to emerge with a front page exposé that undermined everything the American effort in South Viet Nam stood for was almost too much for both of them to bear.

In good military fashion, the barn door was duly locked after the mare had escaped. Orders were issued to ensure that none of our advisors be allowed to keep a diary in the future. And nobody was to profit, dead or alive (Mandelbrot had paid Mrs. Thomas five hundred dollars) from information obtained as the result of the performance of official duties.

Meanwhile, the insurgency droned on in the countryside. The statistics from the field were encouraging on almost every count and seemed to prove conclusively that the Americans were winning. That this was not reflected in the American media was more and more frustrating to the Embassy, whose staff seemed to spend as much time thinking about the press as they did about the war.

At a special Country Team "brainstorming" meeting devoted to the question Bilder suggested that, in order to get a handle on the problem, John Mecklin, the Embassy Public Affairs Officer (PAO), have a report prepared by his staff on the press corps in Saigon who they were, what was eating them and why they were behaving in a manner that many in the mission felt was un-American. To bolster his case, Mecklin was asked to cull the reporters' dispatches to unearth specific instances of misreporting and to determine why errors of judgment were made or errors of fact committed; why these journalists could not see the forest of substantial progress for the trees of minor setbacks.

Mecklin resisted, arguing that such a report would be difficult to do and would have no practical value once done. But he was a minority of one. The rest of his colleagues on the Country Team, even so astute a political observer as Sam Sabo, all felt that Bilder's idea was a good one. The press, they agreed, was the Embassy's thorniest problem, far more vexing than coming to grips with the Strategic Hamlet program, which was progressing nicely—just another of the many encouraging facts that received no coverage in the American newspapers.

Mecklin went through the exercise as if he were walking through a mine field, which he was, and, in collaboration with his press officer, Gil Banks, reluctantly drafted a report that Bilder rejected as "namby-pamby." Mecklin and Banks executed three more drafts—all classified CONFIDENTIAL, EYES ONLY—before they satisfied Bilder. The final version was still too bland for his taste, but it did list all the reporters in Saigon, gave their backgrounds and analyzed their dispatches in terms of their special interests or hobbyhorses, citing instances of misreporting by each of them.

To the Ambassador's aide, the negotiations and counter-negotiations between Bilder and Mecklin were of only marginal interest. Their haggling over drafts was no different than what was taking place on a score of other reports being prepared by various sections of the Embassy. As DCM, Bilder was charged with keeping the paper flowing smoothly to Washington. Like most DCM's, he was a nit-picker. Mecklin's piece was only unusual in that USIS reporting normally did not go through the Ambassador's office, since it was ordinarily not considered important enough.

On the 27th of February, John Henry Mudd, whose tour of duty was up, was leaving Viet Nam. An informal send-off was to be held at four o'clock in the VIP room at Tan Son Nhut airport, the same room in which Admiral McGrath had held his memorable press conference. There had been a large farewell party the previous evening given by his Vietnamese division commander for some seventy of Mudd's military colleagues at the Arc en Ciel in Cholon. The airport ceremony was being staged by his pals in the press. Only two non-journalists had been invited: Marnin and Pepe.

David was the first to arrive. Holding the envelope Mudd had sent him for safekeeping, he sat in the waiting room for fifteen minutes before the others—about a dozen journalists—turned up. They had taken Mudd to a long boozy lunch at the Guillaume Tell and were collectively feeling no pain. When they saw Marnin there was some surly muttering about the presence of "the enemy." But Mudd, who grasped the situation, came over and gave him a warm greeting, which shut them up. David handed him the envelope.

"Thanks, my friend," Mudd said. "I really appreciate your keeping this for me. And I hope you're taking this good preacher's advice and staying away from the local poontang." He gave Marnin a shrewd look and grinned. "Well, boys will be boys."

Mandelbrot, who was making the presentation, called the group to order. "All occasions call for a few suitable words," he began.

"Make sure they're few," Buechner said. "Once you get going he'll miss the afternoon plane."

"I'll make it brief. And I won't tell any dirty stories. I won't even recount some of John Henry's feats of derring-do. You all know them as well as I do. Nobody could exaggerate his courage, or his professionalism, or his effectiveness. And nobody could exaggerate his patriotism. I only mention patriotism—what Samuel Johnson defined as 'the last refuge of the scoundrel'—because that is something which those gathered here today are accused of lacking in official reports sent to the United States government. That there are two views of what is going on in this wonderful country is no secret. But to assert that those Americans on one side of the chasm love their country less than those on the other is an outrage.

"In our dealings with our disingenuous government, the one American we have come to consistently honor and respect is that one standing right there—not because of his physical courage, which is legendary, but because of his moral courage, his willingness to risk everything that he has worked for in his career for the glory and honor of his country. He is not just a fine soldier, but a great teacher. Not only has he taught me more about Viet Nam than anyone else, he has taught me more about honesty and integrity. This is for you, John Henry."

Buechner handed Mandelbrot the package and Billy walked over and gave it to Mudd. It was a silver tray inscribed, "To Lieutenant Colonel John Henry Mudd, A Great Soldier, from the Saigon Press Corps." On it were engraved the names of every American journalist based in Saigon and a few of the regular outsiders like Bob Shaplen, Charley Mohr, and Bob McCabe. There were not many dry eyes in the crowd.

Mudd cleared his throat. "Words haven't failed me in the past," he said. "But they do now. Don't let anyone tell you, though, that this doesn't mean a whole hell of a lot to me, because it does. And that comes from the heart."

With that, he went around the room shaking each man's hand. And then, holding his tray and the envelope he had retrieved from Marnin in his left hand and a new Pan Am flight bag in his right, he walked out on the tarmac and up the ramp, and thus ended his first of three tours in Viet Nam.

After Mudd's departure, Claudio and David played two sets of tennis at the Cercle Sportif, where the Guatemalan easily prevailed. From there they went to the Diamond, where David consoled himself with a dinner of Nha Trang lobster and a splendid bottle of Sancerre, courtesy of Claudio.

"You were awful today. I've never seen you play so badly. You ought to go off to Dalat, to the mountains, for a change of air," Claudio advised his American friend. "Everyone has to do that in the tropics and you're no exception."

"I'm just in a little slump."

David had spent the previous night with Lily, another night of virtually no sleep. Coming home at five for an hour's nap, he had scarcely been able to awaken in time to drag himself to the office to read the cable traffic.

"The game of tennis is played up here." The Guatemalan tapped his temple with his finger. "Not down there with your dick. You're playing tennis like a Mandelbrot. Speak of the devil, look who's here."

Mandelbrot, who was carrying an attaché case, and Buechner, along with five of the other correspondents who had earlier seen Mudd off had wandered into the restaurant. Claudio hailed them and they joined two tables together to seat nine. There was nothing much happening at that point in Viet Nam. So they had gone from the airport to the Hotel Caravelle bar on the top floor of the tallest building in Saigon where they had spent the rest of the afternoon. By dinner time they had all had way too much to drink. Claudio had not met two of the reporters—Bill Spigott of the *Los Angeles Times* and Jack Crawford of the *Christian Science Monitor*. Mandelbrot introduced them.

". . .Crawford of the Monitor. Gets a 'C.' Only four mistakes in reporting on Ap Bac—the best record in all of Saigon. Too bad they weren't marking on a curve. He made the egregious error, however, of quoting the MACV spokesman, instead of checking further with the Embassy."

This was greeted with howls of laughter from the newsmen. Claudio and David were mystified.

"And this is Bill Spigott of the *L.A. Times*. He flunks the course altogether. Never even went to college. A fucking police reporter, for Christ sake."

They redoubled their laughter. Buechner was holding his sides, he thought it was so funny.

"Excuse me," Claudio said. "I know this is all hilarity itself, but I don't quite get the joke."

"You don't," Mandelbrot said. "But Marnin does. He can explain it to you."

"Sorry to spoil the fun," David said. "But I don't get it either."

"You damn well do," Mandelbrot said.

Claudio shrugged. "It's of no importance."

"Yes, it is," Mandelbrot rejoined. "It's damned important."

"What the hell are you talking about?" David asked.

"I'll show you what I'm talking about."

Mandelbrot laid the attaché case, which had been under his chair, on the table. It had a double combination lock and he had trouble getting it open.

"Dammit. . .God dammit," he repeated several times.

All the others were staring in fascination, as though watching a snake charmer luring his cobra from a wicker basket. Finally, he succeeded in getting it open. He extracted a document—a USIA Dispatch ten single-spaced pages in length, classified "CONFIDENTIAL." It began with an additional slug: "SENSITIVE—EYES ONLY." It was Mecklin's report on the Saigon press corps.

PART THREE

FALL FROM GRACE

Monday morning at nine-thirty Marnin was visited by Jim Franco, the wall-eyed embassy Regional Security Officer (RSO), who walked into his office conspicuously clutching a manila folder marked on the cover in bold red letters, "MARNIN, DAVID." Before entering the Foreign Service, Franco had spent a dozen years as an artillery officer in the Army. Judged unfit for command, he was passed over for promotion from Captain to Major. He regularly groused about the Army's mistreatment of him at the bar at the Hotel Rex, where he spent his evenings. It made him a laughing stock among the junior officers at the Embassy.

Luckily for him, however, he was drummed out of the army just at the time when the State Department was making the first of its many subsequent moves to enlarge its corps of security officers. And since the State Department, for reasons which have never been clear, has a proclivity for picking up military castoffs not deemed good enough for retention by our armed services, and since he already had security clearances and could go to work immediately, he managed to land a job in the Foreign Service.

Franco was one of those hearty good old boys, everybody's archetype of a used car salesman.

"Howdy," he said, entering and sitting down. He placed the folder on Marnin's desk so that the name on it was clearly visible.

"Mind if I come in?"

"You're already in."

Franco was no favorite of Marnin's. He was, in fact, the only FSO with whom he had exchanged angry words since his entry into the service. Some "whistle blower" had sent an anonymous letter to Bilder charging that Helen Eng was using her PX privileges to pass on American food and other PX and commissary items to her Vietnamese friends. When this was broached to Helen she refused on principle to confirm or deny an anonymous allegation. In the eyes of Franco, that meant she was both guilty and in violation of army regulations. Pathologically determined to bring her to justice, he had even followed her home from the PX one Saturday and lurked outside her apartment until midnight, presumably in the hope of catching her in the flagrant act.

The following Monday Franco appeared in Marnin's office and confided to him that he was engaged in a "confidential investigation" of Helen's activities. He asked Marnin to "keep an eye" on her. Marnin replied that he would do no such thing. Unable to shuck his army mode of thinking, Franco, a Class Five officer, regarded the response of the junior aide, a Class Eight, as "insubordinate"—analogous to a Second Lieutenant sassing a Major, a court martial offense, and, at the very least, intolerable effrontery.

"You know why I'm here," Franco said.

"I do?"

"Don't be cute with me. You and your friends think regulations and laws are made for other people and that you can—"

"Friends? Laws?"

"I said laws. You heard me. You think this is some kind of joke, a cute college boy prank. But I think you're in big trouble. You're over your head—way over it. So don't be a smartass. Your best bet is to cooperate."

"Cooperate in what?"

"First of all, I'm obliged to tell you one thing and I want you to listen carefully. You're legally entitled to know that what I'm investigating is a felony. You therefore have a right to remain silent and not to incriminate yourself. My own advice as someone who is a fellow officer and has your best interests at heart is that you ought to cooperate to the fullest. You're a young guy and, once you take that great big chip off your shoulder, nobody says you shouldn't have a second chance, whatever you did the first time around."

"A felony?"

"That's right. A federal crime. So this is serious business and I want you to take it seriously."

"What is it exactly I'm accused of doing?"

"I can't let you know as of right now because the investigation is ongoing. It will all come out sooner than you like. I'm not going to get ahead of myself. All I can do now is put some questions to you and get your side of the story. We want to be as fair as possible."

"How can I tell you my side of the story if I don't know what story you're talking about?"

"According to the Ambassador's deposition, it was you yourself who reported to him on Saturday morning that last Friday night you witnessed a highly classified embassy document in the hands of your bosom buddy and college roommate, Willis Mandelbrot."

"Roommate? I knew him slightly at school."

Franco looked through the papers in the manila folder.

"According to my information, you were members of the same fraternity."

"We don't have fraternities at Princeton. We have eating clubs. We ate together. We were in the same club—Colonial. So what?"

"But you've become bosom buddies in Saigon."

"I know him. I've seen him on a number of social occasions. He's a friend of a good friend. But we are not boo-zum buddies."

"I told you not to get smart with me. So I take it that you deny handing over to Mandelbrot the classified document in question when you saw him at the airport during the farewell ceremonies for Lieutenant Colonel John Mudd."

"Absolutely."

"And are you willing to take a polygraph test so that we can get to the bottom of this thing?"

"I don't know. I don't know enough about lie detectors. I hear they're not very reliable."

"That's what I expected. So you refuse to take a polygraph."

"I didn't say that. I said I didn't know. I'll have to think about it.

Are you making this an official request?"

"Not yet. We'll come to that a little later on. Right now I want you
to tell me everything that happened on Friday. Begin with your trip to
the airport to say goodbye to Mudd and then tell me everything that
took place in the restaurant. Be as accurate and as detailed as possible.
But don't forget, I already have the Ambassador's deposition."

"I have absolutely nothing to hide," Marnin said.

Franco took careful notes as Marnin spoke, asked him to stop several times because he was going too fast, and requested clarification of
several of the things he said. When Marnin finished, the security officer looked so pleased that Marnin feared he had somehow compromised himself.

"I'm going to have this typed up," Franco said with a big smile on
his face, his one good eye happily fixed on Marnin. "Then I'm going
to bring it back to you this afternoon and I'll want you to sign it. I
have some more questions. Lots of questions. But those can wait till
later."

"What time will you be coming?"

"Don't you worry your little head—I should say big head—about
it. I'll be back. You can count on it."

He got up and sauntered out of the office.

"I look forward to it," Marnin said to his back, trying to keep up
a brave front. In truth, he was deeply worried and could envision his
career, hardly begun, perhaps already in the process of disintegration.
Was the Ambassador really suspicious of him, as Franco seemed to be
implying? Should he talk this over with him or with Bilder? Was this
something he could confide to Lily? Should he try to find a lawyer? A
felony was a serious matter. Franco kept him on the hook and did not
walk into his office again until five-thirty. He sat down opposite
Marnin, put his feet on Marnin's desk, and began thumbing through
the same manila folder, this time considerably thicker than it had been
in the morning.

"Once more, I advise you to cooperate with this investigation. Do
you have anything further to say to me?"

"Yes. You've got a hole in your shoe."

Franco took his feet off Marnin's desk and handed him a piece of paper. It contained his notes of what had been said to him in the morning. The heading, centered on the top line, was "DEPOSI- TION." "David Marnin, FSO-8" was typed at the bottom. It was a good job. Marnin had no quarrel with it.

"Any problems?" Franco asked.

"No. This is quite accurate."

"Would you mind signing it?"

Marnin scrawled his signature on the bottom and handed the doc- ument back. Franco looked enormously pleased as he put the paper in the rear of the manila folder. His expression said, "Gotcha!"

"First of all, you ought to know that I haven't exactly been sitting on my ass all day. I've been damned busy."

"I'm glad to know the taxpayers have been getting their money's worth."

"Don't you want to know what it is that I've been doing?"

"I have the strangest feeling you're going to tell me anyway."

"That's not far wrong," Franco laughed. "What I've been doing today is contacting every person in this embassy, twenty-one people in all including secretaries and code clerks, who had legitimate access to John Mecklin's Eyes Only dispatch. Do you want to see that list of twenty-one?"

"No."

"Well, would you care to guess as to which one of them would be likely to turn a document like that over to Willis Mandelbrot?"

"No."

"It would certainly be a tough guess. Only five of the twenty-one people involved, other than yourself of course—the Ambassador, the DCM, Sabo, Mecklin, and Bates—even admit to knowing Mandelbrot socially. Mecklin and his press officer are sick over this whole thing. They said that it compromises them completely and that they can no longer deal with the press corps as they're supposed to. They think that whoever did this ought to be hung. I told them not to worry, that he would be. So those two guys are not likely to have turned that dispatch over to Mandelbrot. Do you agree?"

"Yes, I do."

"And you don't think the Ambassador or Mister Bilder or Mister

Sabo would have turned it over, do you?"

"No, I don't."

"Now everybody else who could have given the report to the *New York Times* claims not even to have exchanged a single word with Mandelbrot since Mecklin wrote the dispatch, and most of them don't know him, have never met him, don't even know what he looks like. I have signed statements right here from every one of them. Do you have any reason to doubt that or to think that any of them might be lying?"

"No."

"Well, every one of those people specifically denies they turned the document in question over to Mandelbrot. Are you willing to give me a similar statement?"

"Absolutely."

"Remember that this is equivalent to being under oath."

Marnin pulled out from a drawer a sheet of embassy letterhead stationery and wrote: "I, David Marnin, swear that I have never turned over to anyone in any way, shape, manner or form any US Government classified material."

He signed it and handed it to Franco.

"This is all right as far as it goes," the security officer said. "But it makes no reference to the Mecklin dispatch or to your close relationship with Mandelbrot."

Marnin took out another piece of stationery and made a second try: "I, David Marnin, swear that I did not give to anyone copies of John Mecklin's dispatch on the press in Saigon. Specifically, I did not give it to Willis Mandelbrot of the *New York Times* and have no idea how Mandelbrot, with whom I am acquainted, managed to obtain copies of that document."

"That's better," Franco said when he read it over carefully, "much better. But you can see, can't you, why you're a genuine suspect in this case and that nobody else on this list is even in the running?"

"You don't expect me to answer that, do you?"

"Not really. But I'm happy that we're finally getting somewhere. Now I have some more questions."

"Shoot."

"First of all, the document that you allegedly turned over to Mudd at the airport—what was that document?"

"I don't know. It was sealed. I had no right to open it unless something happened to him. I was just holding it for Mudd."

"You had no curiosity about it? Never asked what it contained? Never discussed it with him? That's awfully hard to believe. And why you, anyway? Here we have maybe the most popular man in Viet Nam—a living legend the *New York Times* called him, a man with hundreds of friends. He was a senior commissioned officer in the United States Army. But when looking for a favor, when looking for someone to leave an important document with, he chose a junior officer from the State Department! Why? Didn't you think it curious that of all the people in Viet Nam that he was so friendly with, he chose to leave this envelope with you, a self-described chance acquaintance?"

"I may have wondered what it contained. I don't have a clue as to why he chose me."

"Do you always accept classified documents from relative strangers? Do you always store classified documents in your desk at home, where they would be available to any servant, to any prowler, to any KGB agent?"

"KGB?"

"You don't think the KGB operates in this country? Well I've got news for you, buddy. It does! If you had any so-called 'curiosity'— what I would call suspicions—about the contents of the document, why didn't you report the matter to your Regional Security Officer, as section 363.8 of the Standard Regs requires you to do?"

"I have no knowledge, not even an inkling, that the envelope may have contained a classified document or any classified material at all. My assumption was and is quite the contrary. Why don't you check all this out with Colonel Mudd? He'll verify everything I'm saying."

"Will he? We'll see about that. You can bet your bottom dollar we'll be checking with your friend Mudd. He might say he doesn't know the first thing about it. That would be a booger, wouldn't it? Now, just to shift gears for a wee bit, when was the last time you saw Mandelbrot before you ran into each other at the airport?"

"I can't remember exactly. We used to bump into each other fairly regularly. Played tennis together. But I. . .haven't been going out much in the evenings these days, and hadn't seen him for about a month."

"Okay. Now we're getting somewhere."

"I don't see where."

"You're not supposed to. You think you're too smart for a dumb hick like me. But we'll just see about that. Now, let's go back to the restaurant. According to the Ambassador's deposition and to your own statement, you say Mandelbrot was drunk, that he pulled out the document, that he flouted it in front of the other reporters, who all seemed familiar with its contents, and in front of a foreign diplomat who's obviously not cleared for access to classified material, that he was—what was the word you used? (He flipped through some papers.) Oh yes, 'pugnacious'—he was pugnacious."

"It means looking for a fight," Marnin said.

"I know what it means! Now, when this pugnacious *New York Times* correspondent waved that sensitive document around a public restaurant, why didn't you take it away from him?"

"Take it away?"

"That's right. Grab it out of his hands. He's a big guy, but you're bigger and, from what I can tell, in better shape. He had something that didn't belong to him. It was the property, in fact, of your employer, the United States government. You had every right to it. You were cleared to read it. You had read it!"

"That's right."

"Furthermore," he continued, "it wasn't a question of rights. It was a question of duty. This was stolen property. You had an obligation to do everything in your power to get it back. Instead, once the brouhaha between you had been papered over as a result of the intercession of the foreign diplomat, you remained—by your own confession. . .I mean deposition—at the same table with him. You even broke bread together. Were you afraid that this pugnacious chum of yours would do you bodily injury?"

Franco, who had a big smile on his face, could see that he was getting to Marnin.

"It never occurred to me to try and grab it," Marnin said. "He already had the dispatch in his possession and had made various allusions to it that the others were familiar with. They had all obviously read it. I had no reason to think this was the only copy. What was sensitive was not the physical document itself, but its contents. And those were already known to everybody present, to all the Americans."

"What you mean to say is that you didn't have the guts to stand up for what you believe. You were afraid to make a scene in a public restaurant—not the sort of thing that's done in the Ivy League."

"What are you trying to say?"

"You've given me one possible interpretation of what happened. But there's another possibility. And that is that you had already given that dispatch to Mandelbrot yourself that very afternoon. So there was not much point in trying to get it back from him."

"That's ridiculous! I had no reason in the world to turn that document over to Mandelbrot. And if I had, why would I then report to the Ambassador that Mandelbrot had a copy of it?"

"In the first place, the Standard Regs stipulate that when an infraction of this kind occurs, an officer should report it not to the Ambassador, but to the RSO, who's got the responsibility to monitor security questions in our embassies."

"Excuse me. I was under the misapprehension that the Ambassador is in charge of everything that takes place in his embassy."

"He is. But security violations are supposed to be reported to the security officer. That doesn't seem very strange, now does it? And as for why you would report the matter—it took place in a restaurant, a public place, with six immediate witnesses and maybe more. So in that situation you had no other choice, no other choice, except to report the matter and try to brazen it through."

"You can make up any story you want," Marnin said. "The fact of the matter is that I never gave Mandelbrot or anybody else Mecklin's dispatch or any other classified document and that I'd cut my wrists before I did any such thing."

"I'm not making up any story. I'm simply putting a logical interpretation on the facts you present in your own deposition. There are some other possibilities too. . ."

"And what are they?"

"I'm not going to tell you what they are for reasons so obvious even an Ivy Leaguer like you could figure them out."

"Look, stop trying to frighten me. It's not a game I'm going to play with you."

"You suit yourself. But just remember that you're young and this is your first post. If you've done something wrong the best way out is to make a clean breast of it. Sure, it might hurt you for a while, but your career will eventually recover."

"Your solicitude is touching."

"Okay. Okay. You just go ahead with being a wiseass. That's your privilege. But if you persist, I'm going to put your ass in a wringer and keep it there. I'll stomp you. And at that point you'll damn well regret you hadn't listened to the good advice I've been giving you this afternoon."

At seven the next morning, Marnin appeared at the Residence as usual with the overnight traffic. Corning was just climbing out of the pool after doing his laps. He first put on his bathrobe and then put a cigarette in his medicated cigarette holder and lit it. Breakfast was served on the glass-topped wrought iron table by Lao Li. The Ambassador had forgotten his fountain pen and asked the houseboy to get it. He then went through all the incoming reading. After finishing that, he dealt with the outgoing cables, making frequent corrections. When he was through with these chores, Marnin put the various papers back into separate folders and started to leave. Corning called him back.

"David, there's something I must talk to you about."

"Yes, sir."

"I think you know what it is. It's about the Mecklin report on the American press in Saigon that you told me about Saturday morning. Naturally you must understand that there is a serious security breach here. Whoever committed it should be found out and punished."

"Yes, sir."

"Now I don't think of you as a possible culprit. We regard you as one of the family. Pattie Lou is very fond of you and so am I."

He peered up at Marnin over his reading glasses.

"Moreover, you've managed to give me over the past five months tangible proof that you are a young man of both energy and integrity. It would pain me more than you can imagine if that integrity were compromised. I don't think for a minute that you'd turn over a classified document to Mandelbrot or to anyone else."

"I would never do that," Marnin said. "Never!"

"And you were wise enough to keep me informed of your interesting encounters with Mandelbrot, and with Mudd as well. I even encouraged you to maintain those contacts. I know that. The question we have to answer now, though, is where do we go from here?"

"Go?"

"As you know, Bilder and I spent an hour with the RSO on this matter last night. Franco has assembled quite a case against you. It's entirely circumstantial and can't be proved in court unless you, Mandelbrot or Mudd own up to it. But it's logically plausible and must be investigated."

"What case? There is no case. I've done nothing wrong."

"I'm convinced of that. And I've every confidence that you're going to be proven completely innocent. But I can't call off the investigation that Franco proposes. And Mudd is unfortunately off on a hunting trip in Alaska and can't be reached for three weeks and won't be anyplace where he can handle classified material for at least a month. Everything will be in abeyance until then. In the meantime, Franco unfortunately is convinced that this is an open and shut case and Bilder believes that, at the very least, the evidence merits investigation."

"What evidence?"

"Franco claims you had an ostensible motive and a perfect opportunity and that you were probably drawn into this thing unwittingly."

"I don't understand."

"Franco's hypothesis—and you must never breathe to another soul that I shared it with you—is that you turned Mecklin's dispatch over to Mudd. We know you admired Mudd for his courage and his soldiering. You've told me so yourself. And since you and Mudd differ about the merits of the Saigon press corps, you decided—according to Franco's theory—to turn over Mecklin's report to Mudd in an effort to convince him that you were right all along. While this is a bad thing to do, it is nowhere near as bad as turning over a report like this to

Mandelbrot, because Mudd had Top Secret and codeword clearances and therefore the legitimate right to read that document if he had a need to know about it."

"I still don't understand. . ."

"Hear me out! What you failed to take into account—again, according to Franco—because you didn't know about it, was Mudd's intimate relationship with Mandelbrot. We know, without any question, hesitation, or doubt, that Mudd on at least five separate occasions had turned over to Mandelbrot highly classified information. Unfortunately, the evidence—and I cannot go into the nature of the evidence—is not admissible in a court of law. It cannot even be entered on Mudd's records. Franco's supposition is that Mudd, in line with his past practice, turned over that report to Mandelbrot without your knowledge, and you were in essence a victim of circumstances of which you weren't aware. It has a certain plausibility."

"It's ingenious," Marnin said. "The only thing wrong is that it isn't true. I never gave anybody anything."

"I believe you. Trust me on that. Nevertheless, we've got to decide what to do about you in the interim."

"What do you want me to do?"

"While the investigation proceeds, and we're talking about four weeks, six weeks at the outside, I'd like to send you up to Hue on TDY to replace Steve Brandon, our Vice-Consul, who was evacuated last week with hepatitis and won't be back for at least another six weeks. It will be interesting for you. You'll learn a lot about Viet Nam and Vietnamese culture that you'd never be able to pick up in Saigon. But you must understand that while a serious allegation of wrongdoing of this nature is being investigated, we can't have you around the front office, the most sensitive spot in the whole Mission."

"Do I have an alternative?"

"Yes. Your alternative is to accept an immediate transfer. If you want to go that route I would do my best to see that it would not prejudice your subsequent career. You can count on that."

"I don't want to leave Saigon," Marnin said, genuinely upset.

The last thing he wanted was a transfer, even a temporary one, since above all it would mean a separation from Lily. Under different circumstances Marnin would, in fact, have welcomed the Hue assignment. He had not yet visited the north and Hue was, after all, the cultural capital of Viet Nam—the seat of the Vietnamese emperors. But this was scarcely consolation.

That evening, while they ate, David told Lily about his sudden misfortune. She listened carefully, without interruption.

"I don't understand," she said, when he had finally finished. "Clearly you don't want us apart from each other. I don't want it either. But what are you so worried about?"

"I'm worried about my career, about my life, about what I'm going to do if I have to resign and leave this embassy."

"But why?"

"Because my integrity has been called into question and the most important thing any diplomat possesses is his integrity."

"But integrity is something that you either have from your bringing up or you're never going to get it. Whether other people think you have it, whatever other people think, should not matter to you in the least. That's the real meaning of integrity."

"That's all very well to say. But in my career you get ahead by what's called your corridor reputation. If that's bad, you don't get the right jobs. And if you don't get the right jobs, you don't get promoted. And everything in a Foreign Service career, the jobs you get and above all the way people think of you, depends on promotions."

"If you even begin to think about things like that," she replied, "you'll become a clerk. That kind of thing is what Lieutenants find interesting. Generals have more important things to occupy them. My husband used to say that good Lieutenants make very bad Generals. The best Lieutenants, he said, are usually stupid and energetic; but the best Generals are always brilliant and lazy. The service you describe is a service of clerks. I would get out of it anyway, if I were you."

"That's all very well. But it's impossible to operate in a bureaucracy without paying attention to its inner workings."

"You're not going to be twenty-nine for several months. There are lots of important decisions you can make at your age that will affect your future. But those decisions almost all have to do with things like sleeping with women and having babies. They have nothing to do with your career. There is nothing you can do at age twenty-eight that anyone in the world, other than those connected to you by blood and semen, will remember when you are fifty. Even your silly fitness reports will mean absolutely nothing by that time. Who remembers what somebody said about somebody else ten years later? Ten years from now your Corning, your Bilder, and your Franco will be ghosts, faces you can just barely remember. . ."

Three days later Marnin flew to Hue on Air Viet Nam to report to the Consulate. His new boss Freddie Loftus, the Consul, was an intelligent, eccentric fellow with a high-pitched voice that seemed always on the brink of cracking with impatience. His edginess was in marked contrast to Marnin's previous chief, the gentlemanly Corning, who spoke to everyone, including his lowliest subordinates, in a soft baritone with exaggerated southern courtesy.

Thrust unexpectedly into the world of Viet Nam, Loftus had labored mightily, he said, during the two months prior to Marnin's arrival to bring some order out of the Augean stables left him by his predecessor, the ill-fated Paul Marks, discovered by the Embassy security people to be a catamite preying on ten year old Vietnamese cigarette vendors. This bit of detective work had earned Franco the first of his State Department Meritorious Honor Awards. He undoubtedly hoped that Marnin's case would garner a second.

Franco may have had some virtues, but discretion was not among them. Thanks to his boozy sea stories at the Rex bar, the account of how our consul in Hue, "the queen of the north," had been photographed with a hairbrush in his hand and a naked Vietnamese boy across his own naked knees was common knowledge in the Embassy. This repulsive incident had also somehow become well known to the Vietnamese employees of the Consulate and filled them with a shame that very few Americans could even begin to imagine. For them Marks, a soft-spoken, rather shy man, not only had disgraced himself by performing the literally unspeakable with children of their own race, but had thereby also brought deep humiliation on each and every Vietnamese in his employ. At the time of Marnin's arrival, a palpable sadness still permeated the Consulate's modest office building.

The expulsion and forced retirement of the unfortunate Marks left Hue in the hands of the Deputy Principal Officer, Steve Brandon, a brand new Foreign Service Officer fresh out of Yale. Providentially, Marks was exposed and punished just as Freddie Loftus, who had perfect French, suddenly became available for reassignment from Hong Kong. Being Principal Officer in a potentially important post such as Hue was by the standards of the State Department a good assignment—in fact, a real opportunity—for a Foreign Service Officer in the political "cone." But no sooner had Freddie gotten there than Brandon came down with hepatitis and had to be medically evacuated.

Left the sole American at the Consulate, Freddie had no choice, he said, other than devote himself to consular affairs. Consuls had to service the public for the forty hour week mandated by the United States Government. (Freddie's alleged need to remain inside the Consulate during its hours of operation became something of a joke in the political section in Saigon, where it was well known that the office hours for the French Consulate in Hue were eleven to one Mondays, Wednesdays, and Fridays, and for the Thai Consulate every other Thursday afternoon.)

Meanwhile, Freddie decided that political and economic work in the northern quadrant of South Viet Nam would have to await the return of Brandon or the arrival of another officer to take up the slack. In a series of irascible cables he petitioned the Embassy for temporary relief. But nobody could be spared until Marnin's misfortune made him available. In the interim, partly out of pique that he was not being adequately supported and partly because Freddie was, in terms of putting pen to paper, one of the laziest officers in the service, he had done absolutely no political or economic reporting. This, of course, was noticed. Political sections in the Foreign Service are like academe— one has to "publish or perish." Political officers distinguish themselves from their colleagues either by the bulk of their reporting or by its quality, sometimes both. To senior officers like Sam Sabo, no reporting at all was inexcusable.

Well before the discovery of the crimes of Paul Marks, Sam had wanted to "jack up" the Consulate's reporting. He therefore was upbeat about Marnin's assignment. "Too much staff work ruins a young diplomat" was an aphorism he had quoted to Marnin, even in better times. And in this worst of times, unlike most of the other senior officers of the Embassy, he had been very good to Marnin—the only person in the Mission, other than Helen Eng and Corning himself, who had taken the trouble to be the least bit kind or encouraging. Everyone else, all the other members of the "Country Team," treated him as though he had just made a bad smell. (If you need a loyal friend while you're in government service, said Harry Truman, get a dog.) Sabo, on the other hand, invited him for a drink, ostensibly to talk over what was needed in terms of political reporting in the Consulate district, but really to encourage him not to lose heart.

"Don't worry about it," Sabo said, after they had settled in on his veranda, drinking camparis and soda. "You're a straight arrow, David. Just pay no attention to this matter and keep your nose to the grindstone and everything will work out. At this stage of your life, nobody remembers what you did at your last post. You've still got the Ambassador's confidence and, for what it's worth, you have mine as well. So look on this as a welcome break. You're a political officer and the assignment to Hue will give you a chance to begin the real apprenticeship in your craft."

"Is there anything special you want from Hue that you're not getting—anything that hasn't been covered in Consulate reporting?"

"The answer to that," said Sabo, "is that nothing has been covered adequately by the Consulate because for three months there's been no reporting whatsoever, just complete silence. Marks was not an adequate reporting officer. Even aside from his special predilections, we were well rid of him. But the only cables we get from Loftus are kvetches that he's not being supported adequately. If he'd let us know what's happening on the local scene up there, instead of just bleating about how overworked he is, we'd all be a lot better off, especially him."

Loftus, an Asian expert who spoke both Mandarin and Japanese, was tall and plump and very white, his whiteness accentuated by a mop of curly black hair. Troubled by a lifelong affliction with eczema, he never exposed his skin to the tropical sun if he could help it. He looked as though if you touched his flesh with your index finger it would leave a permanent indentation. Freddie's specialties were Ming Dynasty and Muromachi art. He owned four paintings by Shang Xi, two by Shen Zhou, and two by Sesshu Toyo, each of which would today fetch considerably more than five hundred thousand dollars on the Tokyo market. During his brief stint in Hue he had already managed to pick up half a dozen lovely Cham heads—the specialty of the local antique dealers.

Marnin moved into Brandon's apartment on Le Loi, not far from the Trang Tien Bridge and a stone's throw from the radio station and tower along the River and, in the opposite direction, the MACV compound along Hung Vuong. As a consular apartment for an unmarried junior officer it was spectacular—three bedrooms, servants quarters, nice living room, separate dining room, and verandas off both with lovely views across bungalow roofs to the Perfume River. At night, sitting on his veranda and sipping a gin and tonic, Marnin would smoke a cigar and watch the fifty foot "long tail" sampans gliding along it, poled by graceful boatwomen standing erectly. In high cricket voices they sang plaintive songs of Vietnamese heroes of old, all of whom, in one way or another, had resisted the encroachments of either the French or the Chinese on their homeland.

Since the flat belonged to the Consulate it cost Marnin nothing, no rent and no utilities, just his housing allowance. In Brandon's absence, he took over his cook, maid, gardener, and driver—all of whose salary, taken together, amounted to fifty dollars a month. Unlike Saigon, there were few foreigners in Hue in those days to compete with each other and jack up prices for servants. Food cost practically nothing.

Hue itself lived up to expectations—to everything that he had read and heard and that Lily, in her tales about her education at the Dong Khanh Girl's School, had told him. Without industry, its rocky environs produced just enough food to support the local population. But with its twelve institutions of higher learning it was the cultural hub of all of Viet Nam. The seat of its last imperial dynasty, the Nguyen, it had for generations been the nation's intellectual center where future rulers of the country were educated—including both Ngo Dinh Diem and Ho Chi Minh.

Hue was a city of scholars and mandarins, of citadels, royal tombs, palaces, pagodas and temples. The ghosts of past emperors haunted the place. There the Tu Duc emperor, the most flamboyant of the Nguyen dynasty, had built a tomb on a thirty acre site containing fifty monuments honoring himself in the hereafter. In his lacquered lakeside pavilion, Tu Duc wrote poetry, drank lotus tea made from dew, ate meals of forty different dishes, enjoyed the dancing of his royal troupe, and sported with his hundred and four concubines, none of whom managed to produce an heir.

With Marnin along to write up the memoranda of conversation, Loftus could finally satisfy the powers that be in the Embassy that he was getting his work done and at the same time go on being the laziest man in town. The ostensible purpose of the appointments he set up was to introduce key people to his new Vice Consul. Heading his list were the two most important political figures in his consular district—Ngo Dinh Can, the "warlord" who controlled the northern region of South Viet Nam, and Ngo Dinh Thuc, the Archbishop—both of them brothers of the President.

But the Ngo Dinh brothers were not immediately available. In fact, Freddie got word back through Mr. Buu, the Consulate's chief local employee, that Can might not see them at all. On the other hand, Buu, a devout Catholic, was happy to report that the Archbishop was eager to meet with them and would grant an audience as soon as he returned from a visit to the shrine of the Virgin at La Vang, near Quang Tri city, where he had gone to give thanks on the twenty-fifth anniversary of his ordination as the Bishop of Vinh Long.

Freddie and Marnin thus began a round of calls on important figures in the consular district. Hue was a somnolent place that seemed fairly untouched by the war. The people were far less open, outgoing, and ready to complain about the Government than those Marnin had become accustomed to in the capital, where one could hardly change clothes in the locker room of the Cercle Sportif or sip a coffee on the "Continental Shelf" without being the object of grumbling from Vietnamese acquaintances about the latest "outrages" of Ngo Dinh Nhu and his wife.

Nothing could have seemed quieter or more under control than the political situation in Hue. Not a single Vietnamese official they talked with expressed the slightest concern that the social fabric of this calm and conservative city might come apart with explosive and unexpected suddenness. So the American Consulate was as surprised as the key Vietnamese officials of Hue when, within a few days, the city unraveled and in the process changed the history not only of Southeast Asia, but of the United States as well.

Chapter 22

THE BIRTHDAY MASSACRE

To the bemusement of the American Consul and his new Vice-Consul, the single exception to the general somnolence they encountered in their political rounds was at the General Association of Buddhists. At the entrance of the Tu Dam pagoda, which was its headquarters, they were met by a young monk, no more than eighteen, his head shaved, dressed in the usual saffron robe and sandals, who had a strong and unpleasant body odor. As they walked with him to the top of the steps, trying to keep up wind, he turned and bowed low and told them, in perfect French, that the Venerable Thich Tinh Khiet awaited. He then ushered them into a small office on the ground floor of the pagoda immediately to the right of the entrance.

Khiet by then was eighty years old, as frail a bag of bones as one could imagine. His voice, which he used sparingly, was never raised above a hoarse whisper. Each rattling word seemed to struggle to get out of a deep cage somewhere in the darkest recesses of his chest. He received the American officials seated in the lotus position in a white, overstuffed rattan armchair, puffing away on a Gauloise. Next to him on a twin armchair, seated in Western fashion with his legs crossed, was Thich Tri Binh, whom Loftus afterward identified as a rabble rousing monk who, in a recent spate of anti-government speeches had mesmerized thousands of Hue residents with his charisma and raunchy humor.

Binh, too, was addicted to Gauloises, which both bonzes relentlessly consumed in tandem. When Khiet finished a cigarette, he would

hand it to Binh, who would light his own from the stub of his colleague's. Finishing his Gauloise, Binh would then return the favor.
The conversation with them lasted well over an hour, with one of
them smoking at all times. And yet neither of them found it necessary
to light a match during that entire period. The room was thick with
the smell of incense and Turkish tobacco.

The interview proved to be lengthy because Khiet spoke no language other than Vietnamese and everything was therefore "translated" by Binh into very fluent but highly idiosyncratic French. And
whereas Khiet never put together more than two sentences at a time,
indeed seemed physically incapable of doing so, Binh's "translation"
was obviously highly embroidered. What took Khiet ten seconds to
say took Binh two minutes to translate. Marnin came away wondering whether Khiet had any idea of what Loftus had said to him or,
more important, what he purportedly had said to Loftus.

Freddie began by thanking His Reverence for receiving them.
Freedom of religion, he pointed out, was a bedrock principle in the
United States, enshrined in our Constitution. Furthermore, it was lit-
tle known in Viet Nam that the United States was a very religious
place. Church attendance in America was far higher than in any
European country. He fished a quarter out of his pocket.

"Look!" he said. "Right there on the coin is our national motto, 'In
God We Trust.'"

Khiet reached into his saffron robe and pulled out a pair of thick
horn-rimmed spectacles, but forgot to put them on. Binh stared at
Freddie for a long time, as if to gauge whether this outlander was
pulling his sarong. Then he took an inordinately long time translating
Freddie's remarks—in the process reaching over and grabbing the coin
away from Khiet—who had been holding it as though he had just
been handed a live frog. Binh then said something in Vietnamese and
both of the monks giggled. He never returned the quarter.

Khiet, in response, said no more than two dozen words that Binh
translated as follows:

"It is great pleasure to make acquaintance of American staff of
Consulate in Hue, seat of national Buddhist movement, and city
where the people, with some notable exceptions, try to conduct them-

selves in accordance with Buddhist precepts. Christian religions pay attention only to what wise men say about what other wise men have said about what Jesus really meant when he said the opposite. You smile when I say that. But Jesus was for peace and against killing. He said the rich can only enter heaven when a camel passes through the eye of a needle. I have read it myself. And how is this interpreted? Your wise men, and your rich, handsome, and pleasure loving President John Kennedy, explain that we must follow teachings of Jesus by getting rich and by making war to ensure peace. We must kill for good of those being killed. Christian wise men say Mister Kennedy will enter heaven with the cleanest of fingernails (and both of these monks had large encrustations of dirt underneath theirs) because he gives out helicopters that kill women, children, and water buffaloes. No wonder Mister Kennedy, he trust in God. For him the birds sing. The sky is blue. Nothing but blue skies from now on."

Freddie looked at Marnin and rolled his eyes.

"Buddhist religion different," Binh continued. "Buddha said what he had to say three thousand years ago and we Buddhists still live by those words. We have no wise men to tell us that black is white or that death is life. The Lord Buddha command us not to kill. So we don't eat meat or kill even insect, even mosquito that bites us and gives us malaria. Have you seen water buffalo shot by fifty caliber bullet fired from helicopter? Buffalo he suffer. Big hunks of steak torn out of his body. Owner of buffalo he also suffer. It break his heart to hear his friend the buffalo screaming and filling rice paddy with his blood. President Kennedy he says water buffalo killed in order help us get rid of Communists. This makes sense to you maybe, but not to Vietnamese farmer. Buddha gave us Four Noble Truths. Very First Truth—man is born to suffer and he suffers in this life and next. Even the Buddha, who was a great prince, greater than Kennedy, suffered until he learned to do away with his desires.

"Second Truth—what is cause of suffering? Cause of suffering is desire. Men crave pleasure. Vietnamese girls beautiful like lotus blossoms. American soldiers see them and crave them. All men crave possessions—gold, servants, houses, and power to tell others what to do. They want beautiful girl to pleasure. Men crave cessation of pain, take drugs into their blood, smoke dope, drink whiskey with Coca Cola, go to massage parlor and have dicks pulled by pretty little Vietnamese girl.

"Third Truth—all craving comes from desire to enhance self. Cure for desire is non-attachment to things, especially non-attachment to self. This is what your President Kennedy should try to do.

"Fourth truth—way to achieve non-attachment, way to cut off self is to follow Lord Buddha's eight-fold path—right conduct, right intentions, right livelihood, right medicines, right effort, right mind-edness, right speech, and right views. Once this is done all desires fade away into nothing. Man enters nirvana, has no need to live any more lives. When we Buddhists see you following eightfold path, we will listen to you very carefully and maybe even do what you say. But when we see dying water buffalo, friend to man, gentle beast, work hard, never hurt anyone, bleeding to death in rice paddy—"

"But the Communists are atheists," Freddie interjected. "They actively persecute religion. Marx said religion is the opiate of the people. They have museums of atheism in every big city in the USSR. Everywhere they rule—in North Viet Nam, in China, in the Soviet Union—they put religious people in labor camps and prisons."

Khiet lit a Gauloise from the stub of Binh's. He shrugged his shoulders. Then, in his hoarse, barely audible voice, a slight smile at the corners of his mouth, he replied to Freddie.

"Venerable Khiet says," Binh translated, "that dragon and eagle are enemies like cats and dogs, but they both like to eat liver of little rabbit. So smart rabbit he does not wander into den of dragons, who can fry him with their tongue and have him for breakfast. This does not mean that when eagle goes hunting for his lunch smart rabbit does not hide under rock. That is general truth, true for all time. Particular truth is that we have been here for two thousand years and will be here for another two thousand. Communists they know that. But Government in Saigon—calling itself Government of Viet Nam, country where huge per cent of people are Buddhists—they persecute us, they spit on us, they dishonor our Lord Buddha."

"I don't know of any persecution," Freddie said.

"That is because there is no persecution in English. And there is no persecution in French. Only persecution is in Vietnamese. In English they say in God we trust and all men created equal. In French they say *liberté, egalité, fraternité,* funniest one of which is *egalité.* But in Vietnamese they tell us we not allowed to honor Buddha on his 2,587th birthday."

"What do you mean?"

"Flags. You know about flags."

"Flags? *Drapeaux?*"

"But surely you have seen flags. They are all over city."

"I don't know what you mean," Freddie said.

"Day after tomorrow is 2,587th birthday of our Lord Buddha. As part of our celebration we have hung out our flags, all to the honor and glory of our Lord. Today we are informed that all these flags, which we have displayed every year for the past fifty years, will have to be taken down. It is edict from Nghia, the Province Chief, direct orders from Saigon, which take direct orders from Archbishop of Hue."

"But why?"

"There is law that only flag to be displayed in public is national flag of Government of Viet Nam. By celebrating birthday of our Lord Buddha we are breaking law. This is what they say. If they are right, we have been breaking law for past fifty years."

"Perhaps there is some sort of misunderstanding?"

"There is no misunderstanding. Bao Dai and De Gaulle have gone. Now we have Ngo Dinh Diem and Kennedy. As far as Pope is concerned, even better. Pair of them not only bigger, stronger, richer, but Catholic as well. Before Buddhists eat dust. Now we eat mud. All same to us, still afraid to open mouth."

"What have the Catholics got to do with it?"

"Take a look! All over town on top of our flags honoring Lord Buddha, the greatest man in all human history, are blue and white Catholic flags celebrating exactly what? Twenty-fifth anniversary of consecration of Archbishop of Hue as Bishop of Vinh Long, which is hundreds of kilometers from here. Who cares what happened in Vinh Long twenty-five years ago? Big riddle we have to solve is why should Buddha flags come down and Archbishop flags stay up? Could answer

not be that this Archbishop, who rides through streets in big black
Buick Roadmaster waving at people who bow down and kiss track
tires make in dust, is elder brother of President and head of his family? During past year whole villages are converting to Catholicism all
at once. They leave Lord Buddha and enter church of Lord Jesus.
When single person alone converts, then it is matter of religious
choice. But if whole village does it, then it becomes political act.
Village wants preference from government. They want loans and sub-
sidies. They think more land will be assigned to them. And why do
they think that? Because it is exactly what that Archbishop, that fat
man, tell them. And Buddhists, we have to eat his dirt. The Lord
Buddha has to eat his dirt. . . ."

The following morning Loftus and Marnin were ushered into the
presence of the object of Thich Tri Binh's wrath. Ngo Dinh Thuc, the
Archbishop of Hue, had a marked resemblance to his younger brother Diem, but was somewhat larger, somewhat rounder, and even more
bubbling and energetic. They were received in the office on the second floor of his large residence next door to the cathedral. The room
was lined with books, most of them leather bound matched sets of
French Catholic philosophers. A volume of Jacques Maritain lay open
on his desk.

They were seated in deep mahogany armchairs covered in red velvet. A noisy window air conditioner was chugging away. Like Diem
and Nhu, Thuc was a chain smoker and during the interview managed to fill a large celadon ashtray with cigarette butts. Unlike his
brothers, he smoked Winstons, in fact displayed them proudly to the
American Consul and Vice-Consul, presumably as a symbol of his
friendliness toward their country. He also made a point of calling
attention to the inscribed photograph hanging behind his desk of
Cardinal Spellman, a great friend of his. He spoke French without the
slightest trace of accent. Freddie began the interview by congratu-
lating the Archbishop on the twenty-fifth anniversary of his consecration. Thuc smiled and shrugged it off.

"The faithful in this area are very devout. But it is not me they are
celebrating. I just happen to be the most senior Vietnamese clergyman

in the country, only the second non-French Bishop ever appointed by
the Church in Viet Nam. The Church, even as late as the 1930s, was
slow in realizing that the French had gone as far as they could in converting this country. The French ruled because they had large cannons. But cannons can only control men's bodies, not men's minds.
This was especially so once it became clear to everyone that the French
were going to pack up and leave, were only a bloody drop in the bucket of Vietnamese history. And so the people celebrate my consecration
not because they love me personally, but because they are proud that
in this whole country there is no longer a single Bishop who is anything other than a Vietnamese."

"You feel that you are being successful, Monsignor, in proselytiz-
ing for the Church?"

"You are Catholic?"

The Americans admitted that they were not.

"But you are Christian and you realize how important the
Christianization of this country is to the future of this entire region.
We are engaged in what I don't have to tell you is a life and death
struggle with our enemies for the soul of my people. The more
Christians we have, the surer we are to win that struggle. I've just
come back from La Vang, the shrine to the Virgin at Quang Tri City.
More than twenty thousand people visited that shrine over the past
year. Only ten thousand the year before. Every month hundreds of
converts come forward to be baptized by the Holy Church. Whole villages are entering *en masse*. Rome is very happy, I can tell you. And so
is the President. He knows we are winning the struggle for this part of
the country. It is a region which, as you know, had for a long time
been sympathetic to the Communists."

"But isn't there resentment from the non-Catholics? Don't some of
the people accuse you of favoritism? We've heard that the Buddhists
are planning a large demonstration to protest against the banning of
flags celebrating the birthday of Buddha," Freddie said.

A dark scowl creased Thuc's face, replacing what had hitherto been
a perennial smile.

"You must remember," he said, "that Buddhism in Viet Nam is not
true Buddhism. It comes from China. It is mixed with Taoist supersti-

tion and tinged with all sorts of crazy beliefs, like that of the Cao Dai, who number Victor Hugo among their saints. Imagine! Victor Hugo!"

"Then you're not concerned about the demonstration? You're not afraid that it could lead to friction?"

Thuc's scowl grew deeper.

"I am very concerned. Just before you came I telephoned to Nghia, the province chief, and told him he should not permit it. When he said he could not do that I told him I would personally call the President to complain. And I will. This is not a Buddhist rally. It is a Viet Cong rally. For fifty years we have not had a political peep out of the Buddhists. They had no organization, no structure, and no spokesmen. Suddenly everything changes. Can that be an accident?"

"They say that tearing down their flags is tantamount to sacrilege, that it demeans the Buddha. They say that according to the law, they are not even classified as a religion, but are described instead as a social organization."

"It's the law that the French left us. If they want the law changed, they should introduce a bill in the parliament. That's how things work in a democracy. I've asked my people to take down my flags. I obey the law. No question. The law is clear. No flags displayed in public except the national flag."

"They say their flags are torn down while yours remain flying."

"Both the Buddhists and we were asked by Nghia, the Province Chief, to take all flags down. The Buddhists refused. We, of course, said we would obey the law and we will. So the Province Chief ordered the police to take down the Buddha flags. He's been assured that our people will remove the ones honoring me, except inside the cathedral, where it is perfectly legal for them to fly."

"When will your flags come down?"

"We don't have the funds to pay people for such work and it is easier to find people to put flags up than to take them down. But I can assure you it will be done. And in the meantime I have asked my brother Can and Nghia, the Province Chief, to investigate how the Viet Cong have come to control these so-called Buddhists."

"Do you have any proof of that?" Freddie asked.

"Think about it," Thuc replied. "For fifty years there is nothing, no organization whatsoever. Buddhist clergy, they never leave the pagoda. Now, all of a sudden, there is an association of Buddhist women, association of Buddhist youth, association of Buddhist farmers, all of them very critical of the Government, mouthing the Viet Cong line not ninety-eight per cent, but one hundred per cent of the time. You have a good saying in English. If an animal looks like a duck, walks like a duck, and quacks like a duck, then maybe it *is* a duck. . . ."

It was May 8, 1963, Buddha's birthday. Five hundred members of the Organization of Buddhist Youth and a sprinkling of monks in saffron robes, carrying signs and placards attacking the Government and chanting anti-Diem slogans, had formed on Dong Da Street, a block from the Consulate, and then marched very slowly past it three times. Loftus had no warning and at first did not know what was happening, but made the natural assumption that the marchers' ire was directed against his office. He had just given orders that the wooden shutters on all the Consulate windows be drawn to protect against stones and broken glass when Mr. Buu, who had been summoned, knocked timidly at the door and was ordered in.

"What's happening Mr. Buu? Who are these young people? Why are they demonstrating against us? I have to call Saigon."

"Nothing to worry about," Buu said. "These are young people in protest march denouncing government treatment of Buddhists on this, Buddha's birthday. They are on their way to the Tu Dam pagoda but are marching by here to make sure that the Americans understand that something important is going on."

"What are they chanting?"

"They are shouting, 'Shame on Ngo Dinh Diem!' 'Shame on Ngo Dinh Nhu!' 'Shame on Ngo Dinh Thuc!' 'Glory to the Lord Buddha!' Interesting they don't say anything about Ngo Dinh Can."

"You're sure they're not going to throw rocks, break windows?"

"No, No. That would be most inappropriate on the birthday of Buddha. They're on their way to the pagoda."

"It'll take them more than an hour to reach it at the pace they're walking," Freddie said. "I was invited to the ceremony, but in the face of this kind of provocative behavior, I'm not going. But I want you to be there, Mr. Buu. Take the car and driver. But don't park close to the pagoda. Walk the last half mile or so."

It was lunchtime when Buu returned. Freddie had gone home to have a siesta and Marnin was the only American in the Consulate. He had spent the morning doing a memo of their conversation with Ngo Dinh Thuc and polishing the one he had done the previous day with Thich Tinh Khiet and Thich Tri Binh. They made interesting reading side by side.

Marnin decided it would be wise to draft a cable alerting the Embassy that trouble might be brewing. Buu, however, said that nothing of great moment had occurred during the ceremony at the pagoda. The Commanding General of I Corps was there, as were the Province Chief, the French Consul, and of course the Thai Consul, who was covering the costs of the celebration. Khiet spoke first about the modesty and piety of the Lord Buddha. Then Binh spoke. And Mr. Buu began to chuckle.

"Binh he is very funny fellow," Buu said and laughed again.

"But what did he say?"

"Oh, he said terrible things, talked about how Viet Nam is supposed to be a democracy and in a democracy the majority rules and in Viet Nam the Buddhists are the majority and not only do they not rule, but they are spat upon."

"That doesn't sound very funny to me," Marnin said.

"What he said was not funny at all. In fact, criminally seditious and very objectionable to us Catholics. The way he said it was very, very funny. The Commanding General, the Province Chief they roared with laughter. There is no way to translate what he said. You have to be Vietnamese to understand."

"And is this the end of it?"

"No. The demonstrations continue. After Binh a monk named Duc spoke. He said that what Binh was saying had been taped. He told the crowd to go home and have lunch and a good siesta. The monks would stay in the pagoda and go on praying to the Lord

Buddha. After lunch they would all meet at the square in front of the Hotel Morin and march on the radio station to demand that Binh's speech be broadcast so that all the faithful have the chance to hear it."

Freddie returned to the office at two-thirty and called Pham Duc Nghia, the Province Chief, who was at the ceremony. "According to Nghia," Freddie said to Marnin afterward, "the crowd was critical, but good natured and far from violent. They'll have a demonstration. And when they get tired they'll disband and go home peacefully, he said. In any case his men will be monitoring the situation and if there's trouble they'll know what to do."

"And will they broadcast the speech?"

"Not a chance," Freddie said. "If that speech is broadcast, Nghia said to me we'll all lose our jobs."

Marnin spent the afternoon drafting a long cable entitled "Religious Tensions in Hue," which then went through Freddie's usual nitpicking. When Marnin wrote "worry," Freddie would cross it out and write "concern;" when Marnin wrote "happy," Freddie would change it to "glad;" when Marnin wrote "stimulating," it would be changed to "exciting." But the gist of the telegram was essentially as Marnin drafted it and the report turned out to be the only document to predict that big trouble could be brewing in Hue. For this Freddie eventually got considerable credit for alert reporting from both the Saigon Embassy and the State Department.

That evening, contrary to his usual custom, Marnin—who was sorely missing Lily—had two whiskeys before dinner as he sat in the rattan armchair on the veranda watching the river traffic float by. After dinner he tried reading in the same chair but the mosquitoes would not cooperate and drove him indoors. He undressed and got into bed and turned on the air conditioner. It was only nine o'clock. He reached for Purcell's *The Chinese of Southeast Asia*, a tome guaranteed to cure anyone's insomnia. Within a few minutes he was sound asleep, the book across his chest, the reading light still on.

The next thing Marnin knew it was pitch dark and he was on his stomach pressed against the back wall of the room, lying on some object and covered from head to foot in broken glass. The sesame taste of the Me Xung that his cook had made for dessert was heavy in his mouth and his heart was throbbing uncontrollably. He did not know where he was or what he was doing. He tried to get up.

He was on his knees when the second explosion threw him back against the same wall in exactly the same position he had been in after the first explosion had blown him out of bed. He reached underneath his body to remove the strange object and found that it was the volume of Purcell torn in half. He looked at it stupidly, trying to grasp what had happened.

"They've torn the book," he said out loud to nobody. "Dammit, it wasn't even mine. It was a library book."

The absurdity of his feeling of outrage at the damage done to Purcell brought him to his senses. For the first time in his life he felt naked fear. With his right hand he grabbed his left wrist and squeezed as hard as he could until he literally managed to get a grip on himself. Was this an assassination attempt? Should he move or stay still? He crawled along the floor into the bathroom, cutting his knees on the broken glass, but not feeling it. He stepped into the tiny bathtub in order to look out the bathroom window. In the street all was quiet. Was this directed against him or was it something else? He passed his hands over his body trying to assess the damage. He was naked and bleeding from many cuts but, except for the heavy ringing in his ears from the force of the two explosions, seemed all right.

Then, as a volley of rifle fire and some more shots rang out in the distance and as the next dozen explosions went off in rapid succession, he dove for cover, flattening himself on the floor of the bathroom. But these explosions had much less force, or perhaps were much further away, than the first two. Whatever was happening was moving away from him. It did not seem to be aimed against him. He lay still for what he thought were several more minutes. In fact, from the first blast that blew him out of bed to the last of the dozen secondary explosions took altogether two and a half minutes, according to the sentry at the MACV compound who made the entries in his log. But to Marnin it had seemed to last at least half an hour. He had no doubt that it was the Viet Cong. Only two weeks before they had attacked a police station on the outskirts of Hue, captured it briefly, and had escaped with a couple of dozen weapons.

Things grew quiet. He crawled back into the bedroom, found some chino pants, a tennis shirt, and tennis shoes and left the apartment. All the windows in the living room had been blown out. But the street lamp outside the entrance to the building was still on. When Marnin reached the front door and stepped outside, he looked at his watch for the first time. It was ten thirty-seven.

His neighbor and landlord, Mr. Hung, who lived in the downstairs apartment of the two story duplex, came running out, a pistol in his hand.

"What's happening? What's going on?" Hung asked in French.

"I don't know. I have no idea."

"Viet Cong?"

"I don't know. Probably."

"Those bastards! I've told my wife and children and the cook to hide under the beds and protect themselves from falling glass."

"Good idea."

Marnin went back to his apartment. The telephone was working. He did not dare turn on a light in a room that was now without a window. He managed fumblingly in the dark to dial the MACV compound. Cursing, he swore to himself that he would never in his life be without a handy flashlight again.

"MACV compound, Hue City, Sergeant Carter speaking, Sir!"

"This is Vice-Consul Marnin. What's happening, Sergeant?"

"Don't know anything yet, Sir!"

"You're not under attack?"

"Negative."

Marnin went downstairs and raced with long strides to the compound. When he got there, however, he discovered there was nothing in his pockets. Without the requisite military ID card the sentry at the gate would not let him pass. Luckily, an officer came by leading a squad that he was deploying in defensive positions around the perimeter. Marnin managed to convince him of his identity.

By that time everyone was following stipulated emergency procedures. Hue was so close to the border of North Viet Nam that an attack by a raiding party infiltrating from the sea was a possibility

American headquarters took seriously. It was a relief to see that the military knew where to go and what to do. Marnin wandered around, still in a daze, still with an awful ringing in his ears. Finally, he made his way to the office of Colonel Harrington, the short, bald artillery officer who was in charge of the advisory effort in this region of I Corps. There was nobody in his outer office so Marnin knocked and walked in. Harrington was on the autovon phone to MACV in Saigon.

". . .Yes, sir. The ARVN is handling it," he was saying, "there doesn't seem to be any reason for us to get involved. . .No, sir . . .No, sir, we're on full alert and will remain that way until we get the all clear from General Nghiem and from you."

He hung up the phone and peered at Marnin.

"Is that you, Marnin? I didn't recognize you. Welcome to Hue City," he said. "What the hell happened to you?"

"Nothing. I'm all right. There was a tremendous explosion near my apartment, two of them. What's going on?"

"You're bleeding like a stuck pig. Go over to the medics. They're playing pinochle waiting for something to do. How did you get cut up like that?"

"Flying glass from my windows. It was quite an explosion. Blew me right out of bed. What's happening?"

"There was some sort of demonstration by Buddhists or Cao Dai, one of the sects, in the square in front of the radio station. The crowd got a little out of hand. Or it may have been the VC."

"Anybody hurt?"

"Sounds to me like there were casualties, but they don't want to own up to them until they know for sure what happened. The Province Chief promised to call me back with a full debriefing. There's nothing to be done here. Get yourself looked at."

Marnin used Harrington's phone to call Freddie at home and told him that he was off to the doctor. Like Harrington, Loftus told him to take care of himself.

There were two doctors, three nurses, and three medics on duty in the infirmary with no patients to occupy them other than Marnin.

Once they established that there was nothing really wrong with him, they all had a fine time. They stood him buck naked in the middle of the examining room and, working three at a time, picked dozens of slivers of glass out of his body, painting each cut with iodine after each removal.

"Pick and paint, pick and paint," said Doctor Brandeis, the surgeon in charge, cheering on his team in high good humor. He was one of those short men who enjoyed taking the mickey out of the tall. "The only damage I can find was to the testicles," he said. "We may have to castrate."

"Very funny," Marnin replied.

They worked quickly and effectively and it was over in twenty minutes. Brandeis handed him a bottle of pills—aspirin mixed with codeine.

"Take one of these every four hours," he said. "And have some brandy when you get home."

"I'm all right. It doesn't hurt."

"It will," he said.

Marnin dressed and wandered through the front gate, this time with nobody paying any attention to him. Troops were lounging about smoking and chatting. The piling up of sandbags that had been in full train when he entered the compound had come to a halt. The excitement was evidently over. It was eleven twenty-five.

Marnin walked down Hung Vuong to the river and turned left on Le Loi and over to the square in front of the radio station, facing the radio tower. The smell of cordite lingered in the tropical air. There were huge craters in the road. The square was ringed by military trucks, all with their headlights on. It was bright as day. Soldiers were everywhere. Nobody was talking. The only sounds were the groans of the wounded. They had been gathered together, twenty to thirty of them, in the lower left hand corner of the square facing the river, waiting for the ambulances to cart them off one by one.

Hundreds of people were in the square—the men in khaki pants and white, short sleeved shirts, the women in colorful pastel *ao dais* chosen to celebrate the birthday of the Lord Buddha, many of them holding small children by the hand. Like Marnin, they all seemed to be wandering around aimlessly in a state of shock. Not far from where the wounded lay a circle of people had formed and were looking down at something on the ground. They were packed in so tightly that he could not at first see what it was.

Marnin edged up and peered over the crowd. Then he pushed through them and looked down. These were the dead, eight of them—six children and two adults, their bodies horribly mangled, arms, legs blasted off, faces obliterated, just flat masses of blood and bone. Only one corpse, that of a boy about eight years old, seemed fairly untouched. He was lying flat on his back, his face expressionless. Then Marnin realized that his head was not attached to his body. Someone had taken his head and placed it against his neck and had flattened out his body to make him look as whole and peaceful as possible.

Marnin thought for a second that he might throw up. He had to get out of there. He ran across the square to Hung Vuong and then back to his apartment. Mr. Hung was still outside the house, sitting on the steps, smoking a cigarette, the pistol held loosely in his left hand.

"What happened?" he asked. "I listen to the radio and they say nothing, just play music."

Marnin looked at him and tried to speak, but no words came. He shook his head from side to side. Tears were coursing down his face. He turned away, climbed the stairs, and walked slowly into his apartment. The front door was open. He had forgotten to lock it. He went into the bathroom, lathered his face, and shaved. Then he lathered and shaved again. He turned the shower on as hot as he could stand it and remained under it until the skin on his hands began to pucker.

He went to sleep on the bathroom floor—the child's severed head before his eyes, creasing his soul.

Chapter 23

"WHO KILLED THOSE PEOPLE?"

The sun streamed into Marnin's bedroom and the ringing in his ears was gone. During the night he had crawled into bed. Something in the room seemed different, but at first he could not identify what it was. Then he realized that there was no glass on any of the windows and the unfiltered morning light and the non-air conditioned morning air that he was breathing were not what he was accustomed to waking up to. The sunlight was reflected from broken shards on the floor and the air conditioner had been blown down and was resting on its face, leaning against the wall.

Marnin awakened feeling as though he were encased in broken eggshells. He was thankful for the pain pills that Brandeis had given him, which after a few minutes did the trick. He managed to get out of bed, do his ablutions, make a pot of coffee, get down some juice and dry cereal, and drag himself to the Consulate.

Freddie and Virginia Thomas, the attractive Consulate secretary, were both hard at work. The Consul had been on the phone and already been briefed by Colonel Harrington, Le Van Nghiem the Commanding General of the region, Nghia the Province Chief, and Major Dang Sy, the latter's deputy for security, who had been in charge of the troops in the square. On the basis of what he had learned Freddie had dictated an "immediate" cable which Virginia was typing.

"What was it?" David asked. "Do we know what happened? Who killed those people? Why?"

"The GVN big cheeses have concocted a cover story," Freddie

replied. "They insist the VC did the killing. But nobody can confirm that even one VC cadre was in the vicinity, much less a squad of soldiers or saboteurs."

"People were just wandering around in a daze when I got to the square," David said. "Nobody seemed to know what was going on."

"According to Nghia, by ten the crowd was getting more and more restless. They'd been in front of the radio station for over eight hours. Nobody seems to be able to explain what caused the damage from the first two explosions—artillery, concealed dynamite, satchel charges, who knows? But those were goddam big explosions."

"They sure were," David confirmed.

"Dang Sy was practically incoherent, babbling like a child, half the time talking Vietnamese to me as though I understood the language. Nghia and Nghiem said they had debriefed the ARVN non-coms and each of the troops who was in the square. They all tell pretty much the same story."

"What story?"

"As best I can make out," Freddie said, "Dang Sy panicked and shot off his pistol, which was the pre-arranged signal for his troops, who were mostly in their armored cars and shielded from the effects of the original blasts, to disperse the crowd. So they followed the procedures taught them. They fired their rifles in the air over the heads of the people—at least that's their story—and then let loose with their grenades and the rest, as they say, is history."

"What a tragedy!"

"Both Dang Sy and Nghia swear that those grenades were non-lethal. Tear gas would have been preferable, but none was available. They insist that these were MK III percussion grenades designed to scare people, not kill them."

"I heard them very clearly," David said. "I heard the rifles being fired and then I counted at least a dozen explosions, which must have been the grenades going off. They were much weaker than the first two. I thought they were further away, maybe across the river."

"Those bastards threw the grenades right into the crowd. Nghia admits that, right where a bunch of children had been playing. And they can say all they want that the grenades were non-lethal, but something sure packed a hell of a wallop. The press reports a dozen dead and more than thirty wounded, with twenty to thirty currently in the hospital. Nghia won't confirm. He says they're still counting."

"I saw about twenty to thirty people wounded and eight dead myself, six of them children," David said. "They were really mangled. It was horrible—severed arms and legs everywhere. One little boy had his head blown off."

Freddie looked at him.

"Are you all right? Maybe you ought to go home and take it easy."

"I'd rather stay here and work. I'll be okay."

"Suit yourself. I'm scheduled to see Dang Sy at nine and Ngo Dinh Can at noon. You're welcome to come along."

At that point Virginia buzzed to say Ambassador Corning was on the autovon line. Freddie picked up the green phone.

"Loftus here. . .Yes, sir. . . I'm just finishing up a cable now. You'll have it within twenty minutes. But the situation is pretty much what I reported in my call to the DCM. . .That's right. . .Unless they're going to make Dang Sy a scapegoat, and I wouldn't rule that out, the official line will be that the Viet Cong set off the explosions and were responsible for the killing. But nobody saw any VC. . .That's right. The Province Chief denies it. They all insist it was the first two explosions that did the real damage and that the grenades they threw into the crowd were non-lethal. . .No, not tear gas, MK III percussion grenades. . .Yes, clearly lots of casualties. . .No VC captured, no VC even sighted by anyone. . .That's confirmed. . .Marnin was in the square and personally saw eight corpses and thirty or so wounded. . . Yes. Horrible. . .The dead were children. . .No. No Americans involved. . . . Only one hurt was Marnin. Brandon's apartment is only a hundred yards from the square. The explosion blew out all the windows in his flat and he got cut by flying glass. . . . He's all right. A grim night, but he'll be OK. . .Yes, sir. . .Thank you, sir. I'll tell him."

"The Ambassador liked our cable on religious problems and Buddhist grievances," Freddie said after he hung up. "He got it in the morning take, said it was policy relevant, a model of what good Foreign Service reporting should be."

Freddie was obviously very happy about that, since the cable had been signed "LOFTUS." And, as the drafter, Marnin felt absurdly pleased as well.

Dang Sy was in terrible shape. A cocky little special forces Major, barely five feet tall, he had been through Fort Benning and was the very prototype of the American-trained "gung ho" ARVN officer. But having had no sleep and having been mercilessly chewed out all night by both Nghia, the Province Chief who was his boss, and Nghiem, the Commanding General of I Corps, he at that point gave literal meaning to the expression "nervous breakdown"—hands shaking, speech stutteringly incoherent, body sweating and moist eyes refusing to focus or meet anyone's gaze head on.

Dang Sy was still in the same sweaty uniform he had worn the previous evening. There were large bloodstains on both sleeves and on his chest—he had held one of the dead children in his arms. He could not sit still. He repeatedly jumped up, paced the room, sat down, and mumbled to himself in Vietnamese. . . .

"The rifles my men fired," he insisted again and again, "were over the heads of the crowd. They did not fire into it. Those MK III grenades could not kill anybody, not even a small child. They could have broken someone's eardrum. But they could never blow people apart."

Dang Sy desperately maintained that he was guiltless. He had done, he said, what any good officer would have done in similar circumstances. The damage, he kept insisting, was caused by the Viet Cong. His men were well trained, had been drilled on what to do in every contingency. His poor wife and his four poor children were going to suffer for something that was neither their fault nor his. He would never be a party to the killing of women and children. These were innocent people. Innocent.

"What's not clear to me," Freddie finally rejoined, "is why you felt it necessary to use your pistol when you knew that this was the signal for your men to fire their rifles and to throw their grenades."

"Yes, that is good point, Mr. Consul. That is the heart of the matter. If only I had not fired the pistol, I would not be bearing this burden. But my men and I had been in that square for nine hours. We hadn't eaten. We were tired. I was tired. Everybody was ready to go home, then all of a sudden, BOOM, BOOM. . ."

He had been pacing the room. He stopped, sat in his chair behind the desk in his cluttered office, picked up the photo of his wife and children that stood on the corner of the desk, got up, went to the window and looked out. He seemed to be reliving his moment of decision. His jaw went slack. Tears streamed from his eyes.

"BOOM, BOOM," Freddie finally said.

Dang Sy looked at Freddie without any comprehension. Then he made the connection. He gazed at them wildly, his eyes rolling, and put the photo of his wife and children back on the desk.

"BOOM, BOOM," Freddie said again.

"Yes. Explosions. Two explosions," Dang Sy said. "BOOM! Knock me down. Then BOOM once more, even bigger BOOM. Sounds to me like artillery. Too big sound for mortar. Must be Viet Cong attack."

"But why fire your pistol?"

"After those explosions, big explosions, everyone in the square knocked down. Hundreds of people yelling, groaning, screaming. If we are under attack, I want to know who is attacking us, from what direction field of fire is coming. I don't want people killed in crossfire. I want square cleared. I fire pistol to disperse the crowd, to get them out of harm's way. It was humanitarian gesture. I didn't want troops to throw grenades directly into the crowd. But even if they did, it should not have mattered much. Grenades were non-lethal. Nobody could be killed by those grenades."

Freddie looked at Mr. Buu skeptically, as if to determine whether another Vietnamese would believe such a story. Dang Sy saw this interplay and fell on his knees and grabbed Freddie's ankles.

"The Americans must believe me. I'm telling you the one hundred per cent truth. I swear it on my mother's grave. I swear it in name of Mary, holy mother of God. I didn't kill those people."

Freddie waited for Dang Sy to let go of his ankles. Then they got out of there as fast as they decently could.

"That was the most awful thing that's happened to me in my entire Foreign Service career," Freddie said when they were back in the car on the way to the Consulate. "When he had his hands around my ankles it literally made my flesh crawl."

"I think he really believes he's innocent of any wrongdoing," David said. "What do you think, Mr. Buu?"

"I think it is too bad he is a Catholic. Much better if he were Buddhist," said Mr. Buu.

"Do you think he was lying?" Freddie asked.

"No I don't," Buu said. "He believed what he was saying. But he is very nervous. Even hysterical. And what else could he say?"

"But you believe him?"

"Yes," Buu said, after a pause. "I do."

"But then what the hell happened last night?" Freddie asked Marnin.

"My guess is that somebody—it could have been the Dai Viet or the VNQDD or even the Viet Cong—planted those charges in the square on a timed fuse. They couldn't have figured in advance that a demonstration like that could last more than a couple of hours—certainly not more than eight hours. How could they know that a demonstration would still be going on late that night? I think those bombs were meant to explode in an empty square as a symbol of protest."

"That's ingenious," Freddie said. "But it's just a little too iffy. We've got to stick to the facts in our reporting."

Chapter 24

THE WARLORD

The sprawling family home in which Ngo Dinh Can lived alone with his aging mother was across the river, about a mile from the Citadel, and was built in the latter half of the nineteenth century. The villa, deceptively modest from the outside, was just two storeys tall and perhaps forty feet wide, without much of a garden. It turned out, however, to be enormously long, extending room after room on both sides of a dimly lit central hallway.

As they pulled up before the house, Marnin had to assume that the person waiting to greet them at the top of the stairs was a servant. But Mr. Buu told them it was Ngo Dinh Can himself. They got out of the car and climbed the steps. There was no security that one could detect.

From Can's reputation, Marnin was expecting to meet a sinister Vietnamese Fu Manchu figure. But of all the Ngo Dinh brothers, Can turned out to be the most self-effacing and soft spoken. He was also the most ascetic—famous for sleeping on the floor without a mattress, his head resting on a ceramic pillow, and for never appearing in public in anything other than traditional Vietnamese garb. The pleasures of the table obviously held no temptation for him. Unlike his brothers, he was cadaverously thin and stooped. Tall for a Vietnamese, about five foot six, he was dressed like a coolie in rope sandals, shiny black pants and a black jacket with a mandarin collar. He wore no wristwatch. Like all his brothers, he was a heavy smoker, lighting one Salem after another with a Zippo lighter, his chain smoking interrupted only by fits of deep wracking coughs.

Can greeted them with a thin, inquisitive smile on his face and shook hands, looking each man gravely in the eye as he did so, as if to gauge their intentions. Then he turned his back on them and had a coughing attack which lasted at least a full minute. Finally under control, he walked several paces down the veranda, gripped the wooden railing, hawked mightily, and spat into the bushes below. Acting as though nothing unusual had happened, Can ambled back over to them and spoke to Mr. Buu in Vietnamese, asking who he was, where he came from, how long he had been in Hue, and who his father and mother were. When Mr. Buu disgorged this information Can commented that he was well acquainted with two of Buu's uncles and one of his cousins, all of whom were in the grocery business in Danang. Only then did Can gesture for them to follow him into the house.

They were ushered into the third room on the right hand side of the dimly lit corridor that looked fifty yards long, and were seated in plush armchairs covered in solid navy blue slipcovers. The sparsely furnished room, like the house, was very long and narrow. It smelled musty from disuse. The walls were hung with Chinese scrolls of meticulously painted birds, monkeys and flowers. The room had only two windows, both half shuttered. It was so dark that it took a moment for Marnin to realize that another person was standing in the far corner, dressed in a Western business suit. Can beckoned him over and introduced him as Dr. Phat, the pathologist from the Central Hospital. Can spoke in Vietnamese, relying on Mr. Buu to translate.

"Dr. Phat was trained in Paris before the war," Can said, and then Buu translated his words into English. "He is an expert in his field, pathology and forensic medicine."

Can asked Buu to translate into French, if he could. Otherwise, Dr. Phat could do the translating. Can explained that while he could not speak French, he could understand it well enough, and it would save time for everyone, if the Americans had no objection, to stick to French and Vietnamese.

"Both Mr. Marnin and I are fluent in French," Freddie said. He added that he appreciated the opportunity of meeting Can, that he had wanted to get to know such an influential community leader ever since his arrival in Hue, but that he was sorry to do so under such tragic circumstances.

"It is a tragedy, indeed," Can said, "the worst thing that has happened to me in all my fifty-seven years in this city."

"These events must have been a great shock," Freddie said.

"Witnessing such slaughter, such gore and savagery, would be an ordeal for anyone," Can said, "even for a foreigner."

He pointed at Marnin. Can obviously was aware that Marnin had been in the square.

"But to you," he continued, "it was an abstraction. To me. . .I wept for the parents of those children. For I knew who they were, where they worked, who their own parents were. . ."

"It must have been a great shock," Freddie repeated.

"If I tell you that my life will never be the same again you will no doubt think I am prone to drama," Can replied. "But you would be wrong."

"I can well understand your distress," Freddie said. "As you undoubtedly understand, I have the responsibility of reporting on what happened here to my government in Washington. Even President Kennedy himself will want to be briefed on this tragic incident. But lots of things are not clear to us. And since you know so much about what goes on in Hue, I was hoping you could help me be as accurate as possible. What do you think happened? Who do you think was to blame? General Nghiem and Colonel Nghia claim the VC were responsible. But nobody seems to have seen any communists near the square."

"I have summoned you here because I have an urgent confidential message to deliver to Ambassador Corning."

"You can be assured of our absolute discretion."

Can looked at Buu questioningly.

"Perhaps it would be better, Mr. Buu, if you waited for us in the car," Freddie said.

Can said something to Buu in Vietnamese. Buu bowed his head and left the room.

"You will find Dr. Phat an excellent translator," Can said. "He speaks French and Vietnamese interchangeably. You ask what happened. You talk about blame. Blame? First of all I blame my brothers. Diem is at fault for being so indecisive, for letting my elder brother Thuc and my younger brother Nhu play their foolish games that are so inappropriate in Annam. Thuc is the guiltiest. He stupidly refuses to acknowledge the differences between us Annamese and the Tonkinese and the Cochinois. The Tonkinese is stubborn as a dog gnawing a thigh bone. The Cochinois is a peasant. If he gets hold of some money he becomes a merchant. He can always be bought. But the Annamese is subtle, sensitive, and proud, attuned to questions of right and wrong. He knows how to bend in the wind like the bamboo. But do him an injury and even if it takes fifty years he will avenge it.

"It is Thuc who made a Buddhist problem where no such problem existed before, who convinced Diem to give the Catholics preferential treatment in land redistribution, in relief and assistance, in commercial and export-import licenses and in government employment. It was Thuc who raised the flags. What difference does it make whether this group or that group flies a flag on a religious holiday? What harm does it do?"

Can paused to light a cigarette, then resumed.

"Every revolution that has ever taken place in my country has started right here, right where you're standing. When I first began to have some authority here in 1954, this entire region was ready to blow up at any time. For seven years I worked to pour oil on these troubled waters. By 1961 things were more quiet than they had been in the past century. Everything was under control.

"Then, all of a sudden the Vatican decides to send my brother Thuc here as Archbishop. My brother Diem asked me what I thought about it when this happened and I said to him that this was a happy day for my family, but a sad day for Hue. Because Thuc never understood that everything was in perfect balance here. This was not because the patient was healthy, but because he was in remission. The cancer could only be kept under control by regulating the fluids. Upset that delicate balance and the patient will die. Last night the balance was upset. And for no reason at all. The result is that we have lost moral authority in this region."

"So essentially you blame this tragedy on the Archbishop," Freddie said.

"If it were only Thuc we could easily have handled the problem. It is Nhu as well. He left this area as a very young man to study in France and has not been back to live here since. It is he who is encouraging Thuc to stir things up. It is he who wants to use the Can Lao Party as his instrument of control and sees all other forces, including myself, as an obstacle to his probing for greater and greater power. He cannot grasp that things have been in remission here precisely because we have managed to eliminate clandestine political parties. Revive them, make the Can Lao strong, and at the same time you'll be reviving the Dai Viet and the VNQDD that we went to so much trouble to be rid of in 1955 and 1956. You'll get Can Lao cells that will be like radishes—Can Lao red on the outside, but Dai Viet and VNQDD white on the inside."

"That's all very interesting," Freddie replied. "But how do you explain the events of yesterday evening?"

"All violent events have a deep cause and an immediate cause," Can said. "The deep cause of the First World War was the rot and the slime within European society. The immediate cause was the assassination of the Archduke at Sarajevo. We understand the deep causes of what took place last night, but the immediate causes are an enigma. The pond is still so full of mud that we cannot see to the bottom."

"Then you don't believe the Viet Cong were to blame?" Freddie asked. "Both General Nghiem and Colonel Nghia blame the communists."

"Somebody was to blame," Can said. "Maybe it was the Viet Cong. Who knows? One way of finding out who caused an event is to determine who benefited from it. Certainly the Viet Cong benefited from what happened last night. But the same can be said for the Buddhists, for the Dai Viet and the VNQDD, for the local Chinese and for all other enemies of the government of Ngo Dinh Diem. The people who did not benefit were those who support that government. And Major Dang Sy, whatever else he is, is a supporter. At three o'clock this morning I convened a meeting of all those responsible for the safety and security of the people in this area. The Province Chief

was there and the Government Delegate and the Commanding
General and a few others. We talked for two hours about what had
happened and tried to find an explanation. We agreed that Dang Sy
did not handle the situation perfectly, far from it, but was not basically to blame. Some thought the Communists were responsible, others
didn't—"

"What do you think?" Freddie asked. "Do you think the communists are to blame?"

"I don't know. I'm not sure. That's why I asked Dr. Phat to give me
a report. The doctor is an expert in forensic medicine. He is also a
Buddhist and their leadership knows him to be an honest man. Kindly
tell our American friends, my dear doctor, what you told me a few
minutes ago."

"It might first be worth pointing out," Phat said in a French tinged
with only the slightest of accents, "that I spent the Second World War
as a doctor fighting with Free French forces, largely in North Africa,
and was in charge of a field hospital there. So gunshot wounds, the
effects of high explosives, of shrapnel, of bombs, on human flesh and
bone are very familiar to me. Last night I was in charge of the team
that carried out autopsies on the six children and two adults who were
killed in front of the radio station. In all my experience I have never
seen such wounds. The force of the explosions literally tore the victims
apart."

"If I understand you correctly," Freddie said, "you're making the
case that Dang Sy's troops could not have inflicted the kinds of
wounds that you examined."

"That is correct. Dang Sy's men were armed exclusively with M-1
automatic rifles and MK III percussion grenades. None of the dead or
injured suffered gunshot wounds. Nor could percussion grenades have
inflicted this kind of damage. Even ordinary hand grenades would not
have been capable of causing such wounds. These were blast injuries,
blasts so powerful that they shattered bones into hundreds of frag-
ments. I am not familiar with explosives that could have caused such
injuries."

"What do you conclude from that, doctor?"

"This must have been some sort of new and more powerful plastique with which I have no previous acquaintance."

"It could have been developed by the communists," Freddie said.

"Or the Americans," Can added.

"The Americans?"

"That's right. A certain American military man, a Captain Scott, was seen walking around the square earlier in the evening observing the demonstration. People thought it strange that he should be there."

"It's more than strange," Freddie said. "It's preposterous. Why would any American want to blow up a group of Vietnamese Buddhists?"

"There are many Americans who are against my brother Diem. The attempted coup in November 1960 was arranged with American backing. When it took place, the American Ambassador Durbrow said he was adopting a neutral position about it. Why should one be neutral about a coup against an ally? There are many Americans who want to stir up opposition to Diem, who want to destroy my family."

"There are many more Vietnamese than Americans who'd be likely to do a thing like that," Freddie said.

"Yes. But those Vietnamese don't have access to new and sophisticated kinds of explosives."

"The communists do."

"Yes. That's true," Can said, with a faint smile at the corner of his mouth. His body was suddenly wracked by deep, wheezing coughs. He extinguished his Salem, took a handkerchief from his pocket, spat into it, and then gazed at the results. "True," he finally continued, "if one can believe the evidence of Dr. Phat, then it was either the Communists or the Americans. In neither case can this country derive much satisfaction. I am a very unsophisticated man and do not have the wit or the understanding to deal with foreigners. But I had to see you today in order to give you two messages that go directly from me to Ambassador Corning. No Vietnamese other than Dr. Phat will know of this. First of all, find out about Captain Scott. . ."

"We will. You can be assured of that."

"Second. This situation is extremely serious. If it is mishandled, everything that you Americans have worked for in this country and all the considerable achievements of this government will be put at risk.

The only way to deal with it is to mollify the Buddhists, to give in to whatever demands they make, just or unjust. My brother Thuc is blind on the issue of religion. My brother Nhu and his wife believe that whatever happens the President should always be what they call strong. They will urge Diem to admit nothing, never to back down, to use force if necessary to keep the Buddhists in line. Such a policy will lead to disaster. But on a matter like this no Vietnamese will be able to convince the President that Nhu and Thuc are wrong. I will try, but I will fail. He no longer listens to me. The President will listen to only one outsider, Ambassador Corning. If Corning fails to convince him, we will all be ruined. Ruined. This is my message."

Two days after the massacre more than twenty thousand people gathered outside the Tu Dam pagoda. (The Hue authorities, wishfully hoping to tamp down the fire that was to come, announced only ten thousand, the figure dutifully reported in the local press.) They were there to vent their wrath on Dang Sy, on the local power elite, on the Catholic Church, and on the government in Saigon. Marnin observed the scene with Mr. Buu at his side giving him a running translation of what was being said. Numerous banners were displayed—"Kill Us, We are Ready to Sacrifice our Blood;" "Buddhists and Catholics are equal;" "Cancel Decree Number 10 of August 6, 1950;" "The Buddhist Flag Will Never Come Down." After the opening sermons by two monks who stressed the non-violent nature of the teachings of Buddha, Thich Tri Binh mounted the platform. There was an expectant hush. Tri Binh kept the message straight and simple.

". . .Innocent people have been killed. Little children have had their heads blown off. There were thousands of witnesses to what happened in that square. All of them saw the troops under the command of Catholic Major Dang Sy fire their rifles and throw their grenades at our women and children. The government says that the Viet Cong was to blame. But can we believe it? We know the Viet Cong. We know their faces. They are our own brothers and fathers and cousins. The VC, whatever one has to say about them, and as you all know I am no friend of the VC, is not in the business of killing innocent

Buddhist children. They want our support. Will we support them if they kill our babies?

"Then if the Viet Cong are not to blame, what horned devil is responsible for those murders? To answer that we must first understand whose cause is helped by what took place in that square on the night of May 8. Only three people stood to gain. Who were these horned devils? The first horned devil is the Emperor Ngo Dinh Diem himself. Those children died in order to show the Buddhist enemy that the Catholic Emperor Ngo Dinh Diem, the first ruler in all Vietnamese history who does not pay tribute to the Divine Buddha, is not to be trifled with. The monkey will only dare to wipe his ass after sundown, when the nuns in the temple cannot be sure whether he is pulling his pudding or scratching his scrotum.

"The second horned devil is Ngo Dinh Nhu. In everything he does he wants to show these foreigners that his new strength is equal to theirs. And what gives more strength than spilling the blood of children on the squares of our city? What did the French do in 1946 in order to hold onto their lucrative colony of Viet Nam? They shelled Haiphong with the big guns of their ships and killed six thousand of our brothers and sisters and maimed and crippled ten thousand more. And what do the Americans who put "In God We Trust" on their coins do in what they tell us is the struggle for peace and religion? They shoot our water buffalo and blow up our women and babies.

"The third horned devil is Ngo Dinh Thuc, the fat man, who glides around our city in his Buick Roadmaster. What does Thuc say to us? He says leave the vineyards of the Lord Buddha and I will use my influence with the Emperor to get you loans from government agencies, to get you cushy jobs in the civil service, to get your son declared unfit for military service. He can do this because his kid brother, the Catholic Emperor Ngo Dinh Diem, has been popped on the throne by the Catholic Cardinal Spellman and the Catholic President Kennedy.

"It is for these three monkey banshees that our little babes were slaughtered in the square before the radio station. And why? Is it because their parents chose to follow the eightfold path of the great Lord Buddha? Is it because our country has been seized by these three monkey kings who came from the same unfortunate womb? Can we, who call ourselves men, who call ourselves Vietnamese, who call ourselves believers in the glory of the Lord Buddha, allow ourselves to be swindled by these three horned devils in such a manner?"

Each day for the week that followed Marnin witnessed a rally of between twenty and twenty-five thousand people, during which Thich Tri Binh roused the crowd with his anti-government tirades. Each day the contingent of police at the back of the crowd grew in number. They listened, very noticeable in their uniforms and their blue riot helmets, but did nothing. So each day Tri Binh jacked his rhetoric and his insults to the Ngo Dinh clan one notch higher. But while Binh repeatedly attacked Ngo Dinh Can's three brothers, he never mentioned Can.

None of this was reported in the press. But the monks of the Tu Dam pagoda and of the Xa Loi pagoda in Saigon used their mimeograph machines to print copies of Binh's speeches, which they handed out to passers-by on the busiest corners of the busiest streets in all the cities of South Viet Nam. Another handout was a list of their grievances, which they boiled down to what they called "The Five Demands."

1) Permit the Buddhist flag to fly on Buddha's birthday.
2) Equalize the treatment between Buddhism and Catholicism.
3) Stop the arbitrary arrests and intimidation of Buddhists.
4) Indemnify the families of those killed on May 8.
5) Punish the officials responsible for the murders.

Each day Freddie and Marnin met at the Consulate at mid-morning, compared notes, got a summary of the local press and some of the local gossip from Mr. Buu, and then Marnin wrote a "sitrep" describing the ever increasing tension in the city.

Hue was moving toward a showdown, and his days were exciting. But the more exciting the days, the more lonesome the nights. He missed Lily fiercely. They could not even talk on the phone, because inter-city calls were known to be monitored and Lily would take no chances. In Hue, moreover, there were no distractions. Unlike Saigon, Hue was a dead city after dark. The demonstrations made it even deader. After ten, the river traffic stopped and the only vehicles on the streets were the regular patrols of the security forces of Colonel Nghia in their white Jeeps.

It was then that he sat on his veranda nursing a gin and tonic, thinking about the sensual nights with Lily and worrying about his future in the Foreign Service. Had he been cleared of all charges? Or was he still under suspicion? Was he now so tainted that, however false the accusations against him, his career was hopelessly compromised?

It was therefore with a sense of vast relief that Marnin heard from Loftus when he arrived at work on the 17th of May that the Ambassador had telephoned to say that he was being recalled to Saigon and should report there as soon as possible.

He arrived at the Embassy at nine the next morning, fresh from Lily's bed, and found Corning hunched over a Sam Sabo cable on the Buddhist crisis. Corning looked up and smiled at Marnin distractedly, not wanting to lose his flow of thought. But then he remembered something he wanted to add to the message.

"Ngo Dinh Can did say unambiguously that he blamed his three brothers for the Buddhist problem in the north, didn't he?"

"He said he needed your help because, for one reason or another, his brothers were ranged against him and you were the only person in this country with enough clout to stand up against all three of them."

Nodding, Corning went back to Sabo's cable, wrote several more sentences in the margin, and handed it to Marnin to give to Helen Eng for retyping. When Marnin reentered the room Corning asked him to shut the door and sit down.

"I'm very happy to say," he said, "that something has happened which made it unnecessary to continue the investigation into that. . . document."

"What was it?"

"It's not something I can talk about."

"But it. . ."

"Some day you'll have an answer to your more than understandable curiosity. But there's nothing further I can say at this point. You'll just have to live with that."

Switching the subject, Corning said he was hoping to go off on leave the following week. The tickets had already been purchased for a cruise of the Greek islands. Patty Lou was insisting on it and so was the Embassy doctor. This was not to be nosed about, but he had a slight blood pressure problem and the doctor felt that a brief respite was in order.

"Sam Sabo and I talked this matter over. We agreed that during my absence you'd be transferred to the Political Section to work on the Buddhist problem. We haven't had anyone in the Political Section exclusively concerned with Buddhism and you've made a fine beginning on the subject in Hue."

"Wonderful," David replied. "I couldn't be more pleased."

Chapter 26

A DÉMARCHE

Since the Buddhist crisis was to be the main subject of the démarche, Marnin accompanied the Ambassador the next afternoon to call on Diem. It took place, as usual, in the corner office on the second floor of Independence Palace. As before, Dinh Trieu Da was Diem's note taker, but took no notes, while for two hours Marnin got writer's cramp in his effort to capture every word exchanged between them. Diem, knowing that Corning had a health problem and was about to go off on leave and that this would be the last audience before his return, was overflowing with courtesy.

"My dear Gus," he said, leading them over to a corner window with a broad, sweeping view of the presidential gardens, "I am delighted that you are taking the opportunity to have some leave. We all need it. I try to do it myself, try to follow the example of the Holy Father and go on retreat at least twice a year. But this office is too much of a burden. My subordinates, they seem to have difficulty even going to the WC without permission of their President."

They both laughed heartily.

"In all seriousness, I'm delighted that you and Patty Lou are getting the vacation you both deserve, both for your own sake and because it shows that you're not overestimating the importance of this Buddhist thing."

"As a matter of fact, Mr. President," Corning said, "I have instructions from the Department to raise with you a few concerns we have about the matter. And for that reason I've brought along Mr.

Marnin, whom I've assigned the responsibility of being the Embassy's Buddhist man, so to speak—the officer charged with following this difficult question."

"I am delighted," Diem said, "that Mr. Marnin is being given such important responsibilities. I was afraid that his tour in Viet Nam was not going to turn out to be a happy one. But he undoubtedly learned a great deal about Buddhism during his time in Hue."

Corning gave Marnin a knowing look.

"There is obviously not much that goes on in this country," he said, "that the President isn't aware of."

Diem gestured in a self-effacing manner. Corning paused and shifted gears.

"Mr. President, I had hoped that this, perhaps our last chat together before my vacation, would be altogether in the nature of a courtesy call. Unfortunately, this is a luxury that life doesn't allow us."

"The Good Lord," said Diem, "moves in mysterious ways. We can no more fathom his aims and purposes than my cat can understand the reasons for my actions. I have a wonderfully intelligent cat, Mr. Ambassador. It is black with a white ruff and white paws and we call it—I think the word in English is Mittens. That cat, Mittens, observes me for hours on end. When I am working at my desk it sits and watches what I'm doing and tries to figure it out. But it cannot. It is a cat. In the same way you and I attempt to understand the meaning and purpose of the Good Lord. And we have as much chance of fathoming his grand design as my cat Mittens does of understanding why I sit for hours hunched over my desk without moving, scratching away at a piece of paper with my pen."

"Indeed," Corning replied, "the events in Hue were difficult to grasp. I have here a cable from USIA summarizing how the deaths there in front of the radio station have been treated by the American press. . ."

Corning handed Diem the cable. Diem passed it on to Da without looking at it.

"I have not seen any of the other American newspapers," Diem responded. "But I have read the stories in the *New York Times* that my embassy has cabled to me from Washington. There is not a single sentence in them that does not contain at least one flagrant lie about what happened."

"I trust I won't be revealing state secrets when I tell you, Mr. President, that I don't disagree. These articles have been entirely unfair to you."

"My government does not persecute Buddhists. My government obeys the law. To say otherwise is a slander. To say that we favor the Catholics over the Buddhists has not the slightest basis in fact. Anyone reading the *New York Times* would think that Catholic troops massacred innocent Buddhists engaged in prayer. Eight people were killed and only five of them were Buddhists."

"Mr. President, the point is that the so-called Buddhist 'five demands,' publicized so widely in my country, have been accepted in our press and by many in our Congress as entirely reasonable."

"Requests are one thing," Diem said. "I can deal with requests. But demands are quite another. Now there are five demands. But if we give in to them, soon there will be a sixth. And after that there'll be a seventh demand and then an eighth. There is only one question that need be answered about the events in Hue. Were my people guilty of illegal behavior? If so, then they should be punished according to the law. But if they were just carrying out their duties as prescribed by the law, if they were placed in an unfortunate position by *agents provocateurs*, and if I throw them to the wolves in order to placate a mob, what will forces of law and order do the next time the Viet Cong organizes demonstrations in their areas?"

"Your point is well taken, Mr. President," Corning replied. "Nevertheless, my government thinks this question must be settled. The aid we are giving your country is substantial, greater than to any other nation. But this aid has to be approved by Congress. That's the democratic way. And if congressional leaders are led to believe that our aid is being used to persecute and oppress a religious minority, then their enthusiasm for making such appropriations will diminish markedly."

"Send your Congressmen here. They will see for themselves that this is a big storm in a teapot."

"We fully understand the difficulties," Corning said. "I've made that as clear to my government as I know how. The main thing, as far as Washington is concerned, is to put to rest the allegations that you're discriminating against a religious minority. Questions of race and religion are particularly sensitive at this time in the United States. The support of our government for any nation that engages in questionable practices in this sensitive area has domestic ramifications that have to be taken into account."

"What is it you want me to do?"

"The so-called 'five demands' of the Buddhist clergy strike Washington as reasonable. Whether they are sincere or not is another question. But if you could adhere to those 'five demands,' in our view the so-called Buddhist crisis would soon be behind us."

"So. To me it is very interesting that Washington has become so expert on our religions. I spent many years in America and found very few of your countrymen there who had even a vague idea of where my country was located. It is surprising that in the short time since I left you've developed such expertise on Viet Nam in your government. Mr. Marnin is now your expert on Buddhism in this country. What is your opinion, Mr. Marnin? If I tomorrow morning call in Thich Tri Binh, that scoundrel, and said to him, Binh my friend, you were right and my people were wrong. I will therefore accede to your 'five demands'. Would that solve the problem for me?"

Marnin looked to Corning for guidance, but the Ambassador's eyes were firmly fixed on Diem.

"Well," Marnin began, "that's hard for me to say, Mr. President—"

"It's impossible for any of us to say," interrupted Corning. "The question that has to be answered in Washington, Mr. President, is what you can do to relieve the pressure emanating from this entirely extraneous question so that we can get on with the business of winning this war. My government feels that you must do something so that we can get on with our main tasks, which have otherwise been going so well lately. After all, we're winning the war. We don't want that obscured."

"The so-called 'five demands,'" Diem rejoined, "merely restate what has always been the policy of my government—equality before the law and non-discrimination for all religions. It's true that currently Buddhism is classified as a sect under our laws. But this was a holdover from the days of the French. It is an anomaly. But I can guarantee that this inheritance from the days of French colonialism will be taken care of at the next meeting of the Assembly."

"That's good. Corning said. "That's certainly moving in the right direction."

"I'll be meeting with key Buddhist leaders tomorrow and will make this all very clear to them. And I will also explain that I cannot accept one of the five demands—that I punish those responsible for the killing in Hue—until that incident is thoroughly investigated. If Major Dang Sy is guilty, he'll be dealt with severely. If not, he'll be free to go about his business like any other citizen."

"That sounds reasonable to me," Corning said.

"This is just a mountain in a molehill," Diem said. "I will take care of it. You have a good holiday, Gus, and free your mind of worries about Buddhism. Mister Marnin and I will take care of that question. On the other hand, there is one problem that I want you to raise with Washington. It is the question of advisors. Since the beginning of this year they are getting out of control. How many are there? Ten thousand? Twelve thousand? Fourteen thousand? None of my people can give me an answer. Hundreds come in every day. They have no passports or visas, just Military Identity Cards. We cannot keep track of them. They misbehave in a way that is intolerable."

"Misbehave? I can assure you, Mr. President, we won't tolerate any wrongdoing on the part of a single American in this country. Americans who misbehave will be out of here on the next plane."

"I have reports of hundreds of examples. Hundreds."

He snapped his fingers and asked Da to bring him one of the folders piled neatly on his desk. Opening it, he put on a pair of black rimmed glasses and began to thumb through it.

"Here is a case I was reading just this morning. It took place in Phu Bai the day before yesterday at the opening ceremony of a new strategic hamlet. The local American Sergeant, a Sergeant mind you, the liaison with the local Popular Forces, was giving out piglets to each of the newly resettled peasants—"

"Is there anything wrong with that?" Corning asked.

"Giving us pigs is fine. We have to learn the modern way to raise livestock. But when your Sergeant gave out those pigs he said to each of the peasants that these animals came from Washington and that if my government should try to seize those pigs he would not let this happen. This American Sergeant would make sure that our peasants weren't robbed by their own government."

"He said that?"

"He said that and more. And with the Province Chief standing there. I have spent my life dedicated to freeing my countrymen from the French colonialist yoke. I do not intend to see a French yoke replaced by an American one."

"But this is just an aberration, a Sergeant who mistakes his own authority. I'll have him transferred immediately if that's what you want. Surely you don't see this as a serious problem!"

"On the contrary, my dear Gus, it is a matter so serious that the existence of my government depends on it. The problem boils down to who exactly runs this country, the Americans or the Vietnamese. I value your help and your training and most of the efforts of your subordinates. But you have to understand first and foremost that when it comes to judging the needs of my people, I am perhaps in a better position than Washington is to make that determination. My government is based on the proposition that the Vietnamese are capable of ruling themselves."

"But there's a war to be won out there. We're not facing a normal situation."

"That is correct. Hundreds of Communists, maybe thousands, infiltrate our country every month. To fight this we need a bigger army, not more advisors, and first class equipment, not your hand-me-downs. This was what you promised to give us in Honolulu a year ago. Instead, you send us your second rate equipment and advisors, thousands of them, so many we cannot keep track of them."

"Your military are very grateful for our efforts."

"Sergeants of one army can tell Sergeants of another army the best way to shoot a bazooka. They cannot tell our peasants what to do with their pigs. You have altogether too many advisers in this country. You ought to scale them back. Add three divisions to the ARVN and give us the infrastructure to support them, and cut the number of your advisors in Viet Nam in half—that's my advice to you."

The Ambassador leaned forward, his head over the lacquer table, not two feet from Diem's.

"Mr. President, let me speak very frankly to you and entirely off the record, as one friend to another."

He looked at Marnin sharply to indicate that he wanted note taking to stop at that point.

"Your message about the Buddhist problem is a very good one and will give me ammunition to demonstrate that your government is politically sensitive to what could be, if we don't watch out, a major international political problem. But what you're telling me about our advisors is not going to be received happily on either side of the Potomac, especially by those who are doing their best to see you get the support you deserve. The advisors we're sending have been carefully screened and are the best people we have available. It's true some of them aren't as sensitive as they could be to the local political scene. And it's up to us to work together to figure out ways to heighten their sensitivity. But for me to go back to Washington to say that you want us to cut our advisory effort in half would send up all sorts of alarm bells that would impinge unfavorably on many of the programs that you cherish most."

"Gus, my friend, your implied threats sadden me. On this matter, believe me, I know what I'm talking about. It is much more serious than you think. But we don't have to resolve this today and I don't want to spoil your nice holiday. Let us put this, how do you say, on the back burner until you return. In the meanwhile, with Mr. Marnin in charge of the Buddhist question in your Embassy I think we will soon bury that particular problem and this will enable us to return once more to the far more difficult question of how to win this war."

"Mr. President, what you're saying is music to my ears. Speaking frankly, I was so concerned about the current situation here that I was not at all sure it would be wise for me to leave."

"It is not only you yourself that you must think about, but Patty Lou as well. The same tensions you feel, she feels with the greater empathy of a woman. You owe her a holiday."

"Well, Mr. President, I'm going to repeat those very words to her on our way to dinner this evening. And I can assure you that they're going to make her a happy woman."

The dark portents on the horizon were nothing novel in Viet Nam, where the question was always not whether the United States was skating on thin ice, but rather how thin the ice actually was. Corning thus went ahead with his vacation plans. On the day of his departure he called Marnin into his office.

"There's one last thing I'd like you to do for me." He pointed to his in-box marked "personal," that had about a foot of file folders in it. "Please go through this stuff and file it back in the top drawer of my safe. I meant to do it myself, but didn't have time. All of it is for your eyes only. I don't want anyone else to have access to it."

"Yes, sir."

It was Marnin's last task for Corning before moving down to the political section. In the course of it he discovered in the back of that safe drawer a manila folder with his name on it. On the front of it, stamped in red ink, was a notation that this folder contained "PENUMBRA" material, a code word he did not have access to, in fact had never heard of before. Marnin knew he had no business reading documents with a codeword designator to which he was not supposed to be privy. But surely Corning could not have forgotten that the Marnin folder was one of the files in the top drawer of the safe he had told him to put in order.

On the other hand, Corning had been enormously busy in those six days before his departure. It could have slipped his mind. In the end, it was a temptation Marnin could not resist. Late the following Wednesday night, after a hiatus of three days, when everybody in the front office, including Bilder, had packed up and gone, he got out that file folder, lit a cigarette, and began to read.

Chapter 27

AN ANONYMOUS TIP

The David Marnin folder contained documents fastened at the top on both the left hand and the right hand sides by two-hole metal clips. It was the same folder he had seen Franco, with a smirk on his face, carry into his office less than two months before, but much augmented. On the right, on top of the pile was Franco's report which concluded that there was almost no likelihood that Marnin was innocent of leaking Mecklin's dispatch. Underneath Franco's report were affidavits from those in the Saigon Mission who had access to Mecklin's dispatch as well as follow-up interviews with others outside of Viet Nam who had been contacted further by SY. Without exception, all those questioned who remembered Mecklin's dispatch (several secretaries had no such recollection) denied showing it to Mandelbrot or anyone else not authorized to see classified material.

Underneath the reports of these interviews were a series of subsequent Naval Investigative Service (NIS) interrogations (Marnin had no idea how the Navy became involved) of people outside the Department who were not available to Franco in Saigon but whom he had specifically fingered for further questioning, including one with Lieutenant Colonel John Henry Mudd. This took place in the "skiff" at Fort McNair in Southeast Washington, where Mudd was a student at the Armed Forces Staff College.

Happily for Marnin, Mudd adamantly denied to the NIS that he had any knowledge of Mecklin's dispatch or that he had at any time passed classified material to anyone. As the report of Mudd's interrogation put it, in its military investigative prose: "Subject used foul and unseemly language in asseverating non-knowledge of said document."

Thus, the papers on the right side of the folder underneath his report in no way backed up Franco and neither did the definitive documents on the left hand side of the folder. These were filed underneath a separate white cover sheet that had "Classified" written in large red letters diagonally across it. On the cover sheet, in its lower left hand corner, stamped in purple ink, was a notation that the documents "contained hereunder include PENUMBRA materials. Nobody uncleared for PENUMBRA is to have access to these documents." Beneath the cover sheet was a white paper which all those who read any part of the PENUMBRA file were supposed to sign and date. The only two names to appear on that sheet were Markoff's and Corning's.

The PENUMBRA materials turned out to be transcripts of telephone conversations. It was not clear who exactly was being tapped, since the identities of the callers were hidden by the use of special code words. There were about a dozen such documents, half of them, the most revealing ones, between "Athos," an American newspaperman, and "Porthos," an Embassy Vietnamese language officer whom Marnin guessed to be Chick Rizzo. The most significant of them, the last document in the folder, was the transcript of a phone call made on April 25, just before Marnin's departure for Hue, from the Embassy officer to the newsman.

"ATHOS: Hello.

PORTHOS: Is that you, [Athos]? This is [Porthos].

ATHOS: How are you, pal?

PORTHOS: I'm no pal of yours, you asshole. I just heard the news. How could you do it?

ATHOS: What are you talking about?

PORTHOS: You know fucking well what I'm talking about. When I passed that stuff on to you, it was with the agreement that you could use it for your own purposes, but that you'd keep it to yourself. (This latter sentence was underlined heavily, and side barred as well, in Corning's violet ink.) It didn't mean you could pass it to the whole

Saigon press corps or flash it in restaurants to other Embassy officers, especially, for God's sake, the Ambassador's aide!

ATHOS: I guess I had too much to drink. We'd been at it all afternoon. Sorry about that. I admit that it was unfortunate.

PORTHOS: Unfortunate doesn't do it, pal. You got that poor bastard fired, and I don't feel too good about it. They're shipping him off to Hue in disgrace. (Heavily underlined in violet ink with triple exclamation points in the margin.) And all because you couldn't handle your liquor.

ATHOS: I tell you I'm really sorry. But there's no way I can change it. He's a friend of mine too, a good friend.

PORTHOS: With friends like you, as the saying goes, who needs enemies?"

ATHOS: I know you're pissed off and I deserve it, but. . ."

Marnin did not bother to finish reading the document. He closed the folder and put it in the back of the top drawer of Corning's safe. He wondered again whether Corning had wanted him to see it. This was irrefutable proof of his innocence, but proof that was both unmentionable and legally inadmissible. Even in those pre-Watergate days an American Ambassador who cooperated in the wiretapping of a *New York Times* reporter would be in major trouble.

Marnin showed up at Lily's that evening with a dozen roses in his left hand and a bottle of Dom Perignon in his right. He was in high spirits as he recounted for her the gist of the exchange between Corning and Diem. His imitation of the language and style of both men made her laugh till her sides ached.

"It's not that funny," David finally said, interrupting himself.

"I'm not just laughing at your imitation of Diem and of Corning too, though it is very good. I am laughing principally at the idea that you are now the American expert on Vietnamese Buddhism. This is not a subject anybody can acquire overnight. Both Viet Nam itself and Buddhism itself, much less a combination of the two, require years of study before they can be absorbed. And here the American Embassy, on whose decisions we depend literally for life and death, turns this matter over in the midst of a crisis to its most junior officer, someone who himself admits that he knew absolutely nothing about this country before his arrival here just months ago."

"I have you to guide me," Marnin replied.

And indeed in the months ahead Lily, whose political shrewdness was apparent in everything she said about the local situation, proved to be Marnin's most valuable tutor as he tried to decipher the Vietnamese/Buddhist puzzle. But that night his interest was in far more than instruction on the religions of Viet Nam. He was not disappointed.

At the office his immediate task was to penetrate the Vietnamese Buddhist community, something no embassy officer had previously bothered to do, largely because there had been no political need to do so. This turned out to be a simple enough task.

Every morning Marnin showed up at the Xa Loi pagoda, where he was taken in hand by one of the four or five English or French speaking young monks detailed to deal with foreigners. These saffron-robed "media manipulators" received scores of visitors—diplomats, newspapermen, even scholars specializing in Buddhist or Vietnamese affairs—during the course of a day. The pagoda itself was a madhouse—surreal in the half light, redolent with the smell of incense. There was activity everywhere and a great cacophony of sound—the swishing of the bonzes' robes as they hurried to and fro, the bronze bells booming and the wind chimes tinkling—this Eastern music mixing with the clack of Xa Loi's bank of manual typewriters and the hum of its four mimeograph machines.

As the acknowledged Buddhist man at the Embassy (several CIA operatives, under various cover stories, were also by this time pounding the pagoda beat) Marnin was treated as something of a V.I.P. and given private daily briefings as well as voluminous, and increasingly polished, mimeographed handouts. Afterward Marnin went back to the Embassy and wrote down his morning notes, passing on any particularly juicy morsels to Sam Sabo or Stu Markoff. He then composed the daily Buddhist Crisis "sitrep."

Having done his duty, he subsequently lunched at the Attarbea Restaurant with various dissident Buddhist politicians, picking up the check, for which he was reimbursed by the "representation" funds doled out to the Embassy Political Section. Many in Saigon at that point, both Vietnamese and foreigners, were accusing Diem of running a police state. And yet one mark of the police state, as Marnin was to learn during two subsequent tours in Moscow, is the citizen's reluctance to criticize his rulers. A good example of how this did not apply in Saigon was his weekly lunch with Senator Vu Ming Mau, who openly claimed that he would be the Buddhist candidate for President once (not "if") Diem was toppled. Mau, a wizened little man who could not have weighed more than ninety pounds, pointed out repeatedly that he had finished higher than the President in both mathematics and French for three years running when they had been in the same Middle School class in Hue. Mau derived from this that he, rather than Diem, should be President of South Viet Nam.

Marnin also lunched regularly with the younger radical Buddhist leaders, including Thich Tri Binh, at a vegetarian restaurant on Le Van Duyet. Mau, whose French was indeed bi-lingual, and whose Gallic logic made some sort of vague sense, at least had the virtue of being easy to understand. But the philosophical vaporings of the radical Buddhist leadership were not. On two separate occasions, Binh, who had moved to Saigon and was camped in the Xa Loi pagoda along with thirty to forty other radical monks from all over Viet Nam, assured Marnin in his elliptical manner that the finest astrologers in Hue had predicted Diem would fall that very year because the stars revealed that it was exactly twenty years since his last orgasm—the product of a wet dream.

Binh was an extremely opaque luncheon companion to someone who felt obliged to go back to the Embassy and write up a memorandum of their conversation afterward. In putting them on paper, Marnin could not help but make Binh's comments more logical than they actually were. Binh's French was not good and his English was non-existent. Taking Marnin by surprise, Binh also turned out to be an avid girl watcher. He did not restrain from interrupting himself in mid-sentence to gaze hungrily, simultaneously picking at his teeth with an ivory toothpick, every time a beautiful mademoiselle on a bicycle rode by—which in Saigon was roughly every thirty seconds.

Despite Binh's lack of coherence, he was a master of the unforgettable off beat phrase, especially when his stream of invective was aimed at Ngo Dinh Diem. And whenever he used a striking expression, within a day or two Marnin was certain to read or hear the same phrase from Mandelbrot, sometimes in context, sometimes not. It was eerie how much they echoed each other. Marnin could never figure out whether Mandelbrot was using the Buddhists, whether they were using him, or whether they were in a state of sublime symbiosis, not knowing where one stopped and the other began.

Marnin was fortunate at that point to begin lunching with Diem's cousin and private secretary Dinh Trieu Da, who was a brilliant sounding board. Da was of course contemptuous of the Buddhists and viewed them as totally irrational. In contrast, he was the ultimate rationalist with the coolest intelligence Marnin had ever come across. Nobody could convey better than he the enormous frustration the Palace felt in trying to come to grips with this enigmatic Buddhist phenomenon. As soon as Diem and Nhu thought they had it stifled within their grasp, it popped in the air like a gigantic soap bubble.

But Marnin's best interpreter of Viet Nam remained Lily. Lying in bed, chuckling to herself, she listened to descriptions of Marnin's various encounters with the bonzes and scornfully analyzed for him what was really happening and why they dissembled in everything they did. In Lily's upper class circle, if you had a religion, then you were a Catholic. And to be secure in that circle it had to have been at least your paternal grandfather who was the first to convert. In fact, much of the legitimacy of Ngo Dinh Diem in their eyes stemmed from his ancestors having been Catholics for six generations. (Later on, nothing marked Nguyen Van Thieu as an arriviste more than his sudden conversion to Catholicism in his forties.)

In Lily's eyes and in those of her friends Buddhism was only practiced by the illiterate, the superstitious, and the uneducated. The shaved heads and the often smelly saffron robes of the Buddhist bonzes, so exotic and striking to the Western newspapermen, were physically repugnant to her. The idea propounded in the American press that these bonzes were not free to practice their beliefs, and that other Vietnamese were indignant about such discrimination, was a joke—further evidence of the *naiveté*, ignorance, and stupidity of the Americans.

"I don't know how we put up with you people," she would say to Marnin in one of her serious moods. "You think you are the leaders of the world, but you are dumb beyond anyone's belief. How can you take what Thich Tri Binh has to say seriously? That man is a clown, a charlatan, a scoundrel. He is as much a holy man as your Bob Hope. And your friend Mandelbrot now actually calls him the Vietnamese Martin Luther King. He writes as though the Buddhists had been slaves to the Catholics and now a new Moses has arisen to free them. What rubbish!"

Lily was at the same time caustically critical of Diem, Nhu, and especially Mme. Nhu, who had been two classes ahead of her in Middle School in Hue. The antagonism toward the Americans in the Saigon press controlled by Nhu and his wife made no sense and served no purpose in Lily's eyes. Nor did she think that Mme. Nhu's campaign to defend the rights and raise the standing of Vietnamese women had any chance of succeeding.

"First, win the war and then worry about women's issues," Lily would say. "Why can't she see that one precludes the other? I can't understand what happened to her after she married Nhu. At school she was shy and demure—very well liked by all of us. But once she hooked up with Nhu she changed completely. Power does strange things to people. It was her duty, she thought, to speak out not just against the way everybody criticizes Diem and Nhu, but also against the way Vietnamese men treat Vietnamese women. She is right, of course, in everything she says. Vietnamese men are pigs. And those who criticize the Ngo Dinhs don't have the brains or stature that Diem and Nhu have. But she comes across to both Americans and Vietnamese as something of a crank, mouthing off on whatever she feels like and doing things like getting dancing in nightclubs banned. The result is that her message, even when it is completely correct, is discounted as bizarre."

"So even though she has organized her corps of hundreds of thousands of women activists, she basically has no appeal to Vietnamese women?"

"Those aren't activists; they are opportunists. We Vietnamese women think that what she is saying is by and large right, but that by saying it so stridently she sets back her own cause. Don't forget that Vietnamese women continue to rule their homes and have been doing so for thousands of years. This is not the first generation of Vietnamese men to be fat, lazy, foolish, and corrupt. It is Vietnamese women who have held the country together and maintained the every day living and the culture of this country."

Within the Embassy the subject receiving the most attention was not the Buddhist problem, but rather the assault that the South Vietnamese were making against the American advisory effort. Stories of misbehavior or of comic ineptitude on the part of advisors who misunderstood local society and local customs were a daily staple in Vietnamese newspapers controlled by Ngo Dinh Nhu. In retrospect, it is hard to deny that Nhu had a point. But at the time the entire community of United States officials condemned Nhu's arrogance and what was considered to be his blatant anti-Americanism. More and more of them became convinced that some way had to be found to separate Diem from the Nhus.

The Vietnamese press campaign against these American military officers was also alluded to by Thich Tri Binh, with whom Marnin had lunch on June 10 in their vegetarian restaurant. Binh had ordered his usual dish of lentils and rice, and picked at it desultorily as he expatiated on the iniquities of his host's compatriots.

"Well, my giant friend, whose countrymen make their living advising us how to kill our brothers, how does the American Embassy think our little movement is progressing?" he asked, once they were seated in their usual sidewalk table.

"Our hope," Marnin said, "is that you'll reach a meeting of the minds with Diem. We're concerned that the Buddhist problem will distract from efforts to win the war."

"And why should we help you in that aim? The Viet Cong, after all, are Vietnamese, even if they are communists."

"And atheists."

"Atheism is for young men with rifles in their hands. When they lay down those rifles, they will leave their atheism in the jungle."

"And how do you feel your struggle is going?"

"Much, much better than all of you think. We have, you see, studied the battles of Napoleon and we know the secret of his success. First you engage the enemy in order to pin him down. You hold your cavalry and especially your artillery, your secret weapon, in reserve. Once he thinks he is about to win, you charge at the weakest point in his line and let loose your secret weapon in a giant barrage and you crush him, stun him, and confuse him. This will happen to Ngo Dinh Diem. You'll see."

Two days later, at nine-thirty in the morning, Marnin got a call from a Vietnamese who did not identify himself. He spoke in heavily accented, barely understandable, French.

"Mr. Marnin?"

"Yes."

"A friend of yours asked me to telephone. I have a message for you and the Lord Buddha will bless you if you respond to it."

"Who is this?"

"You are to be at the corner of Phan Dinh Phung and Le Van Duyet at eleven o'clock. It is important."

And he hung up.

It was a comparatively busy intersection, but not one of the busiest in Saigon. There were four or five jewellery stores in the vicinity and the usual street stalls selling flowers, candy, and cigarettes. At eleven o'clock, as bidden, Marnin arrived. All seemed completely normal. There were no foreigners, no bonzes, nothing at all to suggest that anything unusual was about to take place. Although a row of stately jacaranda trees shaded the sidewalk, it was still very hot. Marnin took off his jacket. He looked at his watch and debated whether to leave or not. Just as he was about to chalk it up to experience and move on to the pagoda, Klaus Buechner drove up in his brand new red BMW convertible and parked at the curb behind a large truck. Making a studious show of not having seen Marnin, Klaus crossed the street to the southeast corner and stood there with the sun behind him, his three Nikons strapped around his neck and at the ready, one of them with a telescopic lens. Marnin decided to stick around after all.

At eleven-thirty an old, light blue Austin sedan drove up and double parked next to Klaus's BMW. There were seven bonzes inside. The first one out raised the hood and left it in the raised position to indicate mechanical problems, presumably so that the police would not bother them. Two of his companions took a loudspeaker system out of the trunk and set it up on the sidewalk. Marnin recognized a twenty year old with horn-rimmed glasses named Bong, who lived at the pagoda and spoke fair to middling English. Once the speaker system was set up and the microphone hooked up to it the others got out of the car. Bong held the microphone. One of them, an old man with skin like parchment, perched in the street in the lotus position and began chanting his mantras. Five of the bonzes held hands and circled him, ensuring that passing traffic gave him a wide berth, while Bong remained on the sidewalk with the microphone in his hand. Then they all began to chant the same mantra, moving around the old bonze in a shuffling step that was not quite a dance.

A Vietnamese girl, about eighteen, came up to Marnin.

"What's going on?" she asked in French.

"I'm a foreigner," Marnin said gratuitously. "I don't have any idea."

She shrugged her shoulders and walked on, as did most of the passers-by during the next quarter hour, paying no attention to the old bonze and his group of fellow worshippers. Finally, one of the monks encircling the old bonze broke off from the group and walked to the light blue sedan. From the trunk he extracted two khaki colored five gallon cans and then passed one to a companion. At a signal from Bong the two of them emptied the liquid contents on the old bonze, dousing him thoroughly. Marnin could smell the gasoline from twenty feet away. Across the street Buechner was getting snapshot after snapshot, only pausing to reload film.

The other monks never stopped their chanting and their dancing, encircling their colleague who by that time looked to be in a deep trance. Then the one who seemed to be in charge handed the old man a large box of wooden matches. Without any emotion or the slightest sound or hesitation the designated martyr lit a match and went up in a pyre of flames ten feet high.

At first Marnin could not believe what he had just seen. Then he moved toward the flaming bonze, with some vague idea of helping, but the fire was much too hot and he had to back off. The Bonze's robes had burned off and Marnin could see his flesh charring and the features of his face melting and the air itself growing wavy from the heat.

Buechner, who kept shooting, got hundreds of photos. Bong on the loudspeaker was saying over and over in English:

"A Buddhist priest burns himself to death! A Buddhist priest becomes a martyr!"

There were at most ten onlookers who had seen the whole performance from the beginning. But during the five minutes the fire burned another two dozen random passers-by stopped to watch. Nobody said a word. The only sounds were the Saigon traffic, Bong on the loudspeakers, and the sizzle of the Bonze's flesh smelling like rancid bacon and frying in the gutter like fat in a skillet. The traffic kept rolling by with none of the drivers able to see what was happening.

By the time the flames subsided the old bonze had turned quite black, but still maintained the lotus position. Finally the fire died altogether and he toppled over on his right side, his legs hooked together for eternity. This impromptu cremation had taken no more than ten minutes. The other bonzes continued chanting their mantras throughout. They had to wait for him to cool off before they could cart him away. (Later they said that his heart remained whole and untouched by the flames—evidence, it was claimed, of his purity. The heart was then placed in a canister and enshrined in the An Quang pagoda in Hue along with the blue Austin they arrived in.)

By the time Marnin returned to the Embassy and reported the remarkable event he had witnessed, first to Sabo and then to Bilder, the wires were already humming with Buechner's exclusive scoop—three main photos, six subsidiary ones, and a two hundred word "Flash" to all Associated Press subscribers. This was followed twenty minutes afterward by a five hundred word story and, in the late afternoon, a two thousand word human interest "I was there" piece, all under Buechner's byline.

Under instructions from Sabo, Marnin drafted a telegram on the burning for Washington and then started to phone Vietnamese contacts for a "reaction cable"—always a frustrating task, given the state of the telephone system in Saigon. There was not much point, he thought, in even trying to call the bonzes. The one telephone at the Xa Loi pagoda, an old-fashioned crank model, was always busy even in slack times. One way or another, the bonzes would somehow be in touch with him, since they were at least as interested in his reaction as he was in theirs. In any case, there could be little doubt how they felt about the matter. Bong's eerie words on that rigged up, crackling loudspeaker just audible over the background of the passing traffic would echo in his memory forever.

"A Buddhist priest burns himself to death! A Buddhist priest becomes a martyr!"

The first person Marnin called was Lily.

"Hello, *petit frère*" she said. "It was so nice last night. I was thinking of calling you myself to tell you so."

"Yes. It was. But something terrible has happened. I want to see you. I need to talk to you about it and get your reaction to it."

"What happened?"

She listened without a word as Marnin replayed the events on Le Van Duyet, the same story he had told Sabo and then Bilder and afterward his colleagues in the political section. When Marnin was finished, she asked him in a flat voice to repeat his tale. After his second recounting there was a long pause. She sighed deeply.

"You are right. This is truly terrible," she finally said.

"Yes, it was awful. Everything was so quiet and seemed so normal and then death came suddenly out of nowhere."

"Old men die all the time. This one even died in a state of bliss. He was lucky."

"What do you mean? Then what's so terrible?"

"I'm thinking of what this will mean. It will have a profound effect here. Giving up one's life for a cause, particularly by fire, has a deep root in our culture. It will be seen as an act of great courage."

"It won't be perceived as the act of a fanatic? Everyone will take this seriously?"

"More seriously than you can imagine. Most of all Diem and Nhu will take it seriously. They will see it as a repetition of the challenge from the Hoa Hao and the Binh Xuyen and wonder whether they can survive it. They will think it absolutely necessary to take some sort of action against it."

Marnin's next call was to Dinh Trieu Da. He explained why he was one of the two non-Vietnamese eyewitnesses. The Palace had just heard about it, Da said. As one of Murray Gell-Mann's best students at Cal Tech, he had been perhaps the first link between physics and Buddhism through the odd circumstance of having been the first person to suggest the "eightfold path" as a means of symbolizing Gell-Mann's breakthrough description of the structure of sub-hadronic matter.

"You say that the bonze Bong was broadcasting on a loudspeaker in English all the time the old man was burning?"

"That's right."

"In English you say?"

"In English."

"Doesn't that tell everything about this? They sacrificed that poor man on the altar of the *New York Times*."

"Then the political effect may not be so serious. People might see this as grandstanding for foreigners?"

"No. That's wrong. It couldn't be more serious. It'll be seen here as the writing on the wall. Maybe we've reached our half life."

"Can I tell people here at the Embassy that you're shocked? Distressed?"

"You can say I'm in despair."

"What about the President? How does he feel about it?"

"My cousin, the President, is an unusual man. At times of real trouble he becomes remarkably calm and soothes everyone around him. He has a deep belief that he is in the hands of forces greater than himself. So as far as he is concerned, what will be, will be. As an unusually religious man, he is of course greatly shocked by this needless loss of life."

Marnin had no sooner hung up the phone with Da when Mandelbrot called in a state of ebullient excitement.

"You were there? You saw it all?"

"Yes."

"I wish I could have been there."

Marnin wondered whether the telephone tip might have come by way of Mandelbrot—perhaps as a way of making amends.

"You should have been," David said dryly. "It was quite a scene."

But the irony was lost on Billy. "Yeah," he said boyishly, "it must have been some sight to see. I'm just back from filing my story at the telegraph office. Do you want me to read it to you?"

"No thanks. I could write it myself. Did you do your story after the event or before?"

"Oh, I had it pretty well written by ten-thirty. There were just a few blanks for Klaus to fill in."

"Does it maybe occur to you that this had been a live human being you were offering to your Gods, whoever they are?"

"Don't give me that shit. You know how many people have been killed in the boonies over the past six months? Five thousand minimum. You can add this bonze to that statistic and now you have five thousand and one. And unlike those other five thousand, this guy was ready to die. Furthermore, the burning was going to happen whether I was in contact with the Buddhist clergy or not."

"You're far too modest," David said.

"I may be a genius, but I'm not that much of a genius. You don't seriously imagine I could come up with the idea myself of having some old bonze burn himself to death on a Saigon sidewalk, do you?"

"Give me a minute. I'll have to think about it."

"Anyway, what are you so pissed off about? You're one of the two white men who actually saw this happen. You were there when history was made—thanks to me."

"Thanks a lot."

"Don't be a bleeding heart! Have you ever seen a village after it's been napalmed? That will give you real nightmares. When babies are burnt black, that is a tragedy. Old men are going to die anyway. This, at least, is going to serve a useful purpose."

"And just what might that be?"

"It's going to play a big part in the dumping of Diem and Nhu. You're the Buddhist expert. This is going to have a profound effect here, not least on the ARVN."

"Do you think that's what the old man was thinking when he lit the match? I'm going to burn so the Americans can win the war."

"What difference does it make what he was thinking, if he was even thinking at all? He was probably high as a kite. Snap out of it, man. You've got to keep your eye on the ball."

Marnin's input to Sabo's cable included, along with some analysis, the enthusiastic reactions of Thich Tri Binh and Senator Mau, both of whom had called him at the Embassy. It was a busy day for Marnin. As the Embassy's so-called expert on the Buddhists, and as the only diplomat in town who had actually witnessed what had happened, he was suddenly in great demand. His phone rang constantly. The Saigon press corps wanted official and unofficial embassy reaction and other embassies wanted his interpretation of events. By the time he could actually get out of the Embassy it was nearly eight o'clock. He was dog tired and had a pulsing headache—the kind that in later life would turn into migraines. He had no interest in going home or in being with anybody in Saigon other than Lily. But Lily had said she could not see him that evening. She and the girls were having dinner with a friend and the engagement could not be broken.

Nevertheless, almost automatically his car drove itself to her compound, although he had no intention of entering it or trying to see her. The gate was open and he gazed at her front door longingly as he passed the house. He continued to the corner and then drove around the block aimlessly. The third time around the block, her black Mercedes was just emerging through the gate. The montagnard guard grinned and saluted smartly when the car appeared, so Marnin knew she and the girls were in it.

The Mercedes turned off Phan Dinh Phung and proceeded for a few blocks, turned right again, then left on Tu Xuong, and onward to the American compound on that street. The compound lay behind a high wall with broken glass cemented on top and contained four spacious "bungalows" that were occupied by high ranking officers of the U.S. Mission, including Bird and Sabo, as well as the swimming pool that all four families shared. The Mercedes turned in at the gate. There was nothing for him to do at that point except to go home, take three aspirins, mix himself a stiff drink, and go to bed.

Bilder was late to the Mission Council meeting, keeping his heads of agency waiting for more than ten minutes. He came into the conference room with a big smile on his pinched face. Everyone rose, giving him the ambassadorial treatment.

"Be seated, gentlemen," Bilder said. "These are momentous times, really momentous times. For those of you who haven't read it yet, I recommend Sam Sabo's cable on the Buddhist question."

Sabo, who was sitting to his left, did not look at him and took no recognition of this accolade.

"Before we go around the room," Bilder continued, "I have a little announcement to make. The reason I was late was that I was on the phone with Roger Hilsman, who was still at his desk at ten-thirty at night. Washington's deeply worried. They think this government has gone out of control and that, as Roger just said, it's time we started playing hardball with Diem and Nhu. Because of that they're appointing a new Ambassador whom the President thinks will be adept at that game. He is a man who unquestionably swings a heavy bat. He's a big man and it'll be a pleasure for all of us to work with him and support him. I'm planning to send him a cable this afternoon telling him exactly that."

Marnin thought of the PENUMBRA documents. The South Vietnamese government that had been tapping the phone of the *New York Times* correspondent would almost certainly be monitoring overseas calls to and from the United States Embassy. Whether Washington thought the Saigon government out of control and in need of "hardball" treatment was one thing, but whether any good purpose was served by announcing this conclusion on the telephone to Ngo Dinh Diem, as it had in effect just done, was another.

"Can you tell us who it is?" Sam Sabo asked.

Bilder looked as coy as a debutante at her first cotillion.

"I can't resist being the person to let this group in on the little secret. And since Roger told me about it on an open international line, I have the feeling you won't be the first to know about it. Not one of you will come even close to guessing who it is."

He paused for effect and chuckled.

"The new Ambassador," he finally said, "is Bascombe Sedgewick!"

There was a loud murmur in the room as the news was being digested. Sedgewick, a Boston Brahmin and rock-ribbed Republican, former Ambassador to France and West Germany, former Senator and Governor of Massachusetts, was a long time political rival of the Kennedy clan. As such, his appointment as Kennedy's most important Ambassador could not be anything other than a surprise—particularly because the usually leaky American ship of state had not produced a hint that this move was in the offing. Everyone thought Corning would be returning for another tour. Indeed, Corning himself had thought so.

Washington is always pleased when the system works and a major new personnel assignment is greeted by the media with as much surprise as this one was—and not only surprise, but approbation as well. The United States was sending one of its mandarins to deal with one of theirs. And Sedgewick was a practical politician, reputed to be pragmatic and tough—Eisenhower's Ambassador to France who had been adept at handling De Gaulle. In the words of an Arthur Krock *Times* column, "It is time to tell it like it is to Ngo Dinh Diem, and there is no better person to do that than one of the true patricians in American politics, Bascombe Sedgewick."

One immediate problem, however, was that in the desire for total secrecy nobody who knew about the appointment had thought to be in touch with the government to whom the new Ambassador was to be accredited. Since the matter had been handled directly by the President through the White House staff, normal procedures had not been followed. As a result, the pending appointment became public in Washington before the Government of Viet Nam had even been asked for *agrément*, much less given it—a violation of diplomatic protocol to which any nation would have been sensitive, and to which the embattled Ngo Dinh brothers were certain to react with dismay, since this was further evidence that the United States regarded South Vietnam as something of a colony.

It was therefore no surprise to anyone who understood anything about the political situation in Saigon when Sedgewick's nomination was greeted with anger in the local press. Long encomiums were printed lauding Corning to the skies, regretting his unexpected departure, saying he was the only American Ambassador who had ever been appointed to South Viet Nam who had made an effort to understand the Vietnamese point of view. These were followed by direct attacks against Sedgewick. Every unsavory dispute in which he had engaged in a lifetime of rough and tumble Massachusetts politics was rehearsed for the Vietnamese reader. The attitude of many Vietnamese was typified by a widely reported remark of Ngo Dinh Nhu. When asked what he thought of the appointment of a new American Ambassador, the President's brother was said to have replied, "Ambassador? You must be mistaken. The Americans are not sending us an Ambassador. They're sending us a Pro-Consul."

Marnin's Buddhist clients were practically bubbling with joy. They had no doubt that they were the direct cause of Corning's removal and that this marked a major change in American foreign policy—two suppositions hard to argue against.

Adding to the flames of impending controversy, with her genius for the wrong word at the wrong time, Mme. Nhu chose that point to make her famous declaration that she, for one, thought it folly to pay attention to this barbecue of an old monk—a declaration that was picked up in bold faced type by a world press which was not slow to discover that the phrase "barbecued bonze" had a certain euphonious ring. No single statement during the entire decade of the Vietnam War made more of a stir than this one careless, foolish characterization. Nothing could have played more into the hands of Mandelbrot and his colleagues in the Saigon press corps, determined as they were to bring down the Diem regime. Mandelbrot, as usual, made no effort to hide his thoughts.

"That's one down," he said to Marnin in the locker room after a tennis match. And three to go."

"Three?"

"That's right. Donnelly, Diem, and Nhu. Make it four. I'll throw in Mme. Nhu as well."

"You take full credit for this?"

"No, no. Not *full* credit."

The supposition—in the dip corps as well as the press corps—that Corning was being fired because he had been too close to Diem, put the Ambassador in a difficult position when he came back to the Vietnamese capital at the end of July, charged by Kennedy and Rusk to use his farewell calls to make one last effort to convince Diem to get rid of Nhu. Whatever Corning thought about the matter—and diplomatic or political observers could only guess because he handled himself with his usual discretion—there was little doubt among those who watched him daily that he was making herculean efforts to bridge the gap between the Ngo Dinh brothers and his successor. In his calls on both Diem and Nhu, in discussion with other government leaders, in backgrounders with the press—even one with Willis Mandelbrot— Corning insisted over and over that he supported Sedgewick and that the new appointment would in the long run turn out to benefit the GVN. Diem needed American help, he said. And the best way to get such help was to have an American envoy in Viet Nam with enough political clout in Washington to ensure that the needs of the GVN were given the highest priority. The fact that Sedgewick was a well-known Republican gave him even more political influence.

In order to allay local skepticism, Corning solicited a cable from Rusk assuring Diem that his departure in no way signified any lessening of American support for the South Vietnamese regime. Diem read this cable and turned to the Ambassador and said, "I believe you and what you say to me. But I don't believe this telegram."

Corning decided to bid a personal farewell to every major figure in the country, both in Saigon and the outlying regions, which he reached in the Air Attaché's C-47. (Hue, the farthest city from Saigon, was less than two hours away by plane.) And Marnin went with him on all of those trips. With every official he called upon throughout South Viet Nam Corning was resolutely optimistic. The extraordinary decline in incidents initiated by the VC and the continued successes of the Strategic Hamlet Program, he said to all, were irrefutable proof that the war continued to go well, despite the political turmoil in the country. This was his public line and his private line as well, and he did not vary it with anyone, including his aide. Nevertheless, late at night when Marnin was working over the memcons and cables that the Ambassadorial farewell activities had generated, he could not doubt that it was only a lifetime's discipline that kept Corning going. He remained the American Ambassador until his successor presented credentials to Ngo Dinh Diem and was going to act out that role to the end. But he was, of course, no fool. All his efforts had come to nothing and he knew it. To pretend otherwise was difficult.

Since the plane on which he was to depart left at midnight, Corning had put out instructions that nobody, other than Bilder, Sabo and Marnin, should go to the airport to see him off. He had bidden Diem farewell that afternoon at Gia Long palace. Corning made no record of the conversation. It was entirely personal, he said. The President and the Ambassador had emerged together, Corning carrying a large black lacquer box which Marnin had subsequently shipped to him through the diplomatic pouch. It contained the following inscription on a brass plate inside its cover:

TO GUSTAVUS HARRISON CORNING III
FROM HIS FRIEND NGO DINH DIEM,
PRESIDENT OF THE REPUBLIC OF VIET NAM;
IN THE COURSE OF A LONG LIFE I HAVE NEVER KNOWN ANY-
ONE FOR WHOM I HAD MORE RESPECT, TO WHOM I LISTENED
MORE CAREFULLY, OR WHO TROD THE PATH OF VIRTUE WITH
MORE NOBILITY.
SAIGON, 7 AUGUST 1963

Da was one of the two Vietnamese at the airport representing his government. The other was Ambassador Luyen, the Chief of Protocol. Bilder, about to assume the mantle of *Chargé d'Affaires* until Sedgewick arrived in Saigon, was there looking very uncomfortable, as were Sam and Grace Sabo and General Donnelly.

"This is the first time in a long career that I've disobeyed orders," Donnelly said. "But I'll be goddamned if I'm going to let you get out of here without seeing you off."

Patty Lou, who had been close to tears ever since Marnin and the driver had picked up the Cornings at the residence, started to bawl. She had been drinking.

"You're a good man, Blix, a dear man," she said to Donnelly. And then, turning to Sabo, "and you're a wonderful guy too, Sam. You're all wonderful, wonderful. . ." She looked around the room and, catching Bilder's eye, fixed a withering gaze on him.

She had not spoken to Bilder since the Cornings' trip through the Greek isles. Someone had tipped her off to Bilder's jubilation at the embassy staff meeting when he announced the impending replacement of her husband. Nor did she appreciate the fact that the first time Corning realized that anything was amiss in Saigon was in Crete when he heard, via the BBC on his short wave radio, that he was to be replaced as Ambassador by Bascombe Sedgewick.

The Sabos had brought along three bottles of Dom Perignon, but no one felt very festive and they barely got through one of them. It was a somber group. Everyone assembled knew that the United States was moving into a period of great difficulty in Saigon when Corning's particular talents could have been of great use to both governments. The usual small talk on such occasions was largely absent. An airport attendant arrived and whispered to Ambassador Luyen that Pan Am wanted the Ambassador and Mrs. Corning on board before the other passengers. There was one final round of handshakes, with Pattie Lou giving Grace Sabo a warm hug and ostentatiously cutting Bilder dead immediately afterward.

The walk to the plane was about fifty meters. Willis Mandelbrot and Klaus Buechner, with his three Nikons, were on the tarmac waiting for Corning. They were the press pool, Mandelbrot explained. Buechner was already going through roll after roll of film.

Patty Lou despised Mandelbrot and had heard her husband say
more than once that Billy and his young colleagues in the Saigon press
corps were largely responsible for curtailing his assignment to Saigon
and besmirching his reputation in Washington. Mandelbrot, she
thought, had not only irretrievably set Corning on a downward trajectory, but had changed her whole life and that of her daughters as well.
She longed to tell Billy what she thought of him—that he was the farthest thing from a gentleman and a disgrace to the *New York Times*
and to the profession of journalism. Here was her opportunity to say
what she deeply felt.

"Mr. Ambassador," Mandelbrot said, "do you have any final words
of wisdom for the readers of the *New York Times* before your departure? I know that you'll certainly be missed by Ngo Dinh Diem."

The two men peered at each other. Mandelbrot, sardonic and
cocky, looked as though he had had a few snorts. This angered
Corning. Marnin had never seen him look so angry. The strain of the
previous two weeks was clearly telling on him. Marnin had never
known him to lose his composure. But Patty Lou unexpectedly
jumped into the fray and by doing so restored it.

"I have some final words to say to you, young man—"

Corning quickly stepped in front of her so that she could no longer
see Mandelbrot. There was a moment's silence. Then the Ambassador
said: "I do have something to say. A great deal in the world will
depend on what the United States can accomplish in this country. On
that outcome, I am convinced, events will turn in far distant lands,
certainly in Asia and maybe even in Europe. We have important and
noble aims here. But those aims won't be accomplished unless we
carry out our programs in full partnership with our Vietnamese
friends and allies. As Ambassador I've been committed to that philosophy, as has been every member of my Country Team. Having had
several telephone conversations with Ambassador Designate
Sedgewick, I have every confidence that he will continue this policy.
And now I bid you farewell."

Holding Patty Lou firmly by her right elbow, Corning steered her
to the plane and then up the stairs. At the top they both turned and
waved. She was crying. And so was he.

PART FOUR

Change of Course

Thich Tri Binh and his followers became bolder as first university and then high school students joined them in demonstrations against the Ngo Dinhs. (For reasons that were never adequately explained to Marnin by Lily or any other of his sources, the most radical of all the students came from the pharmacy faculty of Saigon University.) On instruction from a much exercised John F. Kennedy, Gus Corning in his final three weeks had entreated Diem, Nhu and key members of their government on an increasingly urgent basis to conciliate the Buddhists. But from Marnin's focused vantage point it was apparent that the radical Buddhists would not reach agreement with Diem, no matter what he did. The taste of blood (an unusual taste for a Buddhist) was in their mouths. They could feel the government teetering.

On July 31, the Buddhists held mass meetings in Saigon, Hue, Qui Nhon, Nha Trang, and Dalat, for the first time calling openly for the ouster of the Diem Government. Then, the afternoon of August 4, Marnin received a phone call from Stu Markoff telling him to convey to the *Chargé* that precisely at high noon on that day the novice bonze Huynh Van Le had burned himself to death in front of the *Monument aux Morts* in Phan Thiet, Binh Thuan province. Bilder had been at his home working on a Sam Sabo cable on the mood in Saigon and had left word that he was not taking phone calls. Marnin drove there and gave him the news. Bilder hardly seemed displeased.

The next day the Department, in an unconscious pun that pro-
voked a good deal of laughter in the Embassy, condemned statements
on this second immolation by both Nhu and Madame Nhu as
"inflammatory." It cabled the Embassy that "these statements give us
little ground to hope the GVN is actually interested in carrying out
the conciliatory policy promised by Diem."

Two days after that, on August 7, Ngo Dinh Nhu gave French
Ambassador Lalouette categorical assurances that he fully "and with
both hands" supported Diem's announced policy of reconciliation *vis-
à-vis* the Buddhists. This position was a politically risky course in Viet
Nam, Nhu had said, since many people, including large segments of
the Army, felt that it represented weakness by the government toward
a movement which was subverting the war effort and impeding victory over the Viet Cong. When Lalouette criticized Madame Nhu's
speech to the Women's Solidarity Movement in which she repeated to
her followers the celebrated admonition not to pay attention to
bonzes who insisted on barbecuing themselves, Nhu replied that
nobody realized that Madame Nhu had not seen President Diem for
two months, that he and his family did not have meals with Diem
except on special occasions (a mutually satisfactory arrangement), and
that she was a private citizen who "has the right to express her own
views . . . ."

In response to the Department's condemnation of the Saigon government, on August 8, the *Times* of Viet-Nam carried a defense by
Madame Nhu of her statement that the Buddhists had "barbecued a
bonze with imported gasoline." The Buddhist leaders were neither
true religious figures nor representative of the Vietnamese people, said
Madame Nhu. Their tactics were obviously being dictated by the VC.
The Americans were unbelievably stupid to give this matter any credence.

Bilder complained to the Foreign Minister, deploring the article
and on the next day cabled a Country Team message to the
Department, which stated in part ". . .Madame Nhu is out of control
of everybody—her father, mother, husband and brother-in-law. At the
same time, there have been positive developments on the side of the
GVN: reaffirmation by Diem, as well as Nhu, that the GVN through
the Tho committee intends faithfully to pursue a policy of concilia-

tion; and the Tho committee's announcement of investigation of all complaints will keep the door open for joint investigations—measures which are having a noticeable effect on Vietnamese public opinion."

Marnin had not seen Lily for almost a week. She was in no mood to mollify him when he appeared at her house as scheduled that evening. Somewhat to his surprise, since she was not an admirer of Mme Nhu, she launched into a diatribe at the stupidity of the Americans to give any credence to the Buddhist tactics which clearly had one aim in mind—the downfall of the Diem Government.

"You Americans are beyond belief. And you are as bad as any of them," she said to Marnin.

"It's Madame Nhu who is beyond belief," Marnin replied.

Lily was so upset that David feared he would not get what he came for. He urged her repeatedly to forget about politics and finally she grudgingly acquiesced since she was as anxious for what was to follow as he was. Then, just as they both desired, they spent the night in each other's arms, repeatedly making love.

The next day, on August 11, Marnin's colleagues were displeased to discover that the *New York Times* had carried two related front page stories. The first was by Willis Mandelbrot in Saigon, entitled "Mrs. Nhu Denounces U.S. for Blackmail in Vietnam;" the second was by Tad Szulc in Washington and reported growing concern in the top levels of the Kennedy administration that Diem would not survive unless he compromised on Buddhist demands.

The radical Buddhist response was not long in coming. Two days later, on August 13, in a small village on the outskirts of Hue a third Buddhist bonze burned himself to death. This triggered an impromptu demonstration in Saigon of five thousand of the faithful—a majority of them high school and university students—at Xa Loi pagoda. Marnin attended and was struck by its resemblance to a pep rally before a big American high school football game. Only the cheerleaders were lacking.

Embarrassed not to have predicted this startling turn of events, the mood throughout the Embassy was shifting and even supporters of Diem, such as Sam Sabo, deplored his inability to get a handle on what was now being referred to everywhere as a crisis. This was compounded by bad news from the countryside picked up by the American press. Mandelbrot had a bylined front page story in the *Times* entitled, "Vietnamese Reds Gain in Key Area." In it he asserted that a serious deterioration had taken place in the military situation in the Delta, notwithstanding the United States build-up of South Vietnamese forces there. According to American military sources, the Viet Cong were now operating with well-armed units of 600 to 1,000 men and openly attacking the GVN's regular Armed Forces."

Marnin suspected that Billy's dispatch had more substance in it than the Embassy or our Consulate General in Can Tho were willing to acknowledge, largely because he was told that by Lily, who was following events closely through her ARVN sources. Kennedy, of course, read this article, which contradicted the briefings he was getting from the JCS about how well the war was going. His concern sent out tidal waves within the bureaucracy. When asked by the NSC staff to comment, Donnelly's response was that Mandelbrot, "in his report on the temperature of the battle in the Delta, exhibits a lack of understanding of our entire Viet Nam strategy. From the start that strategy involved a purification process, north to south; driving the Viet Cong southward, away from their sources of strength and compressing them in the southernmost area of the peninsula. This has proceeded. I Corps is fairly clean; II Corps, not much less so; III Corps warmer; and IV Corps, still tough. As General Cao, Commanding General, IV Corps, said in June, 'We want to see all the Viet Cong squeezed into the Ca Mau Peninsula, and then let them rot there.' If Mandelbrot understood this strategy, he might not have written his disingenuous article. . ."

But the bad news for Donnelly and the American mission continued to mount. Marnin spent fifteen hours every day at the Embassy trying to keep track of, and to report to Washington, the way things were going within Buddhist circles. He could not know or predict, however, that on August 15, a Buddhist nun would burn herself to death in the town of Ninh Hoa, near Nha Trang. On the following day, on August 16, an elderly Buddhist monk, the father of a Buddhist scholar studying in Japan, comitted a "pyro-suicide" in the courtyard of the Tu Dam pagoda in Hue. The event had been forewarned. The police were there and watched as the old bonze poured a can of gasoline over his head and set himself on fire.

The political situation was clearly getting out of hand. Three days later, on Sunday August 18, fifteen to twenty thousand people gathered at the Xa Loi pagoda and in the streets surrounding it to hear Thich Tri Binh attack the government. Large banners were displayed calling for Diem's overthrow. Binh hinted for the first time in public (although he had often said it to Marnin in private) that the best political solution would be to neutralize the country. According to the laws of South Viet Nam, advocacy of neutralism was sedition. The radical monk had thrown down a gauntlet that the government, one way or another, had to pick up.

As the "Buddhist Man" in the Embassy political section Marnin was in the middle of this cauldron—heady stuff for a young officer. The Viet Nam story eclipsed all others, not only in the American media, but on the President's desk as well. The Saigon press corps had quintupled. Almost a hundred journalists were registered with USIS. They arrived knowing nothing of the way the Buddhist religion was practiced in Viet Nam and expected Marnin to fill in the gaps in their knowledge (in the land of the blind the one-eyed is king) and to supply them with a scorecard—which bonze was which and which politicians stood to gain most from the explosion that everyone expected imminently.

Marnin was the "expert" on Buddhism in an American Embassy that dwarfed every other mission in town. The next largest embassy was the French, which had not one-fifth the number of people. And this did not include the U.S. military—by that time represented by more than sixteen thousand advisors (two thousand more than was acknowledged to Ngo Dinh Diem, the President of the country.) Marnin therefore became the point man on Buddhism for an American Mission that totaled close to twenty thousand people, about half of whom were reporting back to the Embassy on their relationships with their Vietnamese counterparts.

His enormous frustration was that despite his best efforts to explain to his government what the Buddhist movement was all about, a mythology had taken root in Washington that no reporting of his seemed able to shake. Vietnamese nationalism, so the myth went, was somehow incarnated in Buddhism. The Confucian system that had formed, among others, Ngo Dinh Diem, and had left an indelible imprint on Vietnamese life for two thousand years, was discovered by half-baked Washington socio-anthropologists to be Chinese and therefore foreign. (Catholicism also obviously was foreign.) But Buddhism (although also imported into Viet Nam from China, just as Confucianism was) remained quintessentially Vietnamese, according to this analysis. The policy conclusion drawn from this alleged fact was that the United States should break with the "foreign" Diem, mired in the past, and support the Buddhist representatives of authentic Vietnamese nationalism—the wave of the future.

Diem and Nhu were aware of the growing strength of this line of thought and desperate to get their countervailing message across to Washington. Every American the Ngo Dinh brothers could think to influence was urgently cultivated, including Marnin. In his case their instrument was Dinh Trieu Da. Marnin had, of course, known Da ever since Corning called on Diem. Da was the "note taker" on the other side of the table who never took a note.

Marnin's original assumptions had been that Diem's office was bugged and that Da could at his leisure later listen to the tapes and use them to prepare a written record. It was only after Marnin had occasion to discuss with Da conversations which past American Ambassadors had had with Diem, and then to check Da's recollection of those conversations with the memoranda of conversation still available at the Embassy, that he realized that Da could effortlessly recall important nuances of negotiations held five years before and give back almost verbatim the exact words of each participant. As the most brilliant member of the next generation of the family, Da had been called back to Saigon to help the President (Diem was his second cousin once removed) as soon as he received his doctorate. This obliged Da to give up a post-doctoral fellowship in theoretical physics at Cal Tech. But he could not say no to the head of the family (Ngo Dinh Thuc, not Ngo Dinh Diem). His family had, after all, served Emperors of

Viet Nam for six generations. Now it was his turn.

Da lived quietly on the top floor of a modest house off Tu Do Street with his widowed mother, who was in bad health, and his unmarried older sister Minh, an archivist in the National Library. When he called Marnin out of the blue that Saturday morning to invite him to dinner at his home, David knew that something unusual was going on. They had not talked for a month, not since they had stood together in Diem's office while the President and Corning had their last conversation strolling around the Palace garden.

Da was waiting downstairs dressed in a sport shirt as Marnin arrived just after sunset. There were two frangipani trees in the yard and the air was redolent with their heavy, sweet fragrance.

"The entrance is in the back," Da said. "It would have been difficult for you to find....Watch your step," he said, leading Marnin up the unlighted stairway. "As you shall see, my home is very modest. I would have had you to a restaurant, but they can be too noisy."

"I much prefer eating together here," Marnin replied truthfully.

Despite being forewarned, Marnin was surprised, almost shocked, at the modesty of Da's circumstances. He found himself in a small, crowded living room which contained a sofa and two armchairs covered in a matching faded flowered print and a wooden folding bridge table in the corner laid with a white cloth set for two people. Everything smelled vaguely mildewed and tobacco stained. There were two bedrooms off the living room, one shared by his mother, who never put in an appearance, and his sister, who at the end of the meal emerged from the kitchen with a cigarette in her mouth to accept the two young men's good natured applause.

The largest room was Da's bedroom. It was dominated by a two-sided blackboard on which were chalked in pink a series of differential equations. There was a small bathroom off his bedroom with a stand-up bathtub, and a kitchen where a great deal of activity was going on. Like his cousin the President, Da chain smoked Gauloises and offered one to Marnin.

"If you look around here," he said, "I think you'll see pretty good evidence that the fabled corruption of the Ngo Dinh clan has been somewhat exaggerated by the *New York Times*."

"Nobody who knows anything about your country has ever taken that particular charge very seriously."

"Really? The impression we have is that the *Times* is now not only taken seriously, but is making your entire foreign policy toward this country. For months we've been hearing the *New York Times* correspondent boasting to his friends (he paused and looked at Marnin) around town that he was, as he put it, 'going to nail Corning's ass to the wall.' You had a reasonable Ambassador here and now you've withdrawn him."

"That doesn't mean a change in policy. As you know, we've had a cable from the Secretary denying that any change in policy is in prospect."

"Cables are easy enough to write. And none of us doubt the goodwill of Gus Corning. But there are others in your Mission who behave in a way that would get them expelled from any other country except this one, people who consort with plotters, with criminals. And when these criminals tell them their schemes they solemnly take out their notebooks and write down the plotters' exact words—which these plotters take as encouragement."

"I'm not sure I follow," Marnin said.

"When Mr. Markoff is asked what it is he thinks his people are doing he piously puts his hands up in the air and denies they are up to anything at all. Since the United States, he says, is investing millions of dollars in Viet Nam, it has to know what is going on."

"Well, there is something in that."

"Maybe. Maybe there is. But even you Americans must understand that when you ask a high ranking general whether he continues to support the government which he is sworn to uphold, you are giving him the impression that if he should change his mind about such support the United States would go along with him. Worse than that, if a Colonel tells you that Diem must go, that Nhu must go, and that he is organizing a coup to overthrow them and your reaction is to take out your notebook and write down the Colonel's words and then continue your pleasant social evening, you are giving that Colonel the impression that you approve what he is doing. Much worse than even that, when you ask still a third General what it is that the United

States has to do in order for the ARVN to move against the legally constituted friendly government of an ally, aren't you going beyond disinterested intelligence research, haven't you passed a threshold, aren't you actually encouraging him to move against his own government? I would add that this is not scholarly speculation. All three of these conversations actually took place during the past week."

A servant came out of the kitchen and announced to Da that dinner was ready. Marnin recognized him as one of those who brought in refreshments during the Ambassador's calls on Diem. Evidently he was hired for the evening.

They moved to the table and sat opposite each other. It was a Vietnamese meal, with the china and glassware borrowed from the Palace. They ate with ivory chopsticks emblazoned with red dragons. There were six dishes in all, each of them exceptionally delicate, and a modest bottle of Algerian white wine. Da seemed very pleased that Marnin knew the names of all the dishes, which were standard ones, light on the nhuc mam, and chosen to appeal to the taste of a foreigner. Lily had tutored him well on Vietnamese cookery, which he loved. Da, on the other hand, had the palate of a Gauloise chain smoker and paid no attention to what he was eating.

"Diplomacy is not my game," Da said, midway through the meal. "Theoretical physics is. So I hope you'll excuse me if I seem rather blunt."

"We're friends. We should be frank with each other."

"That's a sentiment we would agree with. You want us to be frank with you, but you seem horrified when we point out that this frankness has been a one way street. Your people, for example, constantly chatter about my cousin Nhu's so-called all-pervasive secret police, but at the same time you flood this country with CIA agents and put half of our government secretly on your payroll."

"I've just been traveling with Ambassador Corning all over this country, talking to scores of your officials. His message at every stop was always the same—Washington and Saigon are friends and allies and have the same aims and goals."

"What's bothering us is how you treat that friend and ally. Your sanctimonious moralizing about how we mistreat this mythically oppressed Buddhist minority literally makes me sick. I've spent seven years in your country. I've been in places where your Negros weren't allowed to piss in the same toilets as white people. So your horror at the brutal treatment of the Buddhists by my family is for me something of a joke. Can you cite one single instance of anyone in this country denied basic human rights just because he's a Buddhist?"

"No, I can't. I'm extremely frustrated, in fact, because people in the States seem to confuse South African treatment of their Negros with what's happening here. But the fact of the matter is that Klaus Buechner's photo of that old bonze setting himself on fire has stirred the United States and the whole world. And when Madame Nhu compounded this by talking about barbecuing bonzes with imported gasoline, she created a situation that's almost impossible to remedy. You all say that she talks for herself, that she's a private citizen, but she's first lady of this country, the President's hostess, for God's sake."

"Madame Nhu does not happen to be my favorite cousin or my favorite human being for that matter," Da said. "She's one of those people who talks first and thinks afterward. But for all that, she's the only person in the world who tells the President exactly what is on her mind. Nhu doesn't do that and neither do Thuc or Can. And certainly neither do I. The fact that he is President stops us from giving him one hundred per cent of what we think. But it doesn't stop Madame Nhu. That's her value to Diem and why he's been reluctant to force her to leave the country."

"You've got to reach some form of reconciliation with the Buddhists and get rid of the Nhus. It's that simple."

"It's not simple at all. Asking Diem to get rid of Nhu is like asking him to cut off his right hand. What if someone were demanding that Jack Kennedy get rid of his brother Bobby? What would be his reaction to that? If Nhu is forced out, the whole strategic hamlet program will go up in smoke within six months. He's the driving force behind it. More than that, Nhu is the President's sounding board. Diem works things out in his mind verbally and Nhu comments as the process is unfolding. Nobody else could do that."

"You could."

"No I couldn't. Both Diem and Nhu," Da said with a smile, "think me too young, too naive, too impractical, too lacking in guile.

Powerful forces within our society have been working for the destruction of our family for eight years. We've kept them off balance. But the cursed thing about this Buddhist mess is that now it is we who are off balance. Our enemies are testing the waters. And if those waters are cleared of Nhu, whom they recognize as a shark, they will be far more prone to act against us."

"You won't be able to handle your enemies if Nhu leaves?"

"That's the question that every American asks us now. It's a false question! The real question is not in the Gia Long Palace, but in the White House. Our enemies are pygmies and Diem is a giant. He would brush them off like ants if they acted alone. But are they acting alone? I need to know why you Americans are prepared to toss this government aside. Who do you think will be a better ruler of this country than Ngo Dinh Diem? What are the forces that are really driving you?"

"Those are not easy questions. But in my mind, it boils down to the Buddhist problem. If you can solve it, if you can somehow conciliate their leadership—"

"You're giving me pat answers out of the Embassy phrasebook," Da heatedly replied. His face had turned red and a large vein stood out in the middle of his forehead. Normally he was the mildest of men.

"We know that you have lunch regularly with Thich Tri Binh. We even know what he says to you. Do you think that there's the slightest chance of reaching reconciliation with that man?"

"No I don't. But there are other Buddhists than Binh."

"We've reached those others. They've made statement after statement calling for such reconciliation. And do you know the net result? The net result has been zero. We've negotiated five separate agreements with the Buddhist leadership and after each one Binh spits in the President's face and the agreement crumbles into dust. This is a society based on relationships between son and father, between the ruler and the ruled. To allow someone to spit in the ruler's face and to do nothing about it is seen as abdicating the reins of power. So far we've let Binh get away with such colossal disrespect because of you Americans. If we got tough and cracked down on Binh, many in Washington would then urge that aid be cut off and that we be shunted aside. But if we allow the Buddhists to spit in our faces and do nothing, then we're certain to be overthrown by those who will use the Buddhist problem as an excuse."

"But you can't just push the Buddhists aside by force. You don't have the power to do that."

"You couldn't be more wrong. We do have the power. We have the troops and we have the rationale. The Buddhists, to quote Chairman Mao, are paper tigers. One push from us and they'd disintegrate."

"At the very least, you have to get Madame Nhu off the stage."

"That will happen. It's a pity, but it will happen. The President has already decided to send her off first to the Interparliamentary Union meeting in Yugoslavia and then on a world parliamentary tour. And she's the only person in this entire country who is saying aloud the truth about the Buddhists. She is right that they are not the majority of the people of Viet Nam, are at most five to ten per cent of the population. She is right that the Buddhist clergy are not comparable to priests or rabbis. She is right that they do not lead their flocks with any temporal authority. And as a result of telling the truth you Americans are insisting she be sent out of the country."

"It isn't what she says, but the colorful way she says it."

"That's true enough. But with the Buddhists it's both what they say and the way they say it that bother us. Do you know about the demonstration today at the Xa Loi pagoda?"

"I attended," Marnin replied.

"And did you listen to the speeches?"

"Yes. My Vietnamese has been getting better and I had a Vietnamese language officer with me and he filled me in on the rough spots."

"And how did you assess the speeches?"

"They're getting much tougher. Before there was a lot of waffling and obfuscation and Buddhist argy bargy. But today was different. Today every speaker without exception called for the overthrow of Ngo Dinh Diem and for a new policy of what they called 'national reconciliation of all factions.'"

"What we cannot understand," Da said, "is that Washington claims to oppose the neutralization of this country. Are you listening to these Buddhists? Are these the people your government wants to take over this country? What are you after?"

"We want an end to this problem and a return to the serious prosecution of the war against the Viet Cong."

"But when our army sees you taking the part of neutralists and worse, people talking outright sedition, then even the best of them will sit back and wait to see how the political situation is resolved before they take any action against the Communists."

"The question remains what action, if any, your family is going to make to resolve the Buddhist problem."

"You were at those demonstrations today along with twenty thousand people. Last week it was five thousand. If we don't do anything in the interim, next week they'll get fifty thousand. There will be violence. And how will that play in your press? How will the hundred twenty-four accredited foreign newspapermen in Saigon write such a story? We both know the answer to that."

"The answer is reconciliation," Marnin said.

"You told me yourself not half an hour ago that reconciliation won't work, that Thich Tri Binh has other aims, that he controls the Buddhist association. We know Binh and we know what he wants. This is not red-baiting or the fevered imagination of a family going down the drain. We know we have to act. This is a fact, a certifiable fact."

"What do you mean?"

"As I never lied to you in the past, I'm not lying to you now. What is important is that the gauntlet has been thrown down. If we don't neutralize these people, our uniformed colleagues will. And they are far more foolish than we. If we don't pick up that gauntlet, we will not survive the year."

Martial law was declared two days after Marnin's dinner with Da. A delegation of seven ARVN Generals met on August 19, first with Nhu, and then with Diem, who was reluctant to take such a drastic step. But in a three hour session Diem was finally convinced that law and order had to be imposed on the pagodas. His main reservation, according to Gascon, who heard from Generals Bich and Kim about the meeting, was concern about the harm that might come to the bonzes. Their safety had to be ensured at all costs, Diem insisted.

The following night Marnin had dinner at Cheap Charlie's in Cholon with Claudio, Mandelbrot, Klaus Buechner, and Frank Gascon. There was nobody else in the place. Their waiter, Chang, and the owner, a fat Chinese in his undershirt, presumably the eponymous Charlie, were serving them. The rest of the staff had been allowed to go home before the newly installed nine o'clock curfew. Because of their diplomatic status, Claudio, Marnin, and Gascon were exempt from its provisions. Whether the curfew included newspaper people was unclear, but Buechner and Mandelbrot chose to interpret the martial law regulations to mean that they and other foreigners were equally exempt.

This was living dangerously. It offered Mandelbrot's enemies, who were legion, a free shot at him. And at that point he had been the target of threatening telephone calls and anonymous letters printed crudely in a childish hand and threatening him with death if he did not leave Saigon. But Mandelbrot did not lack physical courage. He had proved that on the scores of patrols he had accompanied into the jungle chasing the VC. He passed around the choicest of the poison-pen missives.

"Beware Jew!" one read, "Hitler got the rest of you and now we finish the job!" "If you know what is good for you," read another, "you will get your ass out of here. Otherwise, your mother is going to be morning [sic] one dead son!"

"And that ain't all," said Mandelbrot. "I'm followed wherever I go. There are four of them in a black Peugeot. They drive so close I can't put on my brakes for fear they'll rear end me. And what does the Embassy do about it? Absolutely nothing! Not even a protest to the Foreign Ministry."

"Aren't you the guy," Claudio asked, "who's been writing about the insidious South Vietnamese police state run by the infamous Nhu? Either this place is dangerous for dissent, in which case you're either crazy or foolishly brave or both, or else it's rather benevolent compared to most other Third World countries, in which case you're a fucking liar. Which is it?"

"Do I think this place is dangerous?" Mandelbrot replied, raising his beer glass in a toast to the rest of them. "Of course I do. But I'm the best reporter on the best beat in the world. I'm going to take my chances because I'm having too much fun to stop."

"This place is a circus," said Buechner. "This is life under the big top. Wheee!"

"Do you really think," Marnin asked, "that Diem or Nhu would be stupid enough to murder a *New York Times* correspondent?"

"Of course not. It would be an accident. I'd trip in the shower, fall down a flight of steps, or accidentally electrocute myself."

"If you really think that, you shouldn't be out here with us. You ought to be taking some reasonable precautions," Claudio said.

"I am. I'm sleeping at John Mecklin's these days. Even Nhu won't attack me there."

With a curfew in effect they had no onward destination, and there was no reason to hurry. So they whiled away the evening in amiable if heated banter.

"The main advantage of working for the people I work for,"

Gascon said to them, "is that you can tell your wife you're going out on business and she's forced to believe you."

Gascon made no effort to hide from the correspondents the basic nature of his work. In his bluff, conspiratorial manner, when he was not regaling his companions with stories of his days in the French Foreign Legion, he was always alluding to his contacts with the Generals. Half tanked on Four Roses whiskey, he would make no bones about his expectation that his pals would soon be running South Viet Nam and that when they did he would become a very important fellow.

"I can't reveal what these guys say to me," he said to the group, "but I can tell you they're getting more pissed off every day. And when they make the big move at their side is going to be Frank Gascon—who'll be the most influential American in this country."

"You ought to stop smoking dope and stick to whiskey," Claudio commented. "You're getting me nervous."

It was eleven thirty by the time they were ready to pack it in. Claudio agreed to drop Mandelbrot and Buechner at the compound on Tu Xuong where Mecklin lived (and Sam Sabo and Curly Bird as well) and then take Marnin home.

They whisked through the streets of Cholon and into Saigon, the only car on the road. When they reached Tu Do they could see a convoy of five two-and-a-half ton trucks ("deuce-and-a-halves") a quarter of a mile ahead. Mandelbrot, instantly alert, leaned forward from the back seat.

"That's strange," he said. "Trucks moving along empty streets in the middle of a curfew. Catch up with them! See what they're up to!"

"Better stay clear of them," Marnin said.

"Don't be silly!" Mandelbrot rejoined. "Something's happening right in front of us. What are we supposed to do?"

Claudio caught up to the last truck. It was full of soldiers. So were the other four trucks.

"Can you see their uniforms? Can you tell what units they belong to?" Buechner asked.

"No, I can't," Marnin said, as they passed the American Embassy.

"They're regular ARVN troops," Claudio asserted. "At least they're wearing ARVN uniforms."

Claudio dropped back behind the convoy and followed along in its wake.

"What's happening? Where are they going?" Buechner asked.

"I'll be goddamned if I know," Claudio replied.

But Marnin knew. He knew exactly. They were taking the same route he drove every morning. They were heading for the Xa Loi pagoda.

A truck was parked across the middle of the street a block away from the pagoda blocking access to the main road leading to it. Thirty or forty soldiers in field uniforms, wearing riot helmets and carrying M-1 rifles, were milling about aimlessly. Claudio slowed down but did not stop. He tried a side street to the south of the pagoda, but that was blocked as well.

"Go back to the main entrance," Mandelbrot said, "and let us out."

As Mandelbrot and Buechner opened their respective back doors they could hear clearly the incessant beating of the large gongs in the pagoda reverberating in the otherwise unnaturally silent night. Most of the soldiers who had been milling about the truck before had disappeared, presumably in the direction of the pagoda. There were only half a dozen lounging there, blocking the street.

Mandelbrot and Buechner got out of the car and, trying to look as nonchalant as possible, started strolling in the direction of Xa Loi. They were stopped by an unusually short Vietnamese Military Policeman wearing a white helmet and sporting a large, white armband with "MP" written on it. Mandelbrot spoke earnestly and then angrily to the man, gesticulating in that awkward manner he had. He towered more than a foot over him. They were so incongruous together that Claudio and Marnin could not help laughing.

The MP gestured at Claudio's car and Mandelbrot shook his head negatively. The MP then pointed at Buechner's bag, and both Mandelbrot and Buechner started arguing with him. He called over a higher ranking colleague who asked for their identification papers. While the second officer was examining them by flashlight the first started walking over to the Mercedes. Mandelbrot waved Claudio off and the Guatemalan gunned the car away from the curb. The MP gestured at them to stop but Claudio kept going.

They drove to Marnin's place in silence.

"It's the beginning of the end," David said, as he got out of the car.

He went into his house and telephoned Sam Sabo. It rang in their bedroom (phones were hard to come by in Saigon in those days and each embassy residence, other than the Ambassador's and the DCM's, only had one instrument) and awakened them. It was a quarter to one. Grace answered sleepily and passed the phone to Sam. Marnin apologized for the late hour and explained what had happened.

"Call Freddie Loftus in Hue," Sam said, "and tell him to get his ass over to the Tu Dam pagoda and find out if anything's going on over there. If you can't get hold of Freddie, call Colonel Harrington and have him send one of his people. I'll be in touch with Danang, Nha Trang, Can Tho, My Tho, and Bien Hoa myself. After you get off the phone with Hue, I want you to go back to Xa Loi, identify yourself and find out what's happening. I'll meet you in my office. I should be there by the time you get there."

Freddie was at home and sleeping. It took him a few moments to clear his head. Then he grumbled mightily at the prospect of breaking the curfew by driving across the river to the pagoda on what he called a wild bonze chase. Finally he said, "Oh, all right! I just hope a crazy ARVN sentry doesn't shoot me as I drive by."

Marnin drove back to the pagoda, parking next to the same blocked off street just as a group of about twenty bonzes, looking dazed in that special way people have when they're awakened out of a sound sleep, were being herded onto the back of one of the deuce-and-a-halves. Mandelbrot and Buechner were nowhere in sight. Everything was still. Three Vietnamese military policemen in white helmets were in charge and looked to be treating the monks with comparative courtesy. As Marnin stood there watching, an ARVN Captain came up and saluted. He spoke in Vietnamese and Marnin could not catch his meaning.

"American Embassy," David said in Vietnamese, and handed the Captain the diplomatic identification card that he had at the ready. The Vietnamese officer examined it by flashlight, saluted again, and walked away with it in the direction of the pagoda.

The truck with the bonzes in the back drove off and an empty one took its place. Another group of sleepy and dazed bonzes came shuffling up in their sandals, escorted by five ARVN soldiers, who turned them over to the three who were loading the trucks. Last in the straggling line was a bonze who was unable to use his left foot and was hopping along with his arms around the necks of two flanking comrades. His face in the dim light looked bruised, as though he had a black eye. His comrades lifted him onto the back of the truck on his behind. Then they helped him stand on his good leg and brace himself on the side of the truck. When he was settled the truck drove away and a third one pulled up to the curb.

Marnin wondered uneasily if the Captain had forgotten about him. But the latter finally returned after ten minutes with the ID card and a Lieutenant who was linguist enough to have mastered at least one phrase in French—"*Ce n'est pas possible.*"

"I want to inspect what's going on," Marnin said.

"*Ce n'est pas possible,*" the Lieutenant replied with a broad smile.

"I want to speak to the officer in charge."

"*Ce n'est pas possible.*"

"There was an American correspondent and a photographer here half an hour ago. What's happened to them? I want to file a protest."

"*Ce n'est pas possible.*"

As they argued an ambulance drew up and was loaded with two monks carried on stretchers. One of them was in great pain from what looked to be a broken arm or a dislocated shoulder. The other was deeply unconscious or perhaps even dead. Marnin tried to find out what was going on but the military policemen refused, or pretended an inability, to answer his questions. Tiring of this fruitless game, he went back to his car and drove to the Embassy.

It was two o'clock when he reached Sabo's office. Sam was seated at his desk, wearing khaki pants and a batik sport shirt, typing away on his manual, office-sized Remington. (In those days only the secretaries had IBM Selectrics.)

"We've heard from Paul Hare in Nha Trang already," he said, "and from Frank Scotton in Bien Hoa. ARVN troops cleaned out the pagodas in both places. They carried off all the monks, presumably to the local hoosegow."

"That's the way it was at Xa Loi. Was anyone hurt? I saw one monk who was at least unconscious—and maybe worse."

"No. It seemed to have gone pretty quietly in Nha Trang and Bien Hoa. No resistance offered."

Marnin described what had happened at Xa Loi and offered to stay and help. The phone rang and he answered. It was John Mecklin to say that Mandelbrot and Buechner had not returned to his place and were not at the *Times* or the AP offices. When he heard what had happened he said he was going to the Central Police Station to search for them.

As Marnin was talking with Mecklin Freddie called from Hue on the other line and conveyed his news to Sabo. There had been major resistance at Tu Dam and the troops of General Do Cao Tri had been rough. But nobody was reported killed. The monks were being interned in a soccer stadium on the other side of the river, since the jails lacked sufficient room.

In rapid succession calls came in from My Tho and Can Tho confirming that the pagodas in the Delta had also been attacked. As Marnin spoke to Jim Willis in Can Tho, Sabo was typing away and had a cable ready to go by the time the telephone was replaced on the receiver. It had a "CRITIC" designator, reserved for the direst emergencies, the first such cable Marnin had handled. The telegram was addressed to Secstate, rpt info: WHITE HOUSE, DOD, JCS, CIA, and read as follows:

ARVN troops tonight attacked Xa Loi pagoda in Saigon, Tu Dam pagoda in Hue, and pagodas in Bien Hoa, Danang, My Tho, Can Tho and probably a dozen more throughout SVN. Hundreds of monks have been arrested. Pagodas extensively damaged. Monks resisting arrest were beaten up; some severely injured, with possible fatalities. Unless instructed otherwise Embassy plans protest this outrage to highest levels GVN soonest. Please instruct.

BILDER

Sabo then called Bilder, briefed him on what had been happening, and got his approval to send the message, which he read to him over the phone. The Marine on duty had already been instructed by Sabo to summon the duty code clerk, a young black Tennessean with an enormous belly named Pat Patterson, whose ability to chugalug a pint of beer had made him a legend at the Texas Rose. Pat showed up in ten minutes wearing sandals, jeans, and a red T-shirt with four aces on it.

"This is the first time I ever sent a CRITIC message," he said when Marnin handed him the cable.

"The way things are looking around here," David said, "it won't be the last."

The next morning before going to work Marnin drove to the Xa Loi pagoda to survey the damage. There were no guards or police patrols or cars parked in front. From the outside everything seemed normal. But inside the place was a shambles. Tables, chairs, desks, electric fans, papers, leaflets, bits of clothing, scores of safety razors, the occasional toothbrush, and all sorts of other detritus were scattered everywhere. The mimeograph machines and typewriters had been smashed, probably with sledgehammers, and their parts littered the floor of the office and the main hall. Several statues of the Buddha had been decapitated and were lying on their sides, looking forlorn.

He walked through the back door and into the courtyard searching for someone to talk to. The walls, which on the west side separated the pagoda from Curly Bird's USOM compound next door, were covered with bright red bougainvillea. Four frangipani trees graced its dusty center. Flower petals—white and red and purple—were strewn along the ground.

A lone saffron-robed bonze wearing very thick glasses swept the dusty courtyard with a short-handled broom, his shaved head gleaming in the early morning sunlight. A light breeze was blowing and the wind chimes were tinkling. The bonze paid no attention to the foreigner and continued to rake the dust and sweep the flower petals as Marnin walked toward him. It seemed the height of incongruity— tidying the courtyard dust while the pagoda floor inside was covered with every kind of litter. Only when Marnin greeted him did he stop sweeping. Marnin tried English, then French, to no avail, and finally resorted to his weak Vietnamese.

"What happened?" he asked.

"Nothing," the Monk replied.

Marnin looked at him carefully to see if he were joking or being sarcastic. For the first time he noticed a pinkness around the monk's eye that marked him as feebleminded. Because of this the police had evidently let him alone. Marnin waved goodbye to him, turned, and walked back inside. On the steps of the temple he looked back. The monk was sweeping under the west wall, which was covered with lavender bougainvillea. The wind chimes were tinkling. A more peaceful Asian scene was unimaginable.

In contrast, the Embassy Political Section was pulsing with activity. First, Marnin called Mecklin. The police had turned Mandelbrot and Buechner over to his custody at four in the morning on the understanding that they would not breech the curfew further.

"I'm told they attacked thirty pagodas," Mecklin said. "One reporter said scores of bonzes were killed, hundreds injured."

"Are those figures confirmed?" Marnin asked. "I went back to Xa Loi and didn't see anything that would support stories like that."

"No. These are just rumors the press is picking up. There are certainly hundreds of bonzes under arrest all over the country."

Sabo was on the phone talking with Ambassador Luyen, the Chief of Protocol, trying to arrange an appointment for Bilder with Diem. He gestured for Marnin to sit down and handed him a folder of cables. The top one asked Embassy Tokyo to contact Ambassador Sedgewick at the Okura Hotel and to instruct him to get to Saigon "ASAP." Another expressed the Department's "shock" at the "unprovoked attacks" on the pagodas, commended the Embassy for its alert reporting, and noted that the Department spokesman would issue a strong condemnation of this "direct violation by the Vietnamese government of pledges that it was pursuing a policy of reconciliation with the Buddhists."

A third cable, on pink paper rather than white, was an outgoing NIACT (Night Action) message to the Department, sent just forty-five minutes before, at seven AM, drafted by Curly Bird and signed off by Sabo, reporting that in the confusion of the previous evening two bonzes had slipped over the wall of the USOM compound next door to the Xa Loi pagoda and were now requesting political asylum. There were also several cables reporting worldwide press reaction and an incoming from CINCPAC in Honolulu, where Corning was vacationing, transmitting a personal message from him to Diem.

> FOR: PRESIDENT DIEM
> FROM: AMBASSADOR CORNING
> Deeply deplore attack on pagodas, an action that can have nothing but the most negative repercussions in the United States. This is the first time you have ever gone back on your word to me.
> CORNING

Sabo hung up the phone.

"Luyen promises to get back to me. It sounds like a runaround. The Foreign Minister has resigned in protest and shaved his head."

"Shaved his head?"

It was hard to imagine that urbane diplomat with a shaved head.

"That's right. You should have heard Luyen hemming and hawing on that one. I'm insisting that we have to see Diem, especially now that there's no Foreign Minister. The problem, just between you and me, is that Diem has no intention of being bawled out by our *Chargé d'Affaires*. We're going to have to find a way around this impasse."

"Like what?"

"I may work a deal with the Papal Nuncio. He's the Dean of the Corps and this is a religious question. Maybe I can convince him to make a joint demarche with us. We'll see. In the meanwhile, call your friend Dinh Trieu Da and tell him you're on your way to the Palace with a personal message from Gus Corning for Diem. And when you're through with that go over to the USOM compound and talk to

Curly's two monks and get a sense of what's on their minds."

Da was waiting for Marnin in his magnificent office next to the President's. It was the first time the American had seen it.

"Nice digs," he said.

"The French built this place to live in, not to work in. They didn't know the meaning of small rooms."

"Here's the message," Marnin said, and handed it to him.

Da read it, frowned, and tossed it on his desk.

"How are you?" he asked.

"Tired," Marnin said. "I was up all night for the fun at Xa Loi."

"I know," he said. "We have a report."

"Washington is going to issue a tough statement of condemnation."

"That's to be expected," he said. "You warned us August seventh that one would be coming if we did anything foolish."

"Our people read this as a reneging on solemn commitments."

"I'm sure you do. But let me ask you, what is it exactly you would have had us do? If you want the President to resign his office, why don't you just say so? Why do you prefer that he sit at his desk day after day and do nothing, while these people, whom we know to have been infiltrated by the Viet Cong, grow bolder and more provocative? And don't forget that we didn't want to act while your patron, Mr. Corning, was in charge."

"He's still the Ambassador."

"He's technically the Ambassador, but only technically. Would you have wanted us to act after Mr. Sedgewick arrived? How would that look? It all boiled down to one thing. We had to act, and soon. And the only time to act was in between Corning's departure and Sedgewick's arrival. What's wrong with that?"

"What's wrong with thousands of arrests, hundreds of injuries, scores of deaths?"

"As usual, you Americans have it all wrong. There are no arrests as yet. These are all detentions. In ninety-eight per cent of the cases we're going to move the bonzes back to where they work and live. Within two months I promise you there won't be a bonze in Viet Nam behind

bars. As for injuries, it's foolish for monks with sticks to resist combat
police in battle gear. There are nine monks in the hospital in Saigon
and half a dozen in Hue. Several have broken bones, but there are no
deaths. Not a single one."

"Are you sure?"

"Of course we're sure. The President's most urgent order was that
no harm comes to the bonzes."

"But what good did it do? These people will be back on the streets
as soon as they're released?"

"We think that by moving on this broad a scale we have a good
chance of burying this movement once and for all—at least in Viet
Nam. What we cannot control is the American government and the
American newspapermen. We're certain that the Buddhists are paper
tigers. But since we don't know what you Americans will do, we can't
say for certain what the outcome will be."

"Even your friends are shocked at what you've done. You can judge
yourself by the cable from Corning. There's confusion in Washington
about who ordered these raids, who carried them out, and who's really in charge."

A slight smile appeared at the corner of Da's lips.

"Who is in charge?" he repeated. "You can tell your *Chargé
d'Affaires*, Mr. Bilder that, oddly enough, the President of this country, Mr. Ngo Dinh Diem is in charge."

He picked up Corning's message from the desk and walked out of
the room. Marnin rose and went to the window and looked out at the
lovely bank of red cannae lilies that surrounded the north side of the
building. Tired as he was, a feeling of professional satisfaction passed
through him. He thought of his colleagues in the A-100 course stamp-
ing passports and doing notarials in visa mills like Frankfurt and
Mexico City. Life wasn't all bad, he reflected.

Marnin interviewed the two bonzes along with Curly Bird, in
whose compound they were located, and Mr. Phung, his chief local
employee, who interpreted. Neither of the bonzes spoke any language
other than Vietnamese. This was only Marnin's second business
encounter with the Director of USOM. Unless Curly was a consum-

mate actor, he had no suspicion of Marnin's secret life with Lily. He treated him as he would any other junior officer.

The monks were named Bac and Hiep—both in their early twenties and from the pagoda in Nha Trang. They had come to Saigon in mid-June and had spent most of the time since their arrival on the boulevards of Saigon, begging for their food and distributing leaflets cranked out daily on the mimeograph machines at the Xa Loi pagoda. To judge from their conversation, as far as their comprehension of the political issues involved, those leaflets could have as well been written in Greek as in English and Vietnamese.

They were seeking asylum because they were palpably frightened and were adamant that they did not want to be surrendered to the police. The Embassy had by this time received instructions from the Department that their requests for asylum should be honored and that they should not be turned over to the Vietnamese authorities, "unless such action is clearly voluntary on their part." Curly, who had not the slightest desire to host these bonzes, nor adequate facilities in his compound to do so, was determined to explore the extent of their voluntariness to the limit. At the same time, he was very patient with them—kindly and avuncular. Marnin could see what Lily meant. He was a nice man and a gentle one, a literal gentleman.

"The police," he said, "are anxious to speak with you. They assure us that no harm will come to you and that all they require is that you answer a few simple questions. That could be done right here in this room. We would make certain you're treated according to the law if you turn yourselves over to the authorities, who offer you free transportation back to Nha Trang."

Mentioning the return to Nha Trang was a tactical mistake. Bird could see immediately that this was the wrong tack with the two bonzes.

"We don't want to go back to Nha Trang," Hiep, who did most of the talking for the two of them, said. "We want to stay here."

"In Saigon?" Curly asked.

"No. Here. Right here, in this compound" was the reply.

Chapter 33

THE PRO-CONSUL

Sabo's stratagem worked. At two that afternoon Diem received a four man committee led by the Papal Nuncio and including Bilder, French Ambassador Lalouette, and British Ambassador Boggs, all of whom, when Diem allowed them to get a word in, took turns deploring the raids. Diem kept them two and a half hours, while he explained first the political and then the military situation in the country, and capped that with a dissertation on the importation of Buddhism from China, its degeneration, the growth of the sects which were offshoots of the Buddhist tree, their corrupt influence on the politics of Viet Nam, the low esteem in which they were generally held, and finally why his government had no choice but to send the out-of-town bonzes back to their homes.

The martial law decree and the apparent move by the ARVN against the pagodas had led to speculation either that the Generals had taken over or that Nhu had arranged a palace coup. Diem's performance dispelled any such rumors. The envoys emerged from their presidential audience scratching their heads, but convinced that Diem was still in charge of his government.

The pagoda raids brought the students in Saigon and Hue out into the streets. More than a thousand were arrested and were soon keeping company with the fifteen hundred bonzes detained earlier. The jails could not accommodate this sudden influx of people, who were housed in soccer stadiums and schools that had been closed because of the emergency. Four bonzes were reported to have been killed. (This was false. All four of them turned up alive and healthy when a UN investigating team looked into the matter in late October.)

The following night the city was deathly quiet when Marnin appeared at Lily's for their appointed rendezvous. She had believed the story that the army was responsible for the raids and, as always, minced no words. "The stupidity of those men goes beyond belief. They have the brains of a cock in a barnyard. They think only of their rank, their perks, and their privileges. They don't care about their country. They don't care about fighting the Viet Cong. Ten years ago they were all Sergeants. They are still Sergeants! They think like Sergeants and they act like Sergeants."

"But if Nhu goes and Diem goes, they're the ones who are going to end up ruling the country."

"If that happens, God help us all."

"Many in my Embassy think they would have to be an improvement over Diem and Nhu, that nothing could be worse than the existing situation."

"If you want to see Ho Chi Minh taking his morning coffee at the Caravelle Hotel then go ahead and back these Sergeants in their bid for power."

"There is no way the United States is going to let the North Vietnamese take over this country. Peiping cannot be allowed to think that we are the paper tiger Mao says we are."

"For you this is an abstract question. You'll go on to your next post maybe sadder, certainly wiser. But I have the future of my daughters to think about. I cannot allow myself to be caught up in the undertow that my countrymen seem determined to create."

"We can't solve this here. Let's forget about it for eight hours," Marnin urged.

"Maybe even eight minutes," she replied with a coquettish smile.

Only later did it become clear that Nhu had tricked the world by having the Combat Police and Colonel Tung's Special Forces don ARVN uniforms before making the assaults against the pagodas. Nhu had done this so cleverly and had split the army in such a way, in fact, that it took the Generals themselves three days to figure out what had occurred.

Telegram 314 from AmEmbassy Saigon to Secstate
rpt info CINCPAC, August 23, 1963: 8 p.m.
Secret NODIS.
For Hilsman from Bilder.

Despite earlier indications to contrary, we now feel reasonably sure that no military coup has taken place and that Palace is in control. In call I made on Diem to protest pagoda outrage along with Nuncio and British and French Ambassadors (Embtel 298) Diem gave no hint he was not in full command. And lengthy directive (Embtel 293) calling on Republican Youth to support government action would indicate same for Nhu.

Military are ostensibly working together, but they are not monolithic structure. Both III Corps Commander Ton That Dinh and Special Forces Commander Colonel Tung (who are known to detest each other) have forces in Saigon. Should regular Army decide to take over in earnest, i.e. depose Diem, possibility of serious fighting in Saigon would be considerable, as Tung and his Special Forces could, along with Palace Guard, be expected to defend Diem. Tung is disliked and distrusted by Army and would most likely share whatever fate befalls his patrons Nhu and Diem.

                                                            BILDER

Telegram 329 from AmEmbassy Saigon to Secstate
rpt info CINCPAC, August 24, 1963 11 p.m.
Secret; NODIS.
Ref Embtel 314.

We are repeating separately conversations with Dinh Trieu Da (Embtel 318), General Kim (Embtel 320), General Khiem (Embtel 322), and General Bich (CAS Saigon 0265).

These conversations confirm fully conclusions contained reftel. In addition, they indicate that:

a) Nhu, probably with full support of Diem, had large hand in masterminding action against the Buddhists.

b) Generals were genuinely worried about GVN handling of Buddhist situation and ready for decisive action, such as martial law.

c) Regular Army was not cut in fully on planned action against
pagodas, which was carried out by Combat Police and Colonel
Tung's Special Forces dressed in ARVN uniforms.

d) Finally, and most important, we do not conclude that those
with actual military strength in Saigon (Dinh, Tung) are at this
point disaffected with President or with Nhu.

Your 235 implied that U.S. has only to indicate to "Generals"
that it would be happy to see Diem and/or Nhus go, and deed
would be done. Situation is not so simple. Specifically, as indicated (d) above, we have no information that officers with
troops in Saigon are disposed to act in this way or that military have agreed on a leadership.

Action on our part in these circumstances would be a shot in
the dark. Situation does not call for that, in Embassy judgment.
In short, we believe we should bide our time.

(Note: Ambassador Sedgewick has not yet seen this message.)

SEDGEWICK

The cable was signed "Sedgewick," even though it was a Sam Sabo
draft that had been authorized by Bilder, because the new Ambassador
had arrived at 2130 hours at Tan Son Nhut via military aircraft from
Tokyo. Marnin was there along with the whole country team to greet
him. His first duty for Sedgewick was to telephone Pat in the code
room to authorize release of Embtel 331 to the Department, which
read: "Arrived at 2130 hours and have assumed charge.
SEDGEWICK." After that, as long as the Ambassador was at post,
whether he saw the outgoing message or not, all cables were signed
with his name.

The Country Team had gathered on the tarmac awaiting his arrival
on a VIP-configured C-130 after a thirteen hour flight from Tokyo.
The plane was routed to within fifty yards of the VIP room where they
had been waiting for him, along with Ambassador Luyen, the chief of
protocol. The curfew was still in effect and all commercial planes
scheduled to arrive after eight o'clock had been rerouted. So the usual
hustle and bustle of Tan Son Nhut was absent. In light of the curfew,
no wives were in attendance.

The press had also been limited by the curfew and the event was
covered by a pool, consisting of Mandelbrot, Buechner, the AFP correspondent Pierre Delort, and Jim Ballard of the AP. They were

ordered by Ambassador Luyen to wait in a roped off area next to the VIP waiting room. John Mecklin and Marnin went over to greet them. This was the first time Marnin had seen Mandelbrot and Buechner since the raids.

"Those sons-of-bitches almost confiscated Klaus's best Nikon. Good old John came along just in time to rescue it," Mandelbrot said. Then he asked, "Was the Army behind it or not? My sources say Nhu dressed up the Combat Police and Special Forces in ARVN uniforms and turned them loose to have all that fun."

"I don't know," Marnin said. "We've heard that. But it's still in the rumor stage. If true, it was a pretty cute stunt."

"Nhu's smirking now," Mandelbrot said. "But he'll be smiling out of the other side of his mouth pretty soon."

The C-130 rolled up and parked. Mecklin and Marnin disengaged from the press group and joined the other members of the Mission Council waiting at the bottom of the ramp. Ambassador Luyen, representing President Diem, was at the front of the line, followed by Bilder, Donnelly, Bird, Sabo, and the rest. The door opened. A huge spotlight lit up the area. After a prolonged pause Sedgewick emerged, squinting into the light. He waved and the entire group on the tarmac applauded. He smiled and went back into the plane to fetch his wife Penelope. After another pause they emerged together, she with a large straw handbag over her shoulder.

Ambassador Luyen conveyed greetings from President Diem and presented Bilder, whom they had not met, to the Sedgewicks. Bilder then introduced them to each member of the country team, giving names and titles. Although he was tired from the long flight, Sedgewick stopped at each person, looked them in the eye with great sincerity, greeted them warmly and complimented them on the work they were doing. Marnin was, of course, the last in line.

"And this is David Marnin, your Aide," Bilder said.

"How do you do, David?" said Sedgewick, looking at him meaningfully. "I've heard a great deal about you."

Since Marnin was the last person in line, the event was essentially over in the minds of Ambassador Luyen, Bilder, and the rest. But not in Sedgewick's mind. With a troubled frown he turned to Bilder and asked: "And where are the gentlemen of the press?"

Chapter 34

PRESS RELATIONS

If asked what their most difficult problem in Saigon was, Gus
Corning and Blix Donnelly would have unhesitatingly answered,
"press relations." In an attempt to "get a handle" on this problem,
John Mecklin had written memo after memo proposing a campaign
by the Embassy to take the newsmen into its confidence, to co-opt
them. But how could the embassy share its inner thoughts with people like Mandelbrot, Corning would ask Mecklin at Mission Council
meetings, when they live in a fantasy world, refuse to acknowledge the
enormous progress we are achieving in this country, and make no
bones about their advocacy of the overthrow of the very government
that the United States was committed to support?

With Sedgewick's arrival at the airport, however, it became clear
right away that, with him at least, Mandelbrot's view of the South
Vietnamese government had prevailed over Corning's. In one response
after another at the off-the-cuff press conference convened in the VIP
room of Tan Son Nhut, Sedgewick's casually critical remarks about the
regime to which he would soon be accredited delighted the press and
caused Sam Sabo to raise his diplomatic eyebrows practically beyond
his thinning hairline. The new American ambassador made no bones
about his assignment as a "new broom" to sweep away a discredited
policy of "coddling" the Ngo Dinh brothers. He repeatedly referred to
Saigon's current "reign of terror" and the fact that the President was
considering a complete change of course in our policy toward Saigon.

This was amply confirmed four hours later, at three that morning, when Marnin was summoned by Pat Patterson to read a NIACT Eyes Only cable for Sedgewick from the President. It was a bombshell.

Telegram 243 From Secstate to AmEmbassy Saigon
rpt info CINCPAC/POLAD, August 24, 1963, 6:36 p.m.
Eyes Only For Ambassador Sedgewick.
For CINCPAC/POLAD exclusive for CINCPAC. No further distribution.
Ref CAS Saigon 0265, Saigon 322, Saigon 320, Saigon 316, Saigon 329

It is now clear that whether military proposed martial law or whether Nhu tricked them into it, Nhu took advantage of its imposition to smash pagodas with Combat Police and Tung's Special Forces. US Government cannot tolerate situation in which power lies in Nhu's hands. Diem must rid himself of Nhu and his coterie and replace them with best military and political personalities available. If Diem remains obdurate and refuses, then we must face the possibility that Diem himself cannot be preserved.

We now believe immediate action must be taken to prevent Nhu from consolidating his position further. Therefore unless you perceive overriding objections you are authorized to impress on GVN that USG cannot accept attacks against Buddhists taken by Nhu and his collaborators under cover martial law and that prompt dramatic actions to redress situation must be taken, including repeal of decree 10 of August 6, 1950, release of arrested monks, nuns, etc.

We must at same time also tell key military leaders that US cannot continue support GVN militarily and economically unless above steps are taken immediately, which we recognize requires removal of the Nhus from the scene. We wish to give Diem reasonable opportunity to remove Nhus, but if he remains obdurate then we are prepared to accept the obvious implication that we can no longer support Diem. You may also tell appropriate military commanders that if they choose to act we will give them direct support in any interim period of breakdown central government mechanism.

Concurrently with above, Ambassador and country team should urgently examine all possible alternative leadership and make detailed plans as to how we might bring about Diem's replacement if this should become necessary. You will understand that we cannot from Washington give you detailed instructions as to how this operation should proceed, but be assured we will back you to the hilt on actions you take to achieve our objectives.

BALL

On his first morning, tired after his flight, Sedgewick did not show up at the office until eleven. He came in acting like a practicing politician—shaking hands with everyone he saw, including Marnin. He was an extraordinarily handsome man—good looking enough in his youth to have played leading roles in a couple of silent movies. Well over six feet, he carried himself with military bearing and exuded energy and command. Elected Governor and then Senator from Massachusetts, he had resigned from the Senate in early 1942 to accept a commission in the Army and commanded a regiment in the assault on Omaha Beach on D-Day. After stints as Eisenhower's Ambassador to Paris and Bonn, he was thought of as one of the four or five Republican Party leaders with the credentials to be nominees for the presidency in 1964 or 1968.

Marnin gave him five minutes to get himself adjusted in his new office and then entered to find him at the window, staring bemusedly into the kitchen of the apartment across the courtyard where the cook was frying noodles for lunch.

"What a shitcan this place is," he said, the vulgar phrase contrasting markedly with his patrician Eastern accent. "And the security here is appalling. What's to prevent that man frying noodles from picking me off with a high-powered rifle? Rifle, hell! He could do it with a pistol."

"The Vietnamese security people keep a close eye on that building," Marnin replied. "There's a guard at the door twenty-four hours a day to keep the VC from having access to it."

"The VC? It's the Vietnamese security people themselves I'm worried about. Aren't they controlled by Nhu?"

"Yes, sir."

"The last thing Averell said to me before I left Washington was that there was nothing that man wouldn't stoop to, including assassination.

And the first thing I find here is that my office in this rat hole of a building is totally vulnerable."

"Nhu may have many faults," Marnin said, "but he's not stupid. Attempting to kill the American Ambassador would be very stupid indeed."

"But the man is totally irrational."

"No sir," Marnin said. "He's high strung but not irrational."

"Well you seem to know a good deal more about the situation out here than our Assistant Secretary for Far Eastern Affairs or the Undersecretary for Political Affairs."

"For as long as I've been here," Marnin replied, trying to change the subject, "Ambassador Corning has been after FBO to build us a new chancery. I can get the file for you, if you want it."

"Have you got something to write with?"

"Yes, sir."

"This is a cable. Slug it 'TO THE SECRETARY FROM SEDGEWICK. Shocked to discover conditions under which my fine staff is working. These are the best people we have laboring on the front lines and they deserve better. The security situation in this Embassy is intolerable and totally unacceptable. Please send FBO team ASAP to discuss construction of new chancery. Regards. SEDGEWICK.' How's that?"

"Terrific, sir. It's a message that'll buck up everyone around here. And if I may suggest, there's a cable on the middle of your desk you ought to look at right away. That one over there."

Sedgewick walked to the desk and picked it up gingerly. He read it through carefully, pausing to mark important passages. Then he read it again.

"Have you seen this message?" he asked.

"Yes, sir."

"Has anyone else seen it?"

"No, sir."

"In the future," he said, "when an 'Eyes Only' message comes in for me from the President I want it treated just that way. Nobody is to see it before I do. Not even you. Is that clear?"

"Yes, sir, but—"

"But what?"

"The problem is that all these policy messages—and sometimes we get them three times a week—are slugged for your eyes only and arrive in the middle of the night because of the time difference. They're all designated NIACT, and that means somebody has to look at them right away. It could be the duty officer, of course, if you prefer him to read it instead of me. Otherwise, the code room will have to wake you up, which isn't a good idea since ninety-eight per cent of them can wait until morning."

"This is my third Embassy," Sedgewick said, "and I don't need instructions in how to suck eggs. We can return to this problem after I've decided whether you're going to be staying on here."

Marnin's heart sank. He desperately did not want to leave Saigon at that point. Sedgewick leaned back in his chair.

"It's a hell of a cable," he mused, talking more to himself than to Marnin. "Nobody was saying that to me when I left Washington just three days ago. I suppose the pagoda raids have been something of an epiphany. And now here I am. I haven't even presented my credentials, and they want me to overthrow the government I'll be presenting those credentials to. Make a list of potential successors, they say to me. Don't worry about the details. Just go ahead and do it and we'll back you to the hilt, whatever you do. I've heard that song before. If I don't miss my guess, there's a slight confusion in wording. What they mean by backing me to the hilt is that if things go wrong they'll plunge a knife in my back up to the hilt."

Marnin laughed and so did Sedgewick.

"Well, now that you've read that cable, what did you think of it? Thumbs up or down?"

Marnin's sense was that the shape and direction of his tour of duty in Saigon depended on whether or not he gave the right answer. But he was not sure what the right answer was.

"My view," Marnin finally said, "is that it's not wise to jump off an embankment until you've looked over the edge to see how far you have to go before you hit the bottom."

Sedgewick gazed at Marnin skeptically. He gave the impression that he was not pleased. This cable was a license to run and his instinct was to run with it.

"That's the State Department textbook response," he said. "You seem to have chosen the right profession. Congratulations. And now we've got some business to do. You and I are going over to the USOM compound to talk to those bonzes."

Curly Bird had been alerted by a call from Helen Eng and was out in front to greet the Ambassador as the Checker limousine pulled up to the curb. Bird was sweating in the late morning heat. He had been waiting for twenty-five minutes, unaware that they were making an unscheduled stop at the Xa Loi pagoda to survey the damage. A half dozen monks had been on the premises, including Marnin's feeble-minded friend. One of them spoke passable French. Sedgewick, who had as a teenager attended a Paris *lycée* and whose French was bilingual, tried to get the bonze to condemn what had happened to him, but with no success. The bonze had nothing but resolute praise for the authorities. They had handled things beautifully, he said, and had at all times been very proper, even polite. Sedgewick gave up on him and proceeded to the USOM compound.

Bac and Hiep, the two bonzes, were startled in the extreme to have their morning nap interrupted by the newly arrived American Ambassador. When introductions were concluded Sedgewick said, "I arrived in this country last night. My first act, gentlemen, as American Ambassador is to make sure you're comfortable."

The bonzes had been given makeshift housing in one of the compound outbuildings. Two army cots and light blankets had been brought in and a showerhead on a rubber hose attached to one of the two sinks in the bathroom down the hall—a facility that, judging by the smell in their room, they had not been taking advantage of. As soon as Bac and Hiep grasped who their visitor was, they began to exchange nervous phrases under their breaths. In response to Sedgewick's questions, Hiep—so nervous he was stuttering—allowed that his accommodations were more than up to standard. They were palatial.

"And how is your food? Are you getting everything you need?"

"The food is quite good," Hiep said, and then paused. "But much of it we can't eat. We're not used to foreign food and we're forbidden to eat meat."

Someone in USOM had fed them sausages and eggs for breakfast. "You mean to say we're not giving these boys Buddhist meals?" Sedgewick said to Bird. "From now on they're to have Vietnamese vegetarian food. Is that understood?"

"Yes, sir," Bird said, unhappy to be chewed out by the new Ambassador in front of his chief local employee, Mr. Phuong.

In the limousine on the way back Sedgewick asked Marnin to draft a cable about his talk with the bonzes, stressing his demand that they be given Vietnamese vegetarian food. He then dropped his aide at the Embassy and went back to the Residence where, to Marnin's great surprise, he was having lunch with Willis Mandelbrot. Even more surprising was the call Marnin received from the Residence after lunch.

"Please ask Colonel Gascon to come and see me right away," the Ambassador said.

"Yes, sir. Do you want to see him alone?"

"Why do you ask?"

"I was wondering whether you wanted Stu Markoff there as well."

"No I don't," said Sedgewick, and hung up.

Mandelbrot's front page story in the *Times* was headlined, "NEWLY ARRIVED AMBASSADOR HIGHLY CRITICAL OF PAGODA RAIDS." It recounted how Sedgewick's first act in Viet Nam was to visit the Xa Loi pagoda and the two bonzes holed up in the American Embassy and to assure them of protection. The U.S. government, Sedgewick was quoted as saying, was behind those bonzes "up to the hilt." Similar favorable stories about Sedgewick were picked up by AP, UPI, Reuters, and AFP, all emphasizing the American commitment to protect the two bonzes in the USOM compound. Walter Cronkite made it his lead story and the subject of a CBS editorial. It was suddenly clear that the enormous credibility gap that had plagued Embassy Saigon in its dealings with the press—a gap that had contributed vastly to Kennedy's decision to replace Corning—had been bridged with breathtaking speed, literally overnight.

Sedgewick did not return to the office that day. After his talk with Gascon and a subsequent siesta (getting what he called his "beauty sleep" remained a matter of great importance to him throughout his tour in Saigon) he called Helen and asked her to set up half-hour appointments at the Residence with Donnelly, Bilder, Markoff, Sabo and finally with Marnin, in that order. The aide reached the Residence just as Sabo was emerging.

"Things are changing around here," Sam said, as Marnin passed him on the front stairs. "I think we're all going to get the axe."

This dampened Marnin's spirit further. Lao Mi showed him up to the small office on the second floor where the Ambassador was receiving visitors. He gestured to Marnin to sit down.

Marnin handed him the cable, typed "on green," about his visit with the Buddhists. He signed it without comment and handed it back.

"Gus Corning speaks very highly of you," he then said.

"Thank you."

"He urged me to keep you on in your present position and said you'd be enormously valuable to me. How does that strike you?"

"That would be great as far as I'm concerned," David said.

"I told him, however, that it wasn't in the cards, that I already had someone picked out to be my staff assistant. Furthermore, and I want to be frank about this, Gus Corning's recommendation is not much of a qualification with me. There are going to be big changes around here, big changes. People committed to Corning policies might have difficulty with the policies I'm about to implement."

"I don't think that would be a problem with me," Marnin said unhesitatingly.

"That's good. Because the person I had fingered to replace you turns out to be pregnant and you appear to have an important attribute that I wasn't aware of. In fact, I wonder if Corning knew about it."

"What's that?"

"Your close friendship with Willis Mandelbrot."

"He knew about it."

"Well, that close friendship, it may surprise you to know, is of some importance to me. I was quite impressed to hear Mandelbrot praising you to the skies at our lunch today. Willis says you're one of the really valuable people on my staff and a person who knows how to keep a confidence." He paused, indicating he was taking his new aide into his confidence.

"I had a long talk with Jack Kennedy in the Oval Office on August fifteenth, a little over a week ago. It lasted more than two hours. Do you know what we spent half of our time talking about? You guessed it—Willis Mandelbrot. The President said that as far as he was concerned Mandelbrot was my number one problem, that if I could co-opt him, three-quarters of the battle of my Ambassadorship would be won. Well, as you know, Willis and I had lunch today. We agreed to stay in close touch. We also agreed to pass each other information on a regular basis. But for reasons you'll understand, it would not do for me to be on the phone too often with the correspondent of the *New York Times*. Whatever was said in those phone calls would go straight to Nhu. Contact with Mandelbrot will have to be in writing and carried out surreptitiously. In order to make such exchanges without arousing suspicion I'd need to have someone who's already been seeing Willis. You're the obvious person. What do you think of that?"

"I'm your man," David said, feeling much relieved. It seemed that he was going to be staying in Saigon after all.

Chapter 35

SETTING THE COURSE

August 27, 1963. The Country Team was forming up to go over to the Palace in a three car caravan for the ambassadorial presentation of credentials. They were dressed in white suits—Blix Donnelly was in his white dress uniform—and were gathered in the living room of the Residence waiting for the Ambassador to descend from the second floor. Marnin's job was to see that things started on time and he was getting nervous. The departure time was being cut pretty close to the bone. Sedgewick entered the room briskly and went around it, shaking hands with each person. When Marnin's turn came, he said, "We ought to be moving along, Mr. Ambassador."

Sedgewick looked at his watch. Then he raised his hand for silence and addressed the group.

"I've been thinking," he said. "Here we are in a country undergoing revolutionary trauma from pretty sinister forces and within fifteen minutes I and all heads of agency of this mission will be gathered on the home base of those forces. This strikes me as imprudent. We'd look awfully silly if we were captured as a group. So Blix, I've decided you and Carl should absent yourselves from this little ceremony. Go back to your offices and keep the Embassy and the MACV compound on full alert, just in case Mr. Nhu and his cohorts try a little rough stuff."

"Yes, sir," Donnelly said, sounding a bit hesitant.

"Yes, sir," echoed Bilder.

Marnin was astounded. He looked at Sabo and could tell from the expression on his face that he was thinking the same thing—that for Diem or Nhu to sanction acts of violence against the American Ambassador or members of his staff would be tantamount to suicide. Clearly, Sedgewick did not understand that the raids on the pagodas were not the acts of madmen. He was making a wildly wrong estimate of the character and state of mind of Diem and Nhu. Markoff, standing behind the Ambassador, looked at Sabo and rolled his eyes.

"Excuse me, sir," Sabo said tentatively. Sedgewick gazed at him coldly. "The absence of General Donnelly and Mr. Bilder will be noticed at the Palace and eyebrows will be raised, particularly in the case of General Donnelly."

"It seems to me there might be great value in having Mr. Nhu understand that we're on our guard."

"Well then, if I can speak to the local political situation," Sabo persisted. "I don't believe there's the slightest physical danger for any of us in taking part in this ceremony. Diem or Nhu would have nothing to gain from such action. This is your first meeting with the President, Mr. Ambassador, and you'll be having your first substantive talks with him later this afternoon. Both he and Nhu desperately want to get off to a good start with you."

"It's not only that," Markoff added. "I guess I know Ngo Dinh Nhu as well as any American, except perhaps Bill Colby. I see the Counselor, as he's called here, about the Strategic Hamlet Program and other programs we're running at least once a week, and usually more. There's a good deal of talk around town of him being on drugs or crazy or both. Admittedly, he's not enamored with Americans or American policy in this country. But he isn't crazy. I agree with Sam that harming the Country Team, individually or together, would be the farthest possible thing from the mind of either Nhu or Diem."

Sedgewick looked around the room for support, but was greeted by silence. He looked at Sabo and Markoff, from one to the other, gauging how to handle this mini-revolt.

"I'm new," he finally said, "and don't claim to know everything there is to know about this place. But you gentlemen and I obviously have a far different estimate of what's been going on around here these past three months. I've just come from two weeks of briefings in

Washington and have been privy to communications from the President that none of you have seen. From those briefings and those cables I was led to believe that we are dealing with a crisis, that Mr. Nhu is in desperate straits and would not even be above selling out his country to the Commies if that could save his skin. I was told he's a man who would stop at nothing to achieve his ends. Is that incorrect?"

"Well," said Sabo, "not entirely incorrect, but—"

"In that case," Sedgewick said, "it's better to be safe than sorry. What do we lose if we excuse two of our busiest people from an occasion that is strictly ceremonial? Now I see young David looking at his watch. It wouldn't do to be late for a rendezvous in the lion's den."

The group went off and Marnin returned to the Embassy where he hoped to spend the day catching up on his classified reading. Sam Sabo had been scheduled to accompany the Ambassador during his first substantive talks with Diem that afternoon and so Marnin thought he had most of the rest of the day to himself. At noon, however, Helen Eng conveyed the message that Sedgewick had decided that he, not Sabo, should go along with him to call on Diem. In the meantime, the Ambassador would be lunching with Penelope and afterward had a long meeting in his office at the Residence. Marnin was to pick him up at the Residence in the Checker at quarter to five.

"Who's he meeting with?"

"Frank Gascon," she said, with a cocked eyebrow. "That windbag!"

"Alone? Without Stu Markoff?"

"That's right."

Dinh Trieu Da was waiting for them at the foot of the steps. He bowed deeply and escorted them to the presidential office. Diem was seated at his desk when they entered. He rose and greeted them warmly, first Sedgewick and then Marnin by name, and ushered them to the familiar armchairs facing each other, separated by the black lacquer table. The servants came in immediately with their trays of refreshments.

Sedgewick, whose body had not yet acclimatized to the tropics, was perspiring freely. He drank a Fanta while Diem stuck to black coffee and smoked cigarette after cigarette. Diem began the conversation with a warm encomium to his "good friend" Jack Kennedy, without whose support he would never have reached the presidency. He then expressed appreciation for the letter Kennedy had written introducing Sedgewick.

"It is not often," he added, "that a national leader nominates a political opponent for a high position in his administration. This is a great tribute, Mr. Ambassador, to your skills and talents and demonstrates the high regard your President has for you. We understand that you also have great influence among your former colleagues in both parties in the Congress and hope that you will use that influence in order to explain the difficulties we are currently experiencing."

"It was a particular honor," Sedgewick replied, "when President Kennedy offered me the post of Ambassador to your government. I realize, of course, that I know little if anything about Viet Nam. My subordinates," Sedgewick said, gesturing at Marnin, "the professional Foreign Service Officers, claim I have some false perceptions of the local scene."

"Do not trust them, Mr. Ambassador. I hope Mr. Marnin will not think me rude, but we are convinced that many of our problems have been caused by your Foreign Service Officers and your CIA operatives who learn a little very bad, even painful, Vietnamese and then think they know more about this country than we Vietnamese do. They listen to people complaining, making wild charges and wild threats, and they are foolish enough to believe them, and to urge your government to take the tea in the teacup and blow it into a typhoon."

"Many of them are fine young men with good minds," Sedgewick countered. "There are a few rotten apples in the barrel, but we'll nose them out. And though I don't claim to know much about Viet Nam, I know a good deal about how my own country works. I would hope, Mr. President, that you'll allow me to advise you on American affairs."

"You can be sure, Excellency, that everything you say to me, will have my complete attention. I have studied the writings of your founding fathers—great men, all of them—and your constitutional processes as well," said Diem. "There is a well-thumbed copy of *The Federalist Papers* in my library. I don't know who was the greater man, George Washington, Thomas Jefferson, or James Madison. I've read the many volumes of Freeman's biography of Washington and the first two volumes of Malone's biography of Jefferson, so this is not just idle talk. But in order for a system like yours to work, you must have educated and trained individuals—thousands of them. What many of your countrymen fail to understand, Mr. Ambassador, is that we are a backward country. I have to write my own proclamations, to proofread every document that goes out of my office. I am criticized, I know, for holding the reins of power too tightly in my own hands. But given the human clay I have to work with, I have no other choice."

"People in my country know very little about Viet Nam. It was interesting to me in my home state of Massachusetts," Sedgewick said, "that people I had known all my life in politics thought that Madame Nhu was the Chief of State of Viet Nam. People in Boston have read her statements about barbecuing priests and about totally destroying the Buddhists and were shocked."

"This is a problem," Diem said. "And you will not be surprised to know that your predecessor Gus Corning raised this repeatedly with me. I've tried to persuade Madame Nhu to keep quiet. I've done everything I can think of. I've even threatened to take a wife."

Diem laughed in that high pitched chuckle of his, and he was joined by Sedgewick's hearty bass "ho, ho, ho," and even by Da and Marnin.

"But she is stubborn," Diem continued. "She says she is a member of the National Assembly and has a right to make speeches on her own."

"That may be," Sedgewick replied. "But you have to understand that America was founded on the principle of religious toleration. My countrymen were therefore shocked at the idea of official government persecution of the Buddhists."

"I know that," Diem said. "And I hope you will help to explain our precarious situation."

"I can only do that if you give me the proper ammunition. What is needed is a dramatic gesture such as liberating the Buddhist prisoners."

"Half of them have already been screened, released, and returned to their pagodas. You seem to think that our move against the pagodas was 'cruel, brutal, and crazy.' Those are the words Mr. Mandelbrot quotes you as using. But Mister Marnin here can tell you that it was not so crazy, that the provocative meetings at the pagodas, which were growing more disrespectful day by day, and which were simply intolerable, have now stopped and will not be resumed. And as for being cruel and brutal, a few monks got unduly excited and resisted by force. They picked up broomsticks and used them to try and beat the arresting soldiers. This was foolish. They themselves were beaten in turn."

"Our information is that at least four were killed."

"Your information, Mr. Ambassador, is false—lies and calumnies spread by our enemies. Who are these four? What are their names? Where were they killed? Where are they buried? Do you think those people aren't looking for martyrs? If anybody had been killed we'd have had demonstrations at their funerals."

"Be that as it may, the important thing is not so much the truth of what actually happened, but public perceptions. And in the United States it is now widely believed that an oligarchic government is using force to persecute the majority of its citizens."

"Oligarchic?"

Da explained the meaning of the word in Vietnamese.

"More calumny and slander," Diem said.

He snapped his finger and Da went to his desk and brought him a book entitled Buddhism in Viet Nam, published by the Vietnamese Buddhist Association. Diem put on his black-rimmed glasses, turned to page four and read the following to Sedgewick:

". . .under the General Buddhist Association's authority and general direction are grouped three sanghas numbering well over 3,000 monks and about 600 nuns and three communities of disciples which branch out their ramifications as far as to remote hamlets. The figures of adherents to these three lay associations and their affiliates reach about 1,000,000, to which should be added an important number of non-associate disciples by as much as threefold."

Diem removed his glasses and handed the book to Sedgewick, who, in turn, handed it to Marnin.

"So you see, Mr. Ambassador, even the Buddhists themselves only claim a million adherents and three million non-associated disciples, only a quarter of the population—hardly a majority. But claims of this kind are always highly exaggerated. Our estimate is that practicing Buddhists number no more than five per cent of the population—less than the number of practicing Catholics."

Taking religion as his starting point, Diem discoursed on the history of his family going back eight generations, the role of religious beliefs in their philosophy and conduct, their conversion to Catholicism, the arrival of the French, the failure of the French to raise the Vietnamese from their underdeveloped state, the low quality of education, particularly at the university level, and how "inferior persons held posts in universities and turned them into centers of unrest." He said there was a well organized plan to create unrest around the country in order to force the government to pull the troops out of Saigon, leaving the capital defenseless. It was under these circumstances and at the urging of the top generals in the ARVN that he had decreed martial law and approved the "cleansing" of the pagodas.

Sedgewick attempted to interrupt at several points with a comment or question, but, like so many others, found it difficult to rein Diem in. Finally Sedgewick tapped his watch and excused himself for cutting off the President's "fascinating discourse," but noted he was having dinner with Penelope and did not want to keep her waiting.

"Always a good idea, Mr. Ambassador, not to keep a lady waiting," Diem said and chuckled. They all rose. Diem accompanied Sedgewick to the door and then decided to go along with him down the stairs to the front steps.

"One thing," he said on the steps, "I would hope you could instill more discipline among members of your mission, Mr. Ambassador, particularly as regards their mixing into our politics."

"Mr. President," Sedgewick replied, "throughout my career I've based my philosophy on the adage that people know far better than diplomats or intellectuals how to rule themselves. The first three hundred names out of the Boston telephone directory would make a better legislature than the Harvard faculty, and I speak as an overseer of Harvard."

Diem laughed and the two men parted cordially. In the car riding back to the Residence, Sedgewick was quiet.

"That Diem's quite a nice little fellow," he said finally. Then he sighed. "It's too bad. It's really too bad."

Marnin glanced at his handsome, brooding profile and inwardly shuddered.

In his cubbyhole just next to Sedgewick's office that last week in August Marnin watched Gascon, Donnelly, and to a lesser extent Markoff—Sabo was conspicuous by his absence—wheel their marked and ribboned military maps of each of Viet Nam's four military Corps into the office and then come out after lengthy, daily briefing sessions in which the Ambassador was instructed about which Vietnamese General was which, what forces he commanded, and where those forces were stationed. Although a quick study on some matters, Sedgewick was grumbling at that point at having to differentiate "Big" Minh from "Little" Minh—one General Minh was enough for any country—and at the fact that half the population seemed to have the family name of Nguyen. But his difficulty keeping Vietnamese names of people and places straight in his mind did not prevent him from sending the following "back channel" cable to Dean Rusk.

CAS 0292 From Saigon Station to Headquarters
Top Secret. FROM SEDGEWICK. Immediate.
NODIS. August 27, 1963.
FOR THE SECRETARY PERSONAL EYES ONLY
Ref Deptel 0243.

Reftel was on my desk when I arrived in Saigon. It argues that the Nhus have to be forced out, using all means at our disposal, and that it might be preferable to leave Diem in place without them, because with Diem extracted from the scene, no matter how this was accomplished, we would clearly be moving into unknown territory. On the other hand, all my Viet Nam experts believe chances of Diem's removing Nhu and Madame Nhu are virtually nil. At the same time, by making such demands we give Nhu chance to forestall or block such action. Risk, I believe, is not worth taking, since Diem and Nhu are in control of combat forces in and around Saigon.
Best course, in my view, is therefore to go straight to the Generals with our demands without informing Diem. Would tell

them we prepared to have Diem without Nhus but it is in effect up to them whether to keep him or not. . .

The following evening Sedgewick had a long session with Frank Gascon and Stu Markoff in his study in the Residence, after which he signed off on another back channel cable:

CAS 0300 from Saigon Station to Headquarters.
Top Secret. Immediate.
NODIS. August 28, 1963.
Ref CAS 0292, Deptel 0243.

1. Per reftel, Colonel Gascon spoke with JGS Chief of Staff General Tran Thien Khiem 1245 hours and conveyed following from highest levels US Mission:
a. We need further elaboration of ARVN thinking and planning.
b. We in agreement that Nhus must go.
c. Question of retaining Diem or not is up to the Generals.
d. Bonzes and other arrestees must be released immediately.
e. We will provide direct support, including to wives and families, during any interim period of difficulty.
f. Don't expect to be bailed out during initial action of assuming state power. Entirely their own action, win or lose.
g. If Nhus not removed and Buddhist situation not resolved US military and economic support could not continue.
2. General Khiem replied as follows:
a. Generals were in accord with points expressed. Pleased to know Embassy position.
b. These points should not be raised with General Tran Van Bich at this time since Nhu has certain officers on Bich's staff and might become aware of this from them.
c. Colonel Gascon should stand by for later pickup by jeep to meet with General Duong Van Minh and repeat US position to Minh.

The following evening at five Marnin accompanied Sedgewick in his introductory (and only) call on Ngo Dinh Nhu. Stu Markoff was scheduled to go with him, but Sedgewick said he preferred someone more "neutral" than Markoff.

An ARVN Captain met the Ambassador at the gate and escorted

them. Nhu's office, which Marnin was visiting for the first time, was located in the west wing of the Palace. It was much smaller than Diem's, smaller than Da's for that matter, and was crammed with books, files, papers, and reports placed haphazardly on every piece of furniture in the room. Nhu was behind his desk, smoking, reading, and fiercely scowling as they entered. He looked up, saw Sedgewick, leaped to his feet with a big grin on his handsome face and instructed the Captain to clear the papers off the two straight backed chairs in front of his desk so that they could sit down. The conversation was in French.

"So," he said, "you have the courage to come into the den of the big, bad wolf."

"I have the courage of my convictions," Sedgewick replied.

"I'm sorry to hear it," said Nhu. "What is needed on the American side is not so much conviction, but wisdom."

"After a lifetime in public service, I hope that I've accumulated a little bit of that as well."

A servant came in with a pitcher of coffee and three small cups. Nhu poured for them. He did not offer cream or sugar.

"Well, Mr. Ambassador, I hope this marks the beginning of a very fruitful relationship. My hope is that we can work together to surmount the difficulties between our two governments."

"There are those," Sedgewick said, "if I may be so bold, who attribute many of those difficulties to actions instigated by you and to intemperate statements made by both you and your wife."

"It seems I'm destined to be a scapegoat. You people seem to think I'm some sort of master puppeteer and that the President cannot move his arms or legs without my pulling of the strings. But I can assure you that I am what my title implies—a counselor, one of many, although perhaps *primus inter pares*. No, no, no. I'm not the instigator of the current crisis between us. I decline the honor. I would attribute the cause of this crisis to other factors."

"And what are they?"

"Unacceptable interference by Americans, both official and non-official, in the internal affairs of our nation. You decide we need thousands of advisors and you simply assign them helter-skelter all over the country without even consulting us about it. You flood us with people. We don't know how many there are, who they are, what they're doing or where they're located. You tell us there are twelve thousand advisors here, but we learn from others that there are, in fact, sixteen thousand. If we Vietnamese wanted our country to remain a colony, we would have stayed with the French, who had their virtues. Our goals cannot be dictated to us. When you tell us something, wise as you are, you cannot expect us simply to salute and say 'yes, sir.' Nor can your Voice of America issue ultimatums about stopping aid—"

"Ed Murrow, who's very sick by the way," Sedgewick interjected, "wants the Voice to be completely objective in its reporting."

"Objectivity is one thing. But something called the Voice of America is taken by us to be just that—the voice of America—and not some disinterested purveyor of information. When VOA criticizes us you diminish the prestige of this government, prestige we've worked hard to earn. Eighty nations have granted us recognition."

"There is no way that the VOA will be muzzled," Sedgewick said.

"It is not a question of muzzling Mr. Murrow," Nhu rejoined. "At the very least it is not too much to ask that what is reported should be accurate. These statements about the action our government took against the pagodas were wholly false inasmuch as it was the Generals themselves who wanted the action taken."

"I don't know the details," Sedgewick said. "But as a man who has spent many years in public life, I know that no foreign policy can be carried out by the U.S. Government without public support. And our public is much distressed by your treatment of the Buddhists. Nor can we underwrite Madame Nhu's statements about 'barbecuing bonzes' or totally destroying the Buddhists. I'm receiving letters every day about such statements. How do you expect me to respond?"

"She is a member of the National Assembly and a public person in her own right," Nhu replied. "She is entitled to her own opinions, which are not necessarily mine or my brother's. But this is only window dressing. The real question is what is happening in the countryside. Are we winning the war? The answer to that is that although thirty-five per cent of our population is not yet in first class Strategic Hamlets, by the end of the year all of them will be in Strategic

Hamlets of some kind. Then the guerrilla war will be over and the North may decide on a conventional war."

"General Taylor and General Donnelly both assure me that we have adequate resources available here to win any conventional war. The question in Washington is what to do about the Buddhist problem."

"If there is a conventional war," said Nhu, "we will do our best. But we'll need your help. As for the Buddhists, occidental people simply don't understand what's been happening. These suicides are brought about in pagodas filled with incense and incantation. These poor bonzes are hypnotized, intoxicated, and intimidated. This is how these suicides have been organized. But you'll see that the measures we've taken will have their effect. And you must agree that these measures had to be undertaken before your arrival, which we thought would not be until August twenty-sixth."

"It would have been far better for all of us," Sedgewick said, "if you hadn't taken those measures at all. But since you have, it would be very helpful in the U.S. if there could be some dramatic gesture here regarding the liberation of the Buddhist prisoners."

"The Buddhist prisoners are in the process of being released. But we cannot afford to make a dramatic gesture out of it. This would undo all our good work."

"That's too bad," Sedgewick said.

"Please keep in mind in the weeks and months ahead, Mr. Ambassador, the importance of combating worldwide communist objectives. That is where the interests of both our governments lie. We are allies and the government of Ngo Dinh Diem takes our alliance very seriously and will never undermine it. We regard the Russians and especially the Chinese as our bitter enemies. There is an internal problem here, but it is in the countryside, not in the pagodas, We have developed a strategy to deal with that problem—the Strategic Hamlet program. That program is working. And don't forget that it was I who personally invented the Strategic Hamlet."

Nhu stood, to indicate that he had said what he had wanted and that the interview was over. He accompanied Sedgewick to the door, where the ARVN Captain was waiting to escort him out of the building.

"I hope there will be no more threatening statements out of Washington," were his final words.

"I hope there will be no more inflammatory speeches out of Viet Nam," Sedgewick replied.

The two men laughed.

Marnin dropped the Ambassador at the Residence and went back to the Embassy, where he wrote up Sedgewick's conversation with Nhu in cable form. Helen Eng typed it on green and then Marnin took it to Sedgewick's office on the second floor of the Residence. Sedgewick read the message through twice.

"This is fine," he said, and signed it.

He was about to hand it back to Marnin, but on second thought penned a final sentence. It read: "Ngo Dinh Nhu is a highly intelligent and effective man, and would be considered so in any country."

Marnin took the telegram and drove back to the Embassy. As he entered, the Marine Guard told him that the Ambassador had ordered him back at the Residence right away. Sedgewick wanted another look at the cable. He read it through and then added another sentence at the very end: "But my guess is that he is ruthless, not wholly rational by our standards and that he is interested above all in the survival of himself and his family."

Chapter 36

SWIMMING BACKWARD

Kennedy had authorized (Deptel 243) the removal of the Nhus and, if necessary, of Diem as well. But then he waffled. He was not interested, to put it mildly, in presiding over another Bay of Pigs fiasco. So the Embassy was daily queried for "clarification," for endless scorecards describing which Generals and Colonels controlled which brigades that were located exactly where. Over the following week every morning during breakfast—frozen orange juice, All Bran with raisins, black coffee, all preceded by a tablespoon of Maalox—Sedgewick fumed at Marnin about the "goddamned micro-managers" in the intelligence community who seemed to think that they knew more than "the man on the spot."

But in the end his allies, the State Department "activists," Harriman and Hilsman, prevailed and Washington decided to leave the "Diem problem" to the judgment of the Ambassador on the scene. (Like many a neophyte officer before and after him, Marnin was to learn again and again in the course of his career that Washington decisions are made by high policymakers under pressure of hundred-hour work weeks by a logic that is as inaccessible to the uninitiated outsider as the Old Norse texts of the Poetic Edda.)

CAS 0303 from Saigon Station to Headquarters.
Top Secret. NODIS. Immediate. Eyes Only. August 29, 1963.
FOR THE PRESIDENT AND THE SECRETARY FROM SEDGEWICK

It is time to don the life vests. Situation here has reached point of no return. Saigon is an armed camp. Current indications from CAS sources are that the Ngo family has dug in for a last ditch battle. Those Viet Nam experts on my staff whom I trust most estimate that the Generals are determined to push forward. JGS COS Gen. Khiem, the most solid of the Generals, has confirmed to us that overwhelming majority of General officers, excepting III and IV Corps Commanders Dinh and Cao, are united. They know they are on the two-yard line, that the time for long forward passes and end runs is over, and that they have no alternative but to put their heads down and attack the goal line. We believe the Generals will act and that they have a good chance to win.

Bloodshed can be avoided if the Ngo family steps down before the coming armed action. This could still happen. If General Dinh, the mercurial chief of III Corps and military governor of Saigon, joins with the other Generals, it is conceivable Ngo family might surrender without risking a Gotterdammerung. Up to now Dinh has remained firmly on the family's side. But there are signs he is wavering.

Other Generals will be working on Dinh's well-known vanity. Both Don and Khiem are close to him. Meantime, Generals realize the Rubicon has been crossed. It is obviously preferable Generals conduct this effort without apparent American assistance. Otherwise they will be vulnerable to charges of being American puppets, which of course they are not. Nevertheless, all of us understand the effort must succeed and that whatever needs to be done on our part must be done. If this attempt by the Generals aborts or fails, we believe it no exaggeration to say that our entire effort here, and Viet Nam itself, runs serious risk of being lost.

                                                           SEDGEWICK

Mandelbrot and Marnin were in the locker room of the Cercle Sportif having a second *citron pressé*. Marnin had just handed the reporter a large, unaddressed manila envelope—the first of dozens he would pass to him over the following six months.

"The Ambassador says he's entrusting this to your discretion and that you're to guard this stuff like your family jewels."

"Don't you worry your pretty little head about that," Mandelbrot replied. "This priest never violates the secrets of the confessional."

It was four o'clock on a Saturday afternoon and they had played three sets of singles, one more than Marnin wanted on a hot Saigon afternoon. But Billy insisted on a third set after David had taken the first two without loss of a game in less than an hour. Dripping with sweat, they left the court shortly before the afternoon rain came along to cool things off. Dennis Rocard, a rubber planter who cut a wide swath through the nightclubs of Saigon whenever he was in town, was having a drink on the veranda. Pointing the index finger of his right hand to his temple to indicate that they were mad, and waving his Campari at them with the left, he said:

"*Seulment les chiens sauvages et les Américains. . .*"

Mandelbrot, irritated by his lousy tennis, was adopting the patronizing air of the upperclassman with Marnin. The reporter could not stop talking about the prowess of Bascombe Sedgewick. His metaphors all came from the heroic movies of earlier decades. In those days it was still considered bizarre to have actors thought of in political terms, so Marnin was struck when he put Sedgewick's performance in his first week in Saigon in the framework of Alan Ladd in Shane, and then ten minutes later of Gary Cooper in High Noon, and finally, a quarter of an hour after that, of "Errol Flynn leading a cavalry charge." The last was a little too much.

"Errol Flynn, as I recall, played General George Armstrong Custer."

Mandelbrot was taken aback. He eyed Marnin suspiciously.

"You're not pining for Corning, are you?"

"I'm not pining for anybody. I'm just wondering if Rocard is right and you've had too much tropical sun."

"Look, my friend, anybody who understands what's happened this past week has got to gasp in admiration."

"Gasp?"

"Listen, you poor booby, even though you work for it, you seem to have no idea how hard it is for the United States Government to move off its ass and do anything. And what's taken place here over the past week is a fucking miracle!"

"What exactly are you referring to?"

"For eight years the U.S.G. has doggedly pursued one policy in Viet Nam—to sink or swim with Ngo Dinh Diem. As a result we've been stuck in a quagmire. Then Sedgewick arrives on the scene and in one week—one fucking week!—changes the policy of the U.S. one hundred eighty fucking degrees, right on its ass. And this performance has just been for openers. Unless I miss my guess, your boss is operating on his own agenda. It wouldn't surprise me to see him single handedly solve the knottiest problem facing the U.S. Government, and then, when it's all pretty much taken care of, ride off into the sunset next spring to become the Republican candidate for President."

"Now I know you've got sunstroke. Kennedy's got a lock on being reelected. This is Camelot, not the Wild West. Or have you forgotten?"

"Whatever happens, getting the nomination in '64 will give Sedgewick the inside track for '68, when any Republican will have a good shot at the presidency."

"Moreover, even if we did dump Diem, there's no convincing evidence that the situation would improve for us."

"Look, Mr. Eagle Scout, who's kidding who, and why? I know you're in a position to observe what's going on and I know you're observing it. What the hell do you think is in this envelope you've just handed me? I know Gascon's been in touch with Khiem and Khanh and Bich and with Big Minh and that the light he's turning on isn't red or even amber. It's green—bright, fucking green."

Marnin was floored. The most highly guarded secrets of the American mission in Viet Nam were an open book to a *New York Times* correspondent who had proven himself a dozen times over unable to keep a confidence. Marnin had already been burned badly, having been accused of leaking information to Mandelbrot that, compared to this, was anodyne in the extreme. Many hundreds of lives, perhaps thousands, depended on maintaining secrecy. "I don't know what you're talking about," Marnin said to him.

"Look! Spare me an Academy Award performance. You know what I'm telling you is the truth. I know you know. I called you a liar once and lived to regret it. Please don't make me do it again. I don't want to risk breaking up a great doubles partnership."

"Billy, let me assure you I don't have a clue what you're talking about." These were Marnin's last words on the subject. Mandelbrot saw that he could be pushed no further.

Leaving Mandelbrot at the club where he was to meet one of his girl friends, Marnin went to Lily's compound. She had been at a ladies lunch at the Golf Club and greeted him dressed to the nines in an embroidered magenta silk *ao dai* and sporting more makeup than necessary for a woman of her sensational good looks—especially the heavy purple eye shadow that was the latest fashion, but that Marnin disliked.

"Why does the best looking woman in Viet Nam have to make herself up to look like a Las Vegas showgirl?" he asked. "I thought you were at a ladies' tea, not a men's smoker."

"You're a silly boy," she replied. "Women don't fix themselves up for men. They fix themselves for other women. And this means dressing and looking *à la mode*. I wanted to be made up to look exactly the way the other Generals' wives were made up. Since they all come from families that are trash, I cannot look too good or talk too wisely or dress too plainly when I'm with them now that I'm no longer in mourning. Otherwise, they'll say that my nose is stuck too high in the air. And in any case, for once with those empty-headed women who usually talk of nothing but their ailments, their hairdressers, and their husbands' mistresses, the lunch was actually not uninteresting."

"Somebody took a new lover?"

"Better than that," she said with a satisfied smile. "I found out why you've been so busy this past week."

"How's that?"

"Your Mr. Sedgewick seems to be the most dangerous kind of man. My husband used to say there were four kinds of officers. There were the lazy and stupid—the vast bulk of the officer corps. There were the energetic and stupid—people who should be immediately discharged from the service. There was the brilliant and energetic officer, who should be made Chief of Staff. And finally, there was the brilliant and lazy officer, who should be put in command of the army. Your new boss is clearly energetic and stupid, the worst possible combination."

"Why do you say that?"

Lily's girls were visiting relatives for the weekend and they were alone in the big house. Marnin was lounging on the bed in her boudoir. She had removed her tunic and was seated at her dressing table between two large mahogany dressers, in black *ao dai* pants and brassiere, applying cold cream to her face to remove the eye-shadow and other makeup that bothered him.

She laughed.

"It's wonderful seeing little boys dressed up to play Cowboys and Indians, pretending they're big boys."

She came over to the bed and kissed him lightly on the mouth. He could taste the cold cream.

"Everybody in Saigon knows what's been happening this past week," she said. "Even your Embassy must be aware of that."

"I'm not sure I know what you mean," he said warily.

She laughed again.

"I'll tell you what I know," she said, "but only if you tell me what you know."

Marnin fidgeted for a while, kissed her once and then again.

"Your heart is not in those kisses, *petit frère*," she said.

"Things have been happening," he finally said, "interesting things. But I can't tell you about them. I'm sworn not to reveal what I know and I can't violate an oath."

"You are sweet. But then I shouldn't be telling you what I've learned either. I also swore."

"Suit yourself."

"Oh, all right. I'll tell you. But you must promise not to reveal it to anyone. Swear on your mother's grave."

"I swear."

"Your Mr. Sedgewick, it seems he arrived in Saigon determined to overthrow Ngo Dinh Diem. Your General Donnelly, who deals with our top Generals daily, and your Mr. Markoff, who has lunch with Ngo Dinh Nhu every other day, are absolutely opposed to the dropping of Diem. But your Sedgewick, he pays them no attention. He is what is called an elephant running loose in the china shop."

"How do you mean?"

"Within days of his arrival in Saigon, without knowing anything about Viet Nam, your Ambassador Sedgewick sends our mutual friend Colonel Gascon to meet with Generals Don, Khiem, Kim, Khanh, Bich and Minh to encourage them to get rid of the Nhus and in the bargain to cast Ngo Dinh Diem aside. Right away!"

Marnin was thunderstruck. Twice in one day was too much. Was there anybody in town who did not know the most secret plans of the American Embassy?

"How can you know this?" he asked. "How can you believe anyone who tells you this?"

"You Americans don't seem to understand that making a decision on whether or not to organize and support a *coup d'état* against Ngo Dinh Diem is not something these Generals can decide for themselves. It's a family decision. Making the wrong move, turning left when you should have turned right, can cost you not only your life but the welfare of your family for generations ahead. This is important to a Vietnamese. These people, except for General Don, one generation ago were peasants. And if their fathers weren't peasants, their grandfathers were. They come from nothing and if they don't establish their family they're going to remain nothing. They need their own fortunes. And in order to establish such fortunes they have to depend on their wives, who handle their business affairs and who happen to be the ladies I was lunching with."

"And the Generals—they share these Top Secret national security decisions with their wives?"

"Of course they do. What is Top Secret to them, and what only torture will make them reveal, is what brigade is stationed where and the quantity and caliber of ammunition that brigade has. But whether they should stick with Diem or join in a plot to dump him, that is something about which every Sergeant will consult his wife, and at heart these men are still Sergeants!"

"So the people who really decide what's going to happen in this country—the real heavyweights—are a bunch of wives sitting around on a Saturday afternoon having lunch at the Golf Club?"

"They and their Chinese partners. The biggest mistake Diem ever made was to crack down on the local Chinese. If they get the chance they'll take their revenge, just as they already have against my husband. But business is business and the Chinese aren't going to kill the goose that lays golden eggs. The CIP is for them, as you say, a license from the government to print money. If you want to know the truth,

the best way for the Americans to bring down Ngo Dinh Diem is not
to plot with a bunch of fifth rate generals. All you have to do is stop
the CIP. The Chinese will take care of the rest. When Diem becomes
a financial liability to the commercial community, mark my words, he
won't last a week longer."

She began to kiss and caress him. As far as she was concerned, the
conversation was over.

"Wait a minute," David said. "What about the coup? What did
those ladies at the Golf Club say to their husbands?"

"I already told you that."

"No, you didn't."

"Of course I did. What do you think they said? They told them to
grow up and stop thinking they are John Wayne in one of your western movies. They told them to learn how to count before they risked
the fate of the next six generations of their families."

"Learn how to count?"

"To count the numbers—they don't add up. General Ton That
Dinh, for example, commands III Corps and he has lots and lots of
reasons to be grateful to the Ngo Dinh family. What would happen to
him if Diem and Nhu were killed?"

"You tell me."

"I don't think he would live a week. But I don't really know. But
what is more important, he doesn't know either and neither does
Madame Dinh, who also happens to be a very devout Catholic and a
very avid golfer. Furthermore, Colonel Tung—who doesn't belong to
the Golf Club—owes everything to Diem and would be the first one
killed by the Generals along with Diem himself. It is no accident that
his Special Forces are all based in Saigon. And the Palace Guard is
absolutely loyal. So is General Cao in IV Corps, a man of such light
weight that he has to put rocks in his shoes every morning so he won't
float away. Khanh in II Corps will do whatever the Americans tell
him, but he's in Pleiku and won't be able to affect the action for several days after a coup begins. And Do Cao Tri in I Corps—the only
real soldier of them all—is too far away.

"Diem and Nhu," she continued, "have made sure the people
commanding troops in the Saigon area, or in the area that can reach

Saigon by tank or APC within two hours of the beginning of a coup, owe their positions entirely to the Ngo Dinh family. Diem went through a dress rehearsal in November 1960 when your Ambassador Durbrow let him down. He is not going to entrust his destiny to the unreliable. So everything depends on turning Ton That Dinh, whose wife goes to confession to Ngo Dinh Thuc. And there is no sign of Dinh's wavering, nor can the others bring him into the conspiracy without risking that he'll betray them to Nhu."

"So you don't think the Generals will attempt a coup?"

"This is not a question of think. This is a question of know. I know there's not going to be any coup."

"No matter what Ambassador Sedgewick does?"

"Your Ambassador Sedgewick, he can be like Hitler and chew the rug. These Generals on whom you choose to place the fate of my country and the prestige of yours, they are not fit to command a company, much less an entire nation. How can anyone who knows Duong Van Minh—a truly silly man—think of him as a maximum leader of anything other than the orchid horticultural society?"

"And there won't be a coup?"

"Are you deaf? Don't you understand? The coup is dead—as dead as Napoleon, as dead as my husband."

Chapter 37

A BOLT OUT OF THE BLUE

Sedgewick was already in high dudgeon when Gascon burst past Helen Eng into his office to let him know that the coup, which the Embassy had thought was just about to be launched, was not going to take place after all. During the entire conversation that followed, which took so many turns that in other circumstances it would have been comic, Sedgewick kept confusing General Kim, General Don's brother-in-law and the leader of one group of conspirators, with General Khiem, the Chief of Staff of the JGS, the leader of another, and therefore had difficulty keeping straight Gascon's convoluted explanation of why the coup could not take place as planned. Sedgewick felt doubly the fool because not two hours before Marnin had delivered to the code room the following cable to the President:

Telegram 375 from AmEmbassy Saigon to SecState.
Top Secret; Immediate; August 31, 1963—6 p.m.
FOR THE PRESIDENT.

We are launched on a course from which there is no respectable turning back: The overthrow of the Diem government. There is no turning back in part because U.S. prestige is already publicly committed to this end and will become more so as facts leak out. In a more fundamental sense, there is no turning back because there is no possibility, in my view, that the war can be won under a Diem administration, still less that Diem or any member of his family can govern the country in a way to gain the support of the people who count, i.e., the educated class in and out of government service, civil and military—not to mention the American people.

The chance of bringing off a Generals' coup depends on them to some extent; but it depends at least as much on us. Vietnamese Generals doubt that we have the will power, courage and determination to see this thing through. They are haunted by the idea that we will run out on them. We must therefore press on. If proposed action is suspended I believe the respect felt for us by the Vietnamese Generals will be dealt a body blow. I realize that this course involves a very substantial risk of losing Viet Nam. It also involves some additional risk to American lives. I would never propose it if I felt there was a reasonable chance of holding Viet Nam with Diem.

You inquired about the views of General Donnelly. He thinks that I should ask Diem to get rid of the Nhus before starting the Generals' action. But I believe that such a step has no chance of getting the desired result and would have the very serious effect of being regarded by the Generals as a sign of American indecision and delay. I believe this is a risk we should not run.

SEDGEWICK

It was a bad morning for the Ambassador. Just before Gascon burst in, Marnin had informed Sedgewick that the two bonzes, Bac and Hiep, had disappeared from the USOM compound. Curly Bird had phoned first thing that morning. Marnin did not often get calls from him, so when Bird's secretary got on the line Marnin thought it might have to do with Lily. But the call was about the bonzes. Lao Du, the Chinese Buddhist cook had found the room empty when he brought their usual morning fare of congee at seven. They had flown the coop, leaving no note or other indication of what had happened to them. The guard at the gate said they had left at six, carrying nothing but their begging bowls. Since his orders regarding Bac and Hiep were only to stop others from having access to them and said nothing about stopping them from doing anything they wanted, he had made no effort to detain them.

Curly Bird, for one, was relieved. But Marnin knew Sedgewick would be very angry. Bac and Hiep were living symbols, he had said publicly on numerous occasions, of the willingness of his Embassy to stand up for "the little man" against governmental tyranny. They continued to make good copy. Marnin decided to find out what had happened before delivering the news. He drove to the Xa Loi Pagoda, next door to the USOM compound. It was a much different place from the frenetic headquarters of a few weeks before. There were no gongs, no incense, no clacking of typewriters or humming of mimeograph machines. Most of the monks were out on their begging rounds. Those that remained were doing the morning clean-up activities. All the debris had been carted away. It had returned to being a normal Vietnamese Buddhist pagoda.

Nobody Marnin knew from the old days was in evidence. Nor could he find a single bonze who could handle French or English. The one sitting in the office, seemingly in charge, was about forty. He wore steel-rimmed spectacles and had large suppurating carbuncles on top of his shaved head, some of them covered with plastic band-aids. Luckily, he was from Saigon and his spoken Vietnamese was relatively clear and succinct. Marnin identified himself and asked about Bac and Hiep, giving their full names and gesturing toward the USOM compound.

"What happened?" he asked. "Where are they?"

"They're gone," the Bonze said.

"Where did they go?"

"Home."

"To Nha Trang?"

He nodded his head affirmatively and giggled, as though it were all a big joke.

"Why did they leave?"

"They had been there long enough."

"Long enough for what? Who told them to go?"

He shrugged his shoulders and giggled again.

"Was this their idea? Did they want to do this themselves?"

Another shrug. Another giggle.

"How did people manage to talk with them in the USOM compound? They had no phone there."

He pointed at the fence separating the pagoda from the compound next door, gestured with his arm upward and his index and middle fingers moving alternatively and rapidly, to show someone climbing.

"Someone talked with them by climbing over the wall?"

He nodded, and giggled yet again.

Sedgewick was beside himself when he got the news.

"What do you mean, they walked out of the USOM compound? How could they just walk? They were hostages. They were goddamned refugees seeking asylum from an oppressive police state! They were in fear for their lives! Read the *New York Times*! That's how the story was carried on every television network in the world! They were the goddam symbols of the new leaf that's being turned over in this Embassy! I told you to make sure they had everything they needed. I told you to keep them happy! You told me they were happy!"

"They were happy all right. I saw them yesterday and they practically kissed my hands when I walked into their room."

"So why did they leave?"

"Somebody evidently told them to."

"What about the police? I thought they were demanding that we turn Bac and Hiep over to them for interrogation."

"The first three days they kept a couple of cops outside the compound. But after they found out what small potatoes Bac and Hiep really were, they lost interest."

"So they're now presumably on a bus to Nha Trang. And you don't think, the Embassy doesn't think, the CIA doesn't think they were coerced, that there's any goddamned monkey business going on?"

"We're probably never going to know for sure. But as far as we can tell—"

At this point, Helen Eng buzzed to say that Colonel Gascon was on his way in. Gascon paid no attention to Marnin since he knew that one of the aide's duties was to proofread all cables Sedgewick signed.

"It's all over," he said.

Sedgewick rose up out of his chair.

"What in hell are you talking about?"

"The numbers don't add up," Gascon said, echoing Lily's words. "General Minh has called the whole thing off. There was too much uncertainty and no guarantee we were going to win. Without Dinh on board we could have had a bloodbath on our hands, and it wasn't clear where he stood. According to Minh, Nhu had found out about the whole thing and was rubbing his hands waiting for our guys to make the first wrong move. Both Minh and Khiem think they were betrayed to the Palace. They suspect it was by someone in this Embassy close to Nhu."

"Where in hell did they get that idea? Did you have any clue, any inkling this was going to happen?"

"No, sir, Mister Ambassador," said Gascon. "This was a bolt out of the blue as far as I was concerned. A bolt out of the blue!"

Chapter 38

COOL CORRECTNESS

Mandelbrot was as convinced as General Minh that someone within the American Embassy had betrayed the plot to Nhu. "Someone finked," he said to Marnin. His candidates were Sabo and Markoff. Nhu can't take a crap without one of them wiping his behind."

"That's ridiculous," David replied. "First of all, there's no reliable evidence that Nhu had any knowledge that a coup was being planned. Secondly, even if Nhu did find out, it's infinitely more likely that his secret police network or his signals intelligence would have uncovered the information. Why would Sabo or Markoff spill the beans to Nhu? What's in it for them? People who leak information of that kind don't rise very high in the U.S. Government."

"Spare me the Mary Poppins bullshit. The higher they are, the more they leak. Anybody who works for the *New York Times* would confirm that. Why would they tip Nhu off? That's easy. They were on Corning's team and their days are numbered. With the exception of Donnelly, you and Mecklin are the only ones in Corning's inner circle who'll be staying on, and in both cases that's only because of my influence with your boss. You got a reprieve."

"I'm ever so grateful."

"Donnelly can't be fired," Billy continued, intent on letting Marnin know how well he understood the internal politics of the Embassy. "He's too close to Taylor. But he'll be going too. He won't be extended when his tour runs out. He doesn't know it yet, but he's getting a deputy named Westmoreland, a real scrapper who's gonna replace him and win this war. As to your Embassy colleagues, both Sabo and Markoff are acolytes of the Strategic Hamlet program, which almost certainly falls apart as soon as Nhu leaves the scene."

"But you're sure the coup is postponed indefinitely?"

"No. Not indefinitely. The Generals have come this far and they know that if they return to square one Nhu will pick them off at his leisure, eat them one by one like a bunch of grapes. But before the coup can go forward the Generals need a signal that the United States supports it—not just Sedgewick, they know where he stands, but John F. Kennedy, Dean Rusk, and Robert McNamara."

"What kind of signal?"

"Big Minh wants to see three things. He wants American economic aid suspended. He wants Markoff and Sabo fired. And he wants the American Embassy to distance itself from Diem."

"Our economic aid keeps things going here. Without it the place will fall apart."

"There's two hundred million in the aid pipeline. There would only be a real economic crunch when that runs out."

"You know as much about economics as you do about tennis. Just how do you expect the Embassy to 'distance itself,' as you put it, from a government with which we're involved at every level down to the most remote hamlet in the boondocks?"

"The policy will be cool correctness. Don't go after them. Let them come after you. Make them sweat. If they don't do what we've been asking—release the Buddhists and the students, rescind Decree Number Ten, and allow some real democratic freedoms—then we let them dangle in the wind and eventually go down the tubes."

"So we just sit in the Embassy and read the papers."

"If you closed the door of that place one morning and sent everybody away on vacation, do you know what would happen? I'll tell you. Not one fucking thing. And do you know why? Because nobody would even notice, that's why."

They had just exchanged unmarked manila envelopes in the locker room of the Cercle Sportif. Mandelbrot's contained a batch of his latest unedited dispatches from Saigon. He had written nothing about the aborted coup, even though he knew every last detail far better even than the Ambassador, since he could actually keep the actors straight—a spectacular example of Sedgewick's ability to manipulate the press. Instead of the coup, Mandelbrot's story of the week concerned dissension within the American mission. It ran on the front page of the following Sunday's edition of the *Times*.

"Certain senior officials of the mission," he wrote, were desperately unhappy at the new policy of "standing up for American interests" that had been inaugurated by Sedgewick. Having gone to "the Corning school of diplomatic appeasement" dedicated to assuaging the Vietnamese tyrant and his family, these Embassy officers were mistrustful of anyone who demanded that Americans not be pushed around. Luckily, Mandelbrot continued, "we now have at the helm an experienced diplomat who, if necessary, can engage in bureaucratic cut and thrust with the best of them."

Insiders in Saigon, wrote Mandelbrot, were amazed at how quickly Bascombe Sedgewick had seized the reins of power. One high Embassy official was quoted as saying, "the man's amazing. He's done more in one week to make sense of this mess than the rest of us have done over the past five years. What this place needed was a new broom. And thank God we have one."

While Embassy officials, Mandelbrot wrote further—delivering his *coup de grâce*—"are reluctant to name names, it is widely known in Saigon that the two Embassy officials closest to Ngo Dinh Nhu, who have been working hand in glove with him to establish the thoroughly discredited Strategic Hamlet program, are Political Counselor Samuel F. Sabo and Chief of the CIA Station Stuart M. Markoff. It is widely assumed that their tenure of office in Embassy Saigon will not be very lengthy. . ."

The story created a firestorm in every relevant agency in Washington. White House Press Secretary Pierre Salinger reasserted the President's complete backing for both Ambassador Sedgewick and General Donnelly and deplored Mandelbrot's attempt to "fish in quiet waters." Department spokesman Bob Manning expressed unhappiness at anything in the public domain that suggested disunity among American officials in Saigon. There is one team out there, Manning said, working together under the leadership of Ambassador Sedgewick, who "has the Secretary's full confidence." In the Pentagon News Room General Taylor was quoted on background as saying that "Blix" Donnelly was one of the finest officers the US Army had produced over the last half century and what had been accomplished in Viet Nam under his leadership had been nothing short of miraculous.

The Agency with the greatest problem over Mandelbrot's article was the CIA. Everyone in both the diplomatic and press corps in Saigon knew that Markoff was the Station Chief, but Mandelbrot's article broke a taboo in saying so publicly. Sedgewick, in fact, cited his "exposure" in a back channel "more in sorrow than anger" message to John McCone as his main reason for urging that Markoff be replaced. Markoff's future in Viet Nam under Sedgewick was obviously limited in any case. But Marnin's own surmise was that the most important single factor causing him to be the first Country Team member to leave the scene (shortly to be followed by Sabo) was that his dismissal was, as Mandelbrot predicted, a condition laid down by General Duong Van Minh for resuscitating the aborted coup.

On September seventh, General Khiem debriefed Gascon on a meeting the previous evening with Generals Minh, Don, Bich, Kim, and Khanh. They all believed, according to Khiem, that the August coup had been betrayed to Nhu by Markoff. The Generals, according to Khiem, could not even begin to think of a further coup unless they were sure that it would have the full support of a unified American government, including General Donnelly. They set down four preconditions before they could move—three of them the same ones Mandelbrot had forecast to Marnin a week before, i.e., cessation of economic aid, a perceptible cooling of American Embassy relations with Diem and Nhu, and the removal of Markoff (they did not mention Sabo) from Viet Nam. The fourth precondition was denial of direct funding to Colonel Tung's Special Forces and their integration into the command structure of the South Vietnamese Joint General Staff.

Gascon wrote a telegram incorporating what Khiem had said and handed it to Marnin to convey to the Ambassador for his final approval later that evening. As usual, whenever there was something important for Sedgewick to sign Marnin put it on the center of his desk where he could not miss it. But it was still there when he locked the Ambassador's papers up that evening. The next morning he placed it square in the center of his desk once more. But again it was left untouched. This was repeated the following morning. When Marnin went to lock him up that evening, however, the draft cable was gone. He checked with Helen Eng to see if she had brought it down to the code room. She had not. Finally, he looked in the burn bag in the bottom drawer of Sedgewick's safe. There it was, torn in half. He never sent it on to Washington, which therefore never focused on Minh's four preconditions for mounting a coup.

Three of the preconditions stipulated by Minh were already in Sedgewick's hip pocket. First, Markoff and Sabo would soon be leaving. Second, he had been authorized to inform Colonel Tung that American funding would no longer be forthcoming unless his Special Forces were placed directly under the Joint General Staff. Third, Washington had agreed that selected economic aid programs be suspended "temporarily," but put the ultimate decision in abeyance until a fact-finding trip by McNamara and Taylor scheduled for the last ten days of September. The fourth of his preconditions—a show of official coolness to Diem and Nhu—was satisfied at a Country Team meeting September 9.

They all rose when Sedgewick entered the conference room, as was his custom, five minutes after the appointed hour. Gesturing at Bilder to begin, he let each person at the table review events in his area in light of the difficulties then being experienced in relations with the GVN. Each section chief reported that cooperation with the Vietnamese had diminished. Only Donnelly insisted that in his bailiwick the war against the Viet Cong was progressing normally and satisfactorily. John Mecklin reviewed the contents of the local press over the previous weekend. The *Times* of Viet-Nam and the Vietnamese language press had featured excerpts from Mandelbrot's story about dissension within the Mission, and in addition had carried several more direct personal attacks on the Ambassador, whom they dubbed "the Last Colonialist." Sedgewick spoke last.

"Gentlemen," he began, "I've been thinking about how to respond to some of the vicious attacks that have been unleashed against this Embassy, against you, against me, against all of us. One way would be to answer back, but as my old friend Lyndon Johnson likes to say, 'don't ever get into a pissing match with a skunk'! Nevertheless," he continued, "we can't just pretend nothing is happening. So I've decided that the way to meet this challenge is to adopt a new policy. First of all, we're going to cut off aid payments temporarily. Secondly, we're going to maintain cool correctness toward our Vietnamese counterparts to make them understand that we'll not be pushed around a minute longer. Embassy Saigon will henceforth cease communicating with Vietnamese officials professionally or socially. You're not to have them to your house or out to a restaurant. You're to decline invitations from them, and refuse substantive discussion. When you're asked about the aid cutoff, you're to reply with a smile on your face that the matter is under review. If they demand to know when it's going to be decided, you're to say 'soon,' and leave it at that."

Bilder looked as though someone had dropped a rock on his head. This clearly had not been discussed with him before the meeting.

"Mr. Ambassador," he asked tentatively, "is this now open for discussion, or have you pretty much made up your mind?"

"As far as I can see," Sedgewick replied, "there's nothing much to discuss."

"I assume this applies to the Embassy itself and not to the operational missions like USOM," said Curly Bird.

"You assume wrong. This is for everyone," Sedgewick replied.

"Hold on a minute," General Donnelly said. "I'm fighting a war. People are dying out there. I can't bring my operations to a halt."

The Ambassador thought that one over.

"Well, yes," he said. "I suppose we have to make an exception for the military. But that applies just on the operational side and not on policy questions or on MAP funding."

"That's going to be damned awkward," Donnelly said.

"I know it's going to be awkward," responded the Ambassador. "I want it to be awkward. It's the awkwardness that's going to get the message across. And I don't want doubts about what that message is."

"I've got two cabinet ministers coming to dinner on Saturday night," said Sam Sabo. "What am I supposed to do about that?"

"You have two choices. Either you can call and disinvite them or you can cancel your dinner. I'm giving everyone a grace period of three days. Anything within that period that's already scheduled I'm not going to ask you to change. But anything beyond three days you have got to wiggle out of."

"I've got a farewell party at the end of the month," Curly Bird said. "It's a big bash and I expect to invite all the people we've been dealing with, which means two to three hundred Vietnamese. Mr. Ambassador, are you talking about events of this kind as well?"

"I surely am," Sedgewick said sternly.

Bird looked crestfallen.

"Mr. Ambassador," Sam Sabo said, "I understand you've made up your mind on this, but if you'll allow me to play the devil's advocate, I'd like to register a few thoughts."

"Such as?"

"Well for one thing, the effect this will have on the Vietnamese, and especially on Nhu and Diem. They're feeling very embattled. Letting them stew in their own juice seems to me a mistake. We can get them to do what we want. But we can't do it by leaving them to their own devices. We ought to see more of them, not less. We ought to be holding their hands, not letting go. I don't see the point of picking a fight with them."

"We're not picking a fight with them. They've picked a fight with us," Sedgewick replied. "Weren't you in the room when John Mecklin was giving us a rundown on the local press? There's one thing that should be crystal clear to all of you. There is no public figure in the United States—nobody!—who has been more anti-colonialist, more in favor of national self-determination, than I've been over the last twenty years. And yet Nhu is tarring me every day as 'the Last Colonialist.' This is the Hitler big lie technique in spades. Mr. Goebels couldn't do it better. Now I don't care personally. I've been called worse by bigger skunks than Mr. Nhu. But I can't let myself forget that the person they're attacking every day just happens to be the personal representative of the President of the United

States of America. What makes a psychotic pipsqueak like Nhu think that he can get away with a stunt like that? What kind of respect are we going to have from the Vietnamese if they see us subjected to that kind of verbal abuse without replying? I know there are risks. But, goddam it, it's time we took some risks around here. These people have got to stop thinking we're a bunch of gutless wonders. And one more thing. Don't forget that I'm driving this bus. Anybody who doesn't like it should feel free to get off the bus with no hard feelings all around. But I want it understood, and understood clearly. We're not supplicating ourselves to Mister Ngo Dinh Diem or Mister Ngo Dinh Nhu a moment longer. Our policy is one of cool correctness. Is that understood? Is that completely clear?"

"Yes, sir!" Bilder said.

"Yes, sir!" echoed General Donnelly.

Marnin was sitting in his usual seat along the back wall staring at Stu Markoff, who had not said a word during the meeting. It would be very difficult for him to explain to CIA headquarters that their agents had to cut off contacts with the Vietnamese in order to send the correct political message to Ngo Dinh Nhu. This was something he had to take up with the Ambassador and Marnin figured he probably intended to see Sedgewick afterward to talk about new ground rules for his case officers, including Gascon. But Marnin was looking at Markoff carefully for a different reason.

All the others in the room seemed to be accepting Sedgewick's new policy prescription of an aid cutoff and of "cool correctness" at face value. But since Markoff was privy to Gascon's conversations with the Generals, Marnin knew him to be the only other person in the room who would realize that by implementing this new policy Sedgewick had now met all four of General Minh's and General Khiem's September 7 preconditions for moving ahead with the Coup.

Chapter 39

SQUEEZING THE FAT

Markoff tried to see the Ambassador immediately after that staff meeting, but was informed by Helen Eng that Sedgewick was leaving, along with Marnin, to greet the latest Buddhist bonze to seek asylum with the Americans. The Embassy's newest guest had strolled into the consular section the previous afternoon. Marnin had been summoned to peer over a screen and confirm his identity. When the Ambassador heard the news, he felt at last that his luck was changing. The arrival of this particular bonze seemed to him like a media godsend; for he had hooked the big fish himself—Thich Tri Binh.

Sedgewick blew into the basement room where Binh was lodged with a big smile on his face. He stuck out his hand to the nonplussed bonze, who regarded it warily. Instead of shaking the hand, Binh put his palms together and bowed in the age old Buddhist greeting. Since in the course of a hundred sermons he had castigated American conduct in his country—sorely exaggerating the amount of rape, mayhem, and theft committed by the "big noses"—Binh regarded the cordiality being shown him by the number one big nose with understandable wariness. He did not know, of course, that Sedgewick was only vaguely aware of his consistently anti-American vaporings and looked on him not as a foe of the United States, but as an ally in the struggle against Diem.

"Young man," Sedgewick said, "I've spent forty years in public life and I can tell you this is one of the two greatest thrills I've ever had. The only other occasion that compares with this was a fine January

day in 1947 when Lord Mountbatten presented me to the Mahatma
in New Delhi at a small luncheon at the Governor General's palace."

"Who?" asked Binh.

"Gandhi!"

"Gandhi?"

"The Indian leader," Marnin said.

Binh gave him a blank stare. Sedgewick glared at Marnin.

"Gandhi," Sedgewick said, "the man I've always regarded as the
greatest and most fearless political leader of the twentieth century.
And you sir, as far as I'm concerned, are the Vietnamese Gandhi."

"Are you going to ship me to India?" Binh asked. "I've got as much
right to asylum as Bac and Hiep. More."

Sedgewick looked at Marnin helplessly.

"No, Binh, you're not getting the point," David said. "The
Ambassador is comparing you to the great Gandhi, who obtained
India's independence from the British. He says you're the Vietnamese
Gandhi."

"So he will give me asylum?"

The Ambassador heaved a great sigh.

"Of course we will, sir. It's an honor to have you as my guest. I'll
do everything in my power to ensure that you enjoy your stay."

Binh had trouble getting the gist of what Sedgewick was saying.

"I can see," Sedgewick continued, somewhat unnerved by the non-
comprehending stare of his interlocutor, "that this has been a difficult
experience. But you've found a home among friends in your beautiful
native city."

Binh winced. Nothing irritates a native of Hue more than to be
taken for a Saigonese. The Ambassador, oblivious to his *faux pas*,
turned to Marnin and ordered that Binh be given better accommodations. Marnin replied that this was the only available room in the
chancery itself and that if their guest left the building he would be
subject to immediate arrest. Binh looked at them with a puzzled
frown, trying to figure out what was going on.

"Asylum or no asylum?" he asked.

"Asylum, sir, you have asylum," Sedgewick assured him
emphatically. "And now, unfortunately," he said, looking at his watch,

"I have a pressing luncheon engagement with an admirer of yours, Mr. Willis Mandelbrot of the *New York Times*, who'll be delighted to hear of this latest turn of events. And speaking of the press, it's my intention, if this is agreeable with you, to hold a joint press conference together as soon as we find you more comfortable quarters."

Binh nodded his assent, still unsure of what was happening to him.

Instead of accompanying the Ambassador to Tan Son Nhut, where he was to give a speech to the assembled officers at MACV, Marnin spent the afternoon arranging Binh's new accommodations. There was no suitable place for him in the Embassy chancery. So after much agonized discussion back and forth with the mission's Admin Counselor and its General Services Officer, it was finally decided to put him back in the USOM compound where Bac and Hiep had been housed.

Curly Bird was fit to be tied. It was his building paid for by his agency, he said, and he'd be damned if he'd see it used as a hostel for dissident bonzes. But once the Ambassador, at Marnin's behest, called him from Tan Son Nhut, he found himself with little choice other than to acquiesce.

The tricky part was getting Binh to his new quarters, since as soon as he stepped out the door of the chancery he would be subject to arrest. And for all the Embassy knew, the police were outside waiting for him. An emergency Country Team meeting, presided over by Bilder, concluded that this kind of confrontation with the GVN at a moment when our relations were at an all time low should not be risked and that it was better for Binh to remain in the Embassy, albeit in sub-standard quarters.

When informed of that, however, Sedgewick exploded, "I'm the Ambassador here, and I'll decide what we're going to do and what we're not going to do. The *New York Times*, for one thing, has already been informed that Binh is going to be housed at the USOM compound. For another thing, the press is going to want to talk to him. I'm not for one minute contemplating having a joint press conference with him in a goddamned cellar and I don't want the press interviewing him there either. How do you think that would play on the TV networks? I want him in decent quarters!"

Stu Markoff's people were consulted for their technical expertise.

The result was that at six that evening, in the twilight, Binh, wearing khaki pants and a black turtleneck sweater, was lying down on the floor in the back of the Ambassador's Checker limousine, his head resting uncomfortably on Marnin's toes. Marnin and his old nemesis, the Security Officer Franco, wearing a large straw hat and sunglasses, pretending he was the Ambassador, rode together in the rear. The car was fitted out with a small American flag on the front grill, which was always the case when the Ambassador was inside. The gate was then opened and they were driven from the Embassy into the USOM compound. Luckily, the ride was uneventful. They were not stopped, or searched, or even noticed.

It was a day packed with events. Marnin had no sooner gotten home that evening when there was a brisk knock on the door.

"Claudio!" he said. "What's up, my friend? Come on in."

Marnin poured them each a scotch on the rocks and opened a can of peanuts. They sat facing each other, Marnin in an armchair and Claudio on the couch, with the drinks and peanuts between them on a rattan table.

"I'm pretty sure you can't do a goddamned thing for me," Claudio said, "but I'm in a position where I have to touch all the bases and to be seen touching those bases."

"What are you talking about? What's wrong?"

"Well, to put it to you straight, I'm in a little bit of a jam. I've got to come up with a considerable sum of cash very quickly. Either that or convince some fairly disreputable characters that there's no real need for me to do so."

"You can have whatever I've got," Marnin said.

"And what's that?"

"Give me a couple of days and I can lay my hands on ten or fifteen thousand dollars. I can give you a postdated check right now."

Claudio smiled sardonically.

"That's good of you, my friend. But you don't quite get the picture. I need fifty to a hundred times that amount and I need it before the end of the week."

"But I thought all your enterprises were going like gang busters."

"They had been. They are! Our projection as of last Friday was that we'd double our money in the next six months. This, of course, depended on you Americans sticking around—an assumption nobody doubted. But now it's a big fat question mark."

"You don't think we'd put all those resources into this place and then just back out of here, do you?"

"Unfortunately, the people I do business with don't know what to think. They're ready to take a powder."

"Why?"

"Five or six different reasons. But the most important one is the CIP. You're about to cut off your payments. Without the CIP this country goes down the tubes. More important, without the CIP *we* go down the tubes."

The Embassy was not expecting a Vietnamese reaction to the aid cutoff, which had not yet been announced, for weeks. This was supposedly highly privileged, "close hold" information.

"Your friends are exaggerating," David said. "There's no need to panic. The aid shipments will be suspended, only suspended. No decision has been made to terminate the CIP. And there's a couple of hundred million in the pipeline that will carry the CIP for at least another three or four months. There's nothing to worry about yet."

"Nothing to worry about! Tell that to my mother when they fish me out of the Saigon River! You and your countrymen don't know your ass from first base when it comes to economics. The market doesn't give a shit about what's in the pipeline. The market only cares about your intentions. It looks to my people like you're about to pull the rug out from under Diem, and they don't understand it. What for? The one thing a market dislikes is uncertainty. Why should my people leave assets in Saigon that are going to be worthless if the VC takes over when they can reinvest whatever they can get for those assets in Bangkok or Hong Kong and recoup their losses within a year?"

"Nobody's pulling the rug out from under anyone," Marnin said. "And if you're making the kind of money you've been talking about, I don't understand why these friends of yours are so concerned."

Claudio stared at Marnin in seeming disbelief.

"I see I have to spell it out for you in words of one syllable," he

said. "The Chinese are great gamblers. This means that when an unexpected opportunity comes along, like the American build-up in this
country, they play it for all it's worth. They think nothing about bor-
rowing a million dollars at sixty-four per cent interest to build a cigarette factory, because that factory earns them half a million in the first
year of operation, enough to cover their interest payment and make a
profit of one hundred thousand besides on an investment of absolutely nothing except a little collateral.

"Sounds like pretty good business to me," Marnin said.

"That's right. Especially because they borrow money against the
same collateral in three different countries—maybe here and in
Bangkok, or Hong Kong. Could be in Singapore or KL, wherever. As
long as you Americans are here, their creditors are sweethearts—they
don't look too hard at where their payments are coming from. But if
you pull out, or even look as though maybe one day you might pull
out, the whole picture changes. The creditors put on their green eye-
shades. So a cigarette factory that last week was worth two million and
which could have been used as collateral to borrow another ten million, which could have been used, say, to build a bottling plant and a
dozen other enterprises, today that factory is a net liability. You can't
put it in a suitcase and carry it out of here."

"But you still should be making a pile."

"The end of last week, with all our money leveraged to the max,
my group could have liquidated and walked away from Viet Nam
with a minimum clear profit, once we settled our debts, of ten million. A year from now it would have been fifteen—minimum—more
likely twenty-five. That's when there was a market. Today, because
there is no market, our assets are worth shit—less than shit, which can
at least be used for fertilizer. Our creditors, who lend their money by
the week not by the year, want all their dough—every fucking cent—
pronto today. And the fellow whose knees they will break is the front
man of our group, who happens to be me. And all because that prick
Sedgewick decided to squeeze Diem's balls, if he has any."

"Sounds to me from what you say that if we play it cool enough
the financial community will put the kind of pressure on the GVN
that Sedgewick wants to see."

"You couldn't be more wrong. This policy won't just splatter a few golden eggs. It'll kill the goose as well. The reason those Generals couldn't bring themselves to move against Diem two weeks ago is that the people who subsidize their life styles, who know them better than their mothers, realized that those guys couldn't run a hot dog stand, much less a country. Diem might have his problems, but compared to those guys he's just what your Vice President Johnson called him, the Winston Churchill of Asia. If you're going to invest money in this country you want it run, believe me, by Ngo Dinh Diem, who forgets nothing, rather than General Big Minh, who can't remember to zip his fly in the morning."

"I'm very sympathetic," Marnin said. "But you've got a hard row to hoe. Sedgewick isn't going to be moved. The local business community ought to put the pressure on Diem and Nhu to knuckle under."

"The brothers are too stubborn for that. It won't happen. At least it won't happen until it's too late. You were lucky the first time. You almost turned this country over to a bunch of fifth rate, tinpot Generals. You won't be so lucky next time."

"What can I do?"

"Explain to that moron Sedgewick that if he has any idea he can cut the funding of the CIP gradually, so that greater and greater pressure is put on the GVN by the business community to kowtow to the Americans, he's crazy. There are no secrets in this town. What he's doing is destroying the market on which the business community feeds. He won't be squeezing the fat out of this country. He'll be squeezing this country out of existence. Without that market everything dries up, even my balls. *Entiende?*"

Lily was already there as he opened the door, dressed in her pink negligee. But instead of the usual warm and lengthy kiss, with her fingers gently massaging the nape of his neck, she started to admonish him roundly for being what she called an hour, but which he knew to be twenty minutes, late.

"If you're tired of me," Lily said. "Just say so."

"I couldn't help it. Claudio showed up unexpectedly with some real problems. I had to hear him out."

"Claudio! What do I care for Claudio? If your precious Claudio is more important to you than I am, you can turn right around and walk down those steps and get out of my life."

"Look, I'm sorry I'm late. Come on. . ." He tried to kiss her. "Be a nice girl."

"Don't you dare patronize me! If I'm not nice enough for you, why don't you go elsewhere? Maybe one of the bar girls on Tu Do will be nicer."

"Ease up, will you, Lily. It's been a really tough day. . . ."

"*You've* had a tough day? How do you think *I* feel? Yesterday I was a millionaire—thanks to me. Today I'm a beggar—thanks to your Ambassador."

"Lily, what in hell are you talking about?"

"Before he came here, everything was wonderful. People were prospering. . .children going to school for the first time. . . new buildings going up everywhere. Just this morning I woke up singing like a little bird, a perfect day ahead of me. Nothing to do but have a massage, a facial, and spend an evening making love to you. And then what? Before I even get to the beauty parlor, I find out I'm going to lose everything—the farm, the house, the bed you sleep on!"

"But I thought the farm was thriving."

"It was. It is! Only two days ago I signed a new contract with your base at Bien Hoa to supply them with eggs, chicken and pork at a price forty per cent higher than last time."

"So what happened?"

She threw herself on the bed and began to wail. Despite her sobbing, he found himself looking at the enticing curve of her buttocks.

"The Chinese are liquidating," she said, her words punctuated by sobs. "They're calling in their loans."

"You owe them money?"

"Of course I owe money. You can't be in business without owing money. Why do you think God created banks and money lenders?"

"I could let you have what I've got."

She wiped her eyes.

"How much is that?" she asked.

"Well, about fifteen, sixteen thousand dollars."

"I need at least ten times that. Oh, what am I going to do?"

"But do you know why the Chinese are calling in their loans?"

"Of course I know why! Everyone in Saigon knows! They're afraid that Sedgewick's going to dump Diem and turn the country over to those stupid Generals—and then you'll all go away. . . ."

"Lily. . .Lily, this isn't true. . . ."

"Oh, go away! Get out of here! You and your Sedgewick and all you Americans! Go and leave us here pecking in the dirt like chickens, waiting for the Viet Cong to come and chop our heads off!"

Chapter 40

A PLEA

Telegram 536 from AmEmbassy Saigon to SecState.
Top Secret; Immediate; Eyes Only.
Saigon, September 18, 1963—5 p.m.
FOR THE PRESIDENT ONLY. No other distribution whatever.

1. If Secretary of Defense and General Taylor come to Viet Nam, they will have to call on President Diem and I will have to accompany them. This will be taken here as a sign that we have abandoned our policy of "cool correctness," which was instituted to mark our disapproval of the oppressive measures which have been carried out here since last May. It would certainly put a wet blanket on those working for a change of government. The family are anxious to promote the idea that everything has been cleared up and that we should now devote all our efforts to winning the war.

2. Believe, therefore, that Secretary of Defense and General Taylor should come with eyes open knowing that this is what the reaction will be. It is quite impossible at their level to make fine distinctions between the political and the military. The Vietnamese will not see it that way and our press won't buy it.

3. I have been observing a policy of silence which we have reason to believe is getting the family into the mood to make a few concessions. The effect of this will obviously be lost if we indulge in the dramatic gesture of having the Secretary of Defense and General Taylor come out here.

SEDGEWICK

Telegram 431 from SecState to AmEmbassy Saigon.
Top Secret; Immediate; Eyes Only. September 18, 1963—4:52 p.m. FOR
SEDGEWICK FROM THE PRESIDENT. No other Distribution.

I quite understand the problem you see in visit of McNamara
and Taylor. At the same time my need for this visit is very
great indeed and I believe we can work out an arrangement
which takes care of your basic concerns. As our last message
said, my own central concern in sending this mission is to
make sure that my senior military advisors are equipped with
a solid on-the-spot understanding of the situation as a basis
both for their participation in our councils here and for the
Administration's accounting to the Congress on this critically
important contest with the Communists. Having grown up in
an Ambassador's house, I am well trained in the importance of
protecting the effectiveness of the man on-the-spot, and I want
to handle this particular visit in a way which contributes to
and does not detract from your own responsibilities. But in the
tough weeks ahead I do not see any substitute for the ammunition I will get from an on-the-spot and authoritative military
appraisal.

RUSK

Unlike Sedgewick, Donnelly welcomed the McNamara/Taylor
visit. From his own contacts with the highest levels of the ARVN as
well as from what numerous Vietnamese officers were saying to their
American "counterparts," it was obvious that coup plotting continued. But as far as he was concerned, instructions from Washington
were clear—there was to be no direct American involvement in any
coup against Diem. But whether the Ambassador was obeying these
instructions was another matter. And Donnelly did not trust Gascon.
He therefore hoped the correct American role would be cleared up
during the visit of the Secretary and the Chairman. Things were going
well in the field, he felt, and there was no reason to jeopardize progress
in the war by taking political action that would lead the United States
into unknown waters.

Telegram 7356 From Commander MACV to CJCS.
Secret; Eyes Only; Saigon, September 20, 1963—7:47 p.m.
RPT to Embassy Saigon
Exclusive for Ambassador Sedgewick. Personal for Gen. Taylor

1. As everyone else seems to be talking, writing and confusing the issue here in Vietnam, it behooves me also to get into the act. From most of the reports and articles I read, one would say Vietnam and our programs here are falling apart at the seams. We get visitor after visitor from the State Department—all of them so-called Viet Nam experts (experts who speak good French, but cannot even say a few words in the local language)—who reach that conclusion based on conversations with urban intellectuals or the preconceptions they have before they arrive here. Well, I just thoroughly disagree with these "experts" who derive their expertise from talking with old friends from the Frenchified upper classes in Saigon and Hue. Our programs are not falling apart. Far from it.

2. South Viet Nam is divided into two parts—the big city of Saigon with its satellite Hue and the remainder of the country. In Saigon and Hue our press hears every imaginable rumor and grievance. Thank goodness I do not get to read the newspapers until they are at least three days old. If I got the *New York Times* and the *Washington Post* as soon as you do, I would be afraid to go to work and wouldn't know what to do when I got there. So instead I just go to my office, and work darned hard, and find that all is not black. Quite the contrary.

3. As you know, our programs are pointed towards the Vietnamese Armed Forces and the people in the countryside. None are designed for Saigon or Hue. The programs for the Armed Forces are completed or are on schedule. The ones in the countryside continue without let-up. Both are paying dividends.

4. I remain as optimistic as ever, particularly on the military side, and I firmly believe there is reason for optimism in some of the other spheres. Here are some of the indicators.

a. Martial law has been lifted.

b. Press censorship relaxed.

c. The rapid reaction by RVNAF in countering several larger than usual VC attacks and the impressive results obtained by the RVNAF in terms of both VC killed and VC supplies and equipment captured.

d. The voluntary movement by the heretofore reluctant Behnar Montagnard tribesmen in the Pleiku area seeking resettlement and government protection.

e. The obvious interest displayed at all levels of the RVNAF to get on with the war against the VC. This is particularly apparent since the lifting of martial law.

f. The obvious desire by RVNAF personnel to further develop rapport and understanding with their US advisor counterparts.

g. Tam Giang irrigation project in Phu Yen Province officially opened. Project financed by GVN will provide water to irrigate some 2400 hectares of rice lands.

h. The evidence of one's own eyes reveals that Saigon is a prosperous, bustling Southeast Asian city. Except for the problem areas—all of them remote and insignificant—the populated areas of this country are firmly under GVN control and likely to remain that way. One is safer living in Saigon, for example, than in many parts of New York City.

5. These and others are indications that our programs are moving. We must not stop them and let fourteen million people go down the Commie drain. Admittedly we are on the frontline and the VC are using every trick in their bag—murders, ambush, propaganda, Buddhists, and schoolchildren—to thwart us. They know they're losing and are desperate to hang on. We cannot give up now. Regards.

This cable, in which Donnelly for the first time strayed beyond his designated military specialty, marked the beginning of the rift between him and Sedgewick that widened steadily as it dawned on Donnelly that if Sedgewick were allowed to paint the history of the Republic of Viet Nam and its armed forces (RVNAF), his own contribution would be portrayed with Mandelbrot's brushstrokes—not just as minimal, but as negative. When Marnin showed it to the Ambassador over breakfast at the Residence, Sedgewick's reaction was not the usual blowing off steam. He read it once, read it again, and then thought about it.

"You can keep a whore happy by patting her behind for just so long," he finally said with a smile, "But after a while she'll want more than a pat. Donnelly could not be kept on the reservation forever. Before McNamara and Taylor get here, I want you to go through the reports from all the advisors in the boonies. You do that already, don't you?"

"Yes, sir. I screen them all."

"And do these reports support what Donnelly is saying?"

"No, sir. It's a mixed picture. Things are going well in some places and badly in others. The Delta is a particular problem."

"Well why haven't these reports been called to my attention?"

"They're in your long range reading box."

"Goddamnit! Until after we bid farewell to McNamara and Taylor that stuff is short range reading! I want the facts and figures from the USOM and provincial advisors that undercut this Mulligan's stew of glib optimism. Do you get me?"

"Yes, sir!"

On the surface, Saigon diplomatic life proceeded as it usually did—fueled by lunches, receptions, and dinners with colleagues. Sedgewick was being drawn into the Ambassadorial social whirl and was out three times a week to various dinners. Since he had thousands of people working for him and feeding him information, he gleaned little from these social occasions and thought them a bore, but recognized that they were the price one had to pay to occupy his position. An exception to this general rule was his next encounter with Ngo Dinh Nhu.

Telegram 541 from AmEmbassy Saigon to SecState.
Secret; NODIS. September 21, 1963—noon.

Dinner last night with Ambassador and Mrs. Goburdhun (Indian Chairman of ICC in Vietnam), brother Nhu, Foreign Minister and Mrs. Cuu, my wife, and me.

Nhu was extremely talkative. He repeated time and again that it was he who had invented the strategic hamlets, that everyone, including the Americans, had said he couldn't do it but that he had done it. He reiterated over and over that the Buddhists had been hypnotized and then made to kill themselves. They had been murdered, he said, and not committed suicide. He said he could quite understand how Americans were horrified to think that they were supporting conditions which were so bad that Buddhist priests were killing themselves.

I said I was glad he understood it, that I was worried about our joint ability, Vietnamese and Americans, as partners, to carry out the program and that one of the things which endangered the program was the extremely bad publicity since last May which had created grave doubts as to whether the program was worthy of support. I said something should be done to show Americans there had been a real improvement and it was for that reason that I had suggested he go away for awhile. (Nhu did not respond.) I said I realized that President Diem was in favor of atoning to the Buddhists, but that he also had to do something symbolic which would provide material for a photograph of something other than priests burning themselves.

Nhu is always a striking figure. He has a handsome, cruel face and is very intelligent. His talk last night was like a phonograph record and, in spite of the obvious ruthlessness and cruelty, one feels sorry for him. He is wound up as tight as a wire. He appears to be a lost soul, a haunted man who is caught in a vicious circle. The furies are after him.

SEDGEWICK

It was Wednesday, three days before the arrival in Saigon of McNamara and Taylor, and Marnin was looking forward to an early evening and lots of sleep. He had gone directly from Lily's house to the Embassy and spent the day, mostly on the phone with Tom Aylward, nailing down the arrangements for the Ambassador's dealings with McNamara, who was staying with him, and with Taylor, who was quartered with his West Point classmate Donnelly. This was the first visit from an American Cabinet Secretary since Sedgewick's arrival on the scene and, somewhat to Marnin's surprise, given the almost militarily subordinate relationship he had with Sedgewick and the filial one he had enjoyed with Corning, he found that his own role was increased markedly over what it had been under the previous Embassy regime.

During Corning's tenure he had been concerned exclusively with compiling the visit "books," with seeing that the guests were comfortable and well served, and with protocol matters—preparing seating charts for luncheons and dinners, noting when the Ambassador and his guests were to arrive, where they would sit, and who would be seated next to whom. These matters were still within his bailiwick, but under Sedgewick—who now dealt as little as possible with Sabo and Markoff—he was concerned with substance, not just with form.

Marnin arrived home looking forward to an early evening. His

cook had left a *coq au vin* and a salad. He warmed the chicken and
had intended to attack it and then go immediately off to bed. But
there was a knock on the door. It was Dinh Trieu Da. Marnin's face
and demeanor at first indicated that he was not overjoyed to see Da,
who started to make excuses and leave. But Marnin controlled himself
and insisted he come in. Da had already eaten, he said, but could be
persuaded to have a beer. They sat in the dining room and talked
while Marnin ate. Then they each had some fudge ripple ice cream
Marnin had gotten at the base commissary, which turned out to be a
special treat for Da.

"It has been quite a while since I have tasted such ice cream," he
said with a sad smile, "or since we have last talked. Your Ambassador
does not seem to have much business with my President these days.
He has only seen him once of his own volition in the past month, on
September seventh. And that, if our information is correct—and we're
very sure it is—was only in response to direct instructions from
President Kennedy."

"We're very busy getting ready for the big visit," Marnin said, feeling uncomfortable. "What can I do for you?" he asked.

"Something very important. Otherwise I would not be here.
Sometimes things happen that cannot be helped. One crosses the
street and is hit by a drunken man in a pickup truck. On other occasions, however, observing the traffic rules and driving normally will
avoid an accident that is otherwise inevitable. I would therefore like
you, if you don't mind, to explain to me just what the traffic rules are.
Your Ambassador Sedgewick is trying to say something to my cousins.
In the family wireless room our radio operators are picking up that
signal. Unfortunately, however, we don't understand what you're trying to say. I wish to suggest that you may be having the exact opposite effect from what you intend. You are making my cousin Nhu desperate. This is a bad idea, I can tell you."

"I'm not sure I follow you," Marnin stalled, knowing that even in
talking to Da about these substantive matters he was transgressing the
Ambassador's instructions. "And I'm probably not the right person for
you to be talking with. You ought to speak with Sabo or Markoff—
maybe even the Ambassador."

"I could never do that without receiving the express approval of the President. And he wouldn't allow it. He believes everyone has a role in life and that this is not my role. What I say to you isn't to be construed as official in any way. I come to you only because my cousins think of me as their expert, the family's expert, on the United States. Nhu, Thuc, and Can have never even been to your country. Diem spent years there, but in monasteries and retreats. Since I'm a graduate of three American universities and have job offers from half a dozen others they look to me to explain your conduct. They point to specific assurances received from your President, your Vice President, your Secretary of Defense, and your Ambassador, and they don't understand why you're reneging on those assurances."

"What are you talking about?"

"They don't understand why you're pushing a group of indecisive and dishonorable men into overthrowing their government. The United States seems to have no memory! When you were discussing the economic assistance agreement with us just two years ago, Diem foresaw at that time that sooner or later a deep disagreement between us would arise about how we were running Viet Nam. He said to Corning that this was more important than economic aid; that any aid you gave us had to be thought of as primarily in your own interest and not in ours. Otherwise, you'd start giving us orders about the way we run our country and, if we did not obey those orders, threaten us with a cutoff of aid. Pretty soon it would be like having the French back. We needed assurances, Diem said, that you wouldn't interfere in our internal affairs. It wasn't strange for Diem to think like this. After all, we had already experienced your disloyalty during the coup attempt of November 1960. So he insisted on receiving assurances from Kennedy that the United States would never interfere in the internal affairs of this country by supporting his enemies against him."

"I wasn't aware of that."

"We have the letter. Look it up! It's in the record. If you can't find it, let me know and I'll send you a copy of the agreed minutes of that meeting. How can you do what you're doing? I can't explain to my cousins why you think it necessary to support a coup in the expectation that you'll get another government that would allow you to do better against the Viet Cong. Above all, I can't explain to them why you won't lay your cards on the table—simply let us know what it is that's really bothering you."

"I don't know anything about a coup," David said.

"The one thing I've learned in this job," Da said, ignoring Marnin's disclaimer, "is that Heisenberg's uncertainty principle applies to diplomacy as well as to sub-atomic physics. Time and again I'm struck by how difficult it is for one government to convey the most self-evident facts to another and have it taken at face value. So let me try and recapitulate."

"Shoot," David said.

"In the first place, let's start with the events of May eighth, which you yourself witnessed. Before they happened we were working together, your country and mine, to establish a permanent, non-Communist government in South Viet Nam in the face of an insurgency fueled and supported by Hanoi."

"That's right," David agreed. "It's still right."

"It was our further understanding that you felt, along with us, that we were winning the war against the Viet Cong, that through improvements in the ARVN and through the Strategic Hamlet Program we were winning what you call the 'counterinsurgency struggle.' Was that not the view of your government?"

"Yes," David said. "Yes, it was."

"There were those, of course," Da continued, "who maintained the opposite, like your friend Mandelbrot and his colleagues in the Saigon press corps, but we agreed the reporters were young and hot-headed."

"Yes," David said.

"Then came the very unfortunate events in Hue. We should have listened to my cousin Can, who understood his community and could foresee the danger of just such an incident. But nobody wanted that incident to happen and nobody regretted it more than my cousins, all of them—Thuc, Can, Nhu, and, especially, Diem. What your people seem to forget about Diem is that he's a very religious man. You haven't seen him, as I have, poring over the casualty lists of a battle with tears in his eyes or berating an ARVN Colonel for allowing unnecessary casualties to his troops. No one, except perhaps the families of those eight people killed in Hue, wept more for them than Ngo Dinh Diem. Nobody in this country, not his worst enemy, has accused him of approving the events in Hue that evening."

"All right," David said. "But what about Nhu?"

"The same can be said of him, but for different reasons. I was with him when we heard the news from Hue. He immediately saw it as the catastrophe it was. The main thing isn't whether the events of May eighth were mishandled, but whether they had any relevance to the war, the Strategic Hamlet Program, or the economy—all of which are going well. Hue, after all, is in I Corps, the most pacified and peaceful part of the country, several hundred miles from Saigon."

"But the demonstrations spread to the rest of the country."

"That was unfortunate and we deserve blame for not acting quickly enough to tamp a tiny smoldering flame that grew into a great fire. We who know the Buddhists and the insignificant role they play in this country underestimated the harm they could do and the great gullibility of the West. Suicide by fire has been common among the Buddhists in this country for centuries. We know there are Viet Cong agents inside the pagodas stirring things up. We understand how those bonzes were self-hypnotized to die for Buddha. But there is no logical reason to link this to the war or change your previous estimates of how things are going in this country."

"You can't just isolate what happens to the Buddhists from what happens in the rest of the country. There have been demonstrations by students. Middle schools and universities have been closed. We can't ignore that, nor can we ignore our Vietnamese contacts who complain about the arrests of their children."

"It's all regrettable," Da said. "But the fact is the Buddhist issue is now solved. Nobody in Washington seems to have noticed it, but the President met on August twenty-eighth with members of the Vietnamese Sangka, the real representatives of Buddhism in Viet Nam who were shunted aside by Thich Tri Binh and the twenty-four year old Nghiep, who is dignified in the American press with the title of 'Venerable,' but who is an out and out VC agent. This meeting completely solved all points at issue. We can now go back to trying to win the war."

"What about the raids on the pagodas?"

"The actions pursued on the night of August twentieth were only undertaken by President Diem after careful study. Those raids were unanimously requested by all the top Generals in the ARVN. Nhu carried them out. How could the American press and even VOA broadcasts accuse my cousin Nhu and Colonel Tung of being responsible for actions which all the Generals of our armed forces had pressed upon the President? And what had this to do anyway with the earlier assessment that we were winning the war?"

"Events of this importance don't take place in a vacuum."

"We realize that. We've been responsive to every suggestion you've made on how to set things right. But you don't seem to understand that we have to maintain our self respect. We can't just salute, say 'yes sir,' and do what you tell us. How arrogant can you be? We arrived at an agreement with the Buddhists and we stuck to it. It was the Buddhists who broke it. We only attacked the pagodas in the face of insupportable provocations. But now the problem is solved. We want to go back to where things were before this whole mess erupted."

"You can't just turn back the clock."

"We're the same people we were before—only wiser. We won't make the same mistakes again. There is no reason for you to work for our downfall. Look at what's happened in the aftermath! We've appointed a decent Ambassador in Washington. Madame Nhu has been silent. Pro-government rallies have been held—"

"We know you can organize rallies. That's not very significant."

"And the Viet Cong can organize rallies against us. Ours are attended by ten times the number of people as theirs. So why do you pay more attention to theirs? Why do you go there with a notebook and write all their words down, as though Thich Tri Binh were some sort of Hebrew prophet? Why can't your Sedgewick understand the truth about the Buddhists?"

"It's not just the Ambassador. It's Washington and our public."

"But why do your people insist that this young man of no partic-ular theological bent is more of a Buddhist than his older, more cred-ible colleagues who have come out in public in the past three weeks to support us? And what about everything else that's happened? What about the creation of the new inter-sect committee; the release of the students; the reopening of the schools; the easing of the curfew; the return of Radio Saigon to civilian control?"

"All these things have been reported to Washington. I can assure you of that."

"They may be reported, but nobody pays any attention. You continue to work with the Generals to unseat us. You refuse to talk to us, even to tell us what you want. What do you want? Why do you think you'd be better off without us?"

"It's true we've suggested to your cousin Nhu that he take a vacation because, rightly or wrongly, Nhu and Madame Nhu are seen in the United States as the root of the problem." David paused, wondering whether his face would give him away. "But I don't know about any efforts to unseat you."

Da looked at Marnin sardonically.

"I wouldn't expect you to tell me," he said. "But make no mistake about it. We know. Surely your Mister Sedgewick and your Colonel Gascon are not so foolish as to believe that a meeting of ten generals could take place to discuss our overthrow—ten!—without our knowing about it! If that were the case, then we would indeed not be worthy of governing this country. We know these people—a lot better than you do. They are unworthy. Can you possibly believe them when they tell you that they fear that Ngo Dinh Diem and Ngo Dinh Nhu and Ngo Dinh Thuc and Ngo Dinh Can will turn neutralist?"

"We've heard about meetings with the Viet Cong—"

"Of course you have. Nhu meant you to hear about them. This was foolish. He was overplaying his hand, and I told him so. These talks were meant to let you know that our family had other options, if we chose to pursue them. But you know what happened to my oldest cousin, their eldest brother—the head of our family! You heard it from the lips of Diem himself. He was buried alive! Alive! Do you think we've forgotten? Do you think we're about to cut a deal with Ho Chi Minh, the man who buried our family chieftain?"

"Some say the pressure is too much for Nhu, that he's become mentally unbalanced."

"That's nonsense and you know it! Sedgewick talked to him this past week and so have the Italian, French, and British Ambassadors, as well as correspondents from France Soir, Paris Match, and Le Monde. Nhu is high strung and a man under pressure. But he's as rational as your Mr. Sedgewick, maybe more so. As for Diem, the man who runs this country, the man who makes the decisions—he's as calm and as rational as ever. He hasn't changed one millimeter! It's madness for you to consider overthrowing him."

"So there have been meetings with the Viet Cong?"

"This is very secret, for obvious reasons. People's lives depend on it. Yes, there have been meetings. The Viet Cong is tired. The Viet Cong is worn out. It's for exactly that reason that Hanoi has begun infiltrating their people from the North back into this country—to give the Communist movement a shot in the arm. So if the Viet Cong want to talk to us, it pays for us to listen. Our terms are not, like yours in World War II, unconditional surrender. We are all Vietnamese and we're willing to forget past grievances and live together like brothers. We recognize that many Viet Cong are more worthy, more moral, than many of those who claim to support us—certainly more so than these Generals you're backing in a coup against Ngo Dinh Diem—your faithful ally for almost ten years. . ."

Chapter 41

SQUARING THE CIRCLE

Once he got started, Da shared the family weakness for interminable speech. He talked all evening, disregarding Marnin's ever more frequent yawns. For all Marnin's sympathy, there was nothing encouraging he could tell him. It was two in the morning when Da finally left, burdened by the deepening conviction that logic had been outdistanced by events. Marnin observed him from the front window walking into the darkness, his shoulders slumped and for a moment illuminated by a streetlamp. He was an icon of dejection.

Resisting the longing to fall into bed, Marnin jotted down the highlights of their conversation on a yellow legal pad. Punchy after four hours sleep, he drove to the Embassy, picked up the cable traffic, arranged it, and brought it to the Ambassador, who was breakfasting distractedly by the pool reading a week-old copy of the *Wall Street Journal*. Only after he had reviewed all the cables and given the necessary instructions did Marnin tell him about Dinh Trieu Da's call the previous evening.

"So they know all about us," Sedgewick said.

"It looks that way. Yes, sir."

"I've suspected as much. If nothing else, Nhu is efficient, perhaps the only efficient person in this country. And one of the generals, if what you say is right, is clearly a fink."

"As Da said, one out of ten—not bad odds, given the situation and the fact that for them it's a life and death matter."

"Well, that's very interesting," the Ambassador said. "I told

Washington that if we waited them out, they'd come to us."

"I don't want to sound naive," Marnin said. "But I think Da may have been acting on his own."

"That is naive. What kind of secret police does Counselor Nhu run if it doesn't follow the doings of the Private Secretary of the President? We know they're watching the residences of Embassy officers and tapping our phones. I think we have to regard what your friend Da said as a message from Counselor Nhu to me. That's exactly the way I want you to treat it—as a personal message."

"It was more of a plea than a message. In any case, do you want me to do a cable and a memcon or just a cable?"

Sedgewick looked at him quizzically.

"Don't make me repeat myself! It was a personal message. I don't want you to do a goddamned thing! You have enough on your plate getting ready for Bob McNamara and Max Taylor. The only thing I want you to do is see Frank Gascon and tell him everything you've told me. But don't repeat it to anyone else—not to Markoff or to Sabo or to Bilder. You got that?"

"Yes, sir!"

"I don't want anyone to get the idea that this Embassy is encouraging a coup. That would give absolutely the wrong impression in Washington!"

"Yes, sir!"

Standing next to Marnin at the tennis courts of the RVNAF Officers Club in the Southeast section of the city was Nguyen Ngoc Lam, the best tennis player in Viet Nam, who along with his brother Luong had easily eliminated Claudio and Marnin in the quarterfinal round of the national doubles championship in January. They were talking about the recent visit to Saigon of the Australian national junior team, headed by a seventeen year old John Newcombe. Some thirty Vietnamese officers along the sidelines were cheering, applauding, razzing, and heckling "Big" Minh—the GVN's ranking General—as he convincingly took a set from Maxwell Taylor, our ranking General. Whenever Minh muffed a shot, they howled with laughter, hooted at him, made scurrilous remarks, and pounded each other on the back—

all of which Minh took with great good nature. Neither of the Generals hit with much pace or, for that matter, missed easy shots. The result was endless rallies, with the ball often going across the net twenty or more times before somebody made an error.

There were half a dozen American officers there as well, including Tom Aylward dressed in tennis gear, all of them silent until a point was made. Then they would applaud politely, careful to avoid favoritism. This was an interesting cultural difference. It would no more have occurred to any of the American officers to heckle the Chairman of the Joint Chiefs of Staff for netting a backhand than it would to sleep with their mothers. They were as subdued and respectful as they would have been sitting along the back walls of "the tank" in the Pentagon while the Joint Chiefs discussed the potential Soviet nuclear destruction of Norfolk or San Diego.

Seated next to the referee's chair at center court was the Secretary of Defense in a white button down shirt, repp tie, and blue silk suit, his hair slicked straight back, his briefcase at his feet, going through his papers and paying no attention to what was happening on the red clay court. Marnin sensed that the Secretary could tell one exactly what was in those papers, but not whether the sky was blue or grey or whether the grandstand was made of wood or cement.

The schedule McNamara and Taylor were following would have exhausted any five normal men. No day passed without each making half a dozen helicopter trips. As their final report pointed out, in a ten day period they managed between them to visit twenty-four of the forty-two provinces of South Viet Nam where, aside from the usual protocol meetings, Taylor privately interviewed eighty-five ARVN and sixty-one American officers, and McNamara talked with 173 soldiers and civilians of both nations.

The previous evening Claudio and David had discussed their breakneck schedule, geared around no more than five hours sleep and crammed with talks and "events" set up in twenty-minute intervals. Claudio mulled it over and finally asked Marnin, "But when do they get laid?"

The American laughed.

"I'm not kidding," Claudio said. "If I prepared a schedule like that for my Foreign Minister, I'd be fired the next morning. At the very least, you ought to take them downtown to the Black Cat for a ten minute tonsil massage by Hedy Lamarr."

"If your question is a serious one," Marnin replied, "the answer is that, as far as one can determine, neither the Secretary of Defense nor the Chairman will be getting laid during their stay. This might seem strange to you, but my government operates on the theory that a Cabinet Minister can maintain his well-being for as much as ten days without getting laid."

"A very questionable theory," Claudio responded. "More important, a colossal mistake, especially in this country. It means they'll be talking to hundreds of people here, but no women. And it's impossible to understand this place unless you get a sense of the women. When you get to know the men you come away thinking these poor babies need all the help they can get. The soldiers can't soldier, the bankers can't bank, and the leaders can't lead. But the women—they're something else again. All of them learn in the cradle what's important and what's not, how to please and how to instruct, what to know and what to forget. That's as true of Madame Nhu as of the raunchiest bar girl in Saigon."

The Ambassador had been excited about Taylor's tennis match with Big Minh, who ever since the false coup had put out word that it was too dangerous for him to have any more direct contact with Americans. Sedgewick hoped that, by hearing directly what was bothering Minh and his co-conspirators, Taylor and McNamara might be influenced to favor them more. The match had been set up by Blix Donnelly. Word had reached him through General Kim that Big Minh wanted to see General Taylor about an important matter, and without arousing any suspicion. Since both generals were tennis enthusiasts, a meeting was arranged on the courts of the Officers Club. Kim was not clear whether singles or doubles was preferred, so Marnin was rounded up to partner Taylor (with Aylward as his stand-in in case he broke a leg—in the American military one cannot be too careful) and Lam was recruited to partner Minh. But it turned out that the generals preferred singles. So their various entourages all stood around sipping Fantas and watching a tepid match of geriatric tennis.

Kim and Minh must have had something in mind, but what it was the Americans never found out. Taylor at least got his exercise and McNamara managed to get through most of his briefcase. But Sedgewick, when Marnin finally reported to him that it had been a fizzle, was most disappointed. Nothing had happened. Minh—the most ursine and taciturn of men—had remained true to form, made no attempt to draw Taylor aside, and said absolutely nothing. A tennis court, especially a crowded one, was not the best place, in any event, to exchange confidences. So the meeting was considered a total bust by the Americans, who had come to star in a play and discovered they were acting the roles of walk-ons.

In fact, the Minh-Taylor tennis match became in Marnin's mind symbolic of what happened to the thousands of American VIP visitors who traipsed through Saigon and the boonies over a dozen years, punched their tickets and received their canned briefings, and invariably left convinced of the truth and justice of whatever they had believed before they arrived. Sedgewick, who was debriefed each morning at breakfast by McNamara—who proved himself able to soak up information as effortlessly as other men accumulate debts—tried to widen the Secretary's horizons by arranging a private lunch with the enemy, Willis Mandelbrot and Mark Shayne, the UPI bureau chief. But McNamara was not impressed.

During the course of that lunch the Secretary pointed out to them ("fatuously" was the word Mandelbrot used in describing the session to Marnin) that while he did not question their honesty or integrity, their judgments were in no way more valid than the contradictory conclusions of the hundreds of American advisors stationed all over the country. Further, their Vietnamese sources were largely urban intellectuals, whereas the counterinsurgency effort was taking place in the boondocks far from their prying eyes. ("As though we never got up-country!" Mandelbrot said.)

"Given these two conflicting data points," McNamara concluded, he had no choice but to trust the hard knowledge garnered by seasoned officials, many of whom were Viet Nam experts and soldiers with extensive combat experience, rather than the instincts of young reporters who were new to the country, to the area, and to the fog of war.

Marshall Brement

Sedgewick also arranged for McNamara to get an earful at what was billed as a "no holds barred" meeting with junior Embassy political officers, almost all of whom had overnight become extremely critical of Diem, Nhu, and the ARVN now that it was known that this view was shared in spades by the new Ambassador. Morale had gone up for the young political officers in the Embassy since Sedgewick's arrival. Happiness for a junior political officer is to be a sanctified and approved rebel—blessed in your dissidence by your Ambassador and your State Department audience.

Memo (informal) to Amb Sedgewick from DJM.
September 27, 1963.
Subject: Secretary's Meeting with Junior Officers.

As requested, herewith is an account of SecDef's session with Emboffs this afternoon, which turned out more interesting for him than he anticipated. While not quite the "no holds barred" meeting it was advertised to be, few punches were pulled and Washington was generally castigated for promoting policies that were unimaginative and perennially "too little too late."
If my friend Dinh Trieu Da had been there, he would certainly not have been happy. His family took a lot of lumps. Other than to thank the group at the end and to ask mostly monosyllabic questions, the Secretary made no comments whatsoever and maintained throughout what I took to be his usual poker face. But he wrote down everything that was being said to him. The following points were made by various officers, including me:
✔ Buddhist crisis crystallized a general discontent in the cities that had been dormant for some time, but had relatively little effect in the countryside.
✔ Arrests of students have included children of military officers and high-ranking bureaucrats; this will have grave consequences.
✔ Nocturnal arrests have been particularly onerous and have heightened the atmosphere of suspicion; mothers guard their daughters until dawn to avoid rape before they get to prison.
✔ Diem is still respected, but the Nhus are hated by the general populace and by those outside the Can Lao Party and Republican Youth political structure; contrary to what Secretary may have heard elsewhere, it would be very difficult for Nhu to take over from his brother.

✔ Diem is devoted to his country, but wedded to his family. He is admired because of his moral qualities, but people around him are damaging his reputation and this could ruin him; it is a tragedy.

✔ Diem is anxious about the delay in aid, but reluctant to complain for fear of being caught in an American trap.

✔ Generals want to join the cabinet; this causes Diem and others who know them considerable heartburn. Generals are not up to it.

✔ The people are angry and frustrated, especially about the students; they would greet the fall of Diem with jubilation, but after a few months of something worse would probably reconsider.

✔ Some Generals are sex obsessed and venal; Diem's morality acts as a restraint on them—the only restraint.

✔ Responsible Vietnamese are worried about Nhu's anti-American campaign; all agree that the ultimate fate of their country will be decided not in Hanoi or Saigon, but in Washington.

It was time to wind up the trip. McNamara and Taylor had been "in country" ten days. At MACV headquarters they had raked their fine-toothed combs over the operations of each of Donnelly's section chiefs. They had flown everywhere, even over Viet Cong strongholds in the "Parrot's Beak" and the "Iron Triangle"; had talked to everyone (except Nhu), including Thich Tri Binh (whom they could not make head nor tail of) and Willis Mandelbrot; had reviewed all the ARVN troop dispositions as well as the history of all engagements fought over the previous four months above the platoon level; had strategy sessions with the Joint General Staff, the Chiefs of Staff of the ARVN and the various RVNAF Services, i.e., primarily the Navy and the Air Force; and with the four Corps Commanders.

The final report was still to be written. They had reserved their last day in Saigon, the flight from Saigon to Honolulu, and a day at Camp Smith, where the buildings still bore the scars of the Japanese machine gun bullets of December 7, 1941, for the actual drafting. But their conclusions, which they had been very cagy about, were to be delivered at a luncheon of "The Principals" to take place at the Residence.

The rest of the extensive "cast of hundreds" that had come along on the two C-130s they brought with them lunched at the Tan Son Nhut Officers Club with the members of the Mission Council and debriefed them on the preliminary conclusions reached by the Secretary and General Taylor. But "The Big Four"—Sedgewick, Donnelly, McNamara, and Taylor—ate bacon and tomato sandwiches and drank Budweiser beer in the Ambassadorial dining room, while in the study next door a similar table for four had been set up and the same lunch served to Tom Aylward, to McNamara's military aide Marine Colonel "Waxy" Spiers, to Taylor's aide, Air Force Colonel "Hawk" Henderson, and to Marnin.

Although no Viewgraph machine was available at the Residence, no American military staff could let an occasion like that go by without preparing suitable "point papers" and viewgraphs for their principals. Spiers and Henderson offered these mnemonic aids to Aylward and Marnin to read during the course of their lunch. Sedgewick's and Donnelly's aides learned that both their bosses were to receive good report cards. Aylward greeted this with obvious satisfaction, but Marnin knew it would be mixed news for Sedgewick, who had hoped that the McNamara/Taylor visit would cut Donnelly's legs off at the knees. Sedgewick and the conspirators who shared his views in Washington were committed to the ouster of not just Nhu, but Diem as well. Both McNamara and Taylor were skeptical about the necessity of Diem's removal from the scene and the visit to Viet Nam had not changed this. Sedgewick well understood that, after all, if the United States were in the process of winning the war, as Donnelly maintained, then what was the point of taking action against a Chief of State who was not only our ally, but our creation as well?

Of overriding importance for Sedgewick was the judgment of Taylor and McNamara on his policy of "cool correctness." Half a dozen times since its institution he had been urged by Washington to engage in substantive discussions with Diem, to explain where the Vietnamese leader was going wrong, and how he was losing the battle in the United States with the public and the Congress. On each such occasion Sedgewick dodged, and shifted, and squirmed. It was better to "make him come to me," he averred, knowing that the stubborn

Vietnamese President was not likely to do so.

"I do not see the advantage of frequent conversations with Diem if I have nothing new to bring up," he cabled to Dean Rusk in mid-September. What nobody realized at the time—indeed, still do not realize—was that to Sedgewick this was not a matter of tactics, but of strategy. His principal aim was to get the ARVN Generals to act. But how could one mount a coup against a national leader and at the same time be engaged in a constant dialogue with him without giving others who were aware of what you were doing—or who were to become aware of it one way or the other—the impression that you were a thoroughgoing scoundrel? Why would a subsequent President (not only of Viet Nam, but of other countries as well) assume you were being any more honorable to him than you had been to his predecessor? Because of this Sedgewick became a unique figure in the annals of thousands of years of diplomacy—an Ambassador who did everything in his power to avoid contact with the Chief of State of an ally to whom he was accredited.

Marnin had at first not thought it possible that Sedgewick could hoodwink people with the background, command presence, intelligence, and acuity of McNamara and Taylor. But the viewgraphs and point papers made clear that the Ambassador was about to receive what amounted to a total endorsement for his policies from both the Secretary and the Chairman—two officials who, before their arrival on this trip, had been strongly urging a wide-ranging dialogue with Diem. But there it was on the viewgraphs in Marnin's hands. The Kennedy Administration's two most distinguished and effulgent public servants, men who had been intimately following the Viet Nam story from their first days in office, who were in their ninth trip to the country, who had managed in their ten days to go everywhere, see everything, talk to everybody, nevertheless had ended up endorsing the diametrically opposed perceptions, programs and policy approaches of both Sedgewick and Donnelly.

In a nice gesture to their staffs, the aides were asked to join the principals for coffee, brandy, and cigars. The conversation had been animated and the mood in the dining room was one of restrained bonhommie. Both McNamara and Taylor were austere personalities, but they were obviously pleased at the results of their "in country" inspection. Donnelly, who had been apprehensive that their upcoming verdict would be negative, was positively glowing at his vindication and Sedgewick gave the outward appearance of being pleased as well. He called Marnin over and whispered, "Do you have that Young Report with you?" Steve Young was the USOM "Provrep" in Long An Province. Marnin told him it was in his attaché case in the other room.

"I don't want to be too Wilsonian," Taylor was saying as they sipped their coffee and pulled at what Sedgewick laughingly referred to as pre-Castro Montecristos, "but this morning the Secretary and I jotted down fourteen military and five political conclusions of our visit that pretty much covers what Jack Kennedy will want from us. They run over the same ground we've been discussing at lunch, but I'd like to test them out on you, Bascombe, and you too Blix, to see what you think."

"That's fine with me," said Sedgewick.

"Hawk, would you please hand out those papers I had you do up this morning," Taylor said to his aide.

Fourteen Military Conclusions and Recommendations

1. The shooting war is still progressing at an impressive pace. It has only been marginally affected by the political crisis.
2. There is a lot of war left to fight, particularly in the Delta, where the Viet Cong remains strong.
3. Vietnamese officers of all ranks are well aware of the Buddhist issue. Most viewed it with detachment and have not let religious differences affect their military relationships.
4. Vietnamese military commanders are disciplined and obedient and can be expected to execute any order they view as lawful.
5. The US/Vietnamese military relationship has not been damaged by the political crisis to any significant degree.
6. Whatever political dissatisfaction exists among Vietnamese officers is focused far more on Ngo Dinh Nhu than on President Diem.
7. Excluding factors external to Viet Nam, the war will be won if the current US military and sociological programs are pursued effectively, irrespective of the defects of the ruling regime.

8. Improvements in the Vietnamese Government are not going to be brought about by leverage applied through the military.
9. The Viet Cong insurgency in the north and center can be reduced to little more than sporadic incidents by the end of 1964; the Delta will take longer, but should be completed by the end of 1965 provided the GVN cleans up its act, gets rid of ineffective commanders and provincial officials, and restores domestic tranquility.
10. Military emphasis should be on the dangerous situation in the Delta.
11. The tempo of military activities should be increased.
12. Military tactics should be shifted to emphasize "clear and hold operations" rather than meaningless territorial sweeps.
13. The Strategic Hamlet Program should be consolidated, with arms given to the hamlet militias that will make them at least as well equipped as the Viet Cong.
14. We can announce the planned withdrawal of 1,000 US troops by the end of 1964 in connection with our program to train Vietnamese to replace Americans in all essential functions by the end of 1965, when we can pull out of here militarily altogether.

The Five Politico/Economic Pressure Points
1. Full confidence in policies of the Ambassador and the Country Team; Ambassador to be instructed to continue the policy of "cool correctness in order to make Diem come to you," but to be prepared to reestablish contact later if this policy does not work.
2. Suspension of the CIP without public announcement.
3. Selective suspension of PL480, on an item-by-item basis, after referral to Washington for review.
4. Suspension of loans for the Saigon/Cholon waterworks project and for the Saigon Electric Power Project.
5. Further financial support of Colonel Tung's Special Forces to be contingent on their being transferred to field operations outside Saigon as well as on their coming under direct command of the Joint General Staff, again without public announcement."

"This is fine with me, just fine," Donnelly said with a big smile, breaking the silence. "In fact, outstanding! You gentlemen have done a great job, as far as I'm concerned."

"These are both very interesting documents," Sedgewick said. "I certainly appreciate the confidence that you and Bob are placing in me, particularly your support for my ploy to keep Diem and Nhu off balance. I know you both had real doubts about that before you came here. But it's on the military side that I still have a few problems that I've been reluctant to raise in front of others, partly because I think Blix is doing a great job here and I don't want anything I say to detract from his efforts."

"What's on your mind?" McNamara asked.

"Well," Sedgewick continued, "I'm the first to say that I don't understand everything there is to understand about military matters. But there's quite a military tradition in my family. As you know, I served for three years in World War II. So I know something about the way the military mind works. And I've spent my whole life in politics, so I know something about what's useful to politicians. What's been worrying me is that we may inadvertently be giving Jack Kennedy an overly optimistic portrait of what's been happening here."

"How do you mean?" McNamara asked.

"On the one hand, you have mass arrests, assassination threats, what have you—people thrown into jail, tortures, and the worst type of Communist style brainwashing. On the other hand, people from our defense establishment come through here, top flight people like you, and tell me that all this political turmoil is having no real effect on the war or on the fighting spirit of the ARVN. Now I try and put myself in the position of an ARVN Lieutenant whose father has been beaten up and intimidated, whose mother has been denied the God-given right to practice her religion, whose younger brother has been arrested in a student demonstration, and whose younger sister has been sexually molested by one of Nhu's dreaded secret police, and I simply cannot understand how a youngster in that frame of mind can be an effective military officer or how the ARVN, operating in that political framework, can be an effective military force."

"But we've talked to Americans who are in daily contact with hundreds of Vietnamese," Taylor said, "and with hundreds of Vietnamese ourselves, and we've heard nothing which would substantiate that."

"I suppose what I really wonder," Sedgewick replied, "is whether we're taking into account the inclination of these people to tell visitors, particularly high ranking ones, what they think those visitors want to hear. You know as well as I do that what makes our troops the best in the world is their gung ho, 'can do' attitude. Now I'm not implying there's any falsification going on. No, sir, nothing of the kind! But I am saying there's a natural inclination to tell a General Officer or a Cabinet Minister, or an Ambassador for that matter, that things are a damn sight better than they really are."

"Now wait just one cotton-picking minute," Donnelly said. "I have to take real exception to what you're saying. There's no way my people, who are now down to the platoon level, could be wrong about this! What we get comes not just from Majors and Colonels, but from Corporals and Sergeants. Our programs are working! We're winning this darned thing!"

"I certainly hope you're right," Sedgewick replied. "Nobody hopes and prays for it more than I do. But if things are as rosy as you say they are, Blix, then why are we squeezing Diem? Why are we putting the pressure on him to change his government?"

"Sometimes I wonder about that."

"But you do support our policy?"

"Yes. Of course."

"Well my worry is that the two sides of our policy don't square with each other. I'm not so sure we're winning. It appears to me that at best we're just holding our own. We can help these people, but we can't do the fighting for them and we can't make them love their government. Sooner or later hatred of their government is bound to affect ARVN personnel and performance."

McNamara, Taylor, and Donnelly all looked stunned.

"I know you haven't been hearing much of this from me before," Sedgewick continued. "But that's because I was the new boy on the block and I didn't want to sound off on things I didn't know too much about. But if we're doing so well, I wonder why there aren't any mass surrenders. You and I were both in Europe after the Battle of the Bulge, Max. At that time not a day passed without a German platoon, but sometimes a regiment or even a division, surrendering to us. But here we say the Viet Cong is always up to strength and is, in fact, reckoned at a higher figure than it was two years ago, even though 24,000 VC have allegedly been killed during that period. I may be wrong. I'm open minded about it. But let me give you a little recommended reading for the plane trip back to Honolulu. David, do you remember that report from Steve Young in Long An Province?"

"Yes, sir," Marnin said.

"I want you to thermofax two copies and give one to the Secretary and one to the Chairman."

"Yes, sir. I have a couple of extra copies with me."

"You know we have forty-two provinces here and each one of our Provreps sends in weekly and monthly reports. David can tell you I read every one of them religiously, and have done so from the beginning of my tour in Saigon. But this one made my blood run cold. You know the geography around here better than I do. You know where Long An province is. Why, Saigon is practically in Long An. It's the road from here to the Delta. If you control Long An you control Saigon. And what does Steve Young, one of our best people, say about the situation? David, read the summary to us."

Marnin fetched his attaché case from under his chair in the next room and took Young's report out of it. What he read to the Secretary and the Chairman was as follows:

"The past thirty days have produced a day-by-day elimination of US/Vietnamese sponsored strategic hamlets and a marked increase in Viet Cong influence, military operations, physical control of the countryside and Communist controlled combat hamlets. The reason for this unhappy situation is the failure of the government to support and protect the hamlets. The concept of the strategic hamlet called for a self-defense corps capable of holding off enemy attack for a brief period until regular forces (ARVN or Civil Guard) could come to the rescue. In hamlet after hamlet this assistance never came or arrived the following morning during daylight hours.

There are two explanations for this lack of assistance: (a) there are not sufficient troops to protect key installations and district headquarters and at the same time go to the assistance of the hamlet; and (b) movement of troops after dark to assist the hamlets is prohibited.

The strategic hamlet program in this province can be made workable and very effective against the Viet Cong. But help must come immediately in the form of additional troops and new concepts of operation, not in the same reheated French tactics of 1954, beefed up with more helicopters and tanks. The hamlets must be defended if this province is not to fall under complete control of the Viet Cong in the next few months. . . ."

"Well, I don't pay that stuff too much attention," Sedgewick said, knowing when to back off. "But I'd just like to remind all of you gentlemen that we're dealing with a very mixed picture here."

"You certainly have your job cut out for you," McNamara said.

"That's the truth!" Sedgewick replied. "I wake up every morning and wonder to myself what it is exactly I think I'm doing here. But it has its compensations, doesn't it, David?"

"Yes, sir," Marnin said.

"Young David here," Sedgewick said, "I'm told is quite the bachelor around town. Those Vietnamese girls are really something!"

"They surely are," Taylor replied, and joined the others in good-natured laughter.

"Hawk" tapped his wristwatch to indicate to the Chairman that it was time to leave for the airport. Marnin rode to Tan Son Nhut sitting in the front seat of the Ambassadorial limo, with Sedgewick and McNamara in the back. After a good bit of jockeying where each insisted on giving the other the seat of honor, Sedgewick prevailed and was sitting to the Secretary's left. McNamara did not say anything during the ride. He was reading Steve Young's report from Long An Province, a province that was a twenty minute drive from the heart of Saigon.

Chapter 42

AN ENGAGEMENT

The McNamara-Taylor visit had kept Marnin so busy that he had not been able to see Lily since they arrived in Viet Nam. He had phoned her only once and on that occasion she had been cool and showed no interest in another tryst. When he asked if he could see her that evening, she replied that "family business" precluded a meeting. He drove by her house late that night and saw a car with American diplomatic plates parked in the driveway. David had decided his best course was to say nothing about the car, but when they at last got together the night following McNamara's and Taylor's departure, he could not seem to help himself.

"Didn't you tell me you had 'family business' the other night?"

They were in her bedroom, he with his shirt already off and Lily in a peignoir, unbuckling his belt.

"Yes, I did."

"Tell me, do you always have an American diplomat sitting in on your 'family' business meetings?"

David kicked off his shoes and Lily pulled down his pants.

"A diplomat?"

David stepped out of his pants and then sat on the edge of the bed to remove his socks, but Lily knelt and pulled them off.

"I drove by here last night," he said, trying to control himself. "I saw the car in the driveway and the diplomatic plates."

Lily removed her peignoir. They got into bed and she nestled in his arms.

"It was Curly. . .just Curly," she said. "I told you I consult with him, remember?"

"Yes, but not at twelve o'clock at night. What the hell was he doing here so late?"

"Just talking. . .I promise you. Talking and talking. Nothing more."

She kissed him passionately, the first time in more than a week. They quickly made love and then again and again through half the night and it was better than ever.

David awoke. He looked at the radium dial on his wristwatch. It was three in the morning. He could sense she was not asleep.

"Are you awake?"

"Yes."

"Oh Lily, let's go away somewhere. I'll take a few days off. . .a long weekend, the two of us. . . go to Vung Tao and make love on the beach. . .or we could go to Dalat. . .make love by a waterfall. . . anywhere, everywhere. . .Oh Lily, *je t'aime*. . .*je t'aime*. . ."

Lily turned her head away toward the window and for a moment said nothing. Then she turned back to him.

"I love you, too, David," she said. "But I can't go away with you . . .not this weekend. . ."

"Next, then."

"Not any weekend. . .not ever. . .never. . ."

"What are you talking about? Why not?"

Lily sighed, and then spoke slowly and distinctly.

"Because last night. . .I told Curly. . .that I would be his wife."

David was stunned.

"You what! But. . .why, Lily? Why?"

"Because my girls and I," she said calmly, "need someone to protect us."

"You have me!"

"You can't protect us. You can't even support us, David. You have no money."

"I have enough. And in a couple of years maybe. . . ."

"What should I do in the meantime? Soon you'll be transferred. You won't even be here."

"I thought. . .you could join me later."

"I see. I was supposed to wait here. . .to be your Madame Butterfly."

"Some butterfly!"

"Is that what you wanted? If so, you picked the wrong woman."

"Lily, Lily, how could you lead me on like that? We were destined for each other. Think about it. It's not too late to change your mind."

"I've been thinking about nothing else for months. Believe me, it was not an easy decision. But my mind is made up."

David turned the light on, reached for his clothes, and started dressing.

"So when's the happy occasion?" he asked, making every effort to remove the emotion from his voice.

"The 31st of October."

"What's the rush?"

He had his pants and shirt on and stuffed his socks in his pockets.

"We leave the next day for Paris. He's going to be Counselor for Economic Affairs in your Embassy."

"Well. . .*bon chance*! I'm sure you'll be the perfect little embassy wife."

There was a small ceramic ashtray on the night table that had been next to his wallet, his keys, and his money. It had a grey background and hand painted blue swans on it. He picked it up, looked at it, and then threw it against the door, where it shattered into a thousand pieces. Then without looking back at her, he walked out of the room.

Chapter 43
THE PANIC ENDS

Telegram 63560 from White House (Bundy) to AmEmbassy Saigon.
Top Secret. Immediate. CAS Channels.
October 5, 1963.
EXCLUSIVE EYES ONLY FOR AMBASSADOR.

In conjunction with decisions and recommendations taken as result McNamara/Taylor visit and which were discussed with you during course of visit, President today approved policy that no rpt no initiative should be taken now to give any active covert encouragement to a coup. There should, however, be urgent covert effort with closest security under broad guidance of Ambassador to identify and build contacts with possible alternative leadership as and when it appears. Essential that this effort be totally secure and fully deniable and separated entirely from normal political analysis and reporting and other activities of Country Team. We repeat that this effort is not to be aimed at active promotion of coup but only at surveillance and readiness. In order to provide plausibility to denial suggest you and no one else in Embassy issue these instructions orally to Acting Station Chief and hold him responsible to you alone for making appropriate contacts and reporting to you alone.

Telegram 1448 from CIA Station Saigon to CIA headquarters.
Top Secret. October 6, 1963.
Eyes Only Rusk, Harriman, Hilsman, and McG. Bundy
From Ambassador Sedgewick.

Colonel Gascon met with General Duong Van Minh at Gen. Minh's headquarters on Le Van Duyet for one hour and ten minutes morning of 6 October. After usual courtesies, Gen.

Minh said he must know American government position re
change in GVN in very near future. He complained he was getting different signals from General Donnelly and MACV on one
hand and Embassy on other. Gen. Minh said situation is deteriorating rapidly and action must be taken soon or the war will
be lost to the Viet Cong because government no longer has support of the people. He identified among the other Generals par-
ticipating with him a) Maj. Gen. Tran Van Bich; b) Brig. Gen.
Tran Thien Khiem; and c) Maj. Gen. Le Van Kim. Gen. Minh
made clear he did not expect any specific American support,
but he does need reassurances that USG will not attempt to
thwart him. He denied any political ambitions for himself or
his colleagues, with possible exception, he said laughingly, of
Ton That Dinh. His only purpose, he insisted, was to win the
war. To do this, he added emphatically, continuation of
American military and economic aid at the present level of
$1.5 million a day is essential.

Gen. Minh outlined three possible plans for the accomplishment
of the change of government:

a. Assassination of Ngo Dinh Nhu and Ngo Dinh Can, keeping
President Diem in office. This was the easiest to accomplish.

b. Encirclement of Saigon by various military units, particularly Fifth Division elements at Ben Cat (Comment: Commanded
by Col. Nguyen Van Thieu.)

c. Direct confrontation between military units involved in the
coup and loyalist units in Saigon—i.e., dividing the city into sec-
tors and cleaning it out pocket by pocket.

Gascon replied that he could not answer regarding USG non-
interference nor could he give advice re tactical planning. He
could also not advise as to which of three plans was best.

Gen. Minh said that most dangerous men in South Viet Nam
are Ngo Dinh Nhu, Ngo Dinh Can and Ngo Trong Hieu
(Comment: Minister of Civic Action.) Minh said that Hieu was
formerly a Communist and still has communist sympathies.
When Col. Gascon remarked that he had considered Special
Forces Commander Col. Tung as one of the more dangerous
individuals, Gen. Minh stated, "if I get rid of Nhu, Can and
Hieu, Col. Tung will be on his knees before me."

Minh further stated that one of the reasons they had to act
quickly was that many regimental, battalion and company commanders are working on coup plans of their own which would

be abortive and a "catastrophe." Minh appeared to understand Gascon's position of being unable to comment at the present moment.

Telegram 74228 from White House to AmEmbassy Saigon (CAS Channels).
Top Secret. October 9, 1963.
Eyes Only for the Ambassador from Bundy.
Ref: a)Saigon 1448, b)Saigon 1471.

Believe CAP 63560 gives necessary guidance requested reftel b) re upcoming meetings with General Minh and General Don. We have following additional thoughts which have been discussed with President. While we do not wish to stimulate coup, we also do not wish to leave impression that U.S. would thwart a change of government or deny economic or military assistance to a new regime if it appeared capable of increasing effectiveness of military effort and improving working relations with U.S. We would like to be informed on what is being contemplated, but we should avoid being drawn into reviewing or advising on operational plans or any other act that might identify U.S. too closely with change in government. We would, however, welcome information which would help us assess character of any alternate leadership.

With regard to specific problem of how to reply to General Minh, you should consider having Gascon take position that he is unable to present Minh's case to responsible policy officials with any degree of seriousness. In order to get responsible officials to even consider Minh's problem, Gascon would have to have detailed information clearly indicating that Minh's plans offer a high prospect of success. You should also consider with Acting Station Chief whether it would be desirable in order to preserve security and deniability for appropriate arrangements to be made for follow-up contacts by individuals brought in from outside Viet Nam. As we indicated in CAP 63560 we are most concerned about security problem and are confining knowledge these sensitive matters in Washington to extremely limited group of less than ten high officials in State, Defense and CIA, with whom this message has been cleared.

Shortly after the Ambassador and Marnin arrived together at the Republic of China national day reception October 10, always a lavish affair with almost a thousand people invited, Sedgewick seemingly opportunely ran into both Bich and Minh. Marnin could not tell whether it was a planned meeting or not, but inferred that it was. In any case, it was a secure opportunity in the huge crush of people for the Ambassador to assure both of the principal coup plotters that Gascon was his trusted agent and that he himself spoke directly for John Fitzgerald Kennedy, who had after all grown up in an Ambassador's Residence and who consequently made it a practice to preserve the prerogatives and to respect the judgment of the man-on-the-spot.

One of the few advantages of being tall, particularly in Asia where Marnin towered more than a foot over the average man, was to see across crowded rooms. He spotted Lily dressed in a blue silk *ao dai* standing in a corner with Curly. Marnin waited for Bird to wander off with a friend. Then he made his way across the room, determined to greet her.

"What's a nice girl like you doing in a place like this?" he asked.

Lily turned around.

"I hoped I might see you here," she said.

"Did you? Why's that? I should have thought you'd be in a delirium of girlish excitement—last minute fittings, caterers, and bridal showers—all those things brides do."

"Don't be cruel, David. My life is punishment enough."

"Isn't that a line from some play? But you're right. There's no point in recriminations. How are you, anyway?"

"Learning to survive."

"I take it from my invitation that you're having the wedding at the farm."

"Yes. . .One last day at my beloved farm. . ." She sighed deeply. "And then I'm getting out of this country—this lunatic asylum—and never coming back. . .Will you be at the wedding?"

"I wouldn't miss it for the world—anything to see you once more."

"Are you. . . going to Curly's bachelor party tomorrow night?"

"For some reason I wasn't invited."

"Funny. . ." she said, smiling, "neither was I."

"Are you trying to tell me something?"

"I thought. . .well, I thought perhaps you and I. . . ."

"You thought you might have your own little bachelor party, Lily?"

"Something like that. . . ."

"And that I might come to it?"

"Yes. . . ."

"One final fuck, as it were?"

She flinched and looked down. Then she gazed up at him and her eyes were hard.

"If you like."

"Oh yes, I like. Count me in. And have you solved the problems of the farm?"

"Yes. I told Curly about them and he's going to help me."

"That's the least he can do for a wife."

"Not at all. You are a typical male pig living in the last century. It has nothing to do with our personal relations. It is strictly a business proposition."

"What's the deal?"

"We've been working on it all day. He's going to buy out my creditors for $48,000 cash money. This is good business for me because I owe them $61,500. And I'm going to pay Curly back at 20% over a five year period. I had been paying those loan sharks 64%. Now I'm free and clear. And if you Americans come in here in a really big way, as is now the expectation, I'll be able to sell the farm and the livestock for at least a quarter of a million."

Claudio had a similar story to tell over Ba Mi Ba beers on the terrace at the Cercle Sportif the following day. Things had eased up, Claudio said. The Chinese moneylenders had withdrawn some of the pressure and would go along with a cut-rate buyout if the syndicate could come up with $940,000.

"It seemed like a good deal all around. We can borrow half of it in Singapore at forty per cent and put up the rest ourselves. With you people about to come in here in a big way, we should be able to sell our assets for at least three million by the end of next year. In the meanwhile, we'll be netting half a million a year after we pay off the interest, which is not a bad return on an original investment of less than a million."

"So your kneecaps are saved."

"My life, my friend. These guys don't fool around when it comes to a debt of honor."

"But what makes the moneylenders think we're coming in here in a bigger way than we are already?"

"The word is out the Americans are going to dump Diem. That's why the price of gold is rising and the piaster is falling. Just last week the wise money believed you might cut and run and get out of here altogether. That's when the moneylenders put on the squeeze. But now they think you're going to stick around. I think we've seen the end of the great panic of 1963."

Claudio wiped his forehead, downed the last of his beer and ordered another.

Chapter 44

THE AMBASSADOR

AND THE GENERAL

After receipt of Bundy's October 9 cable Sedgewick changed his mode of operations. Before that at least half a dozen other people—Donnelly, Bilder, Sabo, Helen Eng, Markoff before his departure, and Marnin—were in "the loop" and would regularly see all the cable traffic. Afterward, Sedgewick kept detailed knowledge about coup planning from everyone in the Embassy except Gascon and a single CIA code clerk. When the Ambassador wrote anything on the subject it was in his laborious longhand on a yellow lined pad in his study at the residence. Then it was not even retyped. Gascon carried it to the Embassy, where it was transmitted via CIA channels directly from the Ambassador's draft.

Marnin took this as something of a slap in the face. But he soon realized that the person really being frozen out by these new procedures was General Donnelly, who believed that the instructions that had been received from Washington, and specifically from McNamara and Taylor, precluded supporting a coup. Since Donnelly—the official personally and unusually designated by Jack Kennedy to take over the running of the Mission if Sedgewick happened to be absent from the country while a coup was taking place—was not to know what was going on, neither could anyone else, including the Deputy Chief of Mission, and certainly not an insignificant actor like Marnin. The Ambassador did not want Donnelly "blowing the whistle" on him to Taylor and McNamara and to others at high levels in Washington who were skeptical about the necessity for the removal of Diem.

It was a dicey time in Saigon, where the coup machine seemed to be fueled by Sedgewick's fraying nerves. He grew more and more irritable and routinely snapped at his section chiefs and at lesser subordinates like Helen Eng and Marnin. After one tantrum about an insufficient number of sharpened pencils on his desk, things came to the point where Sedgewick had to backpedal and use all his persuasive charm—which was considerable—to dissuade Helen, probably the best secretary in the Foreign Service, from asking for a transfer.

As for Marnin, he had always thought of himself as in control of his destiny. But suddenly, in both his personal and professional lives, he felt himself in the grip of malign forces that he was powerless to govern. Every night after work he downed a couple of martinis and a sandwich, then spent the rest of the evening carousing through the clubs and bars of Saigon, sometimes with Mandelbrot and his colleagues, now and then with Frank Gascon or Chick Rizzo, often with Claudio, and occasionally even alone.

Sedgewick took to leaving for lunch at twelve-thirty and not returning until five. He claimed to be using that time to digest the contents of his long range reading box. But since Marnin was in charge of "locking him up," i.e., securing his various in-boxes both in the residence and then back to the Chancery building, he knew that little long-range reading had actually been done. It was not that Sedgewick was lazy—far from it. Just going back and forth from the Embassy to the residence and then back to the Chancery with cables from and to the President, Mac Bundy, Dean Rusk—cables that required Sedgewick's immediate attention—took up great chunks of Marnin's afternoons.

The ambassadorial study had a small room off it originally designed as a dressing room. It was there Gascon surreptitiously waited after Lao Mi announced Marnin's presence and while the Ambassador and he conducted their routine business. Marnin was not supposed to know Gascon was in the residence, but he could hardly be missed. He drove a beaten up old jeep, painted red, the only one of its kind in Saigon.

Everything Sedgewick was doing depended on the myth that the embassy was neither promoting nor preventing a coup. It was essential to Sedgewick that key officials in Washington did not think he was exceeding his instructions, using Gascon as his instrument. As he cabled McGeorge Bundy on October 25,

". . .It is vital that we neither thwart a coup nor be in a position where we do not know what is going on. We should not try to stop a coup for two reasons. First, it seems at least an even bet the next government would not bungle and stumble as much as the present one. Secondly, it is extremely unwise for us to pour cold water on attempts at a coup, particularly in their beginning stages. When we thwart attempts at a coup, as we have done in the past, we incur long lasting resentments, assume undue responsibility for keeping the incumbents in office, and in general set ourselves in judgment over the affairs of Viet Nam. . . ."

But Bundy was not entirely convinced. He cabled back immediately,

"The President is particularly concerned that an unsuccessful coup, however carefully we avoid direct engagement, will be laid at our door by public opinion everywhere. Therefore, while sharing your view that we should not be in the position of thwarting a coup, we would like to have the option of judging and warning on any plan with poor prospects of success. We recognize this is a large order, but the President wants you to know of our concern."

Meanwhile, it had become apparent to McNamara and Taylor that their man on the spot, General Donnelly, was being frozen out of the action. This was intolerable to them. Taylor cabled his concern in an "Eyes Only" message to Donnelly October 28, using the Defense back channel. In it he stated:

". . .Concern has been expressed by the Secretary over what appears to us to be a continued lack of effective communication between you and the Ambassador. There clearly is a lack of common understanding of something as basic and important as the Washington coup guidance. You have been quoted on sensitive subjects without your specific authorization. There seem to be disagreements on facts which might have been resolved in Saigon by direct discussion between principals prior to messages being sent to Washington. All this and several other indicators suggest a relationship which lacks the depth and continuity required by the complex circumstances in Saigon.

"Related to the foregoing is divergent reporting on the military situation arriving through MACV and Ambassadorial channels. Saigon 768, for example, contains statements on the progress of the war at variance with those we have received from you and with the impression Secretary McNamara and I received in Saigon only three weeks ago (although consonant with our last luncheon conversation with the Ambassador, which we both found disturbing.) Are we correct in believing the Ambassador is forwarding military reports and evaluations without consulting you? If our impressions are correct, I would welcome any suggestions as to how we may help at this end to bring about closer rapport between you and Ambassador Sedgewick.

"Please comment ASAP."

The morning that cable arrived, Marnin received a call from Tom Aylward, who wanted to come to the Embassy to see him. Although they knew each other well and had had many encounters on the residence tennis court and at the Cercle Sportif, this was the first time Aylward had visited him at the Embassy.

"I'll lay my cards on the table," he said, getting right to the point. "The General has been impossible to live with the last couple of weeks, ever since General Taylor and Mr. McNamara left Saigon."

"Life isn't easy for an Aide," Marnin said. "Nobody knows that better than I do."

"The General has the feeling he isn't being cut in on what you political geniuses are up to around here. I'm an artillery officer, not a diplomat like you, so I'll put it to you straight. He asked me to nose around and see if I could find out what's going on. He knows that you and I play a lot of tennis together."

"He thought I might enlighten you?"

"Something like that."

"I would if I could, Tom, but the fact is that I'm as much in the dark as anyone, and certainly more out of the loop than the General. That's not a surprise, is it?"

"It's what I thought you would say," Aylward replied.

Donnelly had to report to Taylor. It was a tough cable to write. He knew that in these circumstances, no matter how much he desired secrecy, whatever he said would get around and make him look bad in the corridors of the Pentagon.

MAC 2028 from Commander MACV to Chairman JCS. Top Secret.
Eyes Only. October 29, 1963—2130 hours.
EXCLUSIVE FOR GENERAL TAYLOR FROM GENERAL DONNELLY.
No Other Distribution.

"Your JCS 4188—63 arrived as I was in the process of drafting a cable for you along the same lines. The fact is I deeply share your concern. I have not as yet seen Embassy Saigon 768—Embassy has not released it—and CAS 1896 was sent first and delivered to me only after its dispatch. Ambassador and I are certainly in touch, but whether we are communicating is something else again.

"I will allow myself to say that Bascombe's methods of operations are entirely different from Gus Corning's. Gus invariably cleared messages concerning the military with me or my staff prior to dispatch. This is not the way things are operating today. You are correct in believing that the Ambassador is forwarding military reports and evaluations without consulting me.

"There is a basic difference apparently between the Ambassador's thinking and mine on the interpretation of the guidance contained in White House 63560 dated 6 October and the additional thoughts expressed in CAS Washington 74228 dated 9 October. I interpret CAP 63560 as our basic guidance and believe CAS 74228 did not change the basic guidance—i.e., no initiative should be taken to give active covert encouragement to a coup. The Ambassador feels 74228 does change 63560, that a change of government is desirable and can only be brought about by a coup. Who is correct? What is Washington's view?

"I'm not opposed to a change of government, no indeed, but am inclined to feel that at this time the change should be in methods of governing rather than in completely changing personnel at the top. I have seen no batting order proposed by any of the coup groups. I think we should take a hard look at the proposed list of players before we make irrevocable decisions about our future in this country. In my contacts here, and I'm not blowing my own horn when I say my contacts with the Generals has been wider and deeper than that of any other American, including Colonel Gascon, I have seen no one with the strength of character of Diem, at least in fighting communists.

"Certainly there are no Generals qualified to take over from him in my opinion. I am not a Diem man per se. I see the faults in his character and know as well as anyone, except perhaps Gus Corning, the difficulties one encounters in dealing with him (difficulties Ambassador Sedgewick does not know too much about personally since he has only had two substantive discussions with Diem since he's been here.) But my mission, as I see it, is to back the 14 million South Vietnamese people in their fight against communism and it just happens that Diem is their leader at this time. Most generals I have talked to agree they can go along with Diem. All say it's the Nhus they are opposed to.

"Turning to my own bailiwick, I do not agree with the Ambassador's assessment in Saigon 764 that we are just holding our own. GVN is way ahead in I, II, and parts of III Corps and making progress in the Delta. Nothing has happened in October to change the assessment you and Secretary McNamara made after your visit here except a series of unhelpful New York Times articles that are at best distortions of the true picture.

"I suggest we not try to change horses too quickly; that we win the military effort as quickly as possible, then let whoever wants to in this country make any and all changes that suit them. After all, rightly or wrongly, we have backed Diem for eight long hard years. To me it seems incongruous now to get him down, kick him around, and get rid of him. For what? With what end in mind? The US has been his mother superior and father confessor since he's been in office and he has leaned on us heavily and tried to do his best.

"Furthermore, if I may be permitted to wander outside the military sphere of Viet Nam itself, it behooves us to remember, as Shakespeare said in "Julius Caesar," that other leaders at other times may some day be watching what we're doing here. And right now heads of other underdeveloped countries will take an understandably dim view of our assistance if they are led to believe that the same fate lies in store for them that may well be experienced soon by our former friend and ally Ngo Dinh Diem.

Chapter 45

THE AMBASSADOR
AND THE PRESIDENT

Sedgewick discovered as October wore on that of all the reasons to pull off his coup as soon as possible, the most pressing and unexpected was that his strategy of "making Diem come to me" had begun to work. The Vietnamese President had seen the writing on the wall and was ready to accept any reasonable solution. If the full import of Diem's decision had become widely known in Washington, its significance would not have been lost on McNamara, Taylor, McCone and Colby, all of whom had been urging that Diem be given another chance. As the Vietnamese conspirators geared up their coup machine, keeping Diem's change of heart from those at the top of the United States Government became increasingly difficult.

The Finance Minister on October 14 told Bob Jaspers that the Bank of Viet Nam was desperately worried about the declining confidence of the business community. The bank had been trying, he said, to ease the pressure on the piaster by tapping the GVN's hard currency reserves. So far it had been relatively successful because those reserves were plentiful. But if the suspension of the CIP were not lifted soon, the value of the piaster could plummet by as much as forty per cent within weeks. He said President Diem wished to discuss this with us. When apprised of this turn of events in a memorandum from Jaspers, Sedgewick scrawled across the top of it, "File this memo. If

Diem is really so worried as all this, then let him summon me to the Palace and we'll talk about it!"

Essentially the same message in a different context was delivered October 19 to Bob Smith, the acting CIA Station Chief, by Nguyen Van Phuong, Nhu's *chef de cabinet*. Phuong said his boss wanted the Embassy to understand that without a further infusion of American funding, the inauguration of six more strategic hamlets in the Delta and four in III Corps by November 1, as scheduled, would be impossible. If things proceeded at their current pace, Phuong claimed the Strategic Hamlet Program would soon grind to a halt. He suggested the Ambassador talk this matter over with Diem or Nhu and that, pending the release of funds, some sort of announcement be made that a dialogue was under way.

Sedgewick refused to act on Phuong's plea. "I'll think it over," he wrote in the margin of Smith's memorandum. "In the meantime, file it." That was the last that was heard of it.

On October 22, an increasingly desperate Nhu told Indian ICC Commissioner Goburdhun that his brother was ready to make the necessary changes of policy and of personnel, including his own transfer, to satisfy the Americans. The important thing, he said, was winning the war against the Viet Cong. Anything serving that cause would be undertaken by the GVN with a "happy heart and a clear conscience." (Nhu was thereby echoing, word for word, the statement on the subject made by President Kennedy at his September 2 press conference—as clear a diplomatic signal as one could give.) But again, when apprised of this by Goburdhun, Sedgewick thanked him, and instructed Marnin to make a memorandum of the Indian's remarks for the record and put the memo in the Embassy files. He did not send it to Washington.

It was therefore no great surprise that in the middle of the following week the Ambassador received a formal invitation from Diem to accompany him to Dalat that weekend in order to inaugurate the GVN's new experimental nuclear reactor. Since the funds for that reactor had been supplied by USOM through a grant from AID, and since the popular Curly Bird was leaving the country at the beginning of November, the inauguration of the reactor was to be accompanied by a ceremony in which Bird was to receive South Viet Nam's highest civilian medal from Diem. In these circumstances, and especially in view of the coup rumors sweeping Saigon with which he did not want to be associated, it was an invitation Sedgewick found imprudent to turn down.

Marnin expected to accompany the Ambassador to Dalat. But he was disappointed to learn on Thursday morning from Bilder that this was not to be the case. It was a small plane, the DCM explained, that only had room for six passengers—Diem, Sedgewick, Penelope, Dinh Trieu Da, and two security agents.

With Sedgewick gone for the day, Marnin had the opportunity that afternoon to pay a farewell call on Sam Sabo, who was leaving Viet Nam the following week. Grace had already preceded him to their town house in Georgetown on N Street next to the Harrimans. The movers—at least ten of them—were at Sabo's home in the embassy compound on Le Qui Don. Packing boxes were everywhere. So the most convenient place for them to talk was on the front porch, where Nhu had held forth at the dinner party a year before. Sabo signaled his number one boy to bring them two Bloody Marys and a dish of cashews.

"I'm really sorry to see you go," David said. "You will be missed around here."

"It's for the best," Sabo replied, "I could never have lasted the way things are going. It's too painful to watch my efforts here becoming irrelevant or, worse yet, going down the tubes."

"I have a problem about that myself," Marnin said.

Sabo gave him a shrewd look. "What's on your mind?" he asked.

"Sam, I'll never forget how you stood by me when I got into trouble. I owe you a great deal."

"Nobody with any integrity would have done any differently."

"It's integrity that's on my mind. Let me give you a hypothetical case. Supposing a junior officer was working for someone who was doing one thing and telling Washington he was doing another. Where does that officer's loyalty lie? What should he do about a situation like that?"

Sabo took a long swig from his drink.

"The answer, my friend, is nothing, absolutely nothing," he said.

"A junior embassy officer simply has no credibility, particularly if he is up against someone powerful. Serious charges require serious evidence. And even if such evidence is produced, the question of how that evidence was obtained has to come up and automatically discredit that hypothetical officer. Nobody in the State Department is going to want to employ him in the future. In any case, nothing your hypothetical officer can do or say will make the slightest bit of difference."

Sabo again looked at Marnin searchingly.

"Just remember," he said, "that whatever is being done around here has to be seen in world-wide terms. The United States simply cannot stand by and allow China to take over Southeast Asia. The basic question is how to go about stopping this from happening. Good men can differ about that. But I don't much like to pontificate, especially so near my departure from this madhouse. I hope this is of some use to you."

"It surely is," David replied.

They raised their glasses to each other in a silent farewell toast.

The Ambassador described his day with Diem carefully, making every effort to convey his total objectivity toward the President. On his return to the Embassy he dictated a cable to Helen Eng, which Marnin had a chance to proofread before it was sent on in an "Eyes Only" message.

Telegram 805 from AmEmbassy Saigon to SecState rpt info Bangkok. Secret; Priority; October 28, 1963—9 p.m.
EYES ONLY FOR THE SECRETARY. BANGKOK EXCLUSIVE FOR CINCPAC
Herewith is a report of my day with President Diem, Sunday, October 27.
We left Saigon and flew to the Dau Nghia Plantation Center where we had a simple Vietnamese lunch. We then flew over the Province of Quang Duc to Dalat. Diem was at his best, surprisingly personable, describing the public improvements he had put into effect. He was constantly saying, 'I had this built,' 'I did this,' and 'I did that.' Despite my previous feelings that Diem was something of a prisoner inside his Palace, he seems deeply interested in agriculture and in developing the country. One feels he is a nice, good man living a good life by his own lights, but also that he is a man living in the past, truly indif-

ferent to people, and unbelievably stubborn.

We dined in the Presidential villa in Dalat. The guest quarters were simple and rustic, quite in keeping with the fact that it had once been a hunting lodge reserved for high French civil servants. Diem mentioned that my distant cousin Teddy Roosevelt hunted tigers there during his round-the-world trip in 1909, after he had relinquished the presidency. Diem seems to have a fund of knowledge about everything in this country and loves to impart it to visitors. Every event and even every dish served to us, and there were a dozen or more, reminded him of something that illustrated the history of his country. After a more than sumptuous Vietnamese dinner he suddenly said in a casual, rather supercilious tone, that he would like to know whether we were going to suspend the CIP indefinitely.

This came out of the blue. In fact, I had hoped to avoid the subject and let our suspension of aid fester a little longer. I replied that I did not know, but asked what he intended to do if our policy changed to one more compatible with his wishes. In that case, would he open the schools, liberate the Buddhists and others who were in prison, eliminate the discriminatory features of Decree Law Number 10?

Diem replied that I seemed to be out of date and suggested we have more frequent contact so I could be sure I was getting both sides of the story and not just swallowing fictions put out by his enemies. He said the schools had been gradually reopening and were already in session in Hue. (I am checking this statement with our Consul there.) The Buddhists, Diem continued, were also being liberated from prison and only a few were left in custody. However, changing Decree Law Number 10 required the assent of the Assembly, and could not be done overnight. He had no authority to change it himself and it was important to maintain legal norms.

He then took the occasion to mention the activities of one CAS Officer who had talked to members of his government about threats (which some attribute to Nhu) to assassinate me and other high-ranking American officials. This CAS Officer allegedly warned that if such assassinations actually took place, we would send the 7th Fleet into Saigon and do what we did in Okinawa in 1945. Diem said such stories were outrageous, slandered him and his Government, and did us both a great disservice. Anyone who knew him would understand, he said, that my safety was a preoccupation of his. I said I had total confidence he did not want me assassinated, but that these rumors were constantly being brought to me.

He said the CIA was openly intriguing against the GVN and conspiring with Vietnamese officers to foment a coup. He said, urging me not to let myself be captured by adventurers, that he knew of at least four such plots. I said: Give me proof of improper action by any US Government employee and he'll be out of here on the next plane. He replied that the war against the communists is the primary aim of both governments and we should not let the focus of our attention be shifted away by the machinations of communist agents.

I said I agreed, but that we both must consider US opinion. We want our relationship to be one of equal partners. We do not want Viet Nam to be a satellite; nor do we want to be a satellite of Viet Nam's. We don't wish to be put in the embarrassing position of condoning totalitarian acts that are against our traditions and ideals. I said that many things have happened which make it hard for us to come to a meeting of the minds with him and his government. We hear of American newspapermen being attacked by Nhu's secret police, of bonzes burning as one just did again on October 5, of children being taken off to concentration camps in American trucks.

Diem replied newspapermen who go into the center of a riot run the risk of being beaten. I said you don't get anywhere in the U.S. by beating up newspapermen. The American public is already so critical of the GVN that I thought if the resolution sponsored by Senator Church cutting off aid to Viet Nam until religious persecution stops came to a vote, a majority of Senators would vote against the GVN.

Diem said the US press is full of lies. This reminded him of the way his brother had been treated by the American media, as though he were some sort of cynical Svengali. Diem talked about the excellent qualities of Nhu—so good, so quiet, so conciliatory, the one person in his government who always saw the American point of view and explained it to his colleagues. I said I would not debate this point and it might well be that Mr. Nhu had been treated unfairly in the world press. But the fact is that Mr. and Mrs. Nhu have had extremely bad publicity. This was why I advised a period of silence for both of them.

Diem said Madame Nhu had more than a hundred invitations to talk to organizations in the United States. He said that the press does not print what Madame Nhu says and that the whole concert of lies is orchestrated by the State Department. It may look that way in Saigon, I said, but the way to stop the bad publicity about Viet Nam is for the forces controlled by Nhu to cease their repressive behavior and for Madame Nhu to stop talking.

Near the end of the conversation I said: Mr. President, every single specific suggestion which I have made you have rejected. Isn't there something you can do that would favorably impress US opinion? He gave me a blank stare and said the important thing was that we were allies united in a worthy and honorable cause—fighting the evils of Communism. We therefore had to work together and trust each other. I replied that he could always count on us to walk the extra mile and thanked him for his courtesy.

Comment: Although the conversation was frustrating and long-winded, the tone was always courteous and restrained. I am convinced we have persuaded him of one thing: that the state of US opinion is very bad from his point of view. For a man who is as cut off as he is, this is something. Perhaps the conversation will give him food for thought and perhaps it marks a beginning. But in itself, I see nothing that offers much hope for change.

SEDGEWICK

Chapter 46

THE BACHELOR PARTY

It was not just Sedgewick whose nerves were raw. Everyone was going a little crazy in Saigon during those last weeks of October. Adding to the nervousness were assassination lists being picked up by the CIA Station. The potential American victims included not only the Ambassador, but all members of the Country Team rumored to be anti-Diem. Nhu was thought to be personally responsible, but some believed his enemies were using this as a device to further split the Ngo Dinh brothers from the Americans. After reviewing one of those CIA reports Sedgewick looked up at Marnin and said, "You seem to be the only American in Saigon who's not ticketed to be killed by Nhu's goons."

"A dubious distinction," Marnin replied.

Blatant coup rumors were everywhere, including the local press, which began to carry dark and barely intelligible diatribes against those venal enough to be seduced by foreign "Judases." Hardly a prominent Vietnamese missed being named in the rumor mills as one of the plotters. Throughout those last weeks of October Marnin could not go out in the evening to a sleazy bar without hearing whispers from one of the "hostesses" of an imminent coup.

Perhaps the most jangled person in town was Willis Mandelbrot, who had at his fingertips a great story that he could not print. This was driving him crazy. Every time he met Marnin he lamented that he could not betray the trust being bestowed on him by the American Ambassador. Sedgewick, in truth, was not taking much of a risk confiding in Mandelbrot. If the *Times* had actually printed what he knew, it would have simply been denied by everyone involved. The plotters might have then changed their plans, but nothing could have been proven. The only beneficiaries would have been Diem and Nhu.

Mandelbrot's tennis not surprisingly was more erratic than ever. He double faulted so much trying for aces on his second serve that Marnin refused to play singles with him. Mandelbrot was only tolerated as a doubles partner because it was from him, more than anyone else, that Marnin could find out what his own boss was up to.

Another companion caught up in these events, but very much outside them, was Claudio. It had been brought home to him by Dennis Chang that the fate of Diem, Nhu, and the Generals could profoundly affect their fortunes. The right scrap of information could turn out to be worth thousands upon thousands of dollars to the syndicate. Claudio began to pump Marnin and to a lesser extent Mandelbrot (he made the mistaken assumption that Marnin knew more than Mandelbrot) about what was going on. This made the aide profoundly uncomfortable. Having knowledge that was worth hard cash to a close friend was a new experience. Marnin began to avoid Claudio.

It was the night before the wedding—the date designated for Curly's bachelor party. Marnin was waved into Lily's compound by the Montagnard clutching his M-16. It will be the last time, David thought morosely, as he, in response, greeted the guard. The maid Ding Ding was waiting for him; showed him down the hall to a room he had not seen before; tapped twice on the door, opened it noiselessly, and then left him.

It was dark and wood-paneled, furnished with a carved ebony opium bed, a man's chest of drawers, a military foot locker, a huge desk and cheval glass. Clearly David was entering a shrine to the former occupant, whose full-length, life size portrait hung on the wall — that of a Vietnamese General in full dress uniform with ceremonial sword, holding an ivory swagger stick in his left hand. The man's face was lean, feral, with watchful eyes and cruel mouth. Hanging next to the painting was a glass case containing a vast array of medals pinned on a backing of black velvet.

On the desk was a phonograph, a silver tray with a champagne cooler and two goblets, and three silver candlesticks whose candles gave the room its only light. Reclining against the burgundy silk cushions of the opium bed was Lily, in a black lace negligee, her hair falling loose over her shoulders.

"Hello, *petit frère*," she said.

"What a place!" David replied, "And that's quite a portrait."

"My late great husband," Lily said.

"I could have guessed. In any case, I know that from the photos. God, look at you! Aren't you a sight! Lucky old Curly! I'll bet he never thought he'd have a little playmate like this in his declining years."

She kissed him lightly.

"Calm down, *mon ami*. Curly will never see me like this."

"What, no black lace and fancy tricks? Just granny gowns and hair curlers and the missionary position once a week?"

"Something like that. But it won't matter because he won't know the difference."

"But you will."

"Yes. I will. Come, let's have some champagne."

She poured them each a glass.

"To the bride!"

Lily did not respond. She led him by the hand to the opium bed and began to unbutton his shirt.

"Is this the right place? In this shrine to Xang?"

She unbuckled his belt, unzipped his fly and pushed him onto the bed.

"I loathed him!" she said. "He was greedy. . .(she stripped off his shoes, socks, trousers). . .corrupt. . .despicable. . .depraved. . .cruel . . . ."

"But here, in front of that painting. . . ."

"I watched for years while he seduced other women. . .degraded me. . .humiliated me. . . . Now let him watch me. . . ."

David peeled off his shirt. She pushed him back on the bed and kissed him passionately.

". . .with my handsome young lover."

She looked up at Xang's painting triumphantly.

"I hope he's writhing in hell, where he belongs!"

"So I'm basically a form of revenge."

"At first, yes. . .But then, to my surprise. . .I began to love you
. . . ."

She kissed him again.

"Come, we have one last night together. Let's use it unwisely."

"What do you suggest?"

"Anything. . .everything. . . . Do to me what you never dared to
do before."

"Is this for him. . .or for me?"

"It's for me."

She walked to the phonograph and turned it on. The song
was "Chieu Mieu Binh Xei."

"Give me a night to sustain me for the rest of my life," she said, as
she walked toward him, dropping her negligee to the floor.

Chapter 47

THE WEDDING

The main house at the farm was decorated in white ribbons and strewn with orange blossoms. Two hundred people were invited—the cream of Saigon society. The Ambassador gave the bride away. He had hoped to see either Big Minh or Bich at the reception, but they were not among the numerous ARVN contingent. Guests were scheduled to arrive at two and depart at six. Everyone knew that the road from the farm to Bien Hoa was unsafe to drive after dark. But there had been few Viet Cong incidents along it during the previous three months. In any case, Lily confided to David that the VC had been paid off—seventy thousand piasters to ensure that no untoward incidents occurred.

Originally, the ceremony was to have been performed by Ngo Dinh Thuc. But at the behest of the Papal Nuncio, and after much consultation with Sedgewick, the Vatican had ordered Thuc to Rome at the beginning of the month, hoping that his absence from Hue would help cool the situation in that hot city. The Archbishop of Saigon therefore officiated. Lily wore a white gown. Her daughters served as bridesmaids, also in white. Her hair was in a chignon, interlaced with sprigs of jasmine. She looked stunning—a radiantly beautiful bride. Curly was in striped pants and morning coat. The Ambassador, and Curly's brother, who had flown in from Kentucky to act as best man, were in dark suits.

Two large tents had been set up, each of them with ten round tables at which ten people were seated. At the center of each table was a pot filled with tiger lily orchids. The wedding was catered by the Nam Fung Restaurant in Cholon. It was a ten course meal, with suckling pig as the *pièce de résistance*. Marnin was in the second tent, seated with Embassy and USOM colleagues, grateful to be separated from the head table. Halfway through the meal Curly and Lily came into the tent and toasted each of the tables, on which stood bottles of Dom Perignon, Martell VSOP, and Johnny Walker Black Label Scotch. This was conspicuous consumption, Saigon style.

"Here's to you, my friend," she said to Marnin, when it was his turn. She sipped some champagne.

"To your health," Marnin replied with tears in his eyes that he did not bother to dab. He was already quite drunk.

After the speeches there was dancing, with two orchestras, one in each tent. Marnin resolutely made his way into her tent. Lily was dancing with an ARVN General he did not recognize. Marnin tapped the man on the shoulder.

"May I have the privilege, sir. . ." he said and paused, "of dancing with the beautiful bride?"

The General looked at him quizzically, trying to decide whether to take offense or not. He resolved to let matters pass and left them alone on the dance floor.

"David, you're drunk," she said.

The band was playing "Somewhere Beyond the Sea."

"I thought white was for virgins. . .and I'm not sure, Lily, that after last night you qualify," he replied.

"In Vietnam, we don't wear white for weddings. We wear it for funerals."

Marnin grasped her and held her close. She squirmed away from him.

"Be nice, David. Please!"

"Here's looking at you, kid," he said in his rather good imitation of Humphrey Bogart. "Well, we'll always have Saigon, sweetheart. We didn't until last night. . .we'd lost it, but last night we got it back. . . ."

And the music stopped.

The bride and groom slipped away at four and drove to Saigon, where they were spending the wedding night at the Caravelle Hotel.

The following day they were to leave on Air France for Paris. The party went on for a couple of hours after their departure. Champagne was plentiful and Marnin drank great quantities of it. At dusk, the guests began to depart. Marnin took an open bottle back to his car, sat in the front seat, finished it off, and passed out.

The next thing he knew a flashlight beam shattered the darkness, shining on him as he slept, hunched over the steering wheel. With a violent start, he came to and looked up. For a moment he was blinded, and then he made out the blurred face leering in through the window. Stupefied, he watched the mouth widen in a gap-toothed grin as the man, one of Lily's montagnard guards, recognized Marnin. The man jabbered something and left.

It was after eleven—much too late and too dangerous to drive back to town. The noise of the cicadas filled the moonless night. It was pitch dark. Luckily, he knew the way to the house. Otherwise, he would have had to stay in the car. He yearned for a flashlight.

There was nobody around. The servants had disappeared to their quarters. The front door was open. Not bothering to turn on a light, he made his way to Lily's bedroom where he had spent so many happy hours, pushed back the mosquito net, let his clothes drop to the floor, and was soon heavily asleep.

PART FIVE

The Coup

November 1 was All Souls Day, *La Fête du Morts*—The Day of the Dead—a national holiday. Fortunately, the Ambassador had told Marnin at the wedding that he did not have to bring the overnight traffic to the Residence until mid-morning. It was already hot as he drove through the rubber plantations and along the river to Bien Hoa, where the road joined Highway One to Saigon. Five minutes after he passed the main entrance to the largest military base in the area, he came abreast of a huge convoy of two-and-a-half ton trucks traveling toward the capital at about twenty-five miles an hour. There was no traffic at all in the opposite direction. The backs of the trucks were filled with soldiers in battle dress and carrying carbines. Seemingly in high spirits, they waved at Marnin as he passed them.

Marnin had never seen such a large convoy. He counted 103 trucks, 14 APCs, and 15 pieces of artillery before he reached the front of the line, where the division commander was leading the way along with his driver and Chief of Staff in a camouflage colored Jeep displaying the national flag on the left side of the bumper and the pennant of the 5th Division—a big red "5" against a yellow background—on the right. Marnin waved as he came abreast. The commander waved back and gave him a big smile. He was a Colonel and a very handsome man.

"I'm from the American Embassy—Ambassador Sedgewick's aide. What's going on?" Marnin shouted at him in French.

"*Nous nous amusons, seulement,*" the Colonel replied, "we're only having a little fun."

He grinned at Marnin and waved again. It was the first time Marnin had ever seen Nguyen Van Thieu.

This was big news. One of the many reasons Washington had been reluctant to commit to a coup was a CIA estimate that the military balance appeared to favor the government. This estimate was based on the supposition that the forces under Ton That Dinh—III Corps Commander and Military Governor of Saigon—would remain at Diem's disposal. The best the coup plotters could hope for, American military analysts believed, was that Dinh, and particularly his strongest force—the 5th Division under Colonel Nguyen Van Thieu—would remain neutral. But Marnin had just seen the 5th in full battle gear barreling down the highway to Saigon.

He drove straight to the Residence. The beaten up old red Jeep was in the driveway. Lao Mi, as befitted a good Catholic, was worshiping at the Saigon Cathedral to celebrate the Day of the Dead. The front door was surprisingly not locked. Marnin raced up the stairs, knocked, and entered the Ambassador's study. Gascon was there. Sedgewick and Gascon looked up at him, both of them not concealing their annoyance.

On the desk were neat piles of crisp, new ten thousand piaster notes. Gascon was counting them, tying together each packet of hundred thousand piasters with rubber bands, noting the serial numbers, and then stuffing them into the compartments of an old-fashioned brown leather briefcase with two straps. Marnin had first noticed that bulging briefcase in the third drawer of Sedgewick's safe when he locked him up two weeks before. It would have been difficult to miss. It had been taped shut with masking tape, locked by key, and then tied up with twine. The key and the twine were on the table next to the banknotes.

"What in hell are you doing here?" Sedgewick demanded.

"I just drove in from Bien Hoa and wanted to tell you without wasting any time that the whole 5th Division seems to be on its way to Saigon," Marnin said. "I counted 103 trucks, 14 APCs, and lots of artillery. The troops were in full battle gear, wearing helmets and carrying M-1s."

Gascon and Sedgewick looked at each other. Gascon allowed himself a smile, but the Ambassador kept a straight face.

"This pretty much confirms it," Gascon said. "I better get down to JGS Headquarters. Can't keep General Minh waiting."

"You should go immediately," Sedgewick said.

"Here, give me a hand," Gascon said to Marnin.

The aide helped Gascon by counting the money—a total of three million piasters—and arranging it in piles. Gascon noted down the amount and the serial numbers of each pile on a piece of yellow paper and then stuffed the currency into the briefcase. It took them about ten minutes to finish up. Sedgewick nervously paced the room as they worked. When finished, Gascon, briefcase in hand, left for Joint General Staff Headquarters at Tan Son Nhut, next to MACV, which had been designated by General Minh as his Command Post.

"David, I don't want you to misconstrue what's happened here," Sedgewick said, as soon as Gascon had left the room. "The money is entirely for humanitarian purposes. In case something untoward happens, the money is to ease the difficulties that the families of the Generals will face. This has been entirely a Vietnamese operation. We've insisted all along that it's up to the Generals to make the necessary decisions. Our role has only been to gather information and not thwart responsible people from taking actions they consider prudent. Do you follow what I'm saying?"

"Yes, sir. I understand completely," David said. And he did.

He was ordered to go to the office, monitor developments, and stay in touch with Sedgewick as the day progressed, but not to overburden him with minutiae. He was to keep a careful log. Gascon reached JGS Headquarters a few moments after Marnin had ensconced himself in the Ambassador's office next to his green secure phone, on which it was permitted to talk about anything up to Top Secret, but not codeword materials.

The first call was from Gascon, who reported that Big Minh had turned over to him the suddenly empty office of Captain Quyen, the Vietnamese Chief of Naval Operations, who had been shot—on his thirty-sixth birthday—in the back of the head without warning in his staff car by his second in command, Commander Lam. The assassination of the South Vietnamese CNO was the crossing of the Rubicon.

There was no retreat for the plotters after that.

Gascon, never squeamish, accepted Minh's offer and used the murdered CNO's phone to keep an open line to the CIA Station, where Barney Maher was on the other end. The pre-arranged signal between them, set up in August at the time of the false coup, was that if a coup were about to commence, Gascon would call in and say, "I need more whiskey." Maher, who had just returned from R & R in Bangkok, had forgotten about the signal in the interim. So when Gascon called him, he replied, "Dammit Frank, it's eleven o'clock in the morning. It's too early for whiskey."

Gascon hung up angrily and called Marnin.

"Would you please explain what's happening to my colleague Mr. Maher," he said. "Tell him what you told Mr. Big and me about what you saw on the highway this morning; that things are going 'CRIT-IC.' Do you read me?"

"Yes, sir. I surely do," Marnin said.

He was worried about Lily and thought of calling Curly Bird at the Caravelle, which was close to where fighting was likely to break out, to warn him and let him know the afternoon flight to Paris might be cancelled. But he decided against it. There were worse things in life, he reflected, than to be stranded in a hotel with Lily on the morning of your honeymoon.

Marnin straightened things out with the CIA Station. Then he called Tom Aylward on the secure phone and told him what was happening. MACV had already been alerted by several advisors with key ARVN units that something was up, but thus far had no confirmation that a coup was about to take place. The first thing General Donnelly had to decide, Aylward explained, was whether to broadcast on the emergency channel of Armed Forces Radio that "Condition Grey" had been declared. This would alert all American personnel to the possibility of impending civil disturbances and warn them off the streets. Marnin checked with the Ambassador, who was concerned that this might in the process be alerting the GVN, and counseled the General to hold off on "Condition Grey" until the troops actually started to move on the Palace.

By that time advance elements of the 5th were forming up near

Tan Son Nhut. Aylward said he could see them from his office window. Gascon reported that Colonel Thuc, the head of Special Forces, loyal to Diem and Nhu, had been arrested and, like Captain Quyen, shot. Ten minutes later, at one o'clock, he called Maher to say that Big Minh—concerned that the executions of the CNO and Colonel Thuc might be discovered and the alarm raised—had given the signal two hours earlier than originally planned. The attack on Saigon had begun.

Sedgewick was having lunch when Marnin called. He could hear the Ambassador chewing something crunchy, probably celery, on the other end of the phone as he gave him a situation report and read the first two "CRITIC" messages to him.

"Fine," he said. "That's fine. Keep me informed. But remember, don't bother me with minutiae."

Ten minutes after the shooting commenced, Helen Eng showed up at the office. Helen was always there when you needed her, Marnin mused. This was a big help—the phones had started ringing non-stop with calls from irate colleagues in the diplomatic corps and from journalists as far away as Sydney. Sedgewick would not talk with anybody. The one exception was Mandelbrot, who reached Marnin at one-thirty.

"Sorry, Billy, the Residence phones have been cut off. The Ambassador is only taking calls through this office, and we're not putting any calls through to him."

"Look, you pissant, you phone him right now! Not five minutes from now, but right now! Tell him I have to speak to him. I've been sitting on this story for a month and now I'm calling in my chips."

Marnin phoned Sedgewick, who sounded annoyed. But Mandelbrot was right. The Ambassador agreed to make an exception for the *New York Times*. The two of them were on the phone for twenty minutes. And, indeed, the coup was portrayed over the next several days on the pages of that newspaper with more of a glow than anything since the successful resolution of the Cuban Missile Crisis. In the process Sedgewick himself was described as probably the country's most effective Ambassador since Benjamin Franklin.

At one-thirty Gascon called to say that the coup committee had announced its intentions to a large group of RVNAF brass gathered at JGS headquarters. One by one, each of the other Generals had been compelled to declare his feelings about the coup. In such circumstances, the responses were unsurprisingly unanimous. Their remarks were taped for later broadcast. A few of those units whose commanders were deemed doubtful were represented by key subordinates, including the Air Force (future Prime Minister Nguyen Cao Ky), the Airborne Brigade, the Marines, and the Special Forces (whose leader had already been shot.)

At one-forty, Aylward called to say that the airport had been seized by rebel troops and was closed until further notice to all incoming and outgoing traffic. There had been no resistance. While still on the line he asked Marnin to hold on and then came back after thirty seconds to let him know that General Bich had called General Stillwell, the American chief of operations, to announce officially that the Army was moving to depose the government. In view of this, Aylward said, General Donnelly had declared "Condition Grey" in effect. This would apply to all Americans, civilian as well as military.

By two, Aylward had reports back from almost every advisor in the vicinity of the capital. All the regular line units of the ARVN were either siding actively with the Generals or remaining passive. General "Tiger" Cao, the Commanding General of IV Corps and former colleague of John Henry Mudd, was the only general of consequence seen as leaning toward the government side. But his deputy and the Commanders of the two major divisions in his area of operations supported the coup. It looked to MACV, Aylward said, as though the Generals clearly had the upper hand.

At two-forty, Gascon announced the insurgents had moved into position to attack the Palace, the barracks of the Presidential Guards, and Special Forces Headquarters. They had already seized naval headquarters, the two radio stations, and the central post office, the site of telephone and telegraph communications with the outside world.

At three, according to Gascon, Diem had called Bich to say that he was ready to form a new government and to announce reforms. "Why didn't you tell me that yesterday?" Bich had responded. "Now, Mister President, it is too late."

A few moments later Aylward called in to say that the 7th Division, which controlled the Northern Delta and the defense of Saigon from the South and West, had joined the coup and were blocking all approaches to the capital from those directions. Colonel Bob Phillips, advisor to General Nguyen Khanh, Commander of II Corps, reported that Khanh had voiced support for the coup, but "was mighty pissed off" he had not had more notice about it. Aylward also reported that Diem and Nhu were desperately trying to rally forces loyal to them. In the process they seemed to have called every major military unit in Viet Nam, with no success at all. The Generals were all standing firm.

Vietnamese-speaking Embassy Officers had been dispatched around town, equipped with two-way radios. By three-thirty the CIA Station reported that all major strategic points throughout Saigon had been seized by the Generals. The 5th Division and a Marine Battalion had surrounded the Palace.

Shortly before four, Aylward called to say all was quiet in I Corps. The Corps Commander, General Do Cao Tri, had gone to Danang to distance himself from Ngo Dinh Can in Hue.

At four, Gascon reported that at least fifteen ARVN Generals were still at JGS Headquarters. The place was a madhouse, with most of them milling around and waiting to be told what to do, and none of them daring to leave the premises. They had placed a call to Diem, each General getting on the phone to confirm his support for the coup and to tell the President he had no choice but to surrender. Big Minh had been the last to talk and Diem had hung up on him.

At four-thirty, Helen Eng signaled Marnin frantically to get on the phone. On the other end was Ngo Dinh Diem.

"Mr. President, is that you?" Marnin asked.

"Is it you, Mr. Marnin?" he asked in return.

"Yes, it is," Marnin said. "I hope you're all right."

"Yes, I'm fine," he replied, and then added with a high pitched chuckle, "at least for the present."

He asked to speak to the Ambassador, whom Marnin reached on the other line. Sedgewick instructed that Helen Eng monitor the call and take down everything that was said.

"This is important," the Ambassador emphasized. "Get it right."

Telegram 860 from Amembassy Saigon to SecState. November 1, 1963--5 p.m.

Secret; Flash; Limit Distribution; Saigon,

FOR THE SECRETARY FROM SEDGEWICK

At 4:30 a telephone call came from President Diem. The following conversation occurred:

Diem: Some units have made a rebellion and I want to know— what is the attitude of the United States?

Sedgewick: I do not feel well enough informed to be able to tell you. I have heard the shooting, but am not acquainted with all the facts. Also it is 4:30 a.m. in Washington and the U.S. Government cannot possibly have a view.

Diem: But you must have some general ideas. After all, I am a Chief of State. I have tried to do my duty. I want to do now what duty and good sense require. I believe in duty above all.

Sedgewick: You have certainly done your duty. We all admire your courage and your great contribution to your country. No one can take away from you the credit for all you have done. Now I'm worried about your physical safety. I have a report that you and your brother have been offered safe conduct out of the country if you resign. Had you heard this?

Diem: No. (Pause) You have my telephone number.

Sedgewick: Yes. If I can do anything for your physical safety, please call me.

Diem: I am trying to reestablish order.

                                                    SEDGEWICK

At four-fifty Radio Saigon returned to the air to broadcast the *communiqué* of the Generals. They had acted "because of the difficult economic situation and because Ngo Dinh Nhu, while pretending to fight the Communists, was trying to contact them. . .The Vietnamese Army controls the situation everywhere on Vietnamese territory. The Army is unanimous in rising up to demand that Diem resign."

At five and again at five-thirty the Generals called the Ngo Dinh brothers to demand that they step down. Minh threatened Nhu that the Palace would be bombarded within five minutes if they did not surrender. On both occasions Diem refused to speak with Minh, a sign of contempt that infuriated the General.

"Big Minh is," said Gascon, "as pissed off as a man can be. They've ordered Thieu to begin the attack. In fact, they're yelling at him because he hasn't begun it already. They promised him that when the Palace falls, he's going to be General Thieu and not Colonel Thieu."

At the stroke of six the bombardment of the Presidential Guards' barracks began, with a shell slamming into the building every thirty seconds. The Embassy was only three blocks away and the ancient chancery building shuddered as each shot hit its target. Mortar attacks on the Palace did not begin until seven-fifteen, when the Generals were finally convinced that Diem and Nhu and the Commander of the Presidential Guard would not surrender.

Gascon called at nine to say that the unopposed shelling of the palace had been taken as a sign of victory at JGS Headquarters. Champagne corks were popping, he said.

The mood within the American Embassy was equally lighthearted at that point. In addition to Helen Eng and Marnin, there were about twenty other officers in the building, most of whom had climbed to the roof to watch the "show," which was spectacular—since from there one had an unobstructed view of the Palace. Someone had unearthed some White Turkey Bourbon and was passing it around in paper cups. There was much nervous laughter between the poundings of the shells. But Marnin was not laughing. He was thinking of Diem and Nhu and of his friend Dinh Trieu Da, trapped in the besieged Palace.

Sedgewick called at nine-thirty and said he was going to bed and did not want his "beauty sleep" disturbed, "unless the roof was about to fall in" and he could do something to stop it from falling. Marnin gave him his final "sitrep" of the day. In the background as he was talking he could hear the Palace being pounded into rubble by the artillery of the 5th division.

"Don't disturb me tonight, if you can help it," Sedgewick repeated. "I want a good night's sleep. Tomorrow's going to be a busy day."

Marnin waited in the command post for the final word on Diem and Nhu, but it never came. The Presidential Guard continued to resist and Thieu, always a cautious man, did not want to take unnecessary casualties. Sooner or later the Ngo Dinh brothers would have to give up or be killed by the bombardment. There was no hurry. Meanwhile Gascon called to say wives and girlfriends were showing up at JGS Headquarters to congratulate the victors. The same was true, to a lesser extent, inside the American Embassy, where all the language officers—every one of them rooting for the coup plotters—who had been patrolling the town with their single sideband radios had returned home to roost because nothing was happening in Saigon other than the bombardment of the Palace.

At ten, Aylward reported that the Presidential Guards' barracks had surrendered. Only the Palace remained under Government control.

"It's all over but the shouting," he said.

"Not quite," Marnin replied. "There's still the President and Nhu."

"That's right. We ought to get them out of here."

"Have you made arrangements to do that?"

"Negative. The Ambassador's plane is gassed up and the pilot is ready to go, waiting for orders. We've asked, but have been told in no uncertain terms to mind our manners, worry about the military situation, and leave the rest to all you political geniuses downtown. That came straight from your boss just twenty minutes ago."

Telegram 678 from SecState to AmEmbassy Saigon.
Secret; Immediate. November 2, 1963--12:35 p.m.
FOR AMBASSADOR SEDGEWICK FROM THE SECRETARY.
Ref Critic 11.

Key to world attitude and most importantly US public and congressional reaction toward coup will depend primarily on Generals' actions. Realize that through wise counsel you are doing whatever possible to ensure Generals take right steps. We understand that this is primarily a Vietnamese affair and Generals appear to know where and how they wish to proceed and may not seek advice or take it if requested. Nevertheless, for guidance, we hope they will bear in mind following points:
1. Practical evidence of determination to prosecute war with renewed vigor.
2. Reprisals at a minimum.
3. Safe passage for Ngo Dinh family to exile.
4. Humane treatment for arrestees.
5. Minimum censorship and maximum press freedom.

6. Minimum period martial law.
7. Prompt announcement re readiness maintain relations and international obligations with states friendly to RVN.

RUSK

In accordance with his instruction from Sedgewick, Marnin saw no point in disturbing the Ambassador with this message, which could wait until morning. But he did call first Bilder and Sabo and then Gascon and read them the seven points. Gascon's reaction was different from that of the DCM or the Political Counselor. He merely chuckled. It sounded to Marnin as though he had not been abstaining from the champagne that was being so plentifully dispensed at JGS Headquarters.

"Did I say something funny?" Marnin asked.

"C.Y.A. buddy, the first principle of any bureaucracy—Cover Your Ass. That message is quintessential Departmental ass covering. You know what that message means? It doesn't mean one single fucking thing."

"What are you talking about?"

"Point three is what I have in mind. We can hear the shelling of the Palace all the way out here. And do you know what happens every time one of those howitzers goes off?"

"You tell me," Marnin said.

"With every explosion these Generals raise their glasses and toast it in champagne. And do you know why? It's because they're hoping that a piece of shrapnel from one of those shells just cracked the skull of Ngo Dinh Diem. Do you think these guys want him in exile in Bangkok or Paris waiting around for them to fall on their butts?"

"Look," Marnin said, "we can each have his own opinion about how to handle the family. But this is official guidance from the Department. You ought to convey this to Minh right away."

"I take orders from Bascombe Sedgewick. When he tells me to say something I do it, and not before. My instructions are to tell these guys that this is a Vietnamese show and that they have to decide for themselves how to settle their own political problems. And what happens to Diem is a political problem."

Marnin thought this over. Then he wrote down Gascon's words on a pad of yellow paper and sat at his desk staring at it. He went so far as to dial the Ambassador's number, but thought better of it and hung up the phone before it could ring at the Residence. He decided not to disturb Sedgewick's "beauty sleep." It all seemed academic anyway, in view of the artillery pounding of the Palace. The brothers could already be dead. Every time a shell was fired the furniture in the Ambassador's office, where Marnin was sitting, rattled and shook. Marnin had already taken down the pictures from the walls.

At ten-thirty, Secretary of State to the Presidency and Deputy Minister of Defense Nguyen Dinh Thuan (Diem was concurrently Minister of Defense)—who ran the South Vietnamese Ministry of Defense—called. The Generals had demanded that those who held high positions under Diem surrender immediately. Those who did not would be treated as enemies. Thuan wanted to know what he should do—surrender or try to escape. He wanted to speak with the Ambassador, said it was a matter of life and death. Bilder, who had returned to the Embassy after dinner to coordinate the voluminous reporting on the coup, had by that time gone home. John Mecklin was the highest ranking officer left in the Embassy command center. Like all members of the Country Team, Mecklin was friendly with Thuan, who was a great favorite of the Americans, their candidate in fact to be Prime Minister had Diem chosen to appoint one. Marnin handed Mecklin the phone.

"Hello, Mr. Secretary," Mecklin said. "It's good to hear your voice. We were worried about your safety. What can I do for you?. . .Yes, I see. . . . Yes, I understand. . . . Well, Mr. Secretary, that puts me in a difficult position. I have my own personal opinions on these matters which I could give you, but these would be nowhere near as good as yours. You know these men. They all worked for you. How can I advise you whether to trust them or not?. . . . Yes, I know this is a matter of life and death to you. . . . I'm sorry, but you're implying that we're somehow involved in the coup. . . . No sir, that's not the case. All we know is what we hear on the radio. . . . Yes, sir, Mr. Secretary, I understand that it may seem that way to you. But I assure you, everything we know we hear on the radio."

Thuan would not get off the phone, kept pointing out to Mecklin more and more insistently that he, of all people, as Undersecretary of

Defense understood that these Generals would not be able to get out
of bed in the morning without the assistance of the Americans. But
Mecklin stuck to his guns. "All we know is what we hear on the radio"
became his leitmotif. He repeated it at least half a dozen times. Finally,
he had had enough. He cut Thuan off firmly.

"Good night, Mr. Minister," he said, and hung up.

Marnin handed him the remains of the bottle of White Turkey
that had been circulating around the room and a paper cup. Mecklin
poured a healthy swig and downed it. Never had Marnin seen a grown
man look so ashamed of himself. The reality of what had at first
seemed something of an adventure was beginning to dawn on everyone inside the American Embassy. Suddenly, Marnin had to get out of
the office. He once more climbed the steps to the embassy roof, going
from the air conditioning into the heavy tropical night air. There were
two dozen people up there—officers, secretaries, code clerks, Marine
guards. The city of Saigon with its broad boulevards and magnificent
shade trees lay before them. The curfew was in effect and nobody was
moving below. The streetlights were turned off. The only illumination
came from the flash of the howitzer shells lazily bombarding the
Palace—one shell every several minutes. The crack of the guns, when
it came, was unbelievably loud.

Although there was no need to do so, people spoke in whispers.
The mood was expectant, charged, and replete with the energy people
feel when they know they are witnessing great events. Marnin suddenly remembered that Lily's African Grey parrot Antoine, whom he had
the night before last agreed to care for until she was settled in Paris,
had not been fed. He had planned to sleep on the couch in the
Ambassador's office, but decided this would be a good opportunity to
take care of the bird, have a shower and change his clothes. It took
him three minutes to drive to his house through the deserted streets.

When he entered the dark living room he was greeted by Dinh
Trieu Da. He turned on a lamp.

"You don't seem glad to see me," Da said with a sad smile. "Your
cook let me in."

"How long have you been here?"

"About three hours."

"I was worried about you," David said. "Every time I heard one of those shells go off I was afraid it had your number on it."

"The shelling was not serious. They weren't trying to kill us, only to frighten us and get us to surrender."

"And the President?"

"He's safe. So is Nhu. At least thus far. The ARVN still thinks we're inside the Palace. We can monitor their radio communications and they don't know it. When we got out, Nhu argued we ought to split up, that one of us would have a better chance of escaping if we weren't all together. He and the President insisted that I try to make it alone. I'm not well known and might be able to slip out of the country when things quiet down."

"What about them?"

"Nhu said they ought to split up, one of them going to the Delta to join General Cao, the other to II Corps, to Nguyen Khanh's headquarters in Pleiku, or perhaps to Hue to join their brother Can. Even if one of them were captured, Nhu thinks they wouldn't kill him while the other remains free."

"It won't work," Marnin said. "The 7th Division has joined with the rest of the Generals and is positioned to the south and west of Saigon. General Cao no longer controls the Delta. And Nguyen Khanh has joined the rebels."

"The President will not abandon his brother. He said the Generals hate Nhu and would kill him. Nhu's only chance is for both of them to stick together. 'We have always been together during these last years,' Diem said. 'How could we separate in this crucial hour'?"

"*Ma foi, c'est très intéressant,*" said Antoine.

They both laughed. But the laughter seemed to cut through Da's reserve and he broke down completely, deep sobs wracking his body. Marnin poured him a glass of brandy.

"Could you give them asylum?" Da asked when he had gotten control of himself.

"I don't know," Marnin said.

"Could you fly us out of the country? The Ambassador told the President that we had been offered safe passage if he would resign."

"Yes—but at that point he wasn't sure whether the coup would succeed or not. If it were up to me—"

"I know that. It's why I'm here. But it's not up to you."

"My best guess is that the Ambassador will do all he can to distance himself from the President."

"That's what Nhu thought. He thinks Sedgewick wants us all dead, that as long as we live the Generals will regard their seizure of power as temporary."

"I don't know what Sedgewick thinks, but I know he wants American involvement to appear as minimal as possible. (As he said this, Marnin was thinking of Mecklin on the phone with Thuan.) Excuse me for a few minutes."

Marnin fed the bird, took a shower, and changed clothes, all the while trying to decide what he could do to help Da. He knew that the CIA station had made provisions to smuggle out of the country a half dozen of their key agents who were Diem supporters and marked for arrest, or worse, by the Generals. Perhaps they would be willing to do the same for Da. As for the President and his brother, he knew from Aylward that the Ambassador's plane was gassed up ready to go. A phone call from him saying that he was acting in response to the Department's instructions might whisk them to safety, if they were still alive. Were he to do that, Sedgewick would never forgive him. He knew that. It could mean the end of his career. He combed his hair distractedly, over and over, and finally concluded that this was something the Ambassador would have to decide.

Rather than disturb Sedgewick—who would be angry to be awakened—Marnin resolved to adhere to his instructions, to go through correct channels. This was clearly a matter which, as the military put it, was well "beyond his pay grade." He would phone Bilder, he determined, tell the DCM about Da, and seek his guidance as to whether he should contact either the Ambassador or Smith, the acting CIA Station Chief.

"Certainly not," Bilder snapped in reply, when the situation was explained to him. "Just do your best to get Da out of your place. I'll take care of the rest. Don't even think of waking the Ambassador. I've seen the Department's instructions. Leave it to me."

Da was in the living room, clutching the brandy, which he had not touched. He had not moved since Marnin left him.

"You're welcome to stay here," Marnin said. "As long as you like."

"The cook has already seen me. It would be sure to leak out. Anyway, I think you and your embassy would be a lot happier if I moved elsewhere."

Marnin did not contradict him, nor did he mention asylum. And he had to get back to work.

"I won't be here when you get back," Da said. "But I do have to make some phone calls. And I cannot leave until the curfew lifts. I brought some black pajamas and a peasant hat I had tucked away for an emergency. I'll try to melt into the crowds as soon as the curfew ends."

They shook hands. The last thing Marnin heard as he left the house was the parrot's refrain.

"*Ma foi, c'est très intéressant.*"

The fresh assault against the Palace began at three-thirty. Marnin was in a pair of chinos, sleeping on the couch in Sedgewick's office. The bombardment woke him up and he looked at his wristwatch, a Breitling with a circular slide rule and a "radium dial." He put on his shirt and climbed up to the roof. He was alone there. To soften resistance before the Vietnamese Marines moved forward, Thieu had unleashed all his artillery, tanks, mortars, and fifty millimeter machine guns with tracer bullets. It was quite a light show. The noise was deafening. Marnin watched for five minutes and then went to the code room and picked up the latest traffic. They were as pleased in the State Department in Washington as Sedgewick was in Saigon.

What none of the Americans except Marnin knew was that the brothers had left the Palace at twelve-thirty by a secret tunnel, and then were joined by Marnin's tennis companion Dennis Chang, who first gave them some tea and biscuits at his home and took them to his "clubhouse," where he met regularly with Claudio and other members of his syndicate, and which was hooked up to the Palace switchboard. It was an escape route prearranged long in advance by Nhu. From the safety of Cholon the brothers were able to use the Palace switchboard to telephone everyone who might be of assistance to them, while giving those on the other end of the line the impression they were calling from the Palace.

After thirty to forty phone calls Diem finally concluded that he was in a hopeless situation. At six-twenty he called JGS Headquarters. He was ready to surrender, he told General Bich, as long as he received "military honors." Unfortunately, Bich said, the fighting had gone on too long and the rebels had suffered many casualties. Diem's surrender would have to be unconditional, he said. Diem then telephoned Colonel Hung, the Commander of the Presidential Guard and ordered him to surrender. Diem apologized to Hung for the loss of life of his men, but commended them for doing their duty. Hung was shot three days later.

At six-thirty-five Gascon called Marnin. He had tried to raise the Ambassador, he said, but Sedgewick was in the bathroom and would not be disturbed. Generals Minh and Bich had asked whether we could give them a plane to fly the Ngo Dinh brothers out of the country. What was he to tell them?

Marnin called Charlie Smith, the acting head of the CIA station. Smith said he had discussed this question with the Ambassador (the context was ambiguous—it was not clear whether he had discussed the matter with Sedgewick the previous evening or that morning) and his instructions were to do nothing about a plane to send Diem into exile unless specifically requested by the Generals. In that case, they were to be informed that there would not be an aircraft available for twenty-four hours, the time required to bring in from Guam a plane with sufficient range to fly directly to Europe. Sedgewick did not want Diem and Nhu to remain in Southeast Asia, where they would be in a position to organize a counter coup.

"What about the Ambassador's plane?" Marnin asked.

"I don't know anything about that," Smith replied. "Presumably it doesn't have the range. Anyway, the Generals are just trying to rope us in and the Ambassador wants to avoid the appearance of any American involvement in this operation. Minh must think we were born yesterday. He could do it himself. If it were just a question of getting them out of here, there are plenty of VNAF planes that could fly them to Bangkok."

Marnin called Gascon back to give him the message. "Twenty-four hours might as well be twenty-four years," Gascon said.

"What do you mean?"

"These guys are going to be making some big decisions here over the next fifteen minutes."

The Ambassador's other phone rang. It was Diem. He sounded very tired.

"Mr. Marnin," he said. "I must speak to Ambassador Sedgewick. I wish to surrender myself to the American Embassy."

"Where are you?"

"You'll be able to reach us at the Don Thanh Chinese Catholic Church in Cholon. I'll be there in a few minutes."

Marnin put Diem on hold and called the Ambassador. His main line was busy, but he got him on his second line.

"Where did you say he was?"

Marnin repeated the information.

"Spell it for me. Hold on a second, I don't have a pen handy . . . OK, now spell it for me slowly and carefully."

The Ambassador told Marnin to keep Diem on the line and hung up. Then Sedgewick went back to his earlier call on his main line. After about a minute, he picked up the phone to speak with Diem. He told Marnin to get off the phone, that he would call him back. Within a minute Marnin's phone rang.

"Is that you, David?"

"Yes, sir."

"That phone call from Diem—who knows about it?"

"Nobody. Just me."

"We never got it. Do you understand me? This is privileged, hush hush information. We never got it."

"Yes, sir. Do you want me to pick them up? I know where that church is. I could drive over to Cholon and have them back here in half an hour."

"That won't be necessary," he said.

His words were cold and final. Marnin never forgot them.

The convoy, consisting of two sedans and an Armored Personnel Carrier, set off from JGS Headquarters at seven-thirty. General Mai Huu Xuan, a former policeman under the French, was in charge. Accompanying him were Colonel Quan, an adjutant on Minh's staff, Major Nghia, an inveterate coup plotter and outspoken foe of the

Ngo Dinh brothers, and Captain Nhung, a montagnard who was Big
Minh's personal bodyguard—known to all the Generals as a professional assassin who notched a mark on his pistol for every man he
killed.   Prior to the departure of the convoy a meeting had taken
place at JGS Headquarters, presided over by Big Minh, in which the
fate of the brothers was discussed. At seven-thirty, just before the
meeting, Gascon left the headquarters. Later he maintained, not
implausibly, that at that point he needed a shower, that he smelled like
a "goat in heat," and that he wanted to check on the safety of his family. He was therefore not at headquarters to notice what all the other
Generals in that room did not miss—that just before the four ARVN
officers left the room, Big Minh gave Nhung a prearranged signal—
left thumb down. Nhung, a wizened little man with gold incisors, in
reply flashed Minh a big smile.

According to the subsequent CIA reconstruction of these events,
the party reached the church at ten minutes to eight. The two brothers were inside praying. When they saw the ARVN officers in combat
uniform entering the church they were surprised. They had expected
someone from the American Embassy.

The brothers followed the four officers outside. In front of the
church was a miniature rocky grotto with a small statue of the Virgin
near the top and "Ave Maria" in red neon lettering above it. They
paused there. Both brothers crossed themselves and looked at each
other. Then they were ushered through a gate and onto the sidewalk
sixty yards in front of the church. A large crowd had gathered. General
Xuan gestured for them to get inside the Armored Personnel Carrier.

"It is not fitting," Nhu said angrily, the first words anyone had spoken since the ARVN officers had entered the church, "for the
President of the Republic of Viet Nam to ride in such a vehicle!"

Nhung struck the Counselor across the back of the head with the
barrel of his pistol, driving Nhu to his knees. There was an audible
gasp from the onlookers who had gathered to witness the scene. A thin
stream of blood issued from Nhu's torn left ear. The brothers offered
no further resistance. They submitted without a word to having their
hands tied behind them and then they were half shoved, half carried
into the front seat of the military vehicle, with Nhung in back and

above them. Nothing more was said. As soon as the APC had turned a corner and was back on the main road from Cholon to Saigon, Nhung emptied the clip of his submachine gun into their backs. Then he took out his hunting knife and, just to be sure, with his left hand grabbed Nhu by the hair and stabbed him three times in the neck.

Thus, after eight years and five days, at exactly eight a.m. on November 2, 1963, the morning following the Day of the Dead, the First Republic of Viet Nam came to an end.

Chapter 50

TIDYING UP

It took a day for the American Embassy to confirm the *New York Times* report that Diem and Nhu had not committed suicide, as was announced by Big Minh's spokesman. Anything could be purchased in Saigon for the right price, and within twenty-four hours Mandelbrot had bought photos of the brothers' mangled corpses for five hundred dollars. Confronted by those photographs, Minh's spokesman was forced to admit that an "accident" had occurred, and promised that it would be "thoroughly investigated." He found it hard to explain how people with their hands tied behind their backs could have managed to shoot themselves.

Aside from this "slip-up," Sedgewick, in both his reporting to Washington and in his comments to the local press and to other diplomatic missions, was elated at the performance of the Generals. Men who can carry out an operation of this kind "almost flawlessly," he cabled Jack Kennedy on November 3, "should have no trouble achieving equal successes in the war against the Viet Cong." (Sedgewick understood that his own political fortunes largely depended on resolute prosecution of the war against the VC by these generals.) But there were still any number of loose ends to tie up—including the care of Nhu's three children (Madam Nhu was in Rome) as well as the fate of Ngo Dinh Can in Hue.

The Embassy received word that Kennedy was upset at the killing of Diem and Nhu and was taking a personal interest in ensuring that no harm came to the rest of the family. "It is urgent," the Department cabled, "that the Nhu children be evacuated immediately." If necessary, they could use the Ambassador's or General Donnelly's personal planes, (planes that could also have transported Diem and Nhu out of the country.)

Telegram 917 from AmEmbassy Saigon to SecState.
November 4, 1963. Secret; Priority.

Herewith is a report of my conversation this afternoon with General Minh and General Bich. Lt. Colonel Gascon was with me.

I stressed repeatedly the importance of publishing a detailed account of their efforts to arrange safe passage for Diem and Nhu; their repeated telephone calls urging Diem to resign; and the provision of an armored car so that Diem and Nhu would not be lynched on the way from the church to the safe haven prepared for them at JGS Headquarters by General Bich. Unfortunately, like many people in this part of the world, they do not appreciate the importance of public relations and Minh is the most inscrutable oriental one can imagine, but I think maybe I made a dent.

I then stressed the need to get the Nhu children out soonest and was told they were now in Saigon and that the Generals also wanted them out as rapidly as possible. On the question of Ngo Dinh Can, they said General Do Cao Tri, the I Corps Commander, had just telephoned that there was a hostile crowd around the house where Can lives with his mother that wanted his skin. I asked whether Can wanted to leave his mother and the country and they did not know. This is a puzzling dilemma. It would obviously be bad if Can were lynched. It would also be bad if we tore him away from his mother.

Minh seemed tired and somewhat frazzled, obviously a good and well-intentionod man. Will he be strong enough to get on top of things? We have to hope so.

Deptel 704 seems to show some divergence between us on significance and merit of the coup. Here is how it looks to us:

a. To anyone who has been involved in either a military or a political campaign, this coup appears to have been a remarkably able performance in both respects. The preservation of secrecy and lack of written communications might be profitably studied by any organization in which leaks and a superfluity of paper are problems. The immediate capture of switchboards, radio stations and communications facilities showed a realism not possessed, for example, by those who attempted the coup against Hitler.

b. Experts in MACV who before were hostile to the coup now say the war can be drastically shortened. One observer said if these men can carry out an operation like this it's reasonable to believe they can do equally well against the Viet Cong.

c. I agree the Generals should make clear they were opposed to any harm coming to Diem and Nhu and that the rest of the Ngo family will be humanely treated. As noted above, I have already urged them in this direction, but I believe it would be an error to push them too far or tell them how to run their own country. I recognize these Generals will make mistakes and I hope they don't start arbitrary arrests and internecine fighting. The best way to avoid this, in my judgment, is to let them work things out themselves and interfere only when our own interests are directly involved.

d. Most important, this coup can shorten the war. Hope we can get behind the new crowd and give them a real chance.

SEDGEWICK

Ngo Dinh Can, his enemies screaming for blood, had taken refuge with the Canadian Fathers in the Redemptorist Seminary on the outskirts of Hue. Priests from the seminary had gone to see Freddie Loftus at the Consulate to determine whether Can could be given safe passage out of the country. The Department replied that "asylum should be granted to Ngo Dinh Can if he is in physical danger from any source. Explain to Hue authorities further violence would harm international reputation of new regime. Also recall to them US took similar action to protect Thich Tri Binh from Diem regime and can do no less for Can. We should make every effort to get him and his mother, if necessary, out of the country soonest; using our own facilities if this would expedite their departure. . . ."

This response from the Viet Nam Working Group in the Department seemed clear enough. But Sedgewick cited these instructions at the first post-coup staff meeting as "the worst kind of micromanaging by Washington pundits who have no feeling for the situation on the ground." Sedgewick said he himself was reluctant to interfere in an internal affair of the new government.

"Hell, these guys know Ngo Dinh Can a lot better than I do. He might be a long term threat to them. I don't want to urge them to give him the kind of whitewash that over the long run will be like a splinter under their fingernails. The only thing I want for him is a fair trial. Public relations-wise that is essential."

Unaware of Sedgewick's views, Freddie Loftus assumed that the cable from the Department was the final word on the subject. Can intended to ask for asylum in Japan as soon as he reached Saigon. He was given to understand that the Americans were guaranteeing his safety, something that was obviously well within their capability to do. After all, he left Hue on an American plane accompanied by an American Consul, two American military policemen, and an American Lieutenant Colonel. That plane could have flown to Bangkok or Vientiane just as easily as it flew to Saigon. But it was only after he reached Tan Son Nhut that Can was informed by Parker Wint, our Consul, that he was being turned over to the Generals.

"I never knew an oriental could turn pale," Wint said to Marnin afterward, "but Can did. His knees buckled and I thought he was going to fall. His face was chalk white. *Je suis un homme mort. Votre Ambassadeur veut tuer la famille entière.* I am a dead man. Your Ambassador wants to kill the whole family,' he said. I felt filthy. It's the worst thing I've ever had to do in my life."

Explaining the Vietnamese turnabout on the question of Can (AmEmbassy Saigon 937 to SecState, November 6, 1963), Sedgewick noted that the Generals, on due reflection, did not think it a good idea to let Can out of the country, as they had Nhu's children. Can had committed crimes for which he should be punished, the Generals felt. Since we wanted to establish a government in Saigon that abided by the rule of law, how could we quarrel with such a decision? At the same time, General Bich had promised that Can would be dealt with "legally and judicially." Therefore, Sedgewick wrote, "it seems to me our reason for giving him asylum no longer exists."

Mandelbrot did not think the turning over of Ngo Dinh Can to the Generals was worthy of the attention of the readers of the *New York Times*. It was, he said to Claudio and Marnin in the Caravelle bar the following night, the right thing to do. "Can was a scumbag," he said. "Anything that happens is too good for him. He was as bad as his brothers and deserves to be exactly where they are—six feet under. Anyway, these Generals are out to establish a new kind of society here. In order to do that you have to abide by the rule of law. They can't let criminals off scot free just to look good in Washington."

"Rule of law?" Claudio said. "You have to be kidding. Do you really think the rule of law has anything at all to do with what's happened? The Generals were going to let Can go because they thought that was what the Americans wanted. But when they saw that Sedgewick didn't give a shit, the '*cailles*' decided they wanted a piece of the big money the family tucked away abroad. The rumors are of sums as high as a hundred million dollars. These guys want to get their mitts on as much of it as they can. So please don't give me any shit about honor, truth, and rule of law."

"I don't believe it. Are you telling me that Minh, Don, Kim, and the rest of them are for sale?"

"Is the sky blue?"

"And that they're in the pockets of Chinese gangsters?"

"Watch what happens here. They've already lifted the ban on dancing. Next week it will be gambling. There's going to be millions of dollars, not piasters, made every week in Saigon over the next five years and maybe longer. Do you think the Chinese won't be controlling it and that the Generals won't be taking their cut? Why do you think the *cailles* have kept the Generals on their payrolls all these years?"

"Wait a minute. These guys aren't all the same person," Mandelbrot said. "Big Minh, as far as anyone knows, is completely clean. That's why the others respect him."

"You've been in Minh's villa. How do you think he paid for that swimming pool? He drives a green Mercedes. His wife's is blue. Do you know what an ARVN General's monthly salary is? Three hundred and fifty dollars—just about enough to pay for the maintenance of that pool. What kind of a shmuck are you?"

"I still don't believe it," Mandelbrot said.

"The word on the street is that they've offered Can his freedom if he'll cough up the family gold, or at least make a deal upward of twenty million dollars. That's their price—twenty million. If he bargains, they may cut it to ten. You'll see. If he doesn't come across, they'll kill him."

Claudio's words filled Marnin with dread—not so much for Can, whose physical safety had at least been guaranteed by Bich, but for Dinh Trieu Da. Nothing had yet been heard about him. He was not well known and had, Marnin thought, a good chance of lying low and then escaping. But if the *cailles* thought that he might be able to lay his hands on millions of dollars, his chances were not good.

Sure enough, on Saturday, November 9, Da was arrested in Vung Tao, betrayed by an informer. He had been hiding out in the villa of a family friend, disguised as a gardener.

First, Da's fingernails and toenails were pulled out one at a time and then the bones in his hands were systematically broken, a new bone day after day for more than a month, in an effort to force him to reveal the whereabouts of the family fortune.

If such a fortune existed, it has yet to be recovered.

Chapter 51

ON THE BEACH AT WAIKIKI

The Vietnamese Generals repeatedly assured their American inter-locutors in their first three weeks in power that they were going to remedy the deficiencies of the previous regime and get on with their top priority—winning the war against the Viet Cong. Sedgewick, as the Godfather of the coup, was of course predisposed to appreciate the virtues and accept the promises of Generals Minh, Bich, Dinh, Don, and Kim. Donnelly, although skeptical about their personal qualities, was anxious to use the opportunity to rid the South Vietnamese armed forces of most of the inefficiencies imposed upon it by the tight controls Diem had exerted from the Palace. Harmony thus for a brief period prevailed once more within the Country Team, much as it did when Gus Corning was in charge of the Embassy. As a result, the Honolulu conference of November 20-22, attended by the entire Country Team and all key Washington policymakers with the excep-tion of the President, was marked by bubbling optimism and a great deal of self-congratulation.

Twenty-four officers and staff from the American mission made the trip from Saigon to Honolulu in a VIP-configured Boeing 707, within which the Ambassador and COMUSMACV (Donnelly) each had compartments to themselves. From there, Sedgewick was going on to Washington in McNamara's plane for consultations with the President. On their arrival the evening of the 19th, the Saigon contin-gent was bussed to Camp Smith, where they were housed in the Bachelor Officers Quarters. Rusk, McNamara, and Bundy were also at Camp Smith in various VIP suites. Donnelly and Maxwell Taylor stayed with Admiral McGrath. Sedgewick, however, always took a suite at the Royal Hawaiian when he was in Honolulu. As his aide, Marnin was happy to accompany him to the famous "pink palace." There were flowers, champagne, and a nice note from the manager in his room overlooking the palms in an inner courtyard when he arrived.

He retired at ten, but with the six hour time difference, it was four in the afternoon in Saigon. At three, Marnin was still wide awake and, deciding the hell with it, went out for a jog in the dark, first along the length of the beach, then doubling back through Fort De Russy behind the Army Museum, with the World War II Japanese tanks on display in front of it. He then ran past the aquarium and the tennis courts along the road out to Diamond Head, and back to the Royal Hawaiian, returning in time to change and be picked up at six o'clock by a very pretty nineteen year old Navy Spec Four driver and taken to the message center at the base to collect the Ambassador's traffic. While Sedgewick answered his mail, Marnin breakfasted sumptuously on the hotel terrace, with the sound of the surf in the background. At seven-thirty he accompanied Sedgewick back to Camp Smith, where the conference was being held. But they had not taken sufficient account of the morning rush hour traffic, which was horrendous.

As a result, Sedgewick was ten minutes late, the last of the principals to arrive. In his inimitable manner he was fussing and fuming at Marnin for keeping the Secretaries of State and Defense and the National Security Adviser waiting. If Marnin had any brains, he would have factored the morning rush hour traffic into his calculations, Sedgewick said. So the Ambassador was distracted and apologetic as he walked into the room and was not expecting what then ensued—a standing ovation. The entire group of dignitaries assembled there, led by Rusk and McNamara and Bundy, rose as one and gave Sedgewick a round of applause that seemed to last five minutes.

Rusk, who was in the chair the first day (McNamara had it the second) made explicit in his introduction what had been implicit in the applause:

"We seemed to be in a blind alley, at a dead end, with no good policy options available to us. Then this man arrived on the scene. Through his dedicated leadership and his boundless energy, he managed in a remarkably short period of time to bring us out of the forest and into a clearing so that we now at least can see the direction where we are heading. Our entire nation owes a boundless debt of gratitude to Bascombe Sedgewick. . . ."

The Ambassador rose to another round of lengthy applause and said he was deeply touched to be greeted so warmly by his peers. Nobody has a monopoly on wisdom in complicated questions such as those they were discussing, he pointed out, and if there was any credit to be garnered from the coup and its aftermath, it should be shared equally with his close colleagues who were with him that morning. Embassy Saigon, he said, operated as a tightly knit family, working together as a team to accomplish its mission. In this regard, a scurrilous, mischievous, and baseless recent article in the *New York Times* implied that General Donnelly was somehow at odds with his civilian colleagues, including the American Ambassador. Nothing, he assured his august audience, was farther from the truth.

Turning to the notes Marnin had prepared for him, Sedgewick described the outlook for the immediate future as hopeful. "The Generals," he said, "appear to be united and determined to step up the war effort. They seem keenly aware that the struggle with the Viet Cong is not only a military problem, but also political and psychological. They attach great importance to social and economic programs as an aid to winning the war. The Generals believe that:

1. The requirement for the population to contribute what amounts to forced labor in connection with the construction of strategic hamlets must be drastically reduced, if not totally eliminated.
2. The Strategic Hamlet Program has been pushed too rapidly and at too great a cost in human effort. Any further wholesale expansion of the program should be deferred.
3. Chinese racketeers and extortionists—the so-called '*cailles*'—must be eliminated.
4. Arbitrary arrests and disregard of habeas corpus must end.
5. The Hoa Hao and Cao Dai sects should be lured off the fence and won over to the side of the government.

"As far as political institutions are concerned, the Generals talk of facilitating the growth of political parties and of creating more courts and judges, but if we can get through the next six months without a serious falling out among the Generals, we'll be lucky. As long as they follow the course they've set for themselves, we should not push them too hard. Since coming to power they've acted with restraint—held down arrests, avoided wholesale purges throughout the government. In fact, they're trying to please the public—a rather new departure in Viet Nam."

General Taylor asked what their present political intentions were. The Ambassador replied that he believed General Minh to be sincere when he described the Military Revolutionary Council as merely a provisional government. On the other hand, there was no civilian political leadership emerging thus far and it was doubtful that one could emerge from the civilian nonentities currently in the Cabinet. The U.S. should not, according to Sedgewick, press the Generals too hard on democratic reforms and early elections. Instead, we should be patient and give them a chance to get on with the war.

After a break for a "pit stop" the conference resumed with General Donnelly as the next briefer. He began by pointing out that despite what had appeared in the press, there was no difference of opinion between Ambassador Sedgewick and himself on the situation in Viet Nam or on the conduct of the war against the Viet Cong. (This was heartily seconded by the Ambassador.) As far as the military situation was concerned, Donnelly said the problem was to win the people over to full support of the war effort. The change of government had had a definite impact at the province level, where everything now depended on the forty-two Province Chiefs. Perhaps even more important than the Province Chiefs were the District Chiefs—253 of them. We had to expect that the new regime would probably want to reassign a goodly number of them.

Within the ARVN itself, Donnelly continued, much remained to be done. Many deserving officers should be promoted. The roles of Generals Khanh and Tri in II and I Corps were not clear, although they had associated themselves with the objectives of the coup. General Minh intended to establish a more direct chain of command

to insure that military orders were carried out when received. This
would be quite a change for the good as in the past a military order
was seldom implemented until the responsible commander had
checked it out through political channels back to the Palace.

In sum, Donnelly stated, the principal problems the Generals
faced were: first, the appointment of new Province and District Chiefs
would inevitably complicate matters until these officials were able to
become acquainted with their areas of responsibility and get on top of
the local situation; second, the establishment of a straightforward military chain of command would, of course, involve some high level
negotiations among the Generals themselves; third, the people in the
rural areas still remained apathetic to the government and the support
of the man in the village would depend on whether the government
could assure his security and improve his living standards.

The conference went on for two days, with each of the
Washington agencies and each member of the Country Team describing his programs and the overall situation from his own perspective.
Marnin attended all the sessions and took notes for Sedgewick. It was
impossible to listen to these energetic and impressive men at the top
of the American government without feeling that the United States
had wisely assembled the very best people it had to deal with its principal national priority. Yet at the same time, Marnin's own eyes and
ears had absorbed impressions that contradicted most of the underly-
ing beliefs about South Viet Nam shared by these same people.

Marnin knew, for example, that the Buddhist problem had not
been a matter of simple religious repression, that the motives of Diem
and Nhu were not those being described at the conference, and that
the picture of Big Minh and the other Generals he had gathered from
Lily and Claudio, and even Billy Mandelbrot, was at sharp variance
with that presented to America's national leaders by Sedgewick and,
to a lesser extent, Donnelly.

Marnin was musing about these discrepancies that last morning in
Honolulu as he drove out to Camp Smith. When he reached the code
room to pick up Sedgewick's traffic, Marnin noticed the code clerk, a
deeply tanned young sailor in white uniform, was unashamedly cry-

ing. He took the folder from him and started to walk away, but then decided to see if there was anything he could do to help him.

"What's the matter?" Marnin asked.

"The President's been shot," the sailor replied.

Kennedy's death was announced by Walter Cronkite on the car radio as they were driving to the military airport. Sedgewick had known Kennedy since the President was a boy. He was in deep shock. So was everybody else on the tarmac when they reached the plane. They were stunned. They stood there in their Hawaiian sport shirts in the blazing sunshine on the runway and spoke in whispers, as though they were in church at his funeral. Marnin shook hands with Sedgewick, bade him farewell, and was driven to the other plane that took the Saigon contingent back home.

That long flight to Viet Nam seemed interminable. They sat in their seats and read or slept or stared vacantly out the window, like strangers on some commercial airliner. It seemed incredible that such a thing could happen to that young and handsome prince—so beyond imagination. All of those passengers sensed that somehow, in a way none of them could define, their lives had irrevocably changed. They sensed, moreover, that the great adventure in Viet Nam in which they were all engaged, in which Kennedy had been their leader, would also never be the same.

Before Kennedy was shot it had been unthinkable to any of them that the United States would emerge from Viet Nam as anything other than victorious. How it was going to win was unclear. That it was going to prevail, as it had prevailed in all the wars it had engaged in during the history of the Republic, was never open to question. But after the assassination in Dallas the unthinkable became thinkable.

PART SIX

The Crime

Chapter 52

THE ELEVENTH MAN

The premonitions triggered by the Kennedy assassination were amply borne out in the days that followed. By every known or imagined statistical indicator the struggle against the Viet Cong took a marked turn for the worse. Yet the Generals seemed content to hunker down and respond only when the odds overwhelmingly favored them, which they seldom did.

With each passing month, the red areas on those familiar MACV charts widened and the blue areas diminished. Nobody in South Viet Nam had any faith in the ability, the wisdom, or the capacity of Generals Minh, Bich, Don, Kim, and Dinh to run a government. Despite the constant encouragement of Ambassador Sedgewick and the entire apparatus of the American Mission, the feeling in Saigon was that their tenure in power would be brief. The question remained: who was competent to replace them?

The resumption of American aid, particularly the $90 million annual CIP appropriation, did much to restore confidence in the viability of the economy, as did the USOM commitment to quadruple the amount of fertilizer used by the rice farmers. USOM estimated that for every seventy dollars invested in fertilizer, the rice yield would increase by $110. But it was not only fertilizer that increased. The level of corruption doubled and then tripled almost overnight. Since no Vietnamese official could be sure of keeping his job for more than a few weeks longer, his natural inclination was to extract the maximum amount of graft before being removed from office.

The Generals became notorious for their unwillingness or their inability to act. The one exception to this generalization was their prompt replacement of the Mayor of Saigon, and Viet Nam's forty-two Province Chiefs and 253 District Chiefs. By the beginning of December, only a month after the coup, every one of those Province and District Chiefs had been fired and a new military officer, anxious to make the most of the opportunity, installed in his place.

The endemic corruption that accompanied even the most minor business with a government functionary became a joke. But the complaints of the Generals, voiced by the Ambassador at the Honolulu Conference, about the depredations of the "*cailles*" turned out to be the biggest joke of all. For as Claudio had predicted, gambling halls were opened and the *cailles* soon ran the entire urban economy. Between the *cailles* in the cities and the newly-appointed Province and District Chiefs in the countryside, South Viet Nam fell into a sink of corruption from which the Viet Cong was not slow to profit.

The ARVN fractured into cliques and the Generals began quarreling over the spoils. The admirable unity the army had displayed during the coup against Diem entirely disappeared and younger officers loudly grumbled at the inefficiency and venality of their seniors. They openly demanded their replacement and urged "a return to democracy." But it was obvious to all that the civilians in the Cabinet, who had been picked specifically for their lack of moral fiber, were not available to step in if the military faltered.

The Catholic minority complained that Christians had been systematically excluded from the top ranks of the new government. Catholics worried about the anti-Christian speeches of Thich Tri Binh and other Buddhist leaders, who were working to make Binh future Prime Minister of a Buddhist-led government. More bonzes, in fact, burned themselves to death in the three months after Big Minh's takeover than in the entire Buddhist crisis of Ngo Dinh Diem, but no one, not even the foreign press, paid the slightest attention to these new "martyrs." Younger officers, outraged that Minh, Bich, Don, and Kim still carried French passports, began to refer to them disparagingly as "the four Frenchmen." Indeed, the CIA station began picking up disturbing reports that these generals were leaning toward De Gaulle's preferred solution of a neutral Southeast Asia. By the beginning of January even Sedgewick, their strongest backer, had begun to entertain doubts because of their neutralist tendencies and their inability to deliver on their promises.

On January 30, 1964 the government of Big Minh and his fellow conspirators was overthrown by the thirty-six year old General Nguyen Khanh, who had been a Lieutenant in the French Army eight years before. The anti-Diem coup leaders—Minh, Bich, Don, Kim, and Dinh—were exiled to Dalat and placed under house arrest. (At the insistence of Sedgewick, Minh was subsequently released and given the ceremonial office of Chief of State.) Khanh pledged that the main aim of his new government would be to clean up corruption and vigorously prosecute the war against the communists.

The reluctant assessment of the American Embassy was that the Khanh government could not help but be an improvement over its predecessor—the same assessment it had made about the government of Big Minh. But it was no surprise to anyone in South Viet Nam that the first act of the new Prime Minister was to replace the Mayor of Saigon, the 42 Province Chiefs, and the 253 District Chiefs that had been appointed by his predecessors three months before. Unlike much else in South Viet Nam, the results of this action were highly predictable.

On May 9 Gascon called Marnin. He had tried to reach the Ambassador, he said, but the boss was not taking phone calls. In truth, as the woes of South Viet Nam mounted and as Gascon's former clients proved themselves over and over unable to handle a worsening situation, his stock with Sedgewick plummeted and the Ambassador became unwilling to deal with the "Colonel" other than through his boss, the new Station Chief.

"What's on your mind?" David asked.

"I've got to get through to the Ambassador right away."

"He's tied up and is not taking calls at this point."

"OK. But he should be interrupted wherever he is and whatever he's doing and be told that Khanh is planning to execute Ngo Dinh Can and Dinh Trieu Da this afternoon at five o'clock."

Marnin's heart began beating so strongly that he thought he would be sick. He hung up the phone and hurried into Sedgewick's office. The Ambassador was working on the "think-piece" drafted by Roy Ewing, Sam Sabo's successor as Political Counselor, entitled "The New Government of South Viet Nam—The First Four Months." The summary paragraph began as follows:

"General Khanh is not everyone's favorite individual and the new team he has gathered is less than ideal. He remains difficult to deal with, difficult to influence, and more pageant-loving and narcissistic than Mussolini. But there can be no doubting his commitment to the anti-Communist cause and his willingness to shake up the ARVN, get rid of timid commanders, and prosecute the war to a successful conclusion. In that sense, he is miles ahead of his predecessors and deserves our sympathy and support. . . . "

"Goddam it, I told you a hundred times not to interrupt me for anything when that door is closed," Sedgewick said.

Marnin gave him Gascon's message.

"Is this some kind of joke?" Sedgewick finally asked.

"I'm afraid it isn't," Marnin replied.

"Does Bilder know?"

"No. I thought you should be informed right away."

"Get him in here. And get me the General. And after I talk with him I want Frank Gascon."

The Embassy had recently installed a direct tie-in to the Palace. Marnin asked Helen Eng to get the Prime Minister urgently on the red phone, reminding her again to make sure he was put on the line first. The Palace operators, especially since the coup, instinctively deferred to the American Ambassador. But Marnin's admonition turned out to be unnecessary. She was informed by an embarrassed interlocutor that the PM was "indisposed" and not taking calls. She handed Marnin the telephone.

"*Ce n'est pas possible. Il est très urgent que l'ambassadeur parle avec le Premier Ministre,*" he shouted. When this did no good, he asked the flustered Major Dong, one of his counterparts on Khanh's staff, to let him speak with Luyen, the Chief of Protocol. But Luyen also, according to Dong, was not available.

Bilder had preceded Marnin into the Ambassador's office. At that point he was suffering from a painful and mysterious allergy to the tropical sun that covered his balding scalp in red blotches and, together with the deteriorating military and political situation and the difficulties of working for Sedgewick, was making the remainder of his tour in Saigon a physical and mental agony. The fact that he was not getting from Sedgewick the respect he thought he deserved sorely rankled him. And it was true that his French accent with its heavy Iowa overtones was a never-ending source of comment from the Ambassador, who was known to have reduced a table of Vietnamese Generals to helpless laughter by a deadpan imitation of his deputy's French pronunciation

The Ambassador told him the latest news. Bilder could not believe it.

"How could this happen without our knowing about it?" he finally asked.

"That's exactly what I want to know," Sedgewick replied, intimating that Bilder had somehow fallen down in his job in allowing this to occur.

Marnin broke the ensuing silence between them. He said the Palace refused to respond, that the Prime Minister was not taking phone calls.

"I made that son of a bitch. When I want to talk to him he will damned well talk to me!" Sedgewick exploded.

He reached for the red phone and barked into it, "This is the American Ambassador. I must speak to General Khanh. It is an urgent matter. . . . I don't care if the General is indisposed. I don't care if he's on his deathbed. I have an urgent message for him from the President of the United States and I have to talk with him!"

But although he undoubtedly scared the hell out of the person at the other end of the line, he was no more successful than Marnin had been.

"That man is a lunatic, a fucking lunatic!" he said, pacing around the room. "He's not going to get away with this! I'll fix him. He'll regret this!"

In those days swearing was frowned upon, especially in front of ladies and subordinates. Although his private speech was liberally peppered with "Goddamns," as befitted a Massachusetts politician, Marnin had never heard Sedgewick use any variation of the word "fuck" in the nine months he had been working for him. And they had already been through three coup attempts and two assassinations, including the President of the country.

Sedgewick flipped on the intercom. "Get me the Foreign Minister," he said to Helen. He paced the room over and over.

"The Foreign Minister is indisposed," she finally replied. "He's not receiving any callers. He's at home in bed."

"You. . .goddamit. . .you call them back and tell them that the Ambassador of the United States of America is going over to the Minister's house this instant to personally pull the son of a bitch out of bed and, if he's not dead already, to strangle him with my bare hands. I'm leaving the embassy in five minutes."

Then, turning to Marnin he said, "You come with me. I want a note taker."

"Shall I call Washington?" Bilder asked.

Sedgewick stopped pacing and drew himself up to his full height.

"You are not even to piss until you have my personal permission! Do you understand me?. . .Do you?"

"Yes."

"Do you think I want orders from the White House to put an end to something I don't have a prayer of stopping? If the worst happens, we knew nothing about it."

The new Foreign Minister, Admiral Nguyen Than Dinh, South Viet Nam's highest ranking naval officer, lived on Le Qui Don, a quiet street near the Embassy in a compound shaded by four magnificent purple-flowered jacaranda trees. A Cadillac limousine and a Mercedes 450 coupe were parked in the driveway. Dinh was unusual for a Vietnamese Flag Officer in that his English was quite fluent, although by no means error free, especially when he got excited. He had, in fact, completed the course for senior foreign officers at the Naval War College in Newport, reportedly finishing at the head of his class. No meeting between them had yet to occur in which Dinh failed to remind Sedgewick, the Boston Brahmin, of his Newport class standing as well as of their close bonds as "fellow New Englanders."

He greeted Sedgewick as though there were nothing amiss.

"My good friend," he said, "welcome to my humble home. This is indeed an honor."

He was wearing a well-tailored dark grey, shiny silk suit, a white on white shirt with black pearl cufflinks, and a solid black satin tie. They had been ushered into the living room by an Ensign who was evidently the Minister's aide. A noisy window air conditioner was going full blast. On the phonograph was Edith Piaf singing, "*Je ne regrette rien.*" Was this an accident? Marnin wondered. The Minister sat in a large, overstuffed armchair and the two Americans on a matching white sofa, both pieces of furniture covered in heavy clear plastic. In the corner of the room stood a two-door refrigerator, a model not very common in Saigon in those days.

"Mister Minister," Sedgewick began, "I am sorry to trouble you at home when you are not feeling well."

Dinh, who never looked healthier, broke into a deep Vietnamese nervous grin.

"Not at all," he said. "What can I do for you? It is always a pleasure to greet fellow New Englanders."

Sedgewick gave him a chilly smile.

"Mister Minister, I am here on a matter of the greatest urgency, one that can profoundly affect relations between our two countries and have the worst possible consequences on our efforts to prosecute this war against our Communist enemies. We are allies, Mister Minister."

"Close allies, Mister Ambassador. Intimate allies."

"Your government, if I am to believe the information at my disposal, is about to make a mistake of the highest order which I must call to your attention and protest in the strongest terms. The late President's brother, Ngo Dinh Can, surrendered himself voluntarily to our Consulate in Hue on November 5, 1963 and requested political asylum. Two of his brothers had already been killed—brutally murdered only two days before. As you know, Mister Minister, the killing of President Diem was a great shock to me as it was to President Kennedy and then Vice-President Johnson. In one of the

most difficult decisions I have had to make during my time as
Ambassador to the Republic of Viet Nam, I personally agreed to surrender Can to your authorities against his will and his expressed
desires."

"I only did so, however, after being assured by General Tran Van
Bich that he would be treated fairly, treated justly, treated according to
internationally accepted standards of jurisprudence and that no physical harm would befall him until he was judged by a jury of his peers.
When the Revolutionary Council handed down death sentences on
Can and Da two weeks ago, I was shocked. I talked with General
Khanh, who told me to see General Minh, the head of state, who had
the power to commute death sentences. So I went to see Minh, who
told me he was powerless, could not even get his old cronies released
from house arrest, and urged me to see Thich Tri Binh about the matter since Khanh was anxious for Buddhist support. I talked to Binh
and again to Khanh and both of them, although they said it was a
complicated situation, gave me to understand that no rash actions
would be undertaken.

"Now, today, I am informed, with no prior warning, that Ngo
Dinh Can and Dinh Trieu Da are to be executed this very afternoon.
How do you think this makes me look? "

"I told General Khanh," Admiral Dinh interrupted, "that it was
foolish in the extreme, to take this action without first clearing it with
the Americans. I said to him that they would not understand, that
they would think just what you said, that it is barbarous."

Once again, he grinned his broad nervous grin.

"It is not only barbarous," Sedgewick said, "it is foolish. It will discredit you in the United States and in the eyes of the world. Let me
remind you, if I may, of the effect that the self-immolation of eleven
Buddhist bonzes last year had in the rest of the world, including
Washington. The question that you and General Khanh should be
asking yourselves is whether or not Ngo Dinh Diem would still be
President of this country if those bonzes had not killed themselves.
Throughout my career I have prided myself on being an anti-colonialist. I have insisted that the peoples of Africa and Asia are fully capable
of running their own affairs. When Washington asked me about those

death sentences, I said that General Khanh and you yourself, Mister Minister, would not allow these sentences to be carried out, that you were members of a new generation of Vietnamese officers who would put the propagation of the war against the VC at the head of your list of priorities."

"You are right, your Excellency, absolutely right," Dinh interjected.

"Furthermore, while one can perhaps understand the case against Can—and I for one do not think he is guiltless of crimes, far from it—the accusations against Da don't make any sense at all. Nothing he could possibly have done would merit execution."

"I agree with you, Excellency, two hundred per cent. Da is a close friend." He smiled again, and then he repeated, "close personal friend." He brushed at his eyes with his right knuckle, as though to dab away tears. But his eyes were as dry as the red dust of central Viet Nam.

"We went to the same middle school in Hue—same school attended by late President Diem. . .And by Ho Chi Minh too," he added and smiled once again. "There is no need to explain to me, Excellency, about virtues of Da. He was great scientist and mathematician. He was OK guy. He is on my list of all time greats. If it were up to me, Excellency, this madness would not even have been considered, much less carried out. I met with the Prime Minister for hours. I begged him. I pleaded. All to no avail, no avail at all."

"When the Revolutionary Council handed down a death sentence," Sedgewick said, "I was certain that you and General Khanh would straighten out this matter. This comes personally at a very bad time for me, Mister Minister, a very bad time."

"You talk frank with me, Excellency. I like that. I talk frank with you. I give you letter which not even delivered yet."

Admiral Dinh reached into his inside coat pocket and handed Sedgewick an envelope with the seal of the ministry in the upper left hand corner. The Ambassador tore it open. It was a hand-written letter in Vietnamese to General Khanh from Dinh. Sedgewick gave it to Marnin, whose Vietnamese after eighteen months commendably allowed him to get around town and kibitz with bar hostesses. But it was not up to official documents with their mandarin turns of phrase.

Marnin handed the letter back to the Minister with a shrug.

"It is my resignation," Dinh said. "General Khanh is crazy man. This is straight revenge. Revenge, Excellency. Difficult to work for man like that. I quit if you tell me. Say the word."

"Your resignation settles nothing. Our problem is to stop these executions, not to remove you from the Government. I don't want you to resign. I want to save Can and Da!"

As the Minister got more excited, his face reddened and his English worsened. "We argue with him for hours. Finally, he get up and say he going hunting. He going to Dalat. And when he come back tomorrow either those bastards dead or he is no longer Prime Minister. If we don't like it, then have another coup and get rid of him. That is what he said—the very words. There is nothing I can do. Nothing. I cannot organize a coup. I'm in the navy, not the army."

"Just arrange for me to talk to the General," Sedgewick said. "We have always gotten along. He'll listen to me."

"He is in the jungle near Dalat hunting tigers with the Montagnards. He has no radio. Cannot be reached. Reason is he doesn't want there to be any way for you to talk to him."

The Ambassador sat silent, his face growing ever more knotted. The Minister fiddled with his black tie. Sedgewick stood up abruptly.

"You goddam people," he said and walked out of the house. Marnin hurried after him.

"Did you notice that tie?" he asked Marnin in the car. "He's in mourning already."

Marnin rode to the Residence with Sedgewick and got his instructions. Back in his office, he made the necessary phone calls. Using the Checker limo and Sedgewick's driver he was taken to the Palace to see Luyen, the chief of protocol. They met just inside the gate. Luyen was clearly conscious that he had Ambassadorial rank, and that Marnin was an FSO-8, the most junior diplomat in the American Embassy.

"So, Mr. Marnin, you have something for me?"

"Yes, Excellency," Marnin responded. "I am under instructions from Ambassador Sedgewick. He gave me this message. He told me to tell you that he is disgusted by this totally illegal and irresponsible act, that his government is disgusted by this, and that we cannot accept or acquiesce in the face of such a barbarous action. He hopes your government will see reason and call this whole thing off."

"There is nothing I can do," Luyen said.

They stood there for a minute. Finally, Luyen turned and walked back to the Palace, without accompanying Marnin the ten steps to the gate, as Asian protocol demanded.

The courtyard faced east and the sun was already low enough to be blocked by the prison walls, shading the bleachers erected for some thirty spectators. By five-fifteen the bleachers were full. No foreigner showed up other than Claudio, presumably representing his business partners. This made it clear to everyone that the *cailles* were behind it; indeed, had insisted on it.

Can was the first. He was carried in on a stretcher and seated on the ground next to the pole by two attendants in white hospital garb and two priests in black cassocks, praying and clutching their rosary beads. Can's diabetes had worsened during his prison ordeal and he had had a heart attack during the trial. His face was lime green. He repeatedly retched, but could not bring anything up. Can, like his brothers Diem and Nhu, was a chain smoker and asked for his last Salem. He smoked it down to the filter. The priests kept up their Latin chant throughout the entire event. Can's final request was to dispense with the hood covering his head. This was refused.

They tied his hands behind him to the pole. Unable to stand, he slumped down into an awkward crouch. They propped him up and tied him under the armpits to the pole to make him a better target. Just before the prison commander, a Major Dong who was in charge of the ceremony, shoved on the hood, Can weakly, barely audibly, cried out, "*Vive la République du Viet Nam!*" The audience clapped politely, as though at a tennis match.

There were ten men in the firing squad. They were not the finest marksmen. Can was hit in the thigh, the abdomen, the chest, and at least twice in the head. It was a good thing they had refused his request to die unmasked.

Major Dong was furious that because Can was already shot in the head the *coup de grâce* was no longer appropriate. He cursed out his men, using the choicest Vietnamese epithets. This was the occasion for raucous laughter from the military audience, which had been embarrassed at the shooting of a man who was clearly dying. The attendants carried Can's corpse back out on the same stretcher. The priests never stopped their praying. (His mother, still living in the family house in Hue which she had shared with Can for a dozen years, died the following week. Three of her sons had been executed within seven months.)

Fifteen minutes went by before Da entered the courtyard, dressed in khaki pants and a short-sleeved white shirt open at the neck. His hands were covered by bandages. He walked with his shoulders consciously drawn back, a contemptuous half-smile on his lips. He had not expected this kind of uniformed crowd to witness his final minutes.

"*Vous êtes tous cochons. Vous êtes tous damnés,*" he shouted at them. ("You are all pigs. You are all damned.")

Until that moment the audience had been subdued, even apathetic. They knew they were taking part in something unclean. Perhaps for that very reason Da's words roused them to fury. They railed at him and cursed him as though he were a goalie who had allowed the other team to score an easy shot to win the game. Da shouted something back at them, but he was drowned out by the crowd, by then stomping their feet in unison to demand that the execution proceed. Da had always seemed the mildest of men. Nobody could recall ever having seen him angry. Like Can, he requested not to be blindfolded. This was again refused.

They tied him up, gave the order quickly, and shot him neatly through the red paper circle pinned to his shirt marking the heart. Although there was clearly no need for it, Dong had the satisfaction of performing the *coup de grâce*. Unlike Can, Da was hauled offstage by a burly jailer clutching him under the armpits, like a bull being dragged out of the arena by a pair of mules. It was all over quickly. The crowd dispersed quietly, some to go home and others to the bars on the Rue Catinat to tell of the afternoon's killing.

Marnin heard about these events that evening from Claudio, who was in an amiable frame of mind. "How often these days do you have a chance to watch a firing squad in action?" he asked Marnin, and then added, "No ears or tail for this one."

They were sitting in the Texas Rose in a booth along with Ruby Ky and Hedy Lamarr and Marnin was getting rapidly drunk, even on the diluted bar whiskey being served him. He had Claudio describe the execution to him three times, until he could see and smell the whole thing.

"The bastards," he kept mumbling to himself. "The dirty bastards."

In that raunchy bar the immensity of his own involvement in these events swept over him like an ocean wave—just as surely as if he had been the eleventh man in that firing squad.

Marnin left Saigon the day after Sedgewick departed, on June 7, on the S.S. American Mail, a freighter traveling to Hong Kong. From there, after three days at the Repulse Bay Hotel, he would transfer to the S.S. President Wilson, a trans-Pacific passenger liner stopping at Yokohama, Honolulu, and finally San Francisco. After home leave he was to report back to the Foreign Service Institute to begin a Chinese language course of thirty months—nine months in Arlington and twenty-one at the State Department Chinese language school in Taichung in central Taiwan. Then he was scheduled to go on to Moscow, where he would be the officer in that Embassy Political Section covering Soviet relations with South and East Asia. Given the Russian he had already learned in the Navy, he would thus become one of the few Officers in the Foreign Service during the Cold War era competent in both Russian and Chinese.

Sedgewick left Viet Nam four weeks after Can and Da were executed, on June 6, 1964—a carefully chosen day. It was the twentieth anniversary of D-Day, the day on which he had landed at Omaha Beach as an Army Colonel. Mandelbrot had said that Sedgewick wanted to use the ambassadorship as a springboard for the Republican presidential nomination. And indeed, his letter of resignation to Lyndon Johnson spoke about leaving his important position in order to play a role in Republican presidential politics.

But the symbolism of that date was lost on the American public. The Honolulu conference had been the high point of Sedgewick's esteem, both in the eyes of his Washington collaborators and even of the *New York Times*. After that meeting Viet Nam policy, and South Viet Nam itself, had turned progressively sour and there was no way for Sedgewick to shed the aroma of failure. The Embassy in Saigon was not to be a way station on the road to the White House. Viet Nam was to be not a precursor, but rather a graveyard, for Sedgewick's hopes.

It certainly was a graveyard for Blix Donnelly, who for three years had confidently predicted victory by the time of his departure, and who retired under something of a cloud. When he left in July and turned his command over to William Westmoreland, neither he nor anyone else was predicting the slightest prospect of an early favorable settlement of the struggle against the Viet Cong.

Gus Corning never got over the death of his friend Ngo Dinh Diem. Blocked from obtaining another suitable post by the same State Department cabal, led by Averell Harriman and Roger Hilsman, that was instrumental in taking Embassy Saigon out of his hands, he resigned from the Foreign Service in mid-1964 in what he described as a protest against America's feckless Viet Nam policy.

But service in Viet Nam was not the kiss of death for all of Marnin's colleagues. Sam Sabo rose steadily through the ranks—DCM in Paris; Deputy Assistant Secretary in the European Bureau of the State Department in charge of West European affairs; Ambassador to the Netherlands; Undersecretary for Political Affairs. Now retired, he spends half his time in his house south of Avignon and half in Chappaquiddick.

After a year as the wife of one of the principal officers in our Embassy in France, Lily followed her husband, who had been named Ambassador to the Ivory Coast. She served in Abidjan with him until 1968, when he retired from the Service and moved back to Paris. Lily and he first lived in, and then inherited, her mother's flat on the Rue Henri Martin in the sixteenth *arrondisement*. Her daughters, both of whom majored in mathematics, graduated with distinction from MIT and are now working for the National Security Agency in Fort Meade, Maryland. Lily watched her husband grow fat and deaf, but they were known throughout the Vietnamese community in France as a singularly devoted couple.

Corning's and Donnelly's *bête noire*, Willis Mandelbrot, left Saigon in much more favorable circumstances than they did. Figuratively clutching his Pulitzer Prize, Billy departed in April for New York to serve his required year on the city desk and then to move onward and upward in a celestial trajectory as the *Times* bureau chief in Bonn, and then as Washington bureau chief.

Claudio showed up in time to share one last copa with Marnin in the ship's "salon"—the last of thousands that they had downed together. He arrived with Hedy Lamarr and half a case of Dom Perignon to further enliven, he said, Marnin's three day journey through the South China Sea with his swinging companions—an ironic reference to Marnin's ten fellow passengers, none of whom saw fit to get off the boat in Saigon because they feared for their safety. They were all elderly retired couples traveling around the world cheaply on freighters. Claudio said he could not imagine why one would voluntarily suffer such a voyage, even as a penance.

In fact, it was a kind of penance. The death of Can, and especially of Da, only a month before, still weighed heavily on Marnin. He would go through life with periodic visions of Da's hunched, small figure slouching away from his apartment under a streetlight at two in the morning.

Sedgewick during this last month had been extremely helpful in pushing Marnin's career forward by getting him into Chinese language training. The Department was reluctant to invest thirty months of study in an officer with only one Fitness Report in his file and who had been in the service less than two years and had originally turned down his application, saying he should apply again after his next tour of duty. But Sedgewick would not take no for an answer. He personally called Harriman and Hilsman and got them to reverse the decision of the Director General's Office. So Marnin ended up owing the three of them—the killers of Ngo Dinh Diem and Ngo Dinh Nhu—a strong personal debt of gratitude.

But having convicted these men in his own mind of first degree murder four times over, Marnin was impelled to move on from there and to reflect on the nature and extent of the crime of which he personally could be accused. This especially bothered him in the case of Da—his friend; someone close to his own age; someone he admired and could have helped. Had he crossed the line and become an accessory to murder? At what point?

Was saving those men beyond his capabilities? He wrestled with that conundrum and on some days concluded that he could not have done so. But on other days he decided that of course he could have. He had the goods on Sedgewick and Sedgewick knew it. With a snap of his fingers Sedgewick could have saved all of them. But at the moment that counted it had been inconceivable for Marnin to cross his Ambassador. Was he a coward or only a nascent bureaucrat? Was it basic weakness of character? Was it the inherent nature of his profession? Or was he one of life's observers? These questions would haunt him through the years.

They certainly dominated his waking hours in June of 1964 as he was leaving Saigon. Weary and overwrought, usually hung over, he looked forward to that long sea voyage. He needed the distraction of applying himself to his Fenn's Handbook, memorizing and learning to write in the correct stroke order his first hundred Chinese characters.

They sailed at noon. Claudio stayed on the dock, waving to him until the ship pulled around the bend and into the deep part of the river. Hedy Lamarr stood beside him holding her conical hat, a graceful figure with her yellow silk *ao dai* billowing in the breeze. As they disappeared out of sight, he had the momentary illusion that she was Lily—that it was Lily bidding him *adieu*.

It took two hours for the tugs to haul the ship down the Saigon River to Vung Tao and the open sea. Marnin stood at the railing and watched as they passed through the jungle shimmering deep green in the midday sun. He tried to reflect on his good fortune, on the opening up of new adventures. Like his country itself, he had come to South Viet Nam as a youth and left it as a man—a man, and a country, burdened with deep unease and sorrow. At first he had wholly enjoyed Saigon, consciously regarding it as part of an exciting rite of passage. For eighteen months he had watched events unfold from the unparalleled vantage point of two American Ambassadors and one of the smartest and loveliest women in the country.

Both Sedgewick and Corning before him, whatever their faults, had seemed a vast cut above anyone Marnin had known before—larger, grander figures engaged in labors that would change the face not only of Viet Nam, but of the United States and even the world. Whether those labors were for good or evil, whether they were moral or immoral, was not a question that at first had even crossed his mind. In everything they did, in everything of which he was a part, these two men were at the vanguard of history—were indeed the stewards of history. Given who he was and where he came from, this in itself was something of a triumph for him. But like his great country, Marnin had begun to learn, and throughout the years that followed bore the scars of that lesson: that in the real world beyond the self-important visions that shield officials from the moral price of their actions, even in the best of times there cannot be victors without vanquished, crimes without consequences, glory without guilt.

AUTHOR'S NOTE

Although the events depicted in this book actually happened, it is a work of fiction. The characters are products of my imagination and have no resemblance to people living or dead. On the other hand, genuine historical figures—e.g., John Kennedy, Dean Rusk, Robert McNamara, Maxwell Taylor—were in the places alluded to in the novel at the date and time given and expressed sentiments consonant with those portrayed.

As an aid to readers unfamiliar with the alphabet soup generated by the U.S. Government (USG), herewith is a selective glossary of acronyms used at the time the novel took place:

A-100—Entering course for Foreign Service Officers
AID—Agency for International Development
APC—Armored Personnel Carrier
ARVN—Army of the Republic of Vietnam
CAP—CIA communication channel serving the White House
CAS—CIA Station in a foreign country
CINCPAC—Commander in Chief Pacific
CIP—Commodity Import Program
CJCS—Chairman of the Joint Chiefs of Staff
CNO—Chief of Naval Operations
CODEL—Congressional Delegation
COMSEC—Communications Security
COMUSMACV—Commander United States Military Assistance
  Command Vietnam
COS—CIA Chief of Station
CRITIC—Designator for Communications of the highest possible
  urgency
DCM—Deputy Chief of Mission
DOD—Department of Defense
FBO—Foreign Buildings Office of the State Department
FSI—Foreign Service Institute, the State Department school
FSO—Foreign Service Officer
GVN—Government of South Vietnam
ICC—International Control Commission (India, Canada, Poland)
JCS—Joint Chiefs of Staff
JGS—Joint General Staff of the armed forces of South Vietnam
KGB—Soviet Committee for State Security (Komitet
  Gosudarstvenoi Bezopasnosti)
M-1—American rifle

M-113—An American APC
M-16—American rifle updating the M-1
MAAG—Military Assistance Advisory Group
MAC—Military Assistance Command
MACV—Military Assistance Command Vietnam
MAP—Military Assistance Program
NIACT—Night Action, i.e., cable designator for message that cannot wait till morning
NIS—Naval Investigative Service
NODIS—No Distribution to other than designated addressees
NVA—North Vietnamese Army
PAO—Public Affairs Officer, chief of local USIS
PCS—Permanent Change of Station
PENUMBRA—Codeword designator
PL-480—Public Law 480, authorizing shipments of surplus agricultural commodities
POLAD—Political Adviser, State Department Officer on CINC staff
RSO—Regional Security Officer, State Department
RVN—Republic of South Vietnam
RVNAF—Republic of Vietnam Armed Forces
SY—Bureau of Security, Department of State
SOP—Standard Operating Procedure
TDY—Temporary Duty
USG—U.S. Government
USIA—United States Information Agency (Washington)
USIS—United States Information Service (in the field)
USOM—United States Operations Mission (AID in the field)
VC—Viet Cong (also known as Victor Charley)
VNAF—South Vietnamese Air Force
VNQDD—South Vietnamese Nationalist Party (suppressed by Diem)
VOA—Voice of America